EDEN

Cordia Byers

FAWCETT GOLD MEDAL • NEW YORK

A Fawcett Gold Medal Book
Published by Ballantine Books
Copyright © 1991 by Cordia Byers

All rights reserved under International and Pan-American Copyright Conventions. Published in the United States by Ballantine Books, a division of Random House, Inc., New York, and simultaneously in Canada by Random House of Canada Limited, Toronto.

Library of Congress Catalog Card Number: 91-92207

ISBN 0-449-14664-2

Manufactured in the United States of America

First Edition: January 1992

"Get myself a man! That's the one thing I don't need, especially if you're a prime example of what western men are like."

Mesmerized, Brand watched Jessie's temper transform her into a vibrant wildcat. Reacting solely on instinct, his body demanding release, he drew Jessie into his arms and silenced her surprised cry with a hard, demanding kiss.

Stunned, Jessie didn't resist. Never had anyone kissed her like Brand Stockton. His exploring, intoxicating kiss stirred things to life within her.

A moment later the impact of her hand against his cheek echoed eerily through the night. "Don't you ever lay another hand on me or I'll kill you."

To Michael, my wonderful son. I love you.

My thanks to Ron Bryce of Oklahoma's Robbers Cave State Park. His information about the area helped tremendously. I would also like to thank Grace Mendez, administrative secretary to Amarillo's Convention and Visitors Council, for the brochures she sent to help me see the lay of the land around Palo Duro Canyon. I can only imagine what they thought the day I called and started asking a million questions about the 1800s. Fortunately they were the type of wonderful, helpful people who understand a writer's need to know the time and place he or she is writing about. Thank you again, Grace and Ron.

Chapter 1

Paradise, Texas, 1877
A ship on a dusty wave, the stage rumbled into town.
A loud "Whoa" from the driver and a screech of brakes against the metal rims of the wooden wheels brought it to a swaying halt in front of the hotel.

Rolling a fat wad of tobacco out of its secure pocket in his jaw, the driver spat the black ooze through a gap in his stained teeth. He wiped a drop off his chin with a gloved hand, scratched at his bearded jaw, and then turned his attention to securing the reins about the brake handle before climbing down. A cloud of dust rose from his buckskin shirt and britches as he moved to open the coach door for his passengers.

"This is the end of the line fer you ladies," he said, making no offer to help them out. Pressing his lips back against his teeth, he squirted another black spurt of tobacco juice over his shoulder into the finely powdered gray clay before stepping aside.

The older woman descended, huffing and puffing. It wasn't until she was safely away from the vehicle and had her feet planted firmly on the planked sidewalk that she glanced back toward the man who had caused her such misery in the last hours. Fanning herself and dabbing at the drops of perspiration beading her brow, she eyed the driver with loathing. Then she turned her attention to her young companion. "Jessica Nolan, had I known what was ahead of us, I would never have agreed to come with you to this godforsaken country. In all my born days I've never seen anything like it. And I would never have believed anyone could endure what we just have and live to tell about it."

Jessica cast the driver a sharp look when she heard him chuckle beneath his breath. The low, throaty sound of satisfaction he emitted served only to confirm her suspicion during the last fifty miles of their journey. The man had taken an instant dislike to Edwina after she'd ordered him to drive safely. And in retribution he'd made the last leg of their journey as uncomfortable as possible. Like most men, he didn't appreciate it when a woman told him how to do his job. And a western man, especially, wouldn't cater to orders given by a woman from back east.

Jessica glanced from the driver to her friend and gave a mental shrug. She feared others would share the driver's opinion, especially when they learned she intended to run her own ranch. As she'd been told in recent months, it was simply something not done west of the Mississippi. Back east you could have your bluestocking suffragettes, but out west men wanted women to stay in their proper place—the home—and do their wifely duties—cooking, cleaning, and having babies.

They are in for a big surprise from me, Jessica reflected. She'd come to fulfill a dream, and she'd not allow anyone to stop her—not Edwina, nor any man who thought she wasn't capable of handling her own affairs. She'd face all of them and not give an inch. However, for the moment she wouldn't bring trouble home before it was necessary. Now she had to concentrate her energy on soothing Edwina's ruffled feathers and getting them both settled.

Flicking her fingers against the cuffs of her muslin gown, Jessica made a moue of disgust at the condition of the soft fabric. What had once been a brilliant white was now a dull gray from the plumes of dirt that had fogged in through the open windows of the stage. Had they been able to endure the heat, tempting heat stroke by keeping the windows closed, she might have saved her gown. However, a piece of clothing, no matter how fine, wasn't worth the torment of being cooked alive. Giving another mental shrug, she smiled at Edwina. "I warned you in Boston that this trip wouldn't be easy," she said, "but you were determined not to let me come alone."

Straight-backed, her huge bustline like an awning shadowing her large, tightly corseted middle, Edwina snapped, "I know what I said, but I didn't know you planned on killing me."

Jessica couldn't suppress her own chuckle at the housekeeper's remark. She had known Edwina Roilings for over ten years, and the woman was at her happiest when she had something to complain about. Edwina had been Kate's housekeeper, and between the two strong-willed women, they had managed to make Jessica as independent as themselves. And were it not for their love and strength, she'd not be here today to try to fulfill a dream lost so many years before.

"Now, Winnie, things won't look as bad when we're

settled. Once I've seen Mr. Langtree at the bank to confirm that my instructions have been followed, we'll be on our way.''

"Don't call me Winnie, Jessica Nolan. You know how I detest that name. And I don't know if my poor old bones can travel another mile. I ache from head to toe. I feel like one big bruise.''

"Then I will rent you a room at the hotel for tonight.''

Edwina cocked her head to one side, eyeing the younger woman. "Don't you mean you'll rent *us* a room for the night?''

Jessica shook her head. "No. I intend to sleep in my own bed tonight. You may remain here in town until you feel you're up to coming out to the ranch, but I intend to go out to Eden this afternoon as planned.''

"Well, you're not going one step without me, young lady. Poor Kate would turn over in her grave if I let you take off on your own. You don't know what could happen out there alone. There might be all kinds of danger, just ready to pounce upon a young, unprotected woman.''

Jessica couldn't hold back her laughter a moment longer. She shook her head. "Edwina, what am I going to do with you?''

"It's not what you're going to do with me,'' Edwina huffed. "It's what am I going to do with you? I'm not the one who wanted to leave civilization to come to this . . .'' She paused and glanced down the street. A wave of her gloved hand encompassed the entire town. "This barren, godforsaken land.'' Her lips curled in disgust. "And they call this place Paradise. It should be named Hell.''

4

The smile faded from Jessica's lips. "This is my home, Edwina, as Boston was yours."

"It was your home as well. Kate left you a fortune so you'd never have to do without a thing. She raised you to be a lady like herself. You never should have come back here."

Jessica shook her head. "You know Boston was never my home. I loved Kate as a mother, and I'm grateful for all she did for me, yet my heart was here where I was born." She cast a sharp glance about, realizing her mistake before the words were completely out of her mouth. She wanted no one to know that she and her two brothers had been the orphans the residents of Paradise had shipped off to the mission in Indian territory ten years ago. But until the time was right, when she would proudly tell everyone that she was the daughter of Earnest and Sarah Fleming, she wanted to keep her past a secret.

Jessica relaxed, seeing no one near enough to overhear their conversation. "Standing here in the middle of town is no place to discuss this matter, Edwina."

Edwina had the grace to blush. "I'm sorry. I'm just overwrought from our harrowing stage ride. The man must be mad to drive like that."

The smile returned to Jessica's sweetly shaped mouth. "He did want to give us a fright. I wonder what could have caused him to act in such a manner?"

"I haven't the slightest idea," Edwina said. Fanning herself rapidly once more, she turned her attention to her surroundings.

Jessica's smile deepened. Edwina knew exactly what had set the man off on his wild tangent. "I'll get you settled in the hotel and then I'll go see Mr. Langtree."

Edwina drew herself up and cast Jessica an indignant look. "As I've already stated, young lady, you're not going anywhere without me. I came here with you and I intend to stay with you, no matter how many outlaws we have to face."

"All right, you win, but don't say I forced you to come. Mr. Langtree may have followed all of my instructions, but I doubt the house will be to your liking until I can hire someone to help us."

"I don't know why we'd need anyone else. I handled Kate's household with no trouble, and I can do the same for yours. And I know you'll not find anyone here who can cook the way I can." Edwina sniffed and raised her chin in the air.

"That certainly is true," Jessica said, giving Edwina a hug. "Now, let's see Mr. Langtree and then be on our way. I can't wait to see the ranch."

Jessica left instructions to have their baggage held at the hotel, then crossed the short span of planking that separated the hotel from the bank. A bell jingled overhead when she opened the door and stepped inside. Glass lanterns helped illuminate the dark-paneled chamber where one clerk worked behind the teller's window. Spectacles perched precariously on the tip of his nose, the teller was bent over his account books. At the sound of the bell he cast a fleeting glance at the two women, finished his column of figures, and laid aside his pen before asking if he might be of service.

"Please tell Mr. Langtree Jessica Nolan is here to see him. I believe he is expecting me."

The clerk nodded, straightened his spectacles and vest, and crossed to the door at the rear of the room. He rapped his knuckles lightly against the frosted-glass panel, on which *Mr. Langtree, Bank President* was printed in bold letters. A moment later he slipped inside and returned with a wide, congenial smile of welcome on his thin face. "Mr. Langtree will be glad to see you, Miss Nolan. If you will follow me." The clerk opened the half door at the side of the counter and stepped back to allow Jessica and Edwina to pass.

"Miss Nolan," Mr. Langtree said, meeting them at the door and ushering them inside his office to the padded chairs in front of his desk. A curt look sent the clerk back to his account books. "I'm sorry I wasn't there to meet your stage. I hope your journey hasn't been too trying."

Jessica glanced at Edwina and saw the other woman stiffen. She smiled at Mr. Langtree. "No. For the most part it has been pleasant."

"Good to hear it. For ladies like yourselves, I know our means of travel can at times be a little harrowing. Now, I realize you didn't come all this way to talk about your travels." Langtree opened his desk drawer and retrieved several papers. He laid them on the desk in front of Jessica. "I think this is what you want."

Jessica picked up the deeds, barely controlling a surge of pure joy. The land was hers! "I hope this didn't cause you too much inconvenience. I understand from my lawyers that the land was open grazing and that you had to acquire it from the state."

Langtree swallowed the uncomfortable lump that rose in his throat and settled back onto his plush leather chair. He crossed his hands over his vested, round middle and cleared his throat. "I had a few complaints, but there was nothing anyone could do to stop me from purchasing the tract of land you wanted. It's been in public domain for nearly ten years, and the state was more than glad to sell it for the price you offered.''

''Have the rest of my orders been followed?''

Langtree smiled, relieved not to have to explain who had been against her. ''To the best of my ability, ma'am. As you instructed, the house, the barns, and the corral were built, and your stock will arrive next week. I sent a few men out to temporarily watch over the place, but I thought it best to wait about hiring the rest of your crew. I figured your foreman would want to hand-pick his own men.''

''Then it seems everything has been done,'' Jessica said with a smile. She opened her purse and retrieved a draft from the Bank of Boston. ''Mr. Langtree, I hope this will be sufficient to show my gratitude.''

Langtree's eyes widened, as did his smile. ''Yes, ma'am. It will do quite nicely. And if there's ever anything else I can do for you, please don't hesitate to ask.''

''There are a few minor things I need to take care of while I'm in town.'' Jessica retrieved another bank draft from her purse and handed it to Mr. Langtree. ''But first I would like to open an account here if it isn't too much trouble.''

Langtree cleared his throat and shook his head as he came to his feet. ''No trouble at all.'' He opened the door and called to the clerk. ''Adams, Miss Nolan wants to open an account. Would you see to the papers?''

''Right away, Mr. Langtree,'' Adams said, jumping to his feet like a skittish rabbit. The motion sent his precariously perched spectacles to the account book on the counter.

When the papers were correctly made out, Mr. Langtree escorted Jessica and Edwina to the door. "Should you need anything, we are at your service."

Jessica extended her hand to the banker, and he shook it exuberantly. Her deposit had just set a record for the Bank of Paradise. Until now, Clint Ramsey had been his best depositor, but even with owning the largest spread in the area, Ramsey didn't have the kind of money Miss Nolan did. Ranchers were wealthy in land and cattle, but few had much cash on hand except after the trail drives. They lived off loans from year to year.

As Jessica stood in the doorway, the man of Langtree's thoughts entered the bank. Wearing a fringed buckskin jacket, expensive boots, and a large Stetson that shadowed his features from view, Clint Ramsey dwarfed the three who stood bidding their farewells. His glance flickered over the two women before settling on the banker. "Langtree, I need to talk to you."

"Clint, I would like to introduce you to Miss Nolan. She's your new neighbor. She's the lady who bought the land down by Little Creek and Mesquite Mountain."

Clint Ramsey turned his glacial blue gaze once more upon the two women, noting for the first time the beauty of the younger. He took off his hat and extended his hand graciously. "Glad to meet you, Miss Nolan. I had heard I'd be getting a new neighbor, but I didn't expect one with such beauty."

Jessica felt an unexpected blush suffuse her cheeks as she took his hand. Unlike the men she'd known in Boston, this Mr. Ramsey didn't mince words, looking her in the eyes as he paid the compliment. His directness was a refreshing change, but it was his ruggedly handsome face that made something deep inside of her tingle strangely.

"Thank you, Mr. Ramsey," she said, slightly breathless.

"Feel free to call upon me if you have any questions about the ranch. My spread adjoins Little Creek to the south of your place. We share the same grazing land."

"Thank you again, Mr. Ramsey. I know I will need all the advice I can get. This is a new venture for me. I have read all the books, but I fear I'm still not going to know everything I need to succeed."

Ramsey's shapely lips curled up at the corners. "I don't believe you can learn to run a ranch from reading a book, Miss Nolan. But you can count on me when you get into trouble."

"I will remember that," Jessica said, giving Clint a brilliant smile. "Now, if you will excuse us, we need to hire a buggy to take us out to the ranch. Good day, Mr. Langtree, Mr. Ramsey."

The two men watched Jessica and Edwina stroll back toward the hotel and disappear from view. Langtree was the first to break the silence. "Clint, I thought you'd be madder than a hornet when Miss Nolan arrived."

Ramsey didn't take his eyes off the vacant sidewalk. "That was before Miss Nolan arrived, Henry." Clint glanced down at the banker and smiled. "And that was before I saw her."

Langtree looked once more past the half curtain that covered the front window. "She is a beauty. That much I can say."

"What else do you know of her?"

Langtree shrugged. "Not much more than I already told you. She's from Boston. She's bought the the land you wanted, and from what I can tell, she's a real lady. That's about it.''

Clint thoughtfully rubbed a lean-fingered hand across his chin and smiled. ''And I got a feeling she'd be my kind of lady.''

''Good to hear it,'' Langtree said, and smiled his relief. He hadn't expected Ramsey to take the news of Miss Nolan's arrival so well. When he'd explained about her buying the land running along Little Creek, he'd thought the man would have a seizure. And for a while he'd wondered if his own life wasn't in jeopardy for handling the transaction.

Langtree placed his hand against the pocket where he'd secured the bank draft and smiled to himself. Ramsey would be fit to be tied if he knew the profit he, Langtree, had made off the deal, and it would serve the bastard right. Ramsey might own the largest ranch west of Fort Worth, but that didn't give him the right to act like he was a king. However, it wouldn't do to flaunt his newfound wealth in front of the rancher, nor to reveal his feelings. He knew when to hold his own counsel. Clint Ramsey wasn't a man to have as an enemy. ''Now what can I do for you, Clint?''

''I came to tell you I'm calling a meeting at the Cattleman's Exchange for tomorrow night. We're going to have to put a stop to that damned half-breed Wade Fleming. Him and that bunch of vermin he leads hit the Lazy L again last night, and it's time we all banded together and put an end to their thieving. I want to see the bastard dead just like his father.''

''There're several other ranchers who feel the same way, Clint. Luke McCoy said he lost twenty head last week, and Nathan Jones lost thirty.''

"That red vermin just hits and runs. He don't take enough head to slow him down, just enough to be a pain in the ass to us."

"He's taking enough to cause a few of the ranchers to default on some of their loans, and that's not good business for them or me," Langtree said, taking two cigars from the inside pocket of his jacket. He offered one to Clint before biting off the tip of his own and spitting it into the cuspidor that sat in the corner near the teller's window. He rolled the cigar between his lips, then retrieved a match from his pocket and lit it. He puffed until the end of the cigar glowed red. Satisfied, he nodded. "Ain't nothing like a good cigar."

Clint Ramsey regarded the heavyset banker with something akin to contempt. The bastard was growing richer by the day from the sweat and toil of the ranchers who had to deal with him. And he'd had the gall to handle the negotiations between the state and the beautiful Miss Nolan, even though he knew Clint had wanted that property.

Clint quelled the urge to hit Langtree in his protruding middle, then smiled to himself. Having Miss Nolan as a neighbor would be interesting for a while. From what she'd already said, he'd get his hands on her land sooner or later. She was as green as a mesquite sapling about ranching. And it wouldn't take long for her to realize that fact when the hard work set in.

"You won't be able to buy your fancy cigars if Fleming is left to steal our herds," Clint said.

"I'm just as concerned about the rustling as you, Clint. I wired the Rangers in Austin last month about Fleming, but they haven't sent anyone up here to help out. I don't know what else I can do."

"You may not know what needs to be done, but I do. And I don't intend to wait around to see if the governor sends the Rangers up here to help out." Clint turned and strode from the bank.

Langtree watched him walk across the street to the saloon. He bit down on his cigar. He knew exactly what Ramsey intended to do, and he was glad he wasn't in Wade Fleming's boots. Turning away from the window, Langtree went back into his office, anxious to undersign the bank draft Jessica Nolan had given him and deposit it into his own account.

"There's our new home, Edwina," Jessica said, drawing the rented buckboard to a halt on the rise overlooking the ranch. Below them, sprawled among the loblolly pines and mesquite, a green ocean of grassy hills surrounding it, stood their newly built house. The timbers, unweathered by the elements, glowed a warm, welcoming gold. However, Jessica knew that would change, as would the vacant look of the empty windows. Soon the frilled curtains, the quilts, the crocheted doilies—starched stiff and white—and the furniture she'd sent from Boston would transform the house into a home. The high-backed rockers she'd ordered would brighten the front porch. There she'd sit in the evenings to watch the sunset and reflect upon the joys of once more being on the land her father and mother had owned before their deaths.

Jessica glanced at Edwina and smiled. She could see the other woman was pleased, even though she would no doubt complain about the austerity of her new home. Soon she'd have colorful flowerbeds edging the porches and sides of the house.

Behind the house a windmill, its tines turning in the breeze, rose high in the air above the well. The pump brought the precious water that would nourish Edwina's plants as well as their livestock. To the left of the house and beyond the barn, with its lightning rod raised toward the heavens, stood the bunkhouse and corrals. The fences would hold the sleek, healthy horses she'd bought to stock her ranch.

Jessica felt her eyes mist as she surveyed the land of her birth. Ten years had separated her from this land—ten long years in which she'd outwardly become a lady, possessing all the mannerisms she'd learned under Kate Nolan's tutelage. Inwardly, though, she had remained the same small, brown-skinned child who had played here without a worry in the world until the night the rustlers had come and murdered her parents. Then she and her brothers had been forced from this land because of their heritage. At that time Texas law prohibited anyone of Indian blood from owning land.

Fortunately, during the past ten years the laws had begun to change. Indians were still despised by many, but since 1875, when the last Comanches were driven out of Texas, the laws had become more lenient to those of mixed blood. Now she had come to reclaim the land that had been taken from her family. She was determined to fulfill her father's dream of owning a successful cattle ranch.

Jessica had another reason for returning to Texas. She wanted to find the man who had shot down her parents in cold blood. She knew nothing of him. The rustler who had killed her parents had been masked, but she had one clue: the intricately carved stock of his rifle. She had watched him raise it to his shoulder and fire, murdering her parents. No, she would never forget that rifle to the day she died, nor would she quit looking for its owner. Reason told her it was an impossible quest she had set for herself, especially after all these years, but her need for vengeance would not allow her to stop.

"You're off in a daze again," Edwina chided, feigning little interest in the view.

Jessica glanced at her friend. "I was only remembering, Winnie."

"Does it still hurt?" Edwina asked.

Jessica nodded and snapped the reins against the horse's back. "Yes, even after all these years. I still miss Mama and Papa and Joseph. And I can't stop wondering what happened to Wade. I don't know if he's alive or dead."

Edwina gave Jessica's arm an understanding squeeze. "I was afraid all of it would come back to you when we came here."

Jessica tried to smile. "I'm not going to let myself dwell on it all the time, but I can't forget. I intend to fulfill Papa's dream here, but I will also keep searching for the man who ended that dream. It's something I owe my family."

Edwina shook her head. "Jessica, I'm afraid for you. Your stubbornness will be the end of you yet."

Jessica looked sideways at Edwina. "And who made me that way? As I recall, I had two stubborn women to tutor me."

"Lord, Kate would die if she knew everything she'd tried to teach you had only brought you back here."

"Kate is already dead, Winnie. And I think she'd be proud of me. She'd not stand in my way. She'd give me that direct, no-nonsense look of hers, stiffen her spine, and raise her auburn head proudly in the air. In her most proper Bostonian accent she'd tell me not to let anyone stop me from what I want to do.''

Edwina nodded. ''You're right. Kate would stand behind your decision one hundred percent. She didn't have a weak bone in her body. When she set her mind to something, nothing in this world could stop her.''

''I seem to recall another woman who has a similar disposition,'' Jessica said as the buckboard rolled along the uneven road to the ranch house.

Edwina sniffed. ''I don't know who you could mean. If you're talking about me, then you are sorely mistaken. I don't have an ounce of stubbornness in me. If I did, I surely would not be here on this bumpy road, adding more bruises to my already abused backside.''

Jessica chuckled. It was good to have Edwina with her, and it was good to be home. Clicking the reins against the horse's back, she urged him down the dusty road.

Chapter 2

Jessie heard the sleeve of her gown rip as she strained to lift the bucket of feed grain. The horses had arrived the previous day, and until she managed to find enough men to work the ranch, many of the chores fell to her.

Disgusted, she glanced at the tear in the soft cotton. It was the third gown she'd ruined in as many days. If things kept going as they were, she'd be naked before the month was out. Mr. Langtree had said it would be an easy matter to hire men to work the ranch, but so far she hadn't found it to be such a simple task. The men he'd hired to oversee the ranch until she arrived had remained only long enough to collect their pay before heading back to town to spend it in the nearest saloon. None had wanted to remain on a permanent basis.

During the past week Jessie had begun to wonder if she'd ever find any men who would work for her. At least a dozen had come to apply, and eleven of those had looked at her as if she'd suddenly lost her mind when they learned she would be their employer. She was beginning to realize western men, more than their eastern counterparts, thought it outrageous to have to answer to a woman.

The only one who had stayed was a young Mexican by the name of Quillon Diaz, and Jessica suspected the motive for his accepting employment was his wife and young child. She had agreed to hire Maria, Quillon's wife, to help Edwina about the house. Fortunately Maria had been a blessing in disguise. With her help, Edwina battled against the dust that layered the furniture she worked to keep polished to a high sheen. Maria's help left Jessica free to concentrate on keeping the ranch going with only herself and Quill to work it.

Jessica wiped the perspiration from her brow with her sleeve and blew irritably at the loose strand of hair dangling before her eyes. She squinted against the blinding glare of the hot sun. Though the day was only a few hours old, the heat was already oppressive. She frowned. Soon the cattle she'd purchased from the King ranch in south Texas would be arriving. Without men to work them, she'd lose all the money she'd already invested. She didn't expect to show any profit the first couple of years but had hoped that by the following spring roundup she'd be able to make a small drive north to break even.

Jessica lifted the bucket of grain and lugged it toward the corral, where the horses waited near the feeding trough for their meal. None of the dreams she'd had while in Boston had touched on the problems she'd encountered during the past week. No, her fantasies had not taken into account the blistered hands, the broken nails, the aching back, the sunburned skin and lips, nor the soreness left in her backside from being in the saddle each afternoon to inspect her property. Riding astride over rough terrain was quite different from the leisurely canters she used to take each afternoon in Boston.

She poured the grain into the trough and patted the bay mare on her sleek neck as she bent her elegant head to eat. She had not anticipated the hardships she'd faced, but she didn't dare complain. Edwina would be the first to say "I told you so" in no uncertain terms while again reminding her she should have stayed in Boston where she belonged.

Jessica smiled with satisfaction as she watched the horse nibble at the grain. Things were hard and she had many lessons still to learn, but she was determined not to give up. Sooner or later she'd find enough men willing to work for a woman. This afternoon she intended to go back into town and once more post a notice for hired hands at the Cattleman's Exchange. Perhaps she'd have more luck than she'd had in the past days.

Hanging the bucket back on the hook behind the barn door, Jessie turned toward the house. She needed a good hot bath to wash away the grime and ease her aching back before venturing into town.

The sound of horses coming down the long drive made Jessie pause in the shade of the porch. When she saw several riders come through the gate, her spirits lifted. Maybe these men had come to work. Her heart sank a moment later when she recognized the handsome rancher, Clint Ramsey.

Suddenly very much aware of her appearance, Jessie quickly tried to tuck a stray curl back into the haphazardly arranged bun at the nape of her neck. She knew she looked a fright with her hair falling about her face, her cheeks smudged with dirt, and her gown torn and sweaty beneath the arms. The thought of Clint Ramsey or anyone seeing her in such a disheveled state brought an unaccustomed blush to her cheeks as she watched him rein his mount to a halt at the hitching post.

Clint dismounted and walked toward the porch. He regarded Jessica for a long moment, inspecting her from head to toe, before a smile brightened his craggy, weathered features. "It looks as if you've been learning how to ranch."

Her cheeks burning even hotter from his accurate assessment, Jessie smiled uneasily and shifted under his direct gaze. "Mr. Ramsey, I'm beginning to see what you meant when you said I couldn't learn to ranch from reading a book."

Clint's laughter spilled into the hot afternoon as he stepped into the shade of the porch and took off his hat. He wiped a sleeve over his brow. His eyes held a knowing look when he spoke. "I'm Clint to my friends, Miss Nolan."

"I'm Jessica to my friends, Clint. Won't you come inside and have something cool to drink," Jessica said, enjoying the sound of his laughter even if it was directed at her.

"I'm sorry, I don't have the time today. I just wanted to stop by and see how things were going." Clint's gaze swept warmly over Jessica. "You should have sent word to the Lazy L if you needed help. That's what neighbors are for. We have to look out for each other."

"I appreciate your kind offer, but I didn't want to impose upon my neighbors so soon after my arrival. I think Quillon and I will be able to handle everything until my stock arrives next week," Jessie said, feeling her cheeks tint once more under his perusal. In all of her twenty years she'd never been affected by a man in this manner before. But she'd never met a man like Clint Ramsey before, either. She sensed his strength by the way he held himself. He exuded the self-confidence she had found lacking in the younger men she had known in the past.

"Then I'll say good day, Jessica. Just remember, my offer still stands. Should you need my help, you only have to ask." Clint gave her one of his most charming smiles. "Maybe one day soon I can take you up on that offer of a cool drink."

"Please do." Jessica returned his smile. "And thank you again for your offer of help."

Clint nodded and settled his hat back on his head. Age had brushed the thick dark hair with wings of gray at the temples, a regal touch that added a distinguished look to his craggy features.

Jessica watched him stride to his horse and ride away before she entered the house. It was odd to find herself finally attracted to a man after so many years of believing it couldn't happen to her. She had begun to think something was wrong. When she'd listened to her girl-friends in Boston as they giggled and swooned over their latest loves, she'd wondered why she'd never experienced such giddy feelings toward the opposite sex. All the boys she knew were exactly that: boys. Jessica thoughtfully considered this new revelation. Perhaps it was Clint's age that had attracted her to him. He was at least twenty years her senior. There was no boyish shyness in the way he looked at her. The expression in his pale eyes was direct: he played no games. He made her totally aware that she was a woman. And she found the sensation as heady as a glass of expensive wine.

"Was that Mr. Ramsey?" Edwina asked when Jessica entered the kitchen and sank the gourd dipper into the water bucket sitting on the dry sink.

"Yes. He stopped by to offer his help should we need it," Jessica said, lifting the refreshing water to her lips.

"Well? Did you accept his offer?" Edwina asked, wiping her floured hands on her apron. She'd been kneading white bread to bake after sunset. Edwina had quickly learned it was much cooler to do her baking in the large iron stove during the evenings.

"No," Jessica said, hanging the gourd dipper back on the nail above the water bucket.

"I didn't expect you would." Edwina shook her head. "You're determined to work yourself into the ground to prove to the world that a woman can run a ranch just as well as any man." Again she shook her head and braced her hands on her wide hips. "Kate made a mistake by making you so independent."

"Kate did what she felt was best for me. She taught me that women have minds of their own and are capable of handling their own affairs, no matter what men may think. And until her death she lived what she believed."

"But Kate never tried to run a ranch with only one Mexican to help her," Edwina retorted, turning her attention back to the dough.

"No, Kate didn't try to run a ranch, but she handled her father's shipping business and cared for me. She never needed a husband or guardian to supervise or approve her every move. And I'm Kate's daughter in every sense of the word except in blood, Edwina. From her I learned not to throw my hands up in defeat at the first little setback. Nor will I ask for help until it is truly needed. Don't you see?'' Jessica said, her hand balling into a fist on the floured table. ''If I want to succeed, I must gain the other ranchers' respect. I can't act like a mewling babe at the first sign of trouble or I'll never be accepted here. This is a hard land, and the people here have to be strong to survive.'' Jessica angrily brushed another stray curl out of her eyes, unwittingly adding a streak of flour to her already smudged cheek. She took a deep breath and offered Edwina a wan smile. ''Will you have Maria prepare a bath for me. I'm going into town to put up another notice for help.''

''Do you think it'll do any good?'' Edwina asked. Noting the circles of fatigue beneath Jessica's eyes and the haggard droop of her slender shoulders, she couldn't chastise the girl further. Jessica was already near the point of exhaustion. The girl's outburst served only to show how close she was to collapse. She was usually even-tempered until she was pushed to her limit. A frown of worry etched a line across Edwina's brow. Until last week Jessica had never done any physical labor. Now she worked from daylight to dark. That alone was enough to concern Edwina for her friend's health.

''I hope it does. If I don't have a crew by next week when the stock arrives, I may have to ask for that help you keep wanting me to get,'' Jessica said, rolling her head from side to side to ease her aching muscles. Her anger had gone as fast as it had come. She wiped the sweat from the curve of her throat as she smiled at her housekeeper. ''Winnie, I'm going to lie down and rest for a little while. Call me when my bath is ready.''

Dressed in a fashionable, drape-skirted gown, a fitted jacket adorned with velvet trim, high boots, and a pert little straw bonnet to shade her face, Jessica drew the buckboard to a halt in front of the general store. She tied the reins to the seat and successfully managed to maneuver herself to the ground without mishap. However, her good fortune did not last. The long train of her expensive gown caught on the corner of the buckboard, and the sound of tearing material echoed through the hot afternoon air.

"Damn, I've had enough of this," Jessica stormed, furious with herself for not buying practical clothing. All the things she possessed were perfect for afternoon teas with the ladies or a stroll through the park. None, however, could withstand the conditions of her new way of life. Like the people in the West, the clothing had to be made of much sturdier stuff. Jerking the offending material free of the splinter that held it, she stalked into the general store. She paused only long enough to give her eyes time to adjust to the dim interior before she made her way to the shelves that contained men's denim work jeans.

"Can I help you, ma'am?" the store clerk asked, emerging from behind the counter. He crossed to where Jessica stood rifling through the pile of trousers stacked on a long table in front of shelves filled with bolts of material.

Jessica glanced at the little man who wore a string tie about his stiff collar and black protectors over his long-sleeved white shirt. "I need a pair of men's trousers."

"What size does your husband wear?" the clerk asked, lifting a pair of Levi's jeans for her inspection.

"I don't have a husband," Jessica said, spying a pair

of denims that looked to be her size. "They are for me."

"For you?" the clerk said. Appalled, he eyed her as if she'd suddenly grown two heads.

"Yes, thank you," Jessica said, her tone short. "And I will also need these items." She handed the Levi's and Edwina's list to the clerk, then marched over to the rack of guns that lined the opposite wall and took down a Remington rifle. She didn't know anything about weapons except that she would need one to protect her livestock from wild animals. She handed the rifle to the clerk. "I'll also take this. Will you add it and the ammunition to my bill?"

The clerk looked up from the list and back to Jessica. He gave her a sheepish little apologetic smile. The woman might be mad, but that was her business. She'd just given him a large order to fill. "I believe I have everything you need, ma'am."

"Good. Then I will be back within the hour. Please see that everything is placed in my buckboard." Without giving the clerk time to reply, Jessica strode from the store, her head high, the hem of her torn gown dragging in the dust behind her.

She ignored the looks she received from the men lounging on the bench outside the saloon, where they hoped to catch a cool breath of air. All conversation ceased as she passed them by without a glance. She made her way along the planked sidewalk to the Cattleman's Exchange to nail up another HELP WANTED notice on the board.

"She's a fine'un, ain't she, Brand?" Slim Johnson said, squinting from beneath his battered hat. His jaw bulged as he rolled the wad of tobacco into the opposite side before squirting a stream of brown juice into the dusty street.

"She'll do," Brand Stockton answered. He stretched his long legs out in front of him and crossed them at the ankles. His dusty boots, faded plaid shirt, and worn denims showed signs of hard wear and lack of care. The Colt in the leather holster at his side, however, gleamed blue-black with fresh oil. Brand wiped the sweat from the back of his neck with a bandanna as he watched Jessica nail up the notice and then haughtily cross the street to avoid having to pass the saloon again. Intrigued by her beauty far more than he wanted to admit, he followed her with his eyes, admiring the sway of her slender hips beneath the layers of material that made up the ridiculously long trained gown. His eyes drifted upward along the expanse of her minuscule waist and then to the ripe curves beneath the frilly blouse.

Brand felt his blood quicken. Slim was right—she was a beauty, he mused as he watched her lift the torn hem of her gown and step up on the sidewalk in front of the jail. His gaze moved upward to her lovely head and he took in her finely sculpted features for a fraction of a second before she turned to look at the WANTED posters tacked to the wall of the sheriff's office. She paused and then moved closer to read. Her curious reaction roused his curiosity.

"I guess the little lady ain't never seen a real criminal before," Slim said, also noting her interest.

"You could be right." Brand watched the young woman stiffen momentarily, then relax with apparent relief. When she turned and walked toward the general store, he managed to glimpse her expression. A provocative smile curled her sweetly shaped lips. "But I feel there's more here than meets the eye."

Slim Johnson glanced at Brand, his weathered features screwing up into a thoughtful frown. "What makes you say that?"

"I don't know, it's just something I feel."

"Damn it, Brand. There you go agin. You talk like one of them damned heathen redskins, always havin' feelin's in your bones and not knowin' what causes 'em."

Brand's head snapped around with the speed of a striking rattlesnake. He eyed his friend coldly through narrowed lashes. "Don't ever say I remind you of an Indian again."

The wrinkles in Slim's face deepened. "Sorry, Brand. I didn't mean nothin' by it. It's just that you always seem to sense things about people before anyone else."

Brand relaxed visibly, the tension draining from his lean body. He understood what Slim had been trying to say, yet he hadn't been able to stop his own reaction. His hatred for the red-skinned devils was far too deeply ingrained within him. Slim comparing him to an Indian was as much or more of an insult than spitting in his face; that would not have rankled half as much. "I didn't mean to jump down your throat, Slim. Let's just forget anything was ever said."

Slim gave Brand an uneasy grin and nodded. He was more than glad to forget his own stupidity in even suggesting Brand had any Indian blood. He, for one, never wanted Brand Stockton angry with him. The man could be lethal when in one of his black moods, and if anyone understood Brand Stockton's moods, he did. He'd been at his side for nearly fifteen years and knew the man better than anyone else alive. You couldn't live together through a war, fighting Indians, Mexicans, and outlaws, without finding out what made a man tick.

Brand turned his attention back to the young woman who was overseeing the loading of her buckboard. "Let's mosey on over to the jail and see what was so fascinating, Slim."

"I was wonderin' how long it'd take you to say that," Slim said. Grinning, he uncoiled his lanky limbs from their resting place on the hard bench. Squirting another stream of tobacco juice into the street, he came to his feet and squinted at his friend. "Are you goin' to look up Ramsey?"

Brand shook his head. "Nope. I'm here to get Fleming and not jump to every damned rancher's tune for miles around. There'll be time enough to tell Ramsey and the others I'm here when I finish what I've set out to do."

Slim scratched his beard-stubbled chin. The gray-and-black whiskers made him look like a dog needing a good mange dip. "I ain't certain the governor or the cap'n'll appreciate the way you're goin' about this job. It ain't like you to sneak around behind people's backs."

Brand stepped up on the sidewalk in front of the WANTED posters, his silver gaze coming to rest on the poster the beautiful young woman had found so interesting. "I know I usually handle things differently, but I don't want Fleming to know I'm here looking for him. He's too damned wily. Until now he's made a laughing-stock out of the law by managing to escape every trap set for him. But that's going to change. I've been a Ranger for nearly twelve years, and I haven't fought Indians and outlaws this long just to let a half-breed

Cherokee be the first to make a fool out of me.'' Brand's features hardened. ''Man with No People may be laughing now because no one's been able to catch him for rustling. But I'm the one who's going to have the last laugh. I'm going to be the one to see him swing, and I won't risk Fleming learning we're on his trail by telling the ranchers we're here.''

''I doubt any of the ranchers'd go out of their way to tell that varmint you're lookin' for him. They want to see him at the end of a rope too bad.''

''I don't say it would be the ranchers,'' Brand glanced down the street to where Jessica stood talking to the store clerk.

''Then who would warn him?'' Slim said, following the direction of Brand's gaze. He looked back to his friend. ''You don't think she knows anything about Fleming, do you?''

Brand shrugged. ''I can't be certain, but I suspect from her reaction to the poster that the young lady knows something about the half-breed.''

Again Slim scratched his chin. ''How you goin' t' find out what she knows when you don't even know who she is?''

Brand smiled down at his friend. ''The first thing I'm going to do is see what she nailed up at the Cattleman's Exchange. If it's a Help Wanted notice, as I suspect, I intend to apply for the job.''

''You what?''

''You heard what I said. I plan on hiring on with the little lady.''

''I ain't no cowhand, Brand,'' Slim said, his voice filling with disgust. ''I ain't never been a cowhand, and I don't never plan to be a cowhand.''

"Then perhaps you can hire on as the cook," Brand said, and chuckled at the look of disbelief that flickered across his friend's leathered features.

"A cook? Damn! That's even worst than being a cowhand."

Brand shrugged. "Look at it this way. It's all part of your job."

"When I joined the Rangers I didn't think I'd have to herd cattle or wear an apron."

Brand gave his friend a wry grin. "Perhaps it won't be so bad."

"Bad? Hell! It couldn't get worst."

Chapter 3

Jessie pushed her way through the thick underbrush and felt her heart lodge in her throat. She drew in an unsteady breath, hoping to ease the constriction that banded her chest at the sight of the dilapidated structure hidden away amid the overgrowth. She had avoided this place since returning to Texas. Until yesterday in town, when she'd seen the WANTED poster of Wade, she'd thought she could keep from coming back here to confront the memories. Each night for the past ten years she'd lived with the nightmare. Now she had to face it in the light of day.

Jessie swallowed again and took the first, hesitant step forward. Tears burned the backs of her lids as she moved slowly toward what had once been her home. The door now hung haphazardly by one hinge, and the glass was gone from the windows. Her breath caught in her throat as she forced her feet to carry her over the leaf-strewn threshold to the main room where she and her family had spent so many happy times together. She fought to suppress a flood of tears, knowing that once she gave way to the memories there would be no turning back. Jessica looked up through the hole in the roof to the pure blue of azure sky overhead. A shroud of darkness dimmed the clear day as the memories of that night gathered like storm clouds, forcing their way to the surface.

Jessie sank down amid the decaying leaves and rotting floorboards. Surrendering to the past, she curled her knees protectively against her chest and wrapped her arms about them before burying her face against the coarse denim. The self-confident Boston lady vanished into the still morning air as the years disappeared. In her place sat the small, barefoot, brown-skinned girl who had lived within these walls until the night she had been dragged abruptly from her innocent sleep to face a horror that would follow her through the years. . . .

"Sarah, keep the children inside," Earnest Fleming said, his worried voice rousing his sleeping children in the small cubbyhole where they slept.

Jessie blinked up through the shadows of night to see her parents standing in the moonlit room beyond the curtain that separated the main room from their sleeping quarters. She watched her father hurriedly drag on his pants and boots. In his haste he took no time to hoist his suspenders over his shoulders, and they sagged to his knees as he reached for the rifle he kept near his bed.

Sarah climbed out of the bed, her bare feet thumping on the floorboards, her face white with worry in the moonlight that streamed in through the window. "You can't go out there by yourself. They'll kill you."

"I can't stay inside and let them steal the herd, either. It's all we've got," Earnest said, loading the rifle and cramming extra ammunition into his pants pocket.

"Earnest, please. Don't go out there," Sarah pleaded.

Earnest paused only long enough to place a tender kiss upon his wife's beautiful mouth. He gazed down into her large blue eyes. Their color was between indigo and sapphire, known to many as Cherokee blue. Momentarily lost in their gentle depths, he brushed his knuckles against the smooth line of her cheek. "I'll be all right. Just keep the children inside and out of danger." With that he turned and walked from the log cabin that he and his wife had built with their own hands after coming to Texas.

"Mama, what's wrong?" Jessie said, padding across the dark room to where her mother stood. Unaware of the silent tears coursing down her ashen cheeks, Sarah watched her husband through the window. Jessie wrapped her small arms about her mother's legs and looked up at her. "Mama, why are you crying?"

"I'm just worried about your pa," Sarah Fleming said, absently caressing the dark hair so much like her own.

"Where has Pa gone?" asked fifteen-year-old Wade, pulling up his suspenders as he entered the room. "What's going on, Ma?"

Sarah Fleming turned to look at her oldest child. "Someone is trying to steal the stock."

"Why didn't Pa call me?" Wade said, reaching for his own rifle on the rack above the fireplace.

"Your father said for me to keep all of you here," Sarah said, not stopping Wade as he rushed out the door, his young chest bare of shirt or the masculine mat of hair that would come with maturity.

"I want to go help Pa, too," Jessie said, hurrying

over to where she and Joe had left the play guns her father had carved out of wood for them the previous Christmas.

"Jessie," Sarah said. "I need you to stay here with Joe."

"But, Ma," Jessie whined, "I'm big enough to help Pa and Wade."

"I know you are, but I need your help here more. I want you to promise me that you'll stay here and keep Joe safe," Sarah said, pulling her shawl about her shoulders. "It's very important that you watch over your little brother. You know he's been sick lately, and the night air won't do his lungs any good. And he'll do as you ask. You know how much he loves you."

"Oh, all right," Jessie grumbled, relenting. "I'll keep Joe inside." And she would. She loved all of her family, and her youngest brother held a special place in her heart. Since the day of his birth he'd never been a healthy child, yet he had a loving nature that couldn't be denied. His little smile seemed to brighten up the gloomiest day. To Jessie, Joe was like one of the angels her ma had told her about from the Bible.

Sarah bent and placed a kiss on her daughter's brow before she hurried in the direction her husband and son had taken. A few minutes later Jessie stood at the window, a silent scream tearing at her throat, her small nails biting into the wood of the windowsill. The light of the full moon hid nothing from her young eyes, and she watched as a masked gunman chased Wade down with his horse. Using the butt of his rifle as a weapon, he felled her brother with one blow to the head. Wade crumbled into the dust, facedown, a dark streak of blood streaming from his temple.

A scream of outrage escaping her, Sarah Fleming, like any animal protecting her offspring, rushed forward toward her son, but she never reached his side. A gunman reined his horse to a halt near the cabin and took careful aim at the woman whose dark hair streamed behind her in a silken cloud. She was knocked off her feet by the bullet to her heart before the sound from the masked man's rifle echoed over the noise the cattle rustlers made as they stole the Flemings' stock. Earnest Fleming, his maddened cry of pain and rage filling the night, raised his own rifle. A gunshot to the temple ended his life instantly.

Her pale face horror-stricken, Jessie watched the armed horseman urge his mount sideways in the moonlight to inspect his victims. Completely unaware that he was being observed or too arrogant and coldhearted to care that the small girl had witnessed her family's annihilation, he called out to the horseman who had downed Wade.

"I guess that shows the Indian-loving bastard what we think of his kind. And this little darling here has served me well once more."

His words as well as his masked, devillike image branded itself into Jessie's brain. Nor would she ever forget how he had lovingly caressed the intricately carved stock of his rifle before slipping it into the sheath at the side of his saddle.

The night was still. The sound of the rustlers and cattle had died away before Jessie could force her small legs to carry her out of the cabin to her mother's side. Six-year-old Joe clung to her tenaciously as she stood gazing down at their mother's body. Sarah lay on her back, a large circle of blood staining the chest of her white nightgown. Joe wept silently, sniffling against Jessie as they stood, two lost and terror-filled souls amid the rustlers' carnage. The moonlight softened Sarah's expression, and she looked to the two children as if she only slept. Jessie knew better, however. Her mother, father, and brother were all dead.

Dry-eyed and in a state of shock, she turned away from the three people who had been so full of life and love only a few short hours earlier. As was their regular routine, they had all gathered about the fireplace after finishing their chores and supper. Each night Sarah Fleming would tell the stories that had been passed down through her people, the Cherokee . . . stories that depicted the history of her people, stories of the trail of tears and the blue mountains in the east, where the Cherokees had lived until the white man had driven them west. When she finished telling of the Cherokee's adventures, she would take down the old, battered Fleming family Bible from its special shelf and read. Before they all went to bed, they would say their prayers together. It had been the same each night for as long as Jessie could remember.

Jessie felt she would explode from the misery welling within her small body, yet she suppressed her tears. She wanted to cry and scream, but Joe was now her responsibility, and in her ten-year-old wisdom she knew she had to be strong for him. She was all he had left.

A moan from Wade brought Jessie to a halt. The sound was like a cleansing wave. It washed over Jessie, relieving her of the burden of the last horror-filled minutes. Her grief and fear rushed to the surface when she saw her brother raise himself on his elbows and shake his head. The tears she'd been holding at bay flooded her eyes as ran to Wade's side and fell on her knees in front of him. She clasped him about the waist, seeking his comfort. Her small body trembling with terror, she cried, "Wade, they killed Mama and Papa! . . ."

The black fog of the past began to clear from Jessie's mind as she raised her head and peered into the shadows of the rotting cabin. Wade—dear, brave, fifteen-year-old Wade—had been made into a man that night, though the world still viewed him as a boy. He'd taken on the burden of burying their parents and trying to keep their family together when the authorities had come to send them to the orphans' mission in Indian territory. He'd done his best to fight for their right to stay on their land, but the men who wanted the Flemings' land for grazing had the power to enforce the Texas law, which forbade them owning land because of the Cherokee blood flowing in their veins. It didn't matter that they were also half white. In the eyes of greedy men who had powerful friends in government, the children of Sarah Fleming were Indians and belonged with their own kind in Oklahoma Territory.

Jessie had watched the impotent fury build within her older brother during the months they had stayed at the mission and then later, when Kate had adopted them. He never accepted the new life he was given when Kate retired from teaching at the mission school and returned them to Boston, where she took over the operations of her family's shipping business. She had wanted Wade to learn and follow in her footsteps, but he never fit into eastern society; he had felt only contempt for it. He'd immersed himself more and more into their mother's people's history, until he had supplanted the white in himself. Wade had been seventeen when he had run away from Kate and Boston and the white man's way of life. When the harsh Bostonian winter had broken the last threads holding Joe's fragile health and he'd succumbed to an infection the doctors had called pneumonia, his death had also severed the last link that had held Wade in Boston. He had stayed only long enough to see Joe buried in the Nolan family plot. Wade had then hugged Jessie good-bye and promised her he would never forget her. That had been the last time she'd seen her brother, and until yesterday afternoon when she'd seen the WANTED poster tacked to the jail wall, Jessie hadn't known if he was still alive.

"Where are you, Wade?" Jessie asked the still morning air. She'd asked the same question all through the long night. Tossing and turning on her soft down mattress, she'd wondered how she could find her brother before he was caught and hanged for his crimes of rustling cattle.

Jessie pushed herself to her feet and dusted off her hands. Her gaze drifted over the small room for any sign of the family who had once resided within it. There was nothing left, nothing to show the love that had existed within its crumbling walls. The only sign of life was a grouse hen's nest in the corner.

Jessie knelt before the leaves and twigs scattered amid the empty shells. Carefully she picked up one of the thin, porcelainlike casements that had nourished the grouse's young chicks until it was time for them to enter the world. She turned it over in her hand and then tossed it away sadly. This cabin, like the grouse's nest, had nothing left except the broken shells of her family's dreams.

Jessie got to her feet, her expression resolute as she once more scanned the place she'd called home in the first years of her life. Everything had decayed except the dream she had nourished since the day she and her brothers had stood over their parents' grave. They had vowed to come back to Texas and take back the land that had been taken from them. Now Jessie would let nothing stand in her way. She had money, and money meant power. She would use it to show the world that Earnest Fleming's family could not be so easily driven from the land they owned.

Jessie drew in a deep breath and stiffened her spine. For now she would continue to keep her identity a secret. She knew that her appearance revealed little of her Cherokee blood. She resembled her mother, possessing the same blue eyes and dark hair. Her features, like her mother's, were finely molded, revealing the interbreeding between Cherokee and white that had once existed before the Cherokee were sent west from their homes in Georgia and Tennessee. And her genteel life in Boston had continued to shield her heritage, causing the sun's tint to fade from her skin.

Yes, for now she would keep her identity secret. When the time was right she would proudly announce it to the world and dare anyone to deny her rights because of the blood within her veins.

Jessie withdrew her riding gloves from where she had tucked them in the back pocket of her denims and slipped them on. She was glad she had come back. Standing amid the ruins of her home only reaffirmed her decision to return to Texas and take back what rightfully belonged to her. Her only regret was that Wade and Joe weren't standing at her side.

"Joe is dead, but Wade is out there somewhere," she said to the rotting logs. "And I intend to find him."

Determination in each step, Jessie left behind the crumbling ruins without bidding a final farewell to the memories. She could only do that when she had succeeded in establishing her ranch and found the man who had murdered her parents.

Jessie hoisted herself back into the saddle and unconsciously made a face at the pain that rippled along her tender backside. She maneuvered her horse along the wash, up the slope, and back in the direction of the ranch house. She'd not come back here until all the scores had been settled. Then she would return and lay the past to rest. Then Eden would truly be the land of a new life and a new beginning for her.

Brand and Slim reined their mounts to a halt in front of the gates. A new sign swayed gently in the Texas breeze, the burned letters black against the wood of warm mellow gold.

"Eden? What kind of name is that for a ranch?" Slim asked, leaning to one side to squirt a stream of tobacco juice into the dust. He rolled the wad into his other jaw and scratched his beard-stubbled chin. "Sounds to me like some prissy back eastern name."

Brand grinned. "What did you expect? The clerk at the store said she was from Boston. It's a wonder she didn't call it Beacon Hill or Tea Party or some other such nonsense."

Slim frowned at his friend, totally misunderstanding Brand's humor. "It's a wonder. Women ain't got no right to be namin' ranches or for that matter running them. Their place is in the kitchen or a man's bed."

"I suspect you're right about that," Brand said, urging his mount forward. After what he'd seen yesterday of the young owner of Eden, he couldn't imagine her running a ranch. In her fancy gown she didn't look capable of doing anything beyond making herself look good. She was a useless tidbit of a woman, something to grace a fancy parlor or, like Slim had said, a man's bed. Brand smiled to himself. He could think of worse things. He wouldn't object to having a few tumbles with the young beauty from back east. And if things went well for them today, he could envision that event in the near future. Few women he'd met had been able to resist him once he set his mind to have them.

"Suspect I'm right? Hell! I am right," Slim grumbled, following suit.

A few minutes later the two men sat staring in surprise at the woman in the paddock, currying a bay mare. A smile of appreciation curled Brand's lips at the sight of the rounded bottom turned in their direction and displayed to perfection by the tight-fitting denims. Perhaps he'd been a little hasty in his judgment about women running ranches, but he suspected his other observations were right on the mark. His smile deepened at the thought. There could be some pleasurable advantages to having a boss lady if she always dressed in men's trousers. Brand watched her brush the horse's flank, allowing his gaze to slide down her slender legs to the small booted feet and then back up over her trim hips past the tiny waist to the full breasts pressed enticingly against the plaid shirt. Yes, he mused, leaning forward and folding his arms across the saddle horn, there could be some very pleasurable advantages.

Brand cleared his throat, drawing the woman's attention. She straightened, brushed a stray curl off her brow, tossed the long braid of dark hair over her shoulder, and gave the mare a sharp pat, sending the animal trotting across the paddock to the water trough. The ebony braid swayed just below her waist as she strode toward them. Her slender hips moved provocatively with each step. Brand had to fight to keep his eyes away from the mesmerizing movement. She braced a booted foot on the lower rung of the fence and looked over the top slat at them, making Brand realize for the first time that she was only a tiny thing. In town the previous day, dressed in her fancy gown and walking with her head tilted haughtily in the air, she'd appeared much larger and much more intimidating.

"Could I help you?" Jessie asked, swiping another ornery curl from her damp brow.

"We're here to see about the job," Brand said, swinging down from the saddle and closing the space between them. "I'm Brand Stockton, and this is my friend, Slim Johnson. We saw your notice at the Cattleman's Exchange."

Jessie felt like jumping for joy but forced herself to maintain a dignified demeanor. After all, it wouldn't impress these men to see her do a little jig. If she wanted them to respect her and remain to work for her, she'd have to act like the proper boss lady.

"I'm Jessica Nolan, and I own Eden," she said, and allowed a long moment to pass so they could absorb that bit of information. "The job pays a dollar a day, and you'll get a bonus for every steer you deliver safely to market."

Brand nodded. "Sounds fair, but my friend here doesn't want to work with the herd."

Jessie eyed the beard-stubbled man who sat regarding her from the shadow of his battered hat. She couldn't read the expression in his narrowed eyes but suspected he didn't like the idea of working for a woman. She shrugged. There weren't many men who did, and as long as he kept his opinions to himself and did his job, it didn't matter what he thought.

"I need men to work the cattle, but I also need a cook for the men." She looked toward the silent man on the horse and then back to Brand. "Can he cook?"

Brand nodded.

Laying aside the currying brush, Jessie removed her gloves and tucked them once more into the rear pocket of her denims before she crawled through the paddock slats to face the two men. She raised a hand to shade her face and noticed for the first time the cool gray of Brand Stockton's eyes. They reminded her of shining silver coins fringed in black silk.

Jessie shook the thought away from her. She didn't know what on earth had gotten into her since coming to Texas. It must be something in the water, because she had never been so obviously aware of men in Boston. First she'd found Clint Ramsey attractive, and now she was assessing an unshaven, long-haired cowhand. Giving herself a sharp mental shake, she said, "You have the jobs. My herd is due to arrive next week."

"Who's your foreman?" Brand asked.

"At the moment I don't have one. How would you like the job? It pays ten dollars more a month." Jessie blurted out.

"I don't know," Brand answered honestly, his expression mirroring his surprise that she would offer him such a position so soon. He'd planned to hire on temporarily as a cowhand, not take on the responsibility of running the place, especially since he'd only be here long enough to learn what Miss Nolan knew of the half-breed rustler. Brand glanced toward Slim, who sat frowning down at him. His friend's eyes plainly indicated his opposition to the idea.

"You don't have to give me your answer now," Jessie said, regaining some of her common sense and feeling completely incompetent. She'd managed to handle every situation that had developed, with the exception of finding men to work for her. Now she had asked this stranger—who looked like a saddle bum with his long black unkempt hair, worn boots, and dusty clothes—to be Eden's foreman. If she wanted to create a disaster, it would be much simpler to place a stick of dynamite beneath the barn and blow it up. Hiring the wrong man as Eden's foreman would ruin the ranch.

Recognizing uncertainty in Jessie's voice, Brand gave her a reassuring smile. "Until I've seen the place and know a little more about it, I won't know if I want the job, Miss Nolan."

"I can understand your position, Mr. Stockton," Jessie answered quickly, relieved that he had not accepted her terms immediately. Though her stupidity didn't deserve it, she had been given a reprieve. Now she would have time to learn more about the man and his qualifications before she placed the ranch in his hands. A foreman could make or break a ranch when it was just getting started. A few bad decisions in the first years could ruin any hope of success.

"You can look the place over this afternoon. I need to ride out to Little Creek to make sure there's enough grass for the herd when it arrives, and I'd appreciate your opinion," Jessie said.

"Be glad to, Miss Nolan," Brand said, admiring her easy way of testing his qualifications for the job she'd offered. The girl might be new at this, but she wasn't stupid. She'd already realized her mistake in offering the job of foreman so quickly. It would be interesting to see how well she'd manage to avoid giving him the answers he needed about the half-breed.

Brand glanced up at his friend, a calculating light gleaming in his silver eyes. "Slim, stow our stuff in the bunkhouse while I ride out with Miss Nolan."

The afternoon sunlight splashed Slim's face, and he squinted against its brightness as he watched Brand and Jessica ride away. He shook his head. Things had gone smoothly—too smoothly, in his opinion. They'd been hired on the spot, and now, within only a few hours of their arrival at Eden, Brand was off with the beautiful Miss Nolan to look at grazing land.

Slim shook his head and ran his hand over the back of his hot neck. That Miss Nolan was something else. She'd been dressed to the nines yesterday in town, looking every inch the easterner. However, when they rode up this morning, she had looked anything but the lady currying down that mare. But that wasn't what had shocked him. The woman had been wearing men's britches just like she belonged in them. Slim sniffed in disdain. She probably did think she should wear men's britches, since she thought she could run a ranch like a man.

Disgruntled, Slim glanced over his shoulder toward the house where the old biddy had marched off to after giving him his orders. She made him regret his statement to Brand that it couldn't get worst if he had to hire on as a cowhand or a trail cook. Meeting Edwina Roilings made him realize things could get much, much worst.

Slim's hackles rose again at the thought of her. That stiff-spined old maid had had the gall to act as if *she* were the boss lady. Without a "thank you" or a "go to hell," she had haughtily informed him of his duties about the ranch—stating coldly that since he didn't plan to help ride herd on the cattle, he was now in charge of the bunkhouse. It was his duty to see that the men were fed.

That in itself didn't surprise or bother Slim overmuch; he'd expected no less when Brand had come up with this harebrained scheme. He could round up a few cans of beans and fry steak as good as the next man. However, when she'd ordered him to make sure the bunkhouse was kept clean and tidy at all times, Slim had thought he'd not heard her right. She wanted a spotless bunkhouse!

With that order Slim had thought he'd explode. The hussy acted as if he were her servant, but if he had his way, Miss High and Mighty from back east would learn that western men didn't turn into parlor maids. He didn't plan to mollycoddle any damn cowhands or anyone else.

"Nope, Miss Winnie Roilings. I ain't no nursemaid nor no dat-blasted housekeeper. I'll do what's expected and no more." Feeling much better, Slim picked up his saddle bags and bedroll and headed toward the bunkhouse. At least tonight he didn't have to cook for anyone but himself and Brand.

When he stepped inside the long building that would

be home to more than ten men when the ranch had an entire crew, Slim couldn't believe his eyes. He gaped at the neat counterpanes covering the bunks, as well as the checked tablecloth and curtains over the windows. There was even a vase of wildflowers in the middle of the table.

Slim rolled his eyes heavenward. It was the darnedest sight he'd ever seen. A bunkhouse for cowhands all rigged out like a woman's tea parlor. He gave a snort of disgust, already suspecting Miss Winnie Roilings's hand in the decorations. Slim tossed his saddle bags onto the floor at the foot of one bunk before he jerked the counterpane from it. He then proceeded to unmake every bed as well as take down the curtains and tablecloth. The wildflowers were tossed out the open door without a second thought.

"Just what do you think you're doing?" came Edwina's strident voice from the doorway.

Slim dropped the pile of stiffly starched material at his feet and turned to look at the furious woman blocking the doorway. She stood rigid, hands on her hips.

"I'm making this place livable. No man worth his salt would sleep in this tea parlor."

"How dare you say such a thing! I personally made those curtains and that tablecloth so the men would feel at home."

"Home, lady? Cowhands only want a place to fill their stomachs and kick off their boots. They ain't got no use for your female gigaws. There ain't a cowhand from here to California that would get a lick of rest in here with it all dressed up like a parlor awaiting the preacher on Sunday. They'd be too afeared they'd get your counterpanes dirty."

Edwina glanced at the pile of material on the floor and realized her mistake. She had hoped her extra effort would help Jessica find enough men to work the ranch. She had been certain when they saw how homey the bunkhouse looked, they'd be more than eager to hire on. She looked back at the man facing her and gracefully accepted his advice. "Skinny, I didn't know. I was only trying to make this place more livable."

"My name is Slim, not Skinny. And as far as making this place livable, I see nothing wrong with it right now. We got everything we need. A place to lay our heads and a place to fill our bellies after a hard day's work."

"Then I'll leave you to get settled," Edwina said, vowing silently that before she made a fool of herself in the future, she'd take the time to ask someone's opinion about things. In Boston, she'd known how to handle every situation. Here in Texas, however, it seemed the rules were completely different. It was a hard life, and the men seemed in no way inclined to make it easier. "Dinner will be ready when Jessica and Mr. Stockton return," she said. "The well is behind the house if you need water to wash."

Scratching his chin, Slim watched Edwina stride back toward the house; he wondered if the old maid was getting sick, to have given up without a fight. He shook his head. Women! They were something he'd never been able to figure out. That was the reason he had never married. He much preferred the company of his own kind. They didn't nag you to death, and when they were angry, you either shook hands and apologized or ended up six feet under. Men were direct and straightforward in their dealing, while women always seemed to have to work their way around you to get their way.

He glanced toward the pile of material. There was only one place in his life for women, and with a ten-dollar gold piece in his pocket and a bottle of whiskey, he could have all he needed for an entire night.

The late afternoon sun splashed Edwina in gold as she stepped upon the porch and made her way into the house. Watching her through the window, Slim couldn't stop himself from wondering how it would be to have a woman like that in his bed. Would she make love with passion, or would she be as cold as a dead cow in a blizzard?

"Well, that's one thing I won't ever know," he said, crossing to the dry sink where the tin bucket sat waiting to be filled. He turned toward the door. He supposed it wouldn't hurt to have a wash before dinner. After all, they would be eating with ladies.

Chapter 4

Clouds of bronze, gold, and vivid rose streaked the
western sky. The plaintiff cry of a young calf in search
of its mother rose above the lowing that filled the evening air. Folding her arms over the saddle horn, Jessie
watched with amusement as the small spotted animal
raised its tail in the air and ran on spindly legs toward
the cow grazing peacefully near the creek. The mother
paid no heed to her hungry offspring and he nuzzled at
her tits and then set about to appease his appetite with
a healthy meal of warm milk. Giving a flick of her tail
to swat away the horseflies that swarmed in a black
cloud about the herd, the cow continued nonchalantly
to enjoy her own meal of sweet grass.

Jessie smiled with satisfaction, enjoying the sight
of the herd grazing on the thick range grass carpeting
the creek bottomland. A sense of contentment spread
through her like a warm breeze. For the first time
since returning to Texas, she felt everything was
going as she had planned. She was now seeing her
father's dream come to life. The herd had arrived
on schedule the previous week, and she now had
enough men to work them, thanks to Brand Stock-

ton's forethought to offer the drovers permanent jobs at Eden.

Jessie glanced once more toward the brilliant sunset and realized that so much had changed at Eden since the arrival of Brand and his friend, Slim Johnson. She could now sit quietly and enjoy a sunset without worrying that the ranch would fall apart without her there to supervise things. It felt good to have a few free moments just to savor life's small pleasures.

Although Brand had not officially accepted the job as Eden's foreman, he had taken on the responsibilities. His actions had relieved Jessie of much of the stress she'd been under since arriving at Eden and had also made her realize that she'd nearly forgotten what it was like to totally relax after a hard day's work.

Jessie glanced at the man of her thoughts. He sat mounted next to her on an ebony Morgan. Jessie allowed her gaze to wander over his sculpted profile while his attention was centered on the drovers settling down the herd for the night. Brand Stockton intrigued her with his good looks as well as his reticence about his past. He'd been at Eden for several weeks, yet she knew no more about him now than she had the first day he'd arrived. She'd quickly learned he knew how to handle cattle as well as men, putting an end to her speculations about his qualifications as Eden's foreman; but the rest of his life was still a mystery.

Jessie shrugged away her curiosity. Whatever was in Brand's past was his own business. He did the job she'd hired him to do, and that was all she asked. In only a matter of days she'd come to depend upon his knowledge and advice.

It was strange to realize how easily she had come to trust this man, a complete stranger. She felt he had dealt honestly with her, and she respected the decisions he'd made about the ranch. It would be hard should he decide to turn down her offer and leave. Struck by the realization of how much she and Eden needed Brand Stockton, Jessie couldn't stay the question that rose to her lips. "Brand, have you thought about my offer?"

"What offer are you talking about?" Brand turned his silver gaze upon Jessie and arched one dark brow.

"My offer of the foreman's job," Jessie said, returning Brand's direct look.

Brand shifted in the saddle and looked once more toward the lazy beasts munching happily near the creek. He rubbed a hand over his beard-stubbled cheek. "I haven't made any decision."

"Well, the job's yours if you want it. You've earned it in the past weeks," Jessie said, feeling a sense of disappointment wash over her. She had hoped for a different answer, but she wouldn't push. It was his decision, and she'd have to respect it.

Brand glanced once more at Jessie. "I just did what I was hired to do."

"No, you've done much more, and I'm grateful. Were it not for you, I wouldn't have anyone to work the cattle."

"I can't take all the credit for that," Brand said, giving her a wry grin.

"You can. As you and I both know, none of the men would have stayed at Eden if you hadn't convinced them it wasn't a disgrace to work for a woman," Jessie said, her lips curling up in a sardonic grin.

"Perhaps." Brand turned his gaze back to the herd. Jessie's gratitude made him uncomfortable. He'd always been straightforward and honest in his dealings with people until he'd met Miss Jessica Nolan. Now the trust she placed in him pricked at a conscience he'd long thought dead and buried.

Unaccustomed to guilt, Brand shrugged off the unusual feeling. He had done only what he'd had to do to gain his own ends. He wanted Fleming, the man the Indians had named Man with No People. And he intended to get him one way or the other. Brand cast a surreptitious glance in Jessie's direction. He'd been sent here to do a job, and he'd damn well do it. And that included making Jessica Nolan trust him enough to reveal what she knew of the rustler. "I think it might be a good idea to put out an extra nightwatch for a while," he said. "I've heard several ranches in the area have been hit recently by rustlers."

"Oh?" Jessie said, her thoughts going immediately to the poster she'd seen of her brother. Her heart began to race, although she forced herself to remain calm and focus her attention on the cattle. She couldn't allow her feelings to show. Any interest she revealed in the rustlers would raise questions she didn't want to answer at the moment. Her relationship with Wade would have to remain a secret for his sake as well as her own. Should anyone find out he was her brother, it could well cost him his life.

"They said it was a half-breed from Indian territory: a man by the name of Wade Fleming," Brand said, watching carefully for Jessie's reaction to the name.

"Indian territory?" Jessie asked evenly, straining to keep any trace of emotion from her voice.

"Yeah, just north of here. They say Fleming has friends there who help him sell off the stock he steals and then they hide him from the law.'' A frown etched a path across Brand's smooth brow. Jessie's cool response puzzled him. There had not been even a flicker of interest in her sapphire eyes when he'd mentioned the renegade's name. The first glimmer of doubt crept into his mind. Perhaps he'd been wrong after all to believe the beautiful Miss Nolan knew something about Wade Fleming.

Jessie's heart hammered excitedly against her ribs. Brand Stockton had given her the first clue to her brother. Wade still had friends in Indian territory, and should she find them, they might help her get a message to him. She knew it was a long shot, but it was the only hope she had of finding her brother.

Anxious now to send word to the mission where she and her brothers had been sent after their parents' deaths, Jessie turned her cool gaze back to Brand and said, ''If you feel the rustlers might strike Eden, then do what you think is best. We can't afford to lose any stock.'' She glanced up at the purpling twilight sky. ''I'm going to ride on back. It's getting late, and I still have to look over the account books tonight. I'll see you tomorrow, Brand.''

Before Brand could say anything more, Jessie drew her mount around and spurred the animal in the side, urging him into a swift trot toward home.

Frowning, Brand watched Jessie ride away. Account books! Something had set the beautiful Miss Nolan's kettle to boiling, but he doubted it was the account books.

Perplexed, Brand thoughtfully narrowed his eyes and considered his young boss lady. He didn't understand her. She was far from what he'd expected when he'd arrived at Eden, and he couldn't deny that she intrigued him. He'd known many women since becoming a man, but she didn't fit into any category or mold like the others. She was a lady, though she wore denims like a man. She was a city-bred girl from Boston, yet he had learned in the past few weeks that she possessed the courage, determination, and spirit of a true Texan. She was wealthy, but she found pleasure in the simple things that money could not buy. He'd seen that tonight, as she'd watched the calf search out his missing mother.

Yes, he mused. Miss Nolan was a mystery, and she was also one of the sexiest women he'd ever set eyes on. Lately he'd found himself hard-pressed to keep his attention centered on his work when she strode about the ranch with her long ebony braid swinging down her back and her tight denim britches hugging her shapely bottom like a second skin.

Brand shifted in the saddle to ease the sudden discomfort created by the images in his mind. This Saturday he'd have to find time for a quick trip into town to see the bosomy redhead at Miss Molly's house. . . .

The lines about Brand's mouth and eyes deepened as he turned his thoughts once more to his purpose for coming to Eden. Instinct told him there was more to the lovely Miss Nolan than just her beauty, but so far his instincts were all he had to go on. He'd seen nothing to confirm his first suspicions.

"And from now on I'll keep my mind on business and my distance from Miss Nolan," he muttered. Drawing his horse about, he headed off in the direction Jessie had traveled only moments before. The lovely Miss Nolan was off limits. She was an enchanting bit of female, but he already knew enough about her to surmise that she wasn't the type of woman who would be willing to fall into his bed and then go about her own business. She'd expect him to put a wedding ring on her finger, and marriage—to any woman—was the one thing he planned to avoid. His life as a Texas Ranger suited him well, and it offered him the only opportunity to finish the mission he'd set for himself twelve years ago.

Brand's mood darkened with the evening sky. He had requested this assignment from his commanding officer at Ranger headquarters in Austin—just like he'd requested every assignment that would take him close to Indian territory since becoming a Ranger soon after the war.

Silver eyes deepening to storm cloud gray, Brand allowed his thoughts to wander back to the day he had returned home to find his family dead. They had been slaughtered by the Comanche, who had cut a bloody path across the frontier during the years of the war. Even afterward, without the federal troops, they had continued to massacre the whites. Years later there were still grizzly reminders of what had happened. The land was dotted with chimneys where the Comanche had burned the homes of those they had slaughtered. After the raid on the Stockton ranch, the bodies of his parents and two younger brothers had been found in the ashes of their cabin. However, his eight-year-old sister, Mercy, his favorite sibling and the joy of his heart, had seemingly vanished from the face of the earth.

Brand looked up at the first stars to stud the night sky and for what seemed like the millionth time wondered if Mercy still lived. He had searched for her for twelve years, but he'd found no trace of the beautiful child he had left weeping on the doorstep when he'd gone off to fight for the South. He remembered well the feel of her plump little-girl's arms about his neck as she'd hugged him good-bye, and he'd never forgotten the pale blue eyes that had glistened with tears. They always reminded him of the Texas sky on a clear day. For three horror-filled years he had held on to the memory. It had been the image of Mercy's sweet innocence that had sustained him during the times when it seemed there was no tenderness or love left in the world. He'd returned home defeated in body and spirit to find the horror had not ended for him when Lee surrendered to Grant at Appomattox.

That day something within him had died. Through the years of the Civil War, watching brother fight against brother, he'd managed to hold on to the softer, gentler side of himself because of the family that awaited his return to Texas. He knew his family's love would help heal his mental and physical wounds. They would give him the solace he needed to · overcome the hatred spawned when he watched his friends die.

However, the Comanches' raid on his family's ranch ended any chance of putting the hatred behind him. Like a wild, writhing thing with a ravenous appetite for revenge, it took hold of him, blinding him to everything but his need to seek those who had killed his family. The monster forced out all the tenderness left within his soul, until a shell formed over his heart that no pain could pierce. When the federal troops failed to put an end to the red scourge swarming over Texas, leaving a bloody path of death and destruction in its wake, he had joined the Texas Rangers to ease his lust for revenge.

With deadly intent, he had sought out his enemy—
the Indian. He had fought with the Rangers, leaving
dead and wounded behind, until now only a few of the
red vermin remained in the high plains of Texas. Yet
his rage had not waned over the years. The need for
revenge still burned within his soul as bright as ever,
driving him on in his search for Mercy.

Brand glanced up at the darkening sky. He knew he
would never live in peace until he found his sister. She
was his beacon, the only hope he had of salvaging a
part of his soul. Until he held her once more in his
arms, he could not live as other men lived, nor could
he look toward the future with any hope.

The last streaks of bronze faded to indigo as darkness
claimed the land. The night was still and quiet. No
moonlight relieved the shadows that obscured the riders
waiting patiently in the stand of loblolly pine on the hill
overlooking Little Creek. No sound revealed their presence to the drovers watching over the herd of longhorns
resting peacefully, unware of the danger lurking beyond
the gurgling stream.

"Wade, are we going to hit 'em tonight?" Renegade
whispered, twisting about to look at the man mounted
Indian fashion on the brown-and-white pinto.

Tense with fury, his icy expression hidden by the
blanket of darkness, Wade gave a shake of his dark
head. "Not tonight. They've posted an extra watch, so
they're expecting trouble. We'll let things settle down
for a few days and then we'll hit them." A cold smile
curled his lips. "But be assured, old friend. When we
return, they'll lose far more than a few head."

Renegade raised a hand and traced the scar that ran

from the corner of his right eye to the edge of his chin. "Then what are your plans? We've come too far to go back empty-handed."

"I don't intend to go back empty-handed. I promised the Comancheros horses, and I plan to deliver. Ramsey has a good stock of prime horseflesh at the Lazy L."

"Aren't you daring the bastard to come after us? We've already hit his spread once this month."

Wade shrugged. "I'd welcome a chance to face Ramsey on my own ground, but I know him better than that. The low-down good-for-nothing is too cowardly to come after me on his own. He's such a fine, upstanding citizen, he won't stoop to dirty his own hands. He'll have a hired gun put a bullet in my back for him."

"You know Ramsey pretty well, don't you?" Renegade said, a grin exposing tobacco-stained teeth.

"I know the bastard too well. He's the man who always thought he was better than us because of my mother. He treated Pa like dirt because he married a woman with Indian blood. And he was one of the ranchers who made sure me, Joe, and Jessie were sent to the mission in Indian territory after our folks were killed. Some of the others said they couldn't see why we had to be sent away because we were just as much white as we were Indian. But Ramsey was the boss. He had the power to make sure he got his way. The few who had spoken up for us had to back down or live to regret going up against him."

"I'd suspected there was something that made you choose this area for our jobs," Renegade said. Wade's revelation didn't surprise him. He'd known there were things in Wade's past that drove him, yet Renegade was wise enough not to pry into any man's past. Being nosy could be hazardous to your health. Many a man had asked the wrong question and had ended up six feet under. On the frontier a man's business was his own, and if you treasured your life, you kept it that way.

"I've a score to settle with Ramsey and a few others in the area," Wade said, turning to look in the direction the man and young woman had ridden earlier. His indigo eyes glittered with suppressed rage. He suspected from the way the two had sat overseeing the herd that they were the new owners of his pa's ranch. He'd heard the state had sold the land, but he'd been unable to learn who'd bought it. But it really didn't matter a damn who they were: he'd still make them pay for believing they could own the land that was his by right.

Renegade accepted Wade's statement without comment. "Then let's get about it. The night ain't getting no younger."

Sitting in the shadows of the porch on one of the high-backed rockers, Clint Ramsey watched Jessica come striding toward the house from the barn. Unaware of his presence, she stopped in the golden streak of lamplight spilling through the windows and nimbly unfastened the top buttons of her shirt. Gazing up at the star-filled sky, she took a deep breath of the cool evening air and absently loosed her thick dark hair from the restriction of the braid. She ran her fingers through the mass of shining silk and gave a toss of her lovely head. The ebony mane spilled carelessly down her back to the waist of the britches hugging her slender hips.

Clint's breath froze at her unconsciously sensuous actions. His rib cage suddenly felt as though it contained a herd of wild mustangs trying to break free. His heart pounded. Blood rushed to his temples and made him feel slightly giddy. He swallowed hard to ease the sudden constriction in his throat.

It had been years since any woman had affected him in such a manner. Since an accident ten years earlier when he'd been gorged in the abdomen by a bull, he'd thought his sexual drive dead. He'd tried to convince himself he would not be left less than a whole man, but since that day no woman had been able to arouse him physically. Finally he'd given up the attempt to reclaim his virility after several embarrassingly futile attempts that had left him too humiliated even to go to the whores at Miss Molly's.

Raging against God and man, he'd turned all his energies to building the finest and largest ranch in Texas to prove to himself and the world that he was still a man. Perhaps he couldn't bed a woman, but he'd found that possessing political and financial power over other men was nearly as heady an experience.

Suddenly a thrill of anticipation shot through him. The way he now felt, he could believe there was nothing physically wrong with him after all. Perhaps it had taken this long for him to heal properly, as well as the right woman to make him realize it. And that woman was Jessica Nolan. She was what he needed to bring all his dead hopes and dreams back to life. She was the one woman who could make him regain his manhood.

The prospect of such an event made Clint's mouth suddenly go dry. Everything was now clear to him, and if he played his cards right, he'd have both Miss Jessica Nolan and the land he needed for the Lazy L. He smiled to himself. That would solve two of his problems at once.

Clint cleared his throat and came to his feet as Jessica stepped upon the porch. Her thoughts still lingering on Wade's whereabouts, she was startled by the rancher's sudden appearance and jumped back with a start, a cry of surprise on her lips.

"Jessica, I didn't mean to frighten you," Clint said. He stepped into the light of the doorway. "Miss Roilings said it would be all right for me to wait for you here. It's much cooler on the porch than inside."

Regaining her composure, Jessie smiled up at Clint. "You did startle me. I thought for a moment you were one of the outlaws Edwina is always worrying about."

"I've been accused of many things," Clint said, the lamplight reflecting off his white teeth as he gave Jessie one of his most charming smiles. "And I'm probably guilty of some of them. But I have yet to rob my first stage coach or train, so you can put Miss Roilings's mind to rest on that matter."

Jessica laughed at the man's humor, enjoying his easy companionship. "I'll tell her the first time I hear her call you an outlaw."

Unable to stop himself, Clint raised a hand and gently traced the line of Jessica's cheek with the edge of his knuckles. He gazed into her sapphire eyes, mesmerized by the shining dark blue pools. "Do you know how beautiful you are, Jessica?"

Jessica felt her cheeks burn with color but could not look away from Clint's compelling gaze. Her mouth went dry, and she had to clear her throat before she could manage a breathless, "No."

"Then you've known only fools. How could any man be near you and not tell you how beautiful you are? I know I'm being forward because we've only known each other for a few weeks, but since the first day I saw you in Paradise, I haven't been able to get you out of my mind.''

A loud ''Ah-hum!'' from the doorway behind them broke the spell. Jessie quickly stepped away from Clint as Edwina came out onto the porch and planted herself firmly on one of the huge rockers like the proper chaperone she thought herself to be. The housekeeper calmly rocked to and fro. ''Mr. Ramsey came over to see if we needed any help with the cattle,'' she told Jessica. ''I said everything was going well since you hired Mr. Stockton to oversee the ranch.''

Jessica looked at her friend and for the first time in her life had a sudden urge to strangle the woman. She couldn't explain the sense of loss she was experiencing, nor did she know what had created it. All the feelings she'd had since coming home were so new to her, she still didn't understand them completely. And given Edwina's timely interruptions, she never would. She gave Clint a resigned glance and settled herself on one of the high-backed rockers. She couldn't stop the smile that curled her lips at the look of exasperation he flashed at Edwina.

''Miss Roilings is right. I did come to see how things were going, but I also had an ulterior motive for my visit tonight,'' Clint said, bracing one wide shoulder against the squared pillar of the porch. An impish grin tugged at his lips as he crossed his arms over his chest and waited for the women's curiosity to get the better of them.

''And what could it be?'' Jessie asked, feeling her cheeks heat from the warm look he bestowed upon her.

''Next month I'm having my yearly shindig at the

Lazy L, and I thought I'd come and extend an invitation to you and Miss Roilings in person. I hope you won't turn me down. It will give you a chance to meet the other ranchers in the area, and they'll be able to satisfy their curiosity about the young woman who has decided to take up ranching on her own.''

"We'd love to come," Jessica said without waiting for Edwina's decision on the matter. "Since everything is running smoothly at Eden, it's time I met my neighbors. I hope they'll not be too disappointed when they meet me and find I don't have two heads."

"Only a fool could be disappointed when they meet you, Jessica," Clint said.

Another "Ah-hum" from Edwina shattered the moment before it could expand into anything more. She glanced meaningfully at Jessica and then at Clint. "Mr. Ramsey, what is a shindig, exactly? I'd like to know before I accept your invitation."

Clint looked at the housekeeper and laughed. "I'm sorry, Miss Roilings. I should have explained. A shindig is what you call a party in the East. All the neighbors get together to dance and enjoy good food and drink. And it's one of the few times in a year that we men get to dance with all the ladies."

Before Edwina could accept or decline Clint's invitation, the sound of a horse's hooves approaching rapidly drew their attention. They watched, curious, as a cowboy galloped straight for them, then drew his mount to a skiddering halt. He tipped his hat politely to the ladies and turned to Clint. "Mr. Ramsey, Payton sent me over to tell you the rustlers have hit us again," he said anxiously.

"What the hell?" Clint was already heading toward

his mount, tethered at the hitching post. "How many head did they get?"

"They took the horses this time," the man said, edging his mount backward. He didn't want to be anywhere near Ramsey when he exploded.

"Damn that bastard to hell! I'll see him dead for this. Those horses were worth a small fortune," Clint growled, jerking the reins loose from the ring and swinging into the saddle. He started to pull the horse's head about when he remembered the two women he'd left sitting on the porch. Edging the animal closer to the house, he looked at Jessica. "I'm sorry to leave in such a rush, but Fleming and his renegade gang have struck again. If their trail isn't too cold, we might be able to overtake them before they can get too far away. Catching the rustlers would give us a real reason to celebrate."

He paused for a moment and glanced at Edwina before looking once more at Jessica. His words were soft and full of promise as he said, "I'll see you next week." He jerked his mount about and spurred him into a gallop down the long drive toward the Lazy L.

Jessie didn't even wait for Clint to ride out of sight before she rushed into the house, retrieved the Winchester rifle from the rack over the fireplace, and ran toward the barn. Sensing something afoot, Edwina followed upon her heels, huffing and puffing from the exertion. She watched Jessica drag the heavy saddle from the tack room toward the stall where her mount was stabled. Hands braced on her wide hips, she blocked Jessie's path and demanded, "What do you think you're doing? Surely you don't intend to help Mr. Ramsey find the rustlers?"

"Edwina, step out of my way. I don't have time to explain things to you right now."

"Then I'm not moving an inch. It's late and I'm not going to let you take off into the night without a good reason."

"I'll explain everything when I get back. Just believe me when I say I'm not going to try to capture any rustlers."

"If you're worried about the stock, then ask Mr. Stockton to go out and check on them."

Jessie rolled her eyes toward the hay-filled loft. "Edwina, it has nothing to do with the stock, and I don't want anyone to know where I've gone. Now please go back to the house."

"Mr. Ramsey called the rustler Fleming," Edwina said, her eyes widening suddenly with understanding. "Is it Wade?"

Jessie nodded. "Now go back to the house and don't let anyone know where I've gone."

"I can't allow you to go," Edwina said.

"You have no choice. Now move out of my way."

"Jessie," Edwina said, "please use your head and be reasonable. You can't go running off after Wade like this. You don't know this country. If men skilled at tracking haven't been able to follow his trail, then you'd never find him, especially at night. You have to find some other way to get in touch with him."

For a long moment Jessie didn't move, torn between her need to find her brother and the housekeeper's reasoning. She knew Edwina was right, but allowing this night to pass without even attempting to follow Wade would be one of the hardest things she'd ever done. He was so close. At last she nodded. "All right, Winnie. I'll do as you ask for now."

Edwina released the breath she'd been holding. "Believe me, it's for the best. Your own actions could cost Wade his life if you're not careful."

Again Jessie nodded and turned to replace the saddle in the tack room. "I know you're right, but damn it! It's been so long."

Edwina crossed to her friend and placed a comforting arm about her slender shoulders. "You'll find him in time, Jessica. You know he's alive now, and that's more than you had before you arrived in Texas."

Giving Edwina a grateful hug, Jessie smiled. "What would I do without you to keep me in line, Winnie?"

"Edwina, Jessica. And I wouldn't like to contemplate such an event. Now let's get back to the house. Your dinner is waiting. I prepared one of your favorites tonight: apple pie."

Brand eased into the deepest shadows and watched Jessie and Edwina walk back to the house. He'd just returned and had begun to unsaddle his mount in the barn when he'd heard the commotion coming from the house. He'd emerged to see what was wrong and had overheard Ramsey telling Jessica about the rustlers. He had waited quietly in the shadows to see what reaction Ramsey's news would create in his lovely boss lady. His patience during the past few weeks had been rewarded when Jessica hurried out of the house with the housekeeper hot on her heels. From what he'd just overheard, he knew his instincts about Miss Jessica Nolan had been right on the money. He'd heard from her own lips that she knew the half-breed.

However, unless she knew exactly where the renegade's camp was hidden, she'd never be able to find him on her own. Brand had already learned that much about the rustler. Fleming was far too clever to leave any trace of prints to reveal his real destination. Even traveling with a herd of horses, he'd be impossible to find once he reached the mountains. It would look as if he'd just disappeared into thin air.

Brand mounted a fresh horse and quietly urged it in the direction Ramsey had taken minutes earlier. He knew it was probably futile to follow the rancher in his search for the outlaw, but he had to cover every lead to trap his quarry. Sooner or later Fleming, like all the rest, would make a mistake, and then Brand would be there to take advantage of it. The sooner it happened the better, Brand thought. He wanted to put Eden and its beautiful owner behind him as soon as possible.

Brand couldn't stop himself from wondering what exactly was going on between the lovely Miss Nolan and the half-breed. His guts twisted into tight coils at the memory of Jessica's voice when she'd spoken of the rustler. There had been so much feeling in her words that he knew she loved the man.

A low growl emerged from deep within Brand's throat. What kind of woman could love a half-breed bastard like Fleming? he asked himself as the horse's hooves ate up the dark miles. A woman who had no respect for herself, he reflected cynically, his prejudice gnawing at him with vicious fangs. No decent woman would allow such a man to touch her. Even the whores at Miss Molly's drew the line at bedding a breed. They had more self-respect than to sleep with red vermin.

Brand's hand clenched about his reins until his

knuckles grew white from the pressure. A muscle twitched in his beard-shadowed jaw. How could Jessica—beautiful, lovely, wise, hardworking Jessica—lower herself to such a degree? Yet from all he'd overheard, she had already degraded herself.

"Damn her," Brand growled, unaware that somewhere deep within his withered soul there were feelings other than his prejudice tearing at him. But they were so new and raw, he couldn't fathom them even if he accepted their existence, which he did not. He only knew the thought of Jessica being held in the arms of the half-breed sickened him until he could taste the bitterness in his mouth.

"Damn her," he muttered again, and spurred his mount onward. He'd find the half-breed one way or the other, and then he'd see how well Miss Jessica Nolan enjoyed seeing her lover swing from the end of a rope.

Chapter 5

The rumble of hooves and a cloud of dust marked the passage of the herd as Wade and his men drove the horses into the pass of Palo Duro Canyon. Through a blaze of late afternoon sunlight, Wade squinted up at the multicolored walls rising to a thousand feet on each side of them. The canyon, carved out of the high plains by a branch of the Red River, was the perfect hideout for the Comancheros when they made their raids into Texas. Its deep arroyos, dug into the canyon walls by centuries of erosion, provided them with the security they needed since the Comanche had been removed from the area in 1874.

Wade's indigo gaze swept along the winding canyon floor. It had only been three years since Colonel Ranald Mackenzie had made the raid on the last Comanche stronghold. The Fourth Cavalry's surprise attack had ended any claim the Comanche had on Palo Duro. Mackenzie's troops had devastated the Indians by destroying their villages and horses. The Comanche had had no recourse but to return to the reservation in Indian territory. Afterward the government, believing the area uninhabited and free of trouble, had withdrawn its troops back to Fort Richardson, leaving the canyon a mecca for outlaws.

A roar of delight and gunfire met Wade and his men as they herded the horses past the camp and into the makeshift corral. Seeing the animals secure, Wade drew his horse about and trotted back in the direction of the Comanchero leader, Sabin Estaban. Drawing his mount to a halt, a wide confident grin breaking across his swarthy features, he slid agilely to the ground, his moccasined feet making no sound upon the hard-packed earth.

"Well, amigo," Estaban said around the *cigarro* he held between his teeth at the corner of this thick-lipped mouth. His words bore the heavy accents of his Mexican and Comanche heritage. He squinted at Wade through the blue haze of smoke. "You brought de horses you promised?"

"*Sí*, and now it is time for you to fulfill your end of our agreement," Wade said, his smile fading as he regarded the Comanchero through narrowed, assessing eyes. Something in Estaban's demeanor roused the rustler's suspicions.

Estaban shrugged. "Never fear, amigo. You will get what you deserve now that I have the horses. But let us refresh ourselves before we conclude our business. We have mescal all the way from Mexico and fine whiskey from Tucson." At Wade's curious look, Estaban chuckled. "The whiskey came in exchange for buffalo hides. The gringos' love for buffalo robes is raising the prices for the hides, so it is profitable for me to deal with the hunters."

"Then you have the money we agreed upon for the horses?" Wade asked. His instincts told him Estaban was avoiding the issue. Yet for the moment, he knew he couldn't accuse the Comanchero of duplicity. Estaban's band outnumbered his men two to one.

Wade glanced at his friend, who stood listening quietly to their discussion. His expression said far more than his words. "Renegade, I want you to see to the horses while we finish our business."

Thumbs linked into the gunbelt swung low on his hips, Renegade nodded. Through narrowed eyes, he watched his friend and Estaban stride toward the camp. He didn't have to be told that Estaban was up to some dirty trick, nor that Wade was already aware of it. The wary look in his friend's eyes told him all he needed to know. When the time came, they'd be ready for anything the Comancheros tried.

Renegade glanced at the sky overhead. Soon night would deepen the shadows already blanketing the recesses of the canyon. He suspected Estaban was biding his time until the dark could cover his moves. Like the rat he was, he'd do his dirty work then. He had the horses he needed, and it would be a simple matter to murder those who had supplied them. Renegade's scarred features hardened. He'd been afraid something like this would happen. He knew the Comancheros couldn't be trusted. They had no loyalty to anything except gold. They traded between the Comanche and the whites or vice versa, selling to the highest bidder. It didn't matter what kind of merchandise they dealt in, be it buffalo hides or human flesh; as long as there was a profit to be made, they would sell.

Renegade ran a callused finger down his scarred cheek and smiled cynically. Estaban thought he had everything well planned, but he didn't know Wade Fleming. He could be just as dangerous and deadly as any sidewinder. Wade Fleming wasn't called Man with No People for nothing. He, too, did what he had to to survive, and it didn't matter whose blood he spilled. He wasn't prejudiced when it came to saving his own skin. Renegade had seen Wade kill red and white alike.

Renegade took a pouch of tobacco from his pocket and slowly rolled himself a smoke. Sticking the slightly crooked cigarillo between his pursed lips, he retrieved a match from the inside of his leather vest and struck it against the bottom of his boot. Like a beacon, it flared in the dusty twilight as he raised it to his cigarillo. Inhaling the strong smoke, he relaxed back against a boulder still warm from the day's sun. The tip of the cigarillo glowed red as he calmly considered Wade's reaction to Estaban's double-dealing. It wouldn't be nice: that he knew for sure. Wade Fleming expected a man to keep his word, and when he didn't, Wade made him pay.

A bottle of mescal was passed between the men while Estaban dug out one of his precious bottles of whiskey. "Drink up, amigo," he ordered as he poured a generous amount into Wade's tin cup. Settling himself on the edge of a large slab of rock, Estaban lifted the bottle to his own lips and guzzled the remainder of the amber liquid. A moment later a loud belch accompanied a satisfied sigh as he wiped the excess liquor from his mouth with the back of one wide, hairy hand. "It is good, no?"

Wade nodded, slowly sipping the whiskey in his cup. He had no intention of drinking too much. Estaban might plan to get him drunk, but Wade had no intention of making it easy for the bastard to try to steal his horses.

"Juanita, bring my amigo some food," Estaban called to the dark-haired woman dressed in a long, coarsely woven, multicolored skirt. She tossed her head haughtily, sending her raven hair cascading about her shoulders like thick, black wool. Through tilted eyes she regarded the Comanchero contemptuously.

"Have your Indian slut serve your friend. I am not your slave." With that she raised her small nose in the air, lifted her skirt to show her sandaled feet, and stalked away.

Estaban shifted uncomfortably on his hard perch and looked at Wade sheepishly. "The woman, she is a hellcat. I will have to beat her again to make her know who is boss."

Wade made no comment about Estaban's methods. From what he had already observed of Juanita, Estaban might be the one to come out the worse for wear when the battle ended. He smiled at the thought as Estaban called to the girl basting the haunch of beef over the fire. "Squaw, bring my amigo food."

The girl started and looked at Estaban with wide frightened eyes before she hesitantly raised a sharp knife to the beef. She sliced off several crusty brown pieces and placed them on a tin plate along with several pieces of flat corn tortillas. Eyes once more lowered, she crossed to where Wade sat and handed him the plate.

Wade couldn't take his eyes off the girl as she moved back to her place near the fire. He had felt the tremor of her hand all the way through the tin plate, and his heart went out to her. The color of her eyes revealed much of her history to him. She wasn't Indian, nor was

she Comanachero. She was white. As such in a Comanchero camp, she would be treated as less than an
animal. She would be used and abused by anyone.

Wade felt a surprising shiver of sympathy race up his
spine. He was half white himself, but until that moment
he'd never felt compassion for any of the captives he'd
encountered in the past. However, there was something
about the fragile girl with the large, pale blue eyes that
reminded him of the Texas sky on a clear day. She was
a tiny bit of a thing, with delicately sculpted features.
She looked so vulnerable and alone here, surrounded
by the dregs of humanity.

"Who is the girl, Estaban?" Wade asked without
taking his gaze off her.

Estaban cocked his dark head to one side, noting
Wade's interest in the white captive. A speculative light
entered his slanted eyes, and his coarse skin creased
above his high cheekbones as he gave Wade a calculating grin. "The Comanches traded her for several
horses."

"Is she your woman?"

Estaban reared back and ran his thumbs beneath the
waist of his striped britches. He gave a loud, dramatic
sigh. One greasy strand of straight black hair fell over
his brow as he shook his head. "Ah, no, amigo. Juanita, she believes the squaw is my woman now, but she
is wrong. The pale-eyes is not for me. I like my women
with a little fire, and the girl, she is ice. She lays beneath a man like a dead woman."

Wade understood Estaban's meaning and cringed inwardly for the girl. The bastard had forced her into his
bed. Wade placed no blame on the girl. She had had
no choice. It was either be used by those more power-

ful, or die. He'd heard many people vow to die before suffering such degradation, but he'd yet to find one of those brave souls. When it came time to make the choice between life and death, only the stupid chose death. For as long as there was breath, there was hope.

Wade eyed Estaban coldly. He clenched his hands at his side and fought to suppress the urge to tightly wrap them around Estaban's neck to squeeze the life out of the little bastard. Such an action would do neither him nor the girl any good. He might succeed in ending the Comanchero's life, but he'd not escape retaliation.

"How much do you want for her?" Wade's voice was hoarse with suppressed emotion as he casually lifted the whiskey cup to his lips.

Again Estaban's thick lips curled into a satisfied smile. "One thousand American dollars in gold."

Wade's expression hardened. The bastard wanted as much for the girl as he was asking for the horses they had delivered. Slowly Wade turned a deadly glare upon the Comanchero. "That is too high. No woman is worth a thousand dollars."

Estaban gave a nonchalant shrug. "True, amigo. No woman is worth that price, though I have already had several offers. The brothel owner in Tucson said he'd take all the white *puta* I could bring him. And he is willing to pay even more than I've asked of you."

"You bastard! You want the horses for nothing, don't you?" Wade growled. Tossing the remaining whiskey into the dust, he surged to his feet.

Estaban arched one dark brow, and his black eyes glowed in the firelight. "The horses in exchange for the squaw?"

"Don't act as if this is the first time the idea has

crossed your mind. You and I both know damn well you never intended to pay us for the horses, and now that you've found a bargaining chip, you're determined to milk it for all it's worth.''

"Amigo, amigo,'' Estaban said, raising his hands helplessly in the air while smiling triumphantly. "I am a businessman, and I must make a profit, *sí* ? And would it not be better to leave Palo Duro with the woman than not to leave at all?'' Estaban glanced into the shadows behind him. The click of rifles being readied to fire echoed eerily in the stillness of the evening air. "Do you understand my meaning, amigo?''

Wade nodded. He and his men were strictly at a disadvantage. They were outnumbered and wouldn't have a chance should there be a fight. "Then I will accept your offer, amigo. The girl for the horses.''

Estaban's grin widened. "I knew you would see reason.'' He looked toward the pale-eyed girl. "Squaw, you now belong to my amigo.''

Wade saw the girl flinch, and his fingers curled again at his side. He itched to end Estaban's miserable existence, but he'd bide his time until his men and the girl were safe. "Then our business is concluded, Estaban.''

The Comanchero nodded smugly. "Perhaps in time we can do business together again. No hard feelings.''

Wade smiled, but the gesture lacked warmth. "I'm sure we will meet again.'' He took the girl by the arm and walked her back to the corral, where his horse was tethered. His men looked at him strangely as he ordered them to mount and ride out, but no one questioned his actions.

They rode in silence until they were safely out of Palo Duro. Wade reined his mount to a halt on a scarp overlooking the pass into the canyon. He slipped from the saddle and reached up to help the girl down. She resisted and slid off the horse's haunch to land lightly on her moccasined feet. She stood poised for flight, reminding him of a frightened rabbit. Wade shook his head. "I won't hurt you." Seeing his words had no effect upon her, he turned his attention to his men. For the moment he didn't have time to worry about the woman. There were far more important matters for him to attend to. "Renegade, I want you to stay here with the girl."

"What do you plan to do?" Renegade asked, dismounting.

"Estaban thinks he's clever, but I intend to make him see it wasn't wise to double-cross me. The bastard thinks he's won, but he'll end up with no horses at all."

Renegade grinned. "You're letting him off easy. I thought you'd kill him instead of just stealing the horses back."

Wade shrugged. "If any Comancheros get in my way, then they will die. For now, I want to even the score by getting our horses as well as Estaban's. By the time the bastard has walked back into New Mexico Territory, he'll know not to play games with Wade Fleming."

Renegade glanced at the girl. "What do you plan to do with her?"

Again Wade shrugged.

"Are you going to take her back to her people?" Renegade asked, puzzled over Wade's decision to buy the girl from the Comancheros.

"I hadn't thought that far ahead. But if something goes wrong and we don't make it back, take her to the Cherokee mission. They'll know what to do with her."

"Damn, Wade. We've ridden together for a long time, and I don't like having to stay here and watch over some half-wild white squaw."

"Old friend"—Wade placed a callused hand on Renegade's shoulder—"you know I wouldn't leave any of the other men with the girl. They'd take off with her, and I've already gone to too much trouble to have that happen."

"Then do you mean to keep her?" Renegade asked, his bewilderment deepening. He'd known Wade for nearly ten years, and this was the first time his friend had ever shown interest in one of the captives they'd seen.

Wade lifted his shoulders again and gave Renegade a pensive look. "I really don't know. But by the time we get back, I'll have figured it out."

Renegade glanced from Wade to the young woman, who still stood poised to bolt at any moment. From the look on her face, he doubted that Wade would have to figure out his feelings. The girl was as skittish as a young colt, and he seriously doubted Wade would have the patience or the time to tame her. He'd never been attracted to women who played hard to get. The women in his past had always been eager to get Wade into their beds or beneath their furs. White or red, they couldn't deny the man's desires.

Renegade nodded, a smile curving his lips. He'd stay with the girl while Wade took care of Estaban. Then he'd sit back and watch the action between the rabbit and the fox. Glancing toward the girl, he knew she'd not make a very satisfying meal for the fox's hungry appetite.

* * *

Dawn crept over the canyon rim to find the bodies of the Comancheros scattered grotesquely about their camp. Mercy Stockton sat warily watching the scarred-faced man who had been left to guard her. He sat with hat pulled low and his back braced against the stump of a fallen mesquite. During the past hour he'd nodded several times, and now she waited, holding her breath, to see his chin finally settle down on his chest in sleep. Unable to see his features clearly beneath the shadow of his hat, Mercy eased to her feet. If she wanted to escape, it was now or never. Once the other men returned, she would have no other opportunity.

Heart in her throat, breath held and nerves screaming with tension, Mercy moved as delicately as the morning dew. During her years of captivity with the Comanche she had learned their stealthy ways. She maneuvered through the grass like a gentle breeze, making no sound to rouse the sleeping man.

Mercy flashed one brief, agonized look across the miles of prairie grass ahead of her. She had little hope of escape, but she had to take the chance. She'd never survive being the captive of another brutal man like Estaban. He was little more than an animal. A contemptuous little smile touched Mercy's lips. People considered Indians savages, but the Comanche were civilized compared with the cruel Comanchero.

The smile faded as Mercy's thoughts turned to the People. Her years of captivity with the Comanche had not been easy. She had been a slave, enduring the insults and beatings from the women along with back-breaking work; yet as the years passed the Comanches had accepted her to a certain degree. She had even been promised to the young brave White Wing, until the medicine man told Long Shadow that her marriage to his son would bring evil upon the tribe. Believing the medicine man's predictions and having no thought to what she would suffer, Long Shadow had traded her to the Comanchero for the horses the Indians needed.

Her eyes burned, but she could not cry. The horror of seeing her family killed and then years of trying to survive had spent all her tears. Her only thought now was of survival.

Mercy speeded up her steps, putting more distance between herself and the rustlers as well as her memories. She had not forgotten her white family, nor the life she had led before her captivity. It had been twelve years, but the pain of their deaths was still a raw wound within her heart.

At last, believing she was far enough from the man called Renegade, Mercy paused to draw in a breath of the cool morning air. For the first time in present memory she felt a glimmer of hope. For years after she'd been taken by the Comanche, she'd prayed her older brother, Brand, would come to rescue her from the savages. However, as time passed, she'd finally had to put her childish hopes away and accept the fact that Brand had not lived through the war. If he had, nothing on this earth could have stopped him from finding her.

Mercy glanced up at the sky and savored the first taste of freedom she'd known in far too many years. She wasn't scared out on the plains by herself. She was used to being alone. Since she was eight years old no one had cared whether she lived or died. She was used to depending upon her own abilities to survive. After her capture she had quickly learned there was no compassion in the Indian camp. Even the squaws who had children had shown no sympathy toward the tiny girl with the large, frightened eyes. It was only her own will to survive that had kept her alive through many harsh plains winters when food and heat went to the People and not their slaves.

No, it hadn't been easy to survive. But staying alive was one lesson she had learned well from the Comanche. They were a tenacious people, one who would not surrender until the last breath had left their bodies.

"Yes," Mercy mused aloud, "I will survive." Another small smile touched her lips.

The girl's sense of freedom ended with the sound of approaching horses. She glanced in its direction and saw the rustlers bearing down on her at full gallop. Like a hare with the dog upon its scent, she ran, heedless of the sharp buffalo grass tearing at her legs. Heart slamming against her ribs, Mercy scanned the wide landscape, searching for any avenue of escape. There was none, but she would not turn and surrender meekly. When Wade's arm came about her and lifted her into the saddle in front of him, she fought like a puma, screeching, biting, and scratching until he finally managed to secure her hands with a rope.

"Damn it, girl! Calm down," Wade called out as he tried to keep the squirming wildcat from falling to the ground. Breathing heavily, he tied her hands to the pommel. He clamped an arm about her middle, bringing her back against him. "I'm not going to hurt you."

The fight suddenly drained out of Mercy, and she slumped in the saddle with head bowed. She accepted her defeat for the moment, for acceptance was one thing she had learned to do well. To survive you had to accept the fate dealt out to you until you found the means to change it.

Wade felt the girl tremble and experienced a strange tug at his heart. She had fought bravely, and she had spirit, but her survival instincts had taught her to succumb to the will of those stronger than she in order to avoid pain.

A muscle in Wade's jaw worked as he ground his teeth together. Damn anyone who would do this to another human being! He knew how it felt to be the victim as well as the victor. He hadn't forgotten when he had been considered less than human because of the Indian blood flowing in his veins. Nor had he forgotten the taunts he'd received in the fancy school Kate had sent him to in Boston. Liberal-minded easterners might boast of their open-mindedness, but let a small half-breed boy enter their strict society and their prejudice would rush to the surface.

Wade looked down at the girl in his arms and saw himself. Kate had never known what had driven him to run away from the lovely home she had provided. He couldn't tell her that narrow-minded people were the same everywhere. There was prejudice even Kate's wealth and power couldn't protect him from. And like the girl in his arms, he'd run away.

Gently Wade raised a hand and touched her tangled hair. She flinched as if he'd struck her. He drew in a deep, resigned breath. Although he knew mere words would not make the girl believe she was safe, he said, "Relax, little one, I mean you no harm." Seeing no sign that she understood him, he repeated it in the soft, guttural language of the Comanche.

Mercy did not respond. She'd been abused too much in the past to believe anything her captor said.

"Do you understand?" Wade asked, and watched as she nodded slowly.

He smiled. A nod wasn't much, but it was better than nothing. He knew it would take time for the girl to realize he had spoken the truth. For now he was satisfied that she was no longer fighting him.

Wade reined in his mount and waited for the rest of his men to catch up with him. Renegade came alongside and shook his head at the sight of the girl tied to his friend's saddle. "Looks like she don't want to travel with us."

"You could say that," Wade replied, and grinned ruefully.

"What do you plan to do with her?"

"For now I intend to take her back to camp with us."

Renegade frowned. "It'd be for the best if you just left her in the nearest white settlement. The people there would see that she got back to her own kind."

Wade glanced down at the bowed head in front of him and again felt his heartstrings pull. He shook his head and looked once more at his friend, his expression grim. "I won't do that to her. She's survived living with the Comanche, and I won't let her own kind destroy her for choosing life instead of death. Until I find her people, she'll stay with us."

"Hell, Wade! We don't need a woman to worry about."

"*You* don't have a woman to worry about, old friend. I took her from Estaban, and she's my responsibility until I find her people. Now that settles it. She'll go back with us to camp and then I'll start making inquiries about where she came from.''

Renegade shrugged. "It's your decision, but I just hope you haven't made the wrong one. It could cost us our necks. All we need is to have the law to think we've turned to kidnapping white women. They hate us enough as is.''

"Renegade, you worry too much," Wade said, and laughed at his friend's sour expression. "Your neck will only stretch so far no matter how many crimes they lay at our door. And I suspect the law doesn't give much of a damn about this girl. If my guess is right, she's been with the Comanche for most of her life, or she'd already be begging us to take her back to her family.''

Renegade rubbed a hand thoughtfully over his scarred cheek. "You may be right. As far as I can remember, the Comanche haven't taken captives since before seventy-five.'' He looked at Wade, his eyes filled with questions. "But if you are right, that means the girl may not have anyone who'll take her off our hands.''

Wade nodded.

"Hell, Wade. You could be stuck with her.''

Again the only answer Renegade received was a nod. He snorted in disgust, wondering at his friend's odd behavior. It wasn't like Wade Fleming to think of anyone but himself.

Wade smiled at the bewildered look that crossed his friend's face. He knew Renegade thought he had lost his mind, and perhaps he had. There was something about this blue-eyed girl that drew him. He had felt it the first moment their eyes had met across the fire in Estaban's camp. Until he could understand why he had abandoned his own code of detachment, he wouldn't let her go. This unnamed girl had managed to find a way down the broken path to his emotions.

"Wade, I wish you'd reconsider," Renegade said, making an effort to reason with his friend. "The decision to keep the girl after you've taken her to our camp may not be left to you. By then it'll be too late to let her go. She'll already know our hideout and can tell the law about it. The men won't let her leave alive."

"I've made my decision, Renegade, and anyone who doesn't agree with it can leave now. I'll be more than willing to pay them for their share in the horses."

"Damn it, Wade. Won't you see reason? What has this girl got that no other woman has?"

"Nothing," Wade said between clenched teeth, and spurred his horse ahead of Renegade. He'd had enough advice for one day. Renegade's argument made sense, but he couldn't heed it. He wouldn't abandon this girl to suffer at the hands of others as he'd abandoned his own sister in Boston. He'd left Jessie because he hadn't been old enough to take care of her. It was different with this girl. He was a man now and not a lost young boy. He would never let anyone abuse the delicate creature in his arms. Confirming his decision, Wade slowly untied the girl's hands and gently massaged the red marks left by the rope. In time he hoped he'd be able to make all the cruel marks in her life disappear until she could look at him with smiling eyes instead of eyes haunted by fear.

Gently he eased the girl back against him, cradling her like a child in the curve of his body. "Given time, all your wounds will heal."

Mercy didn't resist the comfort he offered but stiffly leaned back against Wade. She was still wary of this blue-eyed, dark-haired man with the warm voice, but the previous day's work and the long night's vigil were taking their toll upon her. Her eyes closed slowly, and she relaxed against Wade's hard body.

Wade smiled to himself as he looked down at her sleeping face, then he realized with a start that the girl was beautiful. He saw it through the dirt and soot that smudged the flawless skin. Her delicately sculpted features were as lovely as any painting by the masters. Thick dark lashes hid her eyes as she slept. Her sweetly curved lips were parted slightly and far too tempting to kiss for his peace of mind. Resisting the urge, he allowed his gaze to wander over her velvet skin, tinted a warm hue from years of exposure to the sun. Wade swallowed and his nostrils flared as he drew in a long, cooling breath. He tried to control his response to the woman, yet as his gaze drifted down the dirty white shirt that covered her ripe curves, he couldn't suppress the heat centered in his loins. The girl's body was just as beautiful as her face.

Wade gave himself a sharp mental shake and turned his attention back to the wide plains ahead. He had no right to think of the girl in that manner. He had saved her from the likes of Estaban, and here he was thinking in the same depraved direction.

Wade drew in an unsteady breath and pressed his lips together. Perhaps he had made a mistake by bringing the girl along. She roused things in him he didn't want kindled to life. Still, it was too late to reconsider as Renegade had asked. He had made his decision in Palo Duro Canyon, and he'd not change his mind now. He'd just keep a closer rein on his emotions.

Settling the matter in his mind, Wade turned his

thoughts back to the herd of horses he'd taken from Estaban. He'd drive them north and let his friends find a buyer. That would solve one problem. Then he could concentrate on ruining the people who had bought the Fleming land.

Chapter 6

Standing in the shadows of the barn, Jessie watched the muscles in Brand's back contract and expand as he lifted the bale of hay and tossed it onto the wagon. Naked to his waist, the dark hair at the nape of his neck already damp, Brand glistened with perspiration. It beaded between his wide shoulders and, like drops of golden honey, slowly inched down the curve of his spine. There it disappeared beneath the damp edge of the denims that hugged his lean hips and cupped his firm, muscular buttocks. His powerful thighs bulged against the coarse material as he bent once more to heft another bale. The tendons and veins in his arms and hands stood taut from the exertion, though he moved with such ease that the hundred-pound bale of dried grass seemed weightless.

Jessie's mouth went dry at the display of pure male strength. She couldn't take her eyes off the sun-bronzed back turned to her. Never had she felt such raw animal magnetism. Her hands itched to touch Brand's satiny skin. She stuck the offending members into the pockets of her jeans, wondering again at her strange train of thought. She'd found Clint Ramsey's distinguished good looks and engaging manner alluring, but the mere sight of him did not set her blood on fire.

Jessie forced herself to turn away from the mesmerizing view of naked male flesh. She had to get hold of herself. She didn't want anyone to catch her staring at her foreman with her tongue hanging out on the barn floor. The thought drew a snort of disgust from her as she strode back into the tack room and picked up the can of leather soap she'd been using to clean her saddle. With a vicious swipe she rubbed the grease into the leather, determined not to let her mind dwell upon the man in the barnyard. She had far more important matters to attend to. Brand Stockton wasn't the man for her, even had she time for affairs of the heart.

Jessie gave another snort of disgust. She could almost hear Kate remonstrating with her. In the most regal Bostonian accent she could muster, Kate would tell Jessie that her foreman, no matter how good-looking, was little more than a saddle bum, and she deserved better. And should she intend to show any interest in the men she had met since returning to Texas, it would be the wisest course for her to bestow her feelings on Clint Ramsey. He was well established, owning the largest ranch west of Fort Worth. Furthermore he was a fine specimen of a man with his ruggedly handsome face and dark hair touched with wings of gray at the temples.

Clint Ramsey was the type of man her adoptive mother would have approved of for her. He was settled, rich, and kind. Though there were nearly twenty years' difference in their ages, Kate would not have found anything wrong with Ramsey. She would have said his age gave him the wisdom to treat his wife as she deserved.

From what Jessie had observed of the rancher, Kate would probably have been right.

"But that doesn't change my feelings," Jessie muttered, rubbing the leather harder. Unlike Clint, Brand had an untamed quality that drew her like the proverbial moth to the flame. She honestly didn't know when her attraction toward her foreman had begun. Thinking back, she decided it had always been there, but she had recognized it only during the past few days. Certainly Brand knew nothing of her feelings toward him. They had worked alongside each other now for weeks, and during that time it had been all business. She had thought they were becoming friends, yet he never displayed anything more toward her than casual friendship.

Feeling like a fool, Jessie rubbed more saddle soap into the leather. Brand Stockton didn't give two hoots for her. She was his boss and that was all.

"Then why in God's name do I react the way I do?" she muttered to the saddle. Perhaps her attraction stemmed from Brand's strength. He had come along at a time when she desperately needed someone strong to help her get Eden started. He had filled a need in her life, and she had foolishly let herself react like a schoolgirl with a crush. Jessie didn't try to explain why her blood ran hot and fast at the mere sight of his naked flesh.

Brand collected his shirt from the fence post and used it to wipe the sweat from his brow as he strode into the barn. A sound in the tack room drew his attention and he paused, watching Jessie furiously rub a saddle until it was white with lather. His gaze swept over her, slowly moving down her slender back to her rounded bottom and then sliding along her long, shapely legs. He couldn't stop his mind from conjuring up the vision of her naked before him, her skin warm, her face glowing with passion.

Brand's body reacted spontaneously to his thoughts, and he shifted to ease the pressure mounting in the crotch of his jeans. He frowned at Jessie's back. How could he still find her exciting after what he had learned about her? Yet even knowing her feelings about Fleming and his own prejudice against anyone who possessed Indian blood, he couldn't get Jessica Nolan out of his mind. She was like a whiff of intoxicating perfume drifting upon a sultry summer's breeze. Enticing yet elusive. He was drawn to her against his will.

God, what am I thinking? he censured himself silently. He'd come here to do a job, not moon over a woman who hankered after a half-breed rustler. His problem could be worked out at Molly's when he rode into town tonight. Then he could put Miss Jessica Nolan out of his mind completely.

Clearing his throat, Brand said, "The hay's loaded. Tomorrow I'll have some of the men take it out to Little Creek."

Jessie spun around to face her foreman and again felt her mouth go dry. All rational thought vanished as she watched Brand shrug into his shirt. He made no attempt to button it, exposing much of his wide chest, covered in a thick mat of crisp curls. Her gaze slid along the silken trail of hair that ran down his hard, flat belly to disappear into his Levi's. Jessie jerked her gaze upward and found her eyes locked on to his wide shoulders, where perspiration made the faded material cling damply. The shirt molded to the thick, corded muscles in his upper arms as he casually rested his long-fingered hands against his hips.

Taking Jessie's expression as one of surprise, Brand gave her a slow grin. "I didn't mean to startle you. I thought you heard me come in."

Jessie finally managed to make her throat work. "I'm sorry. As you can see, my mind is on other things." She raised the sticky cloth and tin of saddle soap.

Brand glanced at the saddle Jessie had been working on and chuckled. "From the looks of it, your thoughts weren't on your work. Much more and you'd have worn a hole in the leather."

Jessie cast a sheepish look toward her saddle and blushed. "You're right. I was thinking of the cattle and wondering how long it would be before the herd could be safely moved to open grazing land."

Taking closer note of Jessie's expression, Brand absently buttoned his shirt. Like hell she'd been thinking of the cattle. He'd been around enough to know when a woman was thinking of her lover. They always got that soft expression in their eyes and about their mouths, just like the one Jessie was wearing now. He knew she'd been thinking of Wade Fleming.

"It shouldn't be much longer. With luck the sheriff will catch the rustlers who have been raiding the ranches in this area."

Jessie shifted uneasily and turned her attention to the wagon of hay. "We're supplementing the cattle with hay that should be stored for use in winter while the grass along the northern branch of Little Creek is knee high. That's not good business."

"It's not good business to put the herd on open range

where it can be picked off without a shot ever being fired," Brand said, annoyed.

"That's true," Jessie agreed. "We'll give them until the first of next week, but if we don't hear about the rustlers by that time, I want the herd moved. I doubt the thieves are still in this area, and I can't afford to feed hay to several hundred head of cattle until next spring. It would ruin me."

"You're the boss, lady," Brand said, his tone sharp, his suspicions hardening. Why would she suddenly want to move the cattle? The only answer was that she knew the rustlers wouldn't hit Eden because she was Fleming's lover.

Jessie frowned at Brand. He'd never used such a tone with her before, and she wondered what she had done to cause his anger. "Brand, I don't mean to act like I don't appreciate your advice. You're the foreman, and if you think we should leave the cattle at Little Creek, we will."

"I'm not your foreman," Brand said, abruptly stuffing the tail of his shirt into his britches.

"But I thought . . . I mean . . . you hadn't said you *wouldn't* take the job. I just thought it was settled," Jessie said.

"You thought wrong, Miss Nolan. I don't like to be tied down for long. I like things the way they are now. That way when I get ready to move on, there'll be no hard feelings," Brand said, savagely severing the friendship that had begun to develop between them. Theirs would be a working relationship and nothing more.

Jessie suddenly felt deflated. Everything had been going so smoothly. Brand had the ranch running well, and she'd learned her brother was still alive. She'd hoped with Brand as foreman, overseeing things, she'd have time to search for Wade. "Then that's your decision—you'll work for me until the mood strikes you to move on?"

Brand nodded, her expression leaving a disturbed feeling in his gut. She looked as if he'd hit her. "I'm not leaving right away, so you'll have time to find someone to take my place."

It was Jessie's turn to nod. She knew she would never find anyone to take Brand's place, but she remained quiet. There was nothing more to say. She knew pleading with Brand to reconsider his decision would do no good. That was one thing she had learned about Brand Stockton during the past weeks. When he made up his mind, it was like a rusty bear trap. It didn't budge once he'd set it.

From the shade of the barn, Jessie watched Brand stride toward the bunkhouse. She didn't want to think about his leaving Eden. For a woman who prided herself upon her independence, she'd come to depend upon him far more than she liked to admit. Kate had taught her to be strong and to stand on her own two feet. But Kate's lesson had been shaken when Jessie learned that western men didn't look favorably upon single females such as herself. A rancher's wife worked harder than her husband on the ranch—rounding up and branding cattle and helping with the business side of things . . . while still caring for her own children. She looked after any other livestock about the ranch such as pigs and chickens, and she cooked and cleaned and made sure that they had enough food stored for winter. But what separated Jessie from other women was her marital status. She had no husband to stand back and boast about how he wouldn't have a woman who acted like a man.

The ranchers' attitude, combined with the long, backbreaking hours of work it took to keep Eden going, had nearly defeated Jessie. Brand Stockton had been the answer to her prayers. His presence had made her life much easier and had saved Eden. She feared the ranch would suffer when he left.

Still, losing a foreman didn't explain the hollow feeling that formed in the pit of her belly when she thought of Brand riding out of her life. She couldn't pinpoint the emotion, but she felt as if she'd lost something very special before she even had it to lose.

"I guess I was a fool for thinking we were becoming friends," Jessie mused aloud. She took down the saddle bags from the peg on the barn wall and slung them over her shoulder. She turned toward the house, her thoughts shifting to Wade. Having her brother once more in her life would fill the strange void Brand's news had created. And while Brand was still here to oversee the ranch, she would use the time to search for Wade.

The idea taking firm root, Jessie scuffed her boots on the mat outside the door and entered the house. She tossed her gloves on the table near the door. Dust motes rose in the air and then settled in a thin layer upon the surface Edwina worked so hard to keep shining with polish. Eager to tell the housekeeper of her decision, Jessie walked toward the kitchen, unaware of the dirt. As usual, she found Edwina busy, her hands covered in flour, the week's baking in progress.

"Edwina, I'll need my saddle bags packed with food for several days," Jessie said, dumping the leather pouches over the back of a chair before she crossed to the dry sink and poured several dippers of water into a tin pan. She splashed her face and then dried it with the towel that hung on the peg by the sink.

''And may I ask exactly why I should pack your saddle bags?'' Edwina asked, kneading the white dough vigorously with the heels of her hands.

''It's time I found Wade,'' Jessie answered, tensing for Edwina's reaction.

Silence greeted her announcement. The only sound in the kitchen for several long minutes was the slapping of dough on the table. Venting her frustration on the bread, Edwina slammed it on the table one last time. Puffs of flour filled the air about her as she finally turned to look at Jessie. ''Have you lost your mind?''

''No. I've just made up my mind, and there's no use trying to dissuade me. I won't listen to any arguments. Wade's my brother and I intend to find him one way or the other.''

''Jessica, I know your feelings, but you don't have to risk your life trying to find Wade. You can send a message to the Indian mission through Quillon or one of the other men.''

Jessie shook her head. ''I won't risk it. The only hope I have is to go myself. Wade would never believe a message left at the mission by one of the men. He'd think it was a trap.''

Edwina flopped the large lump of dough into an earthen bowl and covered it with a checkered cloth to let it rise. She wiped her floured hands on her apron and released a resigned sigh. When she looked at Jessie her fifty years were reflected in her lined face. ''I knew it would come to this after the other night. It's just taken you a day or two longer than I expected to come up with this harebrained scheme.''

"It's no scheme. My brother is out there living by his wits when I have all the money I could ever need to help him. Since we lost Kate, I would think you, most of all, would understand why I have to go. He is my family, Edwina. I love you dearly, but Wade and I share the same blood. This land is half his.''

Edwina sagged in defeat. "Then go and find your brother. I'll worry myself sick until you're back here where I can keep an eye on you.''

Jessie crossed to her friend and hugged her. "Edwina, you are also my family and I love you.''

Edwina nodded and gave Jessie's hand a motherly pat. "And I love you in all your stubbornness. My prayers go with you.''

"I'll leave at dawn, but first I need to ride into town to get directions to the Indian mission.''

"Do you think that is wise?'' Edwina asked. "Shouldn't you just ask one of the men to tell you how to get there?''

"It may not be wise, but I prefer to have a map. I don't want to get lost. And should anyone ask my reason for needing directions, I can always say I want to send food to the orphanage. Such an excuse won't seem strange since I'm a woman. They'll just think it's another of my harebrained ideas.'' Jessie chuckled at the thought. She could almost see the gossips with their heads together, talking about that odd woman from back east who wanted to feed the savages. She probably would be able to hear their outrage all the way to Indian territory.

* * *

Edwina punched the yeast dough with the force of a boxer getting ready for a championship match, then covered the bowl with the checkered cloth. It had to rise once more before it could go into the oven. Her mind already on other problems, she dusted her hands together to rid them of the excess flour and turned to wash them in the tin pan of the dry sink. A movement in the doorway caught her attention and she turned to find Slim Johnson leaning casually against the door frame, arms folded over his chest. He smiled at her and tipped his battered felt hat.

"Good day to you, Miss Edwina. Just come over to see if there was anythin' you need me to pick up at the mercantile in town. Me and Brand are goin' that way."

"There are a few things I need, Mr. Johnson. Won't you come in and have a cup of coffee while I make out a list," Edwina said, using the same polite but impersonal tone that Slim had used with her. Since their first encounter on the day he and Brand had arrived at Eden, an unspoken truce had developed between them. So far it had worked out beautifully. They'd had no further disagreements. However, their peaceful coexistence relied on their efforts to avoid each other unless communication was absolutely necessary.

"I'd enjoy a cup of coffee," Slim said, eyeing Edwina suspiciously. He didn't understand the invitation. It was the first time she'd ever asked him into the kitchen without Miss Nolan present. Slim took a seat at the table and watched Edwina pour a cup of the steaming dark brew. She absently put it before him before settling herself across the table. She picked nervously at a loose thread in the tablecloth with two fingers but seemed not to notice that she was creating a hole in the material.

"Somethin' troublin' you, Miss Edwina?" Slim asked when the housekeeper continued to stare at the ever-widening space and made no attempt to make the list she'd promised.

"I'm sorry, Mr. Johnson. Did you say something?"

Slim leaned back in his chair and took a long sip of coffee before answering. "I asked if there was somethin' troublin' you."

Edwina frowned at Slim, her expression puzzled. "Why would you think anything was troubling me?"

"For starters you're not actin' like yourself, and you said you wanted to make me out a list of supplies to pick up at the mercantile in town."

"A list of supplies?" Edwina said, and then nodded briskly. "Oh, yes. I do need a bag of salt and I'm nearly out of flour."

"Is that all?" Slim asked, glancing in the direction of the covered bowl. Something akin to disgust flickered over his face as he thought of the sickly white bread the woman was so fond of making. For the life of him, he didn't understand why Miss Nolan liked it. It didn't stick to a man's ribs like good sourdough biscuits. And anyone with a lick of sense knew a man needed good nourishing food if he intended to do a hard day's work.

"Yes, of course, what more would I need?" Edwina said. Her voice trailed off, her mind once more on Jessie.

Slim frowned, dragging his thoughts away from the bowl of dough and back to Edwina. "Woman, I can see there's somethin' botherin' you. It might help if you talked about it."

Edwina snapped back to the present and drew herself

up. "Mr. Johnson, you will refrain from calling me 'woman.' My name is Miss Roilings or Miss Edwina, thank you."

"Dat blast it! Don't you go gettin' all uppity on me. I only wanted to know what was troublin' you, and you ain't got no call to go jumpin' down my throat when I was extendin' my hand in friendship."

Chagrined by his censure, Edwina nodded. "I apologize. I shouldn't have spoken so harshly."

"You're right about that. But I can see you've got your mind on other matters, so I'll accept your apology. Is there anythin' I can do to help you?"

Edwina shook her head. She couldn't tell him Jessie planned on riding alone into Indian territory. Nor could she tell him she'd argued until she was nearly blue in the face and it had done no good. The girl was determined to find her brother, no matter how much danger she was putting herself in. No, she couldn't tell Slim Johnson what caused her worry. Nor could she tell anyone else without revealing Jessie's secret.

"Thank you, Mr. Johnson, but I'm afraid there's nothing anyone can do to change things. If you'll stay right here, I'll write the supply list and you can be on your way."

His face screwing up thoughtfully, Slim scratched at his chin as his gaze came to rest on the saddle bags draped over the chair. Something was going on here. He'd have to ask Brand if he had any inkling of what the boss lady and her bossy housekeeper were up to.

He frowned and pursed his lips to one side at the thought of Brand. Of late it wasn't easy for him to talk to his partner. The boy was so ill tempered that he acted as if he had a hard-on all the time. Slim shook his head.

He didn't know what had gotten into Brand, but Slim knew he should wait until they started back from Miss Molly's tonight before bringing up the subject of Miss Nolan and Winnie. The boy would be in a much better humor after a good tussle with one of Molly's whores.

Morose, his head pounding from the effect of the cheap whiskey he'd drunk at the whorehouse, Brand squinted up at the dawning sky through bloodshot eyes. He mounted his horse, then kicked the animal in the side, urging it none too gently in the direction of Eden. His mood had not been improved by his visit to Miss Molly's house of pleasure, and he swore under his breath, recalling his own reaction to the heavy-breasted, red-haired woman who had led him upstairs to her bed. He didn't know what had gotten into him. Last night had been the first time in his life that he'd not been able to respond to the expertise of a lady of the evening. Her fingers had tried to work their magic, but he had lain there like a rag after a heavy rain, limp and lifeless.

Disgruntled by the memory, Brand ran his hand across his unshaven cheek and glanced at his friend. Slim hadn't had any problems with the ladies at Molly's. He'd taken two of her spriest girls upstairs and hadn't been seen again until nearly dawn. He was still grinning from ear to ear over his adventures between the sheets.

"You don't have to look so damned pleased with yourself, old man," Brand grumbled. "You didn't win a prize for endurance back there."

Slim's grin deepened. "Myrtle and Madge might disagree with you on that. Did you know those girls are sisters? Damned if they can't do some of the wildest things. It's just like two good cowhands workin' with a steer. They know their jobs down to the letter.''

Brand's frown deepened. He tipped his hat to the back of his head and gently massaged his aching temple. ''I'm afraid I'm not in the mood to appreciate the details of your night with the sisters. Save them for a time when my damned head doesn't feel as if it's going to explode between my ears.''

Slim's grin faded. Brand's behavior puzzled him. His friend had often suffered hangovers, but even then he was usually in good humor after enjoying himself with a woman. ''How was your redhead? She looked as if she knew how to please a man without any help from her sister.''

''She did,'' Brand said curtly. Slim would laugh himself silly if he learned how the night had really gone. A muscle worked in his jaw as he clenched his teeth against the throbbing in his head. Damned if he didn't feel as if there were a cattle stampede behind his eyes.

''So you had a good time?'' Slim questioned, watching Brand anxiously.

Brand grunted an affirmation and Slim released a relieved breath. ''Then I thought you ought to know that I think somethin's afoot with Miss Nolan. That housekeeper of hers was actin' strange yesterday. She even invited me in for a cup of coffee.''

Brand turned his bloodshot gaze upon Slim, his frown deepening into a grimace. ''You suspect something is amiss at Eden because the housekeeper invited you in for a cup of coffee?''

''I don't rightly know what to think. I just know that there were saddle bags in the kitchen and Winnie was upset. And it takes somethin' powerful to make that straightlaced old woman absentminded. I figure there's only one thing she cares enough about to upset her in such a way. And that is our boss lady.''

Brand came completely alert. His head still ached, but he ignored the pain, sitting straighter in the saddle. "I think it's time we get back to the ranch. Our Miss Nolan may be planning to meet her rustler, and I want to be on her trail the minute she sets out.''

"Won't your bein' gone raise a bunch of questions?'' Slim asked, urging his horse to keep pace with Brand's.

"No, because you're going to explain that I decided to stay in town for a couple of days. That should satisfy anyone's curiosity. Every cowhand has to take time to spend his wages on liquor and women.''

"What will you do if she leads you to Fleming? Do you plan on arrestin' her, too?''

"If you lie with dogs . . .'' Brand let the words trail off.

"She sure don't seem the type to be involved with the likes of Fleming,'' Slim said, scratching absently beneath his arm. "But I've known from the first minute we set eyes on her wearin' men's britches that she's different from any other woman I ever seen. From one minute to the next you don't know what to expect.''

Another frown etched a path across Brand's features. Slim's words echoed his own thoughts about Jessie. She was different from any woman he had ever met. He feared if he stopped to rationalize the reason for his lack of response at Molly's, he'd have to lay the blame at his boss lady's door. She had him so damned mesmerized that he couldn't think straight.

Brand urged the Morgan to a faster gait. With luck his patience was about to be rewarded. Once Jessica led him to Fleming he could finish his job and put her behind him—before he revealed his desire and made a fool of himself. The woman could scramble up his insides with a mere look from her expressive eyes.

"She's different all right. There aren't too many women who are willing to be involved with the likes of Fleming," Brand said, and galloped ahead of Slim to end their conversation. In his present frame of mind he didn't want to talk or think about Jessica Nolan and her involvement with the half-breed. If he thought too much on it, he feared he wouldn't bring Fleming back alive to stand trial.

Chapter 7

A blaze of scarlet and gold streaked the western sky as the sun sank slowly below the rolling hills blanketed with cottonwood and pine. Twilight's indigo shadows were already claiming the land beneath the trees and stretching their tentacles across the valley floor. The lonely sound of a wild turkey calling to its mate echoed through the evening air, reflecting Jessie's feelings as she maneuvered her mount along the narrow trail to the small stream flowing peacefully over a rock bed.

Agilely Jessie slipped from the saddle and dropped the reins. The horse, eager to quench his thirst after the long day's journey, slurped the cool water and flicked its tail against horseflies as his rider hunkered down beside him and cupped her hands to drink. Thirst satisfied, Jessie splashed her face to rinse away the dust and dried it absently on the sleeve of her shirt as she surveyed her surroundings.

The valley had ample grass for her horse and the trees provided protection, but Jessie had no idea where she was. Irritated, she dragged her saddle bags from the horse and tossed them against a fallen log. She'd been so certain she could reach Indian territory without involving anyone else in her plans. "And I should have had a map," she muttered. Her trip into town had only gained her incompetent directions at best. The clerk at the general store had said it would be easy to find the orphanage on the Choctaw reservation. All you had to do was go directly north. And like a fool she had believed him.

Jessie glanced once more at the sky and, though the air was still warm, shivered. She rubbed her arms absently as the first stars appeared on the eastern horizon. The luxurious life Kate had provided had weakened her natural instincts for survival, overshadowed her Indian heritage and the things she had been taught as a child born on the frontier. In Boston she'd had no need to hone such skills. Had she any doubt of the direction back to Kate's mansion on Beacon Hill, all she'd had to do was pay a cab to take her there. Everything she'd needed had been provided by others. Now, because of her own lack of ability, she was hopelessly lost.

"And I believed I could find Indian territory without a guide because I'm half Indian," she muttered, and gave a snort of disgust at her own stupidity. Even a full-blooded Indian reared in Boston wouldn't know which way to go without a map. Only those raised in this country knew the challenges and the dangers facing them. The word *danger* seemed to echo ominously through Jessie's mind, and she quickly turned to start a fire. She didn't want to think of what she might have to face, lost and alone at night in the wilderness.

By the time night completely shrouded the valley in its ebony folds, the dry sticks Jessie had gathered cracked and popped from the flames licking greedily about them. Satisfied with a job well done, Jessie dug a pot out of her saddle bag and filled it with water from the stream. She tossed in a handful of coffee beans and set the pot at the edge of the fire to brew. She opened a can of beans and warmed them near the flames until the coffee was ready. Then she unwrapped the last biscuit Edwina had sent along and consumed her bland meal. She told herself she wasn't afraid to be alone at night in the wilderness despite the eerie shadows that formed beyond the circle of firelight.

A twig snapped and she jerked about, her hand going to the rifle that lay at her side. She saw the brief gleam of eyes beneath a bush before the small, frightened rabbit scurried back into the darkness.

Jessie laughed aloud with relief and felt her rapidly beating pulse begin to slow. She drew in a deep, steadying breath. She was acting foolish. There was nothing here to harm her. The little furry beast reminded her of some advice Wade had given her when she was a little girl: "Always remember, Jessie. Animals are far more frightened of you than you are of them, so there's nothing to worry about in the dark."

The memory made Jessie smile as she recalled how she had placed her faith in Wade's advice. He had been nearing his fourteenth birthday, and in her nine-year-old mind he was nearly a grown man. She had believed every word he spoke.

Jessie relaxed and laid the rifle aside once more, caught up in her memories. Knees bent and arms looped about them casually, she raised her face toward the star-filled sky and again wondered where her brother might be at that moment. Was he holed up like an animal, waiting until the night gave him the freedom to plunder the countryside, raiding ranches?

At the thought of the life her brother led, Jessie felt a lump rise in her throat. Being reunited with Wade would not solve all their problems; it would only be the beginning. Her brother would still be considered an outlaw, and it would not be a simple matter to make things right for him.

"Oh, Wade. Why did you have to turn to rustling to make your living? Why couldn't you have stayed with Kate and me? You would now be rich and respected with everything you desired."

Unaware of the silver eyes watching her from the shadows, Jessie dashed the dampness from her lashes. It was useless to think of what might have been. She had to find Wade first before she could help him set his life to rights.

A twig snapped close by, jerking Jessie from her reverie. She expected to see another rabbit scurrying into the darkness. Instead she caught sight of a tall figure just beyond the circle of firelight. Her eyes widened with fear. Her mouth suddenly a desert, her fingers boneless, she fumbled for the rifle at her side while she scrambled to her feet. Finally she managed to aim the rifle at the shadowy intruder. She swallowed several times and felt her blood run cold as the tall figure moved slowly toward her. Gripping the rifle trigger, she closed her eyes and squeezed.

Nothing happened.

Her eyes flew open and she stared in dismay at the man who approached her, a curious smile curling up his sensuous mouth at the corners.

"I believe you have to put a round in the chamber for it to work properly," Brand said, taking the Winchester from Jessie's shaking hands. Expertly, and with the ease of much experience, he worked the lever action, settling a cartridge into the chamber before he raised the rifle to his shoulder. The explosion that followed startled Jessie's mount, who shifted wildly, straining against the ropes that secured him to a nearby tree.

Calmly Brand set Jessie's rifle aside. The smile he had worn a moment earlier had vanished, leaving only a deepening scowl. "What kind of fool would come out here and not know how to use a rifle? Don't you realize I could have been an Indian or any one of the outlaws who freely roam the countryside just looking for simpletons who don't have any better sense than to put themselves in dangerous situations?"

Brand's stinging censure burned along Jessie's nerves like a whip tipped in salt. What he said was true. She was a fool for not knowing how to use the rifle and for getting herself lost. However, he had no right to chastise her like a child. She was a grown woman, and he worked for her.

Stiffening, she looked up at Brand, her eyes snapping with blue fire. "And what kind of fool comes sneaking into camp without letting his presence be known? As I see it, Brand Stockton, you are fortunate I didn't know how to use the rifle or you would now be dead."

"I didn't sneak into camp. I spoke to let you know I was here, but you were too damned busy trying to shoot me."

Jessie felt her cheeks flush with embarrassment. "I thought you were an outlaw."

"I damned well could have been. Don't you know you shouldn't be this far from the ranch? If I hadn't been out looking for strays and smelled your smoke, you could have gotten lost."

Her blush deepening, Jessie looked at Brand sheepishly. "I was already lost."

"Lost?" Brand said, eyeing Jessie skeptically. If she thought she'd throw him off the trail by saying she had been riding over her land and then lost her way, she had better think again. He wasn't stupid.

"I was riding out to see about the line shacks near the north range and didn't realize how far I'd gone or that I'd taken the wrong direction until it was too late."

Brand ground his teeth together to keep from confronting her on the feeble lie. His fingers itched to shake the truth from her, but he managed to suppress the urge. He had to act as if he believed every word she said, or he'd have to tell her he'd been following her since she'd left Eden at dawn.

"Well, I guess you're lucky I came along. You're in Indian territory."

"Yes, I'm grateful you're here, though you did nearly frighten me to death," Jessie said. "Have you had anything to eat?"

Brand shook his head.

"There's an extra can of beans in my saddle bag," Jessie said without thinking. "And I believe there's still some coffee in the pot."

Brand opened the leather flap and took out the beans. He stared down at the tin in his hand for a long moment before he looked once more at Jessie. "At least you came prepared to get lost."

"I—I— Oh, all right," Jessie said, unable to find a reasonable excuse for having two saddle bags filled with enough food to last her several days. "I wasn't riding the range but going to the Indian orphanage at the mission. I heard about it when I was in town and wanted to make a donation.'' Satisfied with her new lie, she waited for Brand to speak.

Brand didn't say a word but continued to regard Jessie skeptically. After what seemed an eternity, he shrugged. ''What you do with your money and time is your own business. But you should have asked me or Slim to escort you. That way you wouldn't have gotten lost.''

Jessie breathed a sigh of relief. ''I know that now.''

Brand finished the coffee and the beans and laid out his bedroll on the opposite side of the fire from where Jessie had settled. The fire slowly burned down, leaving only a reddish glow of coals to light the ebony night as he tried to sleep.

Jessie, too, was unable to sleep, though the sound of the nearby stream soothed the tension from her body. She lay, head resting on her arms, staring up into the black velvet sky, thinking how beautiful the night had become since she was no longer alone. The soft hoot and a flutter of wings in the shadowy pines drew her attention to an owl searching for his nightly meal of fat mice. His dark shape swooped overhead, circled their camp, and then sailed once more toward the security of the trees. Jessie smiled to herself. Poor owl, she thought, he's disappointed we're not mice.

Her smile deepened with contentment. She rolled onto her side, where she could see Brand. Stretched out, his head resting on his saddle, his Stetson pulled down over his eyes, his lean body relaxed, he still seemed to exude power. Jessie's gaze moved over his chest to the hand lying relaxed on his hard, flat abdomen. He had beautiful, masculine hands. Strong and long-fingered, they possessed the strength to rope a steer and easily bring it down.

Jessie's smile faded with the thought. Something Brand had said earlier niggled at the back of her mind. He had told her he'd been out searching for strays. Frowning, she went over their conversation once more in her mind. Her eyes widened and she gasped. Her movement roused Brand and he immediately reached for his revolver.

"What's wrong? Did you hear something?" he asked, peering cautiously into the night.

"You lied to me," Jessie said, indignation filling her voice.

Brand blinked at Jessie. "What are you talking about?"

"You know exactly what I'm talking about, Brand Stockton," Jessie threw back her blanket and got to her feet. Hands on hips, she glared at him.

Brand yawned and slipped his revolver into the holster at his side. "Jessie, it's been a long day. Couldn't we discuss this in the morning?"

"There is nothing to discuss. You lied to me about the reason you're here. You weren't out searching for strays. We're too far from the ranch for that. You were following me, weren't you?"

Brand tossed another stick on the glowing coals and watched it blaze before he looked up. He shrugged. "You're lucky I followed you. Look what a mess you got yourself into on your own. If I hadn't been close by, there's no telling what might have happened to you."

Jessie eyed Brand coolly and raised her nose in the

air. "For your information, Mr. Stockton, I can take care of myself."

"Certainly you can." Brand laughed, coming to his feet. "I saw how well you take care of yourself today while I followed you in circles. And as for tonight, I found you're also an expert with a rifle."

"How dare you laugh at me!" Jessie cried, her irritation mounting.

Brand couldn't stop himself from chuckling at the look on Jessie's face. "You might be able to take care of yourself in Boston, but I'm afraid the things you learned in those fancy schools back east won't help you when you come up against roving Indians or a hungry puma. You should realize it by now. If tonight is any example of how you can take care of yourself, I suggest you do like the rest of the women out here and get yourself a man to keep you out of trouble."

"Get myself a man!" Jessie sputtered, struggling desperately to hold on to her temper. Eyes snapping blue fire, breasts heaving against the thin material of her shirt, she stamped her foot in frustration. "Oh! You sneaking, lying, conceited, egotistical, swell-headed, dunderbrained idiot! That's the one thing I don't need, especially if you're a prime example of what western men are like."

Mesmerized, Brand watched Jessie's temper transform her into a vibrant wildcat, exuding fiery sensuality as she stood facing him in all her fury. His senses stirred and he felt himself swell in answer to the beauty before him. He'd been attracted to Jessica Nolan from the first, but now he felt an undeniable need to strip her naked and press her satiny length against his flesh while he kissed away her protests.

Reacting solely on instinct, his body demanding release from weeks of torment, Brand closed the space between them. In that moment all thoughts of her involvement with Wade Fleming vanished from his mind. He drew Jessie into his arms and silenced her surprised cry with a hard, demanding kiss.

Stunned, Jessie didn't resist. Her experience with the opposite sex had been limited to the boys who had come to call on her in Boston. She'd received only a few innocent pecks on the cheek and light brushes on the lips by a suitor who had been bold enough to chance her wrath. Never had anyone kissed her like Brand Stockton. His lips moving hungrily over hers, his tongue demanding entrance as he forced her mouth open to accept his intimate caress. To her bewilderment, before she could regain control and push herself out of his arms, his exploring, intoxicating kiss stirred things to life within her. In watching Brand work, she'd felt only a glimmer of the sensation that now coursed through her, starting at the very core of her being and radiating outward until every inch of her body tingled.

Intrigued yet frightened by the new sensations, Jessie thrust herself out of Brand's arms. A moment later the impact of her hand against his cheek echoed eerily through the night. She wiped her mouth on the back of her hand, her eyes full of accusations. "Don't you ever lay another hand on me or I'll kill you."

Brand's narrowed eyes glowed in the firelight like newly minted coins. Lips firmed into a thin line, Jessie's handprint white against the dull flush that tinted his face, he rubbed his stinging cheek. His voice was a low, ominous growl. "You bitch."

"Call me anything you like, but k-keep your distance,'' Jessie stammered. She suddenly realized the precariousness of the situation. She was alone in the wilderness with a man who could easily overpower her. Her safest course of action was to put as much distance between herself and Brand as possible. Slowly she backed away from him.

Incensed, Brand snaked out a hand, his fingers like bands of steel about her wrist as he drew her back to him. ''You don't have to be afraid I might soil your lovely lips again with my kisses, Miss Nolan. I wouldn't kiss you if you were the last woman in Texas. Or the world, for that matter.'' Brand snapped his mouth shut before he added, ''Because you're a breed's whore.''

Forcing down the fear that made her insides quiver, Jessie jerked her arm free of Brand's fingers. Determined to brazen it out, she stiffened her spine and glared up at him. She'd never let him know how his kisses had affected her. ''That's exactly how I want to keep things.''

''I'm glad we both agree on something,'' Brand said, turning his back before he strangled her. His cheek still burned from the blow she'd given him, and he was in no mood to wrestle with his temper. No one had ever struck him before without paying dearly for the insult, and it took every ounce of willpower he possessed to keep himself from tanning Miss Jessica Nolan's haughty little backside. He could nearly imagine the pain she'd feel when his hand came into contact with her tight Levi's. Pushing the enticing thought away, he stretched out on the woolen blanket of his bedroll and covered his eyes once more with his hat. His voice was cold as he said, ''I suggest you get some sleep. We leave at dawn.''

Jessie glanced uncertainly at her own bedroll. How could she sleep after what had happened? Her nerves were as taut as a piece of wet rawhide left to dry all day in the sun. Emotions tumbled about inside her like an avalanche of boulders down a steep hillside. She didn't understand how she could feel so angry with Brand for kissing her and at the same time feel distressed because he'd agreed to keep his distance. Confused, Jessie sat down and drew the blanket up around her shoulders. Hours later she finally slept, her body curled up under her blanket, completely unaware of the silver eyes that watched her from the other side of the campfire.

At dawn, their moods as black as the roiling clouds moving in from the west, Jessie and Brand started back to the ranch. She wanted to go on to the mission to leave a message for Wade but realized without Brand's help she'd risk getting herself lost once more. After what had transpired between them the night before, she couldn't ask the detestable man to guide her, not even if her life depended on it. She would just have to find some other way to get in touch with her brother.

Jessie glanced toward her silent companion. For the moment she had no recourse but to travel back to Eden with Brand. However, once she was back at the ranch their association would come to an end. She intended to fire Brand Stockton immediately.

Several hours later, the sky, the color of an angry sea, opened up. Heavy drops of rain drenched the two riders before they could retrieve their oilcloth rain slickers from their saddles. They continued on, riding silently through the downpour until the lightning began to spread eerie fingers across the hillsides. A fiery blue bolt struck a clump of nearby mesquite as the two passed. The trees shattered, exploding into the air, sending a current of electricity and bark over Brand and Jessie.

Shaken, Brand looked about for shelter. Spying a dark outline in the distance, he altered course, praying it was a line shack. Wind whipping about them, sending dead branches and leaves scurrying across the ground like misshapen animals, Brand shouted at Jessie, "We've got to find someplace to get out of this storm. It's too dangerous to keep on traveling."

A loud crack of thunder nearly drowned out his words as Jessie nodded her agreement. The force of the wind had risen to such a degree, it was taking all her strength just to handle her mount and stay in the saddle. Seeing her dilemma, Brand reached down and grabbed her reins.

"Hold on, Jessie. I think I see a line shack up ahead." Jessie clung to the pommel while Brand urged their mounts forward into the biting rain.

Relief swept over Brand as they neared the dilapidated building. Bringing the horses around to a lean-to behind the shack, he dismounted, tied them securely to the side of the shelter, and then turned to help Jessie down. She slipped easily into his arms, and he drew her protectively against him as he braved the torrent of rain to reach the sagging porch. He kicked open the door and set Jessie on her feet, then took in their surroundings.

"It looks like Lady Luck is with us today," Brand said, crossing to the rusty, potbellied stove sitting in the corner. He lifted the round iron lid and peered into the dark cavern half-filled with ashes. With a flick of a hand on the bottom grate, he sifted the gray dust out of the stove and within minutes had a fire blazing in its round belly. Warmth spread over the cabin as he turned to find Jessie still huddled by the door, trembling from cold.

"I think we'd best take off our wet clothing," Brand said, already shrugging out of his rain slicker. His shirt came next as Jessie stood and gaped if he'd suddenly gone mad.

"I have no intention of taking off my clothing with you here," she sputtered.

Brand rolled his eyes in disgust and ran a hand through his damp hair. Lack of sleep, the storm, and a stubborn woman did little to induce a good mood. A wayward curl fell over his brow as he shook his head. "Rest assured, Miss Nolan, I have no ulterior motives. I won't try to seduce you. My only thought was to keep you from coming down with an infection of the lungs. But by all means, stay wet if it pleases you. It's none of my concern."

Jessie watched in dismay as Brand strode across the cabin and picked up a rough woolen blanket from the narrow cot. He tossed it to her before he turned his back and pulled off his boots. Next, without a glance in her direction, he shucked his britches. Jessie's eyes widened in shock as the pale skin of his firm buttocks came into view. She quickly shifted her gaze in the opposite direction and felt her skin heat with embarrassment even as the blood began a furious race through her veins.

Nearly strangling on the riot of conflicting feelings within her, Jessie clutched the blanket to her chest as if it were a lifeline. Her world had totally gone berserk.

She no longer felt like the confident young woman Kate had taught to manage her own life; instead she was a spoiled child being denied a treat. She knew she should be glad that Brand had staunchly reaffirmed his lack of interest in her, though to her dismay she found herself piqued by his vows and wondered what he found so distasteful. When he had kissed her the previous night, he hadn't thought her so repulsive. What had changed in only a few hours?

Jessie's dark brows knit over the bridge of her slender nose as she absently worked loose the buttons on her rain slicker. Perhaps the kiss they'd shared hadn't affected Brand in the same way it had her. Perhaps he had only been playing with her emotions, as Kate had warned her men often did with inexperienced women. Kate had told her men would say or do anything to get their own way and then leave the woman to suffer the consequences.

Eyes sparkling with annoyance, Jessie glanced at her silent companion. He stood with his back to her, a woolen blanket wrapped about him, his hands held out to the warmth of the stove. Quietly she slipped out of her rain slicker and then her soggy clothing. She wrapped a blanket around her body and tied it in a knot over one shoulder. The makeshift garment curved inticingly about her bottom in back, while the front of the thin wool hugged her breasts, emphasizing their lush fullness below the creamy skin of her bare shoulders and throat. Her eyes still on Brand, Jessie unbraided her hair and ran her fingers through the mass of damp silk. It hung about her in a wavy, dark curtain, contrasting starkly against her fair skin. Unconscious of the provocative sight she made, Jessie raised her head in the air and crossed to Brand's side. If he tried to touch her again, she'd give him a setdown that would singe the hide off a buffalo.

Brand kept his eyes leveled on the wall behind the stove. He had heard Jessie undress, and his imagination had betrayed him by creating images of her body naked and glistening with raindrops. Struggling to keep a tight rein on himself, he ignored Jessie when she came to stand beside him. He jumped with surprise when she accidentally brushed against his side as she leaned forward to warm her hands. Swallowing with difficulty, he looked down at his half-dressed companion and felt the heat surge into his loins.

Standing close enough for him to smell her lilac fragrance, her small toes peaking from beneath the blanket draped about her, Jessie looked like a pagan deity with her hair a mass of wild waves about her bare shoulders. Brand cleared his throat, causing her to look up. In that moment he felt he would drown in the soft blue velvet pools. His heart began to hammer against his ribs as if trying to escape the confinement of his chest.

Struggling with the turbulence of his emotions, Brand forced himself to look away from the alluring sight. He had vowed to keep his distance, and he would. Before he could step away from the stove, however, a loud crack of thunder shook the cabin. Jessie jumped instinctively, the movement sending her once more against Brand.

Brand's groan of despair sounded to Jessie's ears like a roar of disgust as his large hands gripped her firmly by the arms to set her away from him.

"Woman, won't you be still! You're stepping all over my feet."

Jessie's temper flared. "Oh, I think it's time I stepped on your toes, Mr. Stockton." Jessie said, and proceeded to carry out her threat.

Dancing out of the way of her small feet, Brand growled, "Sweet Jesus, woman! What's gotten into you? Has the rain washed away what little sense you had?"

"Don't talk to me like I'm some brainless half-wit. Remember you work for me, Brand Stockton, and I will be treated with respect."

"Respect?" Brand repeated, glaring at Jessie as he rubbed his aching toes. "How can you expect me to show respect for a woman who attacks me without the least provocation? If you think your actions deserve respect, then you must have eaten some locoweed while you were out getting yourself lost."

"Attack you? As I recall, you were the one who attacked me last night without provocation," Jessie snapped, eyeing Brand furiously.

"I've had damn well plenty of provocation," Brand stormed in self-defense. "You've strutted around Eden without a care, wearing those tight little britches. It's enough to entice any man into wanting you."

"I wasn't trying to entice you or anyone else. I wore the britches because they're far more durable when I'm working."

"A good excuse. But you damn well should have realized the consequences. You're just lucky someone hasn't taken you up on your offer way before now and tossed you into the hay for a little fun."

"I've made no offer," Jessie blustered, feeling the first glimmer of uncertainty.

"Hell, you don't have to say a word. A man reads what he sees in the hand he's dealt. A spade is a spade

122

until he learns otherwise. But usually by that time it's too late to change things.''

His words cut her to the bone. Jessie felt her cheeks burn with embarrassment. Had her attraction to Brand made her unconsciously send out an invitation to him to overstep the bounds of propriety? ''No,'' Jessie said firmly, shaking her head in denial. ''You're wrong. I should be allowed to wear whatever I want without men believing I'm trying to get them into my bed.''

Brand nodded. ''You're right, but damn it, Jessie, that's not the way things are. Last night is a prime example. I forgot everything except my need to taste your lips. And other men will do the same or a lot worse when they get excited.''

Jessie stared at Brand for a long, thoughtful moment before lowering her eyes to the blanket draped about her. It was ironic, but to a certain degree he was right. Even now she was dressed—or should she say undressed?—to arouse him. She'd been piqued by his vow not to touch her and unconsciously or perhaps consciously—she honestly didn't know which at the present moment—she'd set out to make him regret his decision.

The heat rose in her cheeks. She'd been honest about why she wore men's britches. She'd had no ulterior motive in mind other than the comfort and ease they provided. Swallowing the sick feeling that rose in her throat as her eyes filled with tears, Jessie turned away from Brand.

''I'm sorry. I didn't realize,'' she muttered, too humiliated to remain a moment longer with the man she had unwittingly set out to seduce. She couldn't face him, knowing that he knew what she had done. Before

Brand could stop her she crossed to the door and fled into the storm.

"Damn," Brand muttered, realizing the mistake he'd made by laying all the blame at Jessie's door. His reaction to her had nothing to do with the clothes she wore. He knew he'd still desire the little termagant had she been swathed from head to toe in layers of burlap feed sacks. He'd lashed out at her from jealousy, because the man for whom she'd traveled so far away from Eden was Wade Fleming.

Tossing aside his blanket, he jerked on his wet britches and boots before going after Jessie. He stopped on the porch, where a leak thumped against the floorboard. He called her name but received only the steady drum of the rain on the tin roof in answer.

Cursing again, he stepped into the downpour. Water ran into his eyes and streaked down his face as he squinted into the gray gloom of the stormy day. He had to find Jessie before she got too far away. It was too dangerous for her to be out in the elements alone. She could be struck by lightning or washed away in one of the flash floods that often occurred when rain became too heavy to be absorbed into the ground.

"Jessie," he shouted again, spying a dark shape huddled at the base of a low-limbed mesquite. Mud squelching underfoot, he crossed the rivulets of water between the tufts of range grass to where Jessie wept like a beaten child, her blanket soggy and mud-splashed, her dark hair sticking to her face like a silken web. His heart thudded against his ribs as he knelt by her side. Gently he placed a hand on her dark head and murmured, "Jessie, love. I didn't mean what I said."

Slowly Jessie raised her head and looked at him, her

glistening eyes sad, her lower lip trembling. At the sight, Brand lost the battle with his emotions. He lifted Jessie into his arms and cradled her against his chest as he walked back into the line shack. All his resolutions were washed away by the torrent of rain drenching the Texas earth.

Brand laid Jessie on the narrow cot and tenderly wiped the tears and rain from her face. "I'm sorry, Jessie. I didn't mean all the things I said. I just wanted to . . . Oh, hell," he said quietly, "I don't really know what I wanted."

"But you were right," Jessie admitted. "I can't deny it. I wanted your kiss as much as you wanted to kiss me."

Brand cupped her cheek in the palm of his hand and peered into her sapphire eyes. "Do you mean it, Jess?"

Jessica could only nod. Her wild flight into the storm had taught her one startling lesson, and she had wept with the realization. It had not been merely physical attraction that had drawn her to Brand Stockton. Without even being aware of it, she had fallen helplessly in love with him.

Jessie's nod made Brand's mouth go dry. He could no longer suppress the desire that had begun upon his first glimpse of Jessica Nolan, haughtily passing the saloon, her head raised regally in the air. He trembled from the force of his feelings for this woman who had bewitched him so thoroughly. She made him forget everything but his need of her. He felt something stir deep within him that he couldn't put a name to. Somewhere in distant memory he had known a similar feeling, but he pushed the thought aside. All he needed for the moment was Jessie. Slowly he lowered his mouth to hers and thrilled as she opened her lips to him in tentative response. Her arms stole about his neck, drawing him down.

The warmth from the potbellied stove and the heat of their passion spread over the two lovers, drying their rain-drenched bodies as Brand stretched out beside Jessie on the narrow cot. Hungrily he devoured what he had only tasted once before. A moan of pleasure escaped him as Jessie molded her body to his. She clung to his shoulders, her fingers working the corded muscles beneath the tanned flesh. Dragging his mouth away, chest rising and falling with his labored breath, he looked down into Jessie's passion-filled eyes before allowing his gaze to travel over her.

"Jessie, my angel. God, how I've wanted you. I've wanted to feel the silk of your skin beneath my hand." He stroked the curve of her throat. "To feel your heart beat beneath my fingers." Slowly, provocatively, he moved his hand along her collarbone to her cleavage. "To touch the satin of your breasts." Ever so slowly he moved his fingers along the edge of the blanket and untied the knot. He eased back the damp material, leaving her naked before his eyes. His voice grew hoarse with desire as he continued. "To taste the sweetness of their coral peaks." He lowered his head and brushed his lips against a nipple as his fingers gently teased its twin. "To suckle your sweetness." He opened his mouth and took the nipple, his tongue lavishing it lovingly before he began another erotic torture, drawing against it until Jessie moaned with pleasure.

Burying her fingers in his dark hair, Jessie arched her back to give him complete access to the bounties he craved. Until this moment she had thought she knew what love and life were all about. Now, she realized how naive she had been. The fancy girls' school she'd attended in Boston had left her totally ignorant of the pleasure a man's caress could give. This man she knew so little about, this man who had stolen her heart, was teaching her about life. His touch made every nerve in her body tingle. To ease the gentle ache mounting deep in the core of her being, she instinctively thrust her hips against the leg Brand pressed between her thighs.

His hunger for Jessie consuming him like a prairie fire in a drought, Brand raised his head and looked once more into her slumberous eyes. "Jessie, you are the most beautiful woman I've ever seen. I crave you like a bee hungers for the essence of a blossom. I want to taste your honeyed skin until I know all of you."

Mesmerized by the magic of his touch and soft voice, Jessie caressed his beard-stubbled jaw. She thought she would die from the fire licking her body. She needed him as she'd needed no other person in her life. Only he could fill the aching void his touch had created. He was the maestro and she the violin; together they would make a passionate melody that their hearts alone could hear and understand.

"Love me, Brand," she whispered, her voice husky with passion.

Jessie's request shattered his desire to prolong their loveplay. Eager to feel himself buried deep within her warmth, Brand quickly stripped himself naked and rejoined her on the narrow cot. Cradling her face in his hands, he captured her mouth in a soul-shattering kiss as he eased her thighs apart. He felt the hot, wet warmth of her against his sex and trembled from the searing sensation.

"God, how sweet you are," he murmured against her lips, dropping heated little kisses along her cheeks. "Nothing in your past matters to me, Jessie. Only this moment means anything to us. Take me now, love."

Unable to deny himself further, Brand thrust within the moist sheath and felt the barrier tear away. Jessie flinched but made no sound as she surrendered the gift of her virginity to the man she loved. Stunned, Brand looked down into her tear-bright eyes and felt as if he were being torn asunder by the emotions warring within him. He wanted to laugh and cry at the same time. He had received the greatest gift any woman could bestow upon a man, and he had taken it without a thought.

Winding his hands in her damp hair, he kissed her swollen lips and murmured, "Forgive me, Jessie. I didn't want to hurt you."

In answer to his heart-wrenching plea, she wrapped her arms about his neck and moved against him, her body accepting his as a part of her own. The stinging pain receded, and other, far more pleasant sensations replaced it. The tiny embers of passion that Brand had fanned with his lips and hands now burst into flame. A wildfire in her blood that only Brand could quench, she moved restlessly, urging him to fulfill his own needs.

Unable to deny himself or Jessie, Brand began to move, thrusting within Jessie's satiny warmth with long, slow, tantalizing strokes. She pulsed about him, caressing his length until all coherent thought vanished under the deluge of sensation.

Jessie gasped as Brand touched the depth of her being. A great scorching wave consumed her. Every muscle in her body trembled, engulfing her in a fiery explosion.

Their breathing ragged, their bodies damp with perspiration, they raced toward the horizon and leapt together into the burning sunset of golden rapture. A crash of thunder rocked the cabin as their bodies shook with fulfillment.

"God, you're wonderful," Brand breathed before collapsing over her, his face cradled in the curve of her neck. Legs entwined, bodies still joined, they lay together until their hearts slowed to normal.

Chapter 8

The dawn of a new day found Brand standing on the line shack's porch, coffee cup in hand, one shoulder braced against a pillar. His shirt hung open to the waist revealing the hard planes of his chest as he stared into space. Completely unaware of the hot, bright orb creeping over the horizon to chase away the lingering shadows of night, Brand looked morose.

"Damn," he muttered as his thoughts turned to the previous night spent in the narrow cot with Jessie. He squeezed his eyes closed and sought to control his body's reaction to the memory. In all the years since he'd bedded his first woman, Jessica was the only one able to affect him with only a thought.

Brand's expression turned grim. Yesterday his need of Jessie had driven him to lose sight of his job as well as her involvement with Wade Fleming. Even though she had unexpectedly gifted him with her virginity, her innocence didn't belie the love he'd heard in her voice when she'd spoken of the rustler. The memory was like the sharp blade of a knife in his gut. It twisted and sliced, leaving his insides feeling like mush.

How could the woman he had taken to his bed, the

woman who had captivated him with her innocent passion, care for a half-breed?

"For God's sake, she's a lady, not a tramp," he muttered, tossing out the dregs of coffee in his cup. He'd tried to reconcile the Jessie he found so enchanting with the one he'd overhead talking about the rustler, but to no avail.

The knife twisted deeper as Brand ran a long-fingered hand through his hair. In less than twenty-four hours he had broken every rule he'd set for himself. He'd become involved with a woman who very well could be on the wrong side of the law. Even worse, her association with the half-breed made her a part of everything he despised. She was no better than a half-breed herself. That alone should have been enough to turn him against her.

"But it didn't," Brand said through clenched teeth. He shook his head at his own foolish assumption that once he had bedded Jessie she'd be like all the rest of the women in his past and he could put her from his mind. Ironically, making love to Jessie just made him need to have her again and again. Even now, knowing what a mistake last night had been, he wanted to go back into the shack and kiss her awake before sinking himself into the moist warmth of her luscious body.

"Damn her," Brand muttered, disgusted at his body's response. He had to get control of himself or he'd never be able to stay around Jessie long enough to capture Fleming.

Jessie stretched her arms over her head and curled her toes, arching her body like a satisfied kitten. A tiny smile tugged the corners of her lips as she opened her eyes to the new day. Her body still replete from lovemaking, she looked at her surroundings with the eyes of a woman in love. The line shack—their lover's haven—was bathed in gold, the narrow cot warm and comfortable. Had she a choice, she'd never leave the paradise she'd found.

Smiling, Jessie tossed back the blanket and slid her feet to the floor. Behind the potbellied stove, she noted, her clothes had been hung to dry on a makeshift line. Her smile deepened: Brand had thought of her well-being even while she slept; he had not found his pleasure and then put her from his mind. Warmed by the thought, Jessie slipped on her pants and shirt. Yesterday morning she would never have dreamed she'd find such happiness with Brand Stockton nearby.

Through the open doorway she saw Brand on the porch. Barefoot, she crossed the cabin and stepped out to join him. She slipped her arms about his waist and pressed her cheek against his back, hugging him close. "Good morning, Mr. Stockton."

Deep in thought, Brand started. He hadn't heard Jessie behind him until it was already too late to prevent her from touching him. He was well aware of his weakness for her and knew the only way he was going to maintain his distance was to remain aloof. Struggling with his emotions made his voice harsh. "It's time we got moving."

Jessie frowned at his tone but shrugged it aside. Her contentment was too great to allow herself to pick up on every little inflection in her lover's voice. She hugged him tighter and moved closer, seductively aligning her body against his. "What's the rush? I thought we might stay here a little longer."

Suddenly Brand gripped her arms and jerked them

from about her waist. Before Jessie could protest, he stepped away. "I don't have time to be out gallivanting around. I've been away from the ranch too long already."

Jessie looked up at Brand, hurt by his violent reaction to her touch, and wondered where the man of the previous night had gone. There was no tenderness in his face. They were back to being hired hand and boss. Swallowing the tears that clogged her throat and threatened to choke her, Jessie nodded. Her own voice was gruff when she finally managed to speak. "You're right. We've been away from the ranch far too long."

Jessie turned and quickly strode back into the cabin. A wayward tear escaped and traced a crystal path down her cheek as she bent to pick up her boots. She brushed away the offending droplet and rubbed her eyes free of excess moisture. She'd not allow Brand to see her pain. Never would he know how much his careless disregard had hurt her.

She sat down on the side of the bed and jerked on her boots. Slowly self-preservation set in, the hurt becoming anger. Jessie's eyes sparkled with ire, and her lips, still slightly swollen from Brand's passionate kisses, pursed into a thin line. Kate had warned her to be wary of men, but she had been foolish enough to allow passion to override common sense. The man she had fallen in love with was no different from other men after all. He had enjoyed the pleasure of her body and now had no more use for her. She was once more his boss lady.

"He didn't even have to say he loved me! Just give the dumb little easterner a kiss and she falls into your bed without an argument!' Jessie muttered, disgusted with herself. She grabbed her saddle bags and started toward the door, impatient now to get away from the dilapidated shack. At the door, she paused for one brief glance back at the place where she had truly become a woman. There was no enchantment left in the grubby cabin, only a rusty stove and a narrow cot with sagging ropes and moth-eaten blankets. A furry-legged spider was already making a new trap for another unwary victim.

Jessie released a long breath and turned away. The cabin looked as bleak and barren as her heart felt. Outside, Brand was already mounted and waiting with her horse. Tossing the bags behind the saddle, Jessie mounted and without a word urged the horse in the direction of home.

It was late afternoon when Jessie and Brand arrived at Eden. Edwina, her face flushed from running to the corral, met her as she dismounted. Eyes glassy with tears of relief, she held Jessie at arm's length, inspecting her thoroughly before hugging her against her ample bosom. "Jessica, are you all right? I've been so worried."

"I'm fine, Edwina," Jessie said, pulling free of the housekeeper's smothering bear hug. "I'm just tired. We've ridden all day."

"We?" Edwina said, noting Brand for the first time. She frowned at Eden's foreman. "Skinny told me you were staying in town for a few days."

"That was my plan until I saw Miss Nolan ride out. I decided I might be needed to see that she didn't get hurt or lost," Brand said without elaborating. He turned his attention to unsaddling his horse.

Edwina's worried gaze swung back to Jessie. "Jessica . . . ?"

"Winnie, everything is fine. It was fortunate Mr. Stockton decided to follow me because I did get lost. I never reached the orphanage to make my donation." Jessie gave Edwina a meaningful look that silenced further questions from the housekeeper. She stretched her aching back. "Now all I want is a nice hot bath to wash away the dirt from the trail."

"I'll have Maria see to it immediately," Edwina said, casting another anxious glance toward Brand. She couldn't pinpoint exactly what was disturbing her, but something just didn't sound right. Why would he follow Jessica when he had no reason to assume she was leaving Eden? And why hadn't he told anyone where he was going? At last Edwina shrugged and put the questions from her mind. She was too grateful for Jessica's safe return to worry about Brand Stockton.

Wet hair wrapped in a towel, Jessie stepped from the tub and dried herself briskly. She glanced at the image reflected in the armoire's mirrored doors and saw her skin blush as she remembered Brand's caresses. She inspected herself closely. Could Edwina see the change in her? Was her body different now that it had known passion? Would people know what had transpired between herself and Brand? Jessie shook her head. There were no physical signs left of her night of lovemaking with Brand Stockton. The only evidence was on the inside, and only she knew of its existence. The heart of the young girl who had left Eden now lay in fragments within the woman who had returned.

Jessie turned away form the mirror, her eyes burning,

her throat clogging with tears. She didn't want to think of the previous night, nor of the man who had claimed her as his own in the raging storm. She had to concentrate all her energies toward finding her brother and making Eden prosperous. She had to put Brand Stockton out of her mind. Last night had been a horrid mistake that she couldn't afford to dwell upon. In the heat of anger she had planned to tell Brand he was no longer needed at Eden, but common sense had prevailed. No matter how she felt about him, she wouldn't jeopardize the ranch. She would come to terms with her wayward emotions without destroying the promise she and her brothers had made at her parents' grave. Her father's dream would survive even if her own heart was destroyed in the process.

"At least that much of your good sense rubbed off on me, Kate," Jessie murmured as she slipped on the soft linen camisole and chemise before stepping into a simple blue muslin gown. The scooped neckline and puffed sleeves were edged in hand-worked lace and tiny pearl buttons accented the front of the bodice to the waist. Fastening the gown, Jessie once more regarded her image in the mirror. She smiled. "I might not have any sense where men are concerned," she said, "but you did make me understand not to mix business and pleasure, and I'm grateful to you for that lesson, Kate."

She sat down at the dressing table and towel-dried her hair before arranging it in a simply chignon at the nape of her neck. Then, reminded of the fact that she had not eaten all day, she followed the heavenly scents coming from the kitchen and seated herself at the table. Edwina had already piled a plate high with hot fluffy biscuits, white gravy, fried chicken, green beans, creamed potatoes, and dried-apple pie.

Edwina gave her time to finish the last bite of her meal before she launched into the questions that had been burning in her brain since that afternoon. She folded her arms over her heavy breast and asked quietly, "Are you ready to tell me exactly what happened while you were away?"

Jessie glanced at her friend and then busied herself stacking the dishes. Her actions didn't put off Edwina.

"I'm waiting for an explanation, Jessica Nolan."

"I've already told you what happened," Jessie said. Getting to her feet, she carried the dirty dishes to the sink.

"I heard what you told me, but that doesn't mean I believe you. Did you get a message to Wade?"

Jessie relaxed visibly as she sat back down at the table. She shook her head. "I managed to get lost before I reached the mission."

"Then Mr. Stockton doesn't know the real reason for your foolishness?"

Again, Jessie shook her head. "No. I told him I was on my way to the Indian orphanage to make a donation."

Edwina frowned. "Didn't he think it odd that you decided to go yourself instead of sending your donation by mail or messenger?"

"He didn't ask any questions," Jessie said.

"That's strange. Why would he follow you for nearly two days before he let you know of his presence?"

Jessie shrugged and looked away. She suspected the reason behind Brand's actions, but she couldn't explain herself to Edwina without revealing her own foolish behavior. Edwina would never understand what had made her react like a wanton under Brand's tutelage into the world of passion. She loved her housekeeper dearly, but in all the years she'd known her, Edwina had never shown any interest in men. In most instances she displayed only contempt for the opposite sex. Jessie didn't understand what lay behind Edwina's attitude, and she certainly couldn't ask. Like Jessie's, Edwina's private feelings were her own.

Unable to discuss the events of the previous day with Edwina, Jessie feigned a wide yawn behind her hand. "I believe I'll go to bed. I'm exhausted. Riding for days at a time doesn't do wonders for a person's backside." She moved around the table to Edwina and hugged her fondly. "Thank you for the wonderful welcome-home dinner." Before Edwina could say anything more, she hurried from the kitchen.

Upstairs, Jessie closed her bedroom door behind her and leaned against it. She'd answered all the questions she could for Edwina as well as herself. There was no other explanation for what had transpired between herself and Brand except that she had been a fool to give her heart to a man who cared nothing for her.

Tears brimming in her eyes, Jessie crossed to the window and pulled back the lace curtain to stare into the ebony night. She leaned her brow against the cool wood of the facing as her gaze traveled to the moon-silvered bunkhouse beyond the barn. Unlike herself, Brand probably slept undisturbed by the events of the previous night.

Jessie turned away from the window. Her gaze swept over the room, taking in the high square postered bed and coming to rest on the mirrored armoire that reflected the image of a haggard-faced young woman. Jessie quickly looked away from the haunted sapphire eyes gazing back at her. She didn't want to see the misery she had brought upon herself by giving her heart to Brand Stockton.

Unable to bear being confined with her thoughts a moment longer, Jessie crossed to the door and opened it quietly. The house was dark and silent except for the slice of light that filtered from beneath Edwina's door. Slipping past, Jessie made her way out of the house and into the quiet, moon-drenched night with the hope that the cool night air would clear her mind.

She paused near the windmill, absently rubbing her arms against the night's chill as the soft *swoosh* of the blades whirling in the breeze drew her gaze upward. The constant motion of the windmill was comforting and oddly symbolic. It proved life went on even when hearts broke. Disgusted, Jessie turned away. She'd wanted to clear her mind, but getting Brand out of her thoughts was no simple matter.

"Jessie, what are you doing out here this late?" The softly spoken question came from the shadows of a loblolly pine.

Jessie halted, instantly recognizing Brand's voice. She didn't turn in his direction but stared straight ahead. "I might ask the same of you."

"I couldn't sleep," Brand answered honestly. A match flared in the dark, momentarily splashing his features in golden light as he lit a cigarillo.

"I couldn't sleep, either." Jessie's voice was little more than a strained whisper as she struggled with the emotions whirling within her. She had the wild desire to throw herself into Brand's arm and beg him to make things right between them again. However, logic won out. She wouldn't humiliate herself again with Brand Stockton.

"Why couldn't you sleep?" Brand asked quietly, crushing out the cigarillo beneath his boot. He hadn't meant to ask, but the question slipped out before he could stop it. He didn't want to know why Jessie couldn't sleep. It was enough to know she was the reason sleep had eluded him. He had tossed and turned on his narrow bunk until several of the men had begun to complain about the noise. At last he'd given up. He'd walked out of the bunkhouse, hoping the night air would clear his thoughts or at least cool his blood.

"It was too hot to sleep," Jessie lied, straining for a glimpse of the man whose voice made her pulse race.

Against his better judgment, Brand closed the space between them. "Jessie, I want to apologize for everything that has happened. I didn't mean to let things go as far as they did between us."

"It's too late for apologies, Brand," Jessie said, turning away from him, a dead weight sinking in the pit of her belly.

Brand captured her shoulders and drew her back against him. "I know it's too late for apologies, but I had to say it. I couldn't leave things as they were between us today, not if we want to keep working together."

Brand's hands seemed to burn Jessie through the material of her gown, but she resisted the temptation to turn in his arms and put an end to the agony in her heart. Her back stiff and head high, she stared off into the ebony night. Her voice was cool when she finally managed to speak. "Brand, it is best that we both forget what happened last night. As you said, we can't keep working together unless we do."

Something in her tone snapped what little control Brand had managed to retain over his emotions. He raised one hand to her hair and curled his fingers in the silken mass, drawing her head back against his shoulder. He inhaled her tantalizing fragrance as he leaned his cheek against hers and asked, "Can you honestly tell me you can forget what we shared?"

Jessie swallowed her tears and whispered, "I have to. You and I both know what happened between us was a mistake."

"Jessie," Brand said, his voice an agonized groan of defeat as he surrendered to his desire. She turned to face him. "I want to forget, God knows I do. But I can't." Her hair a silken leash, he drew her near and lowered his head to capture her lips in a devastating kiss.

The feel of his mouth upon hers dissolved all protests, and Jessie wrapped her arms about Brand's neck. She had lived through hell since that morning, believing Brand no longer wanted her. Now she was back where she belonged. Clinging to him, she gave herself up to his heady kiss, freely opening her lips to his exploring tongue and returning his hungry caresses with her own.

Brand moaned his pleasure but didn't release her mouth as he lifted her into his arms and strode purposefully toward the barn. He left her mouth only long enough to jerk a blanket from the shelf in the tack room before effortlessly carrying her up the ladder to the hayloft. After another debilitating kiss that sent her blood racing, he set her on her feet and spread the blanket over a mound of soft straw.

The sweet scent of fresh hay filled the air as Brand turned back to Jessie and lifted her once more into his arms. Gently he lowered her to the bed. "God, I can't seem to get enough of you."

He gave Jessie no time for coherent thought, swooping down, capturing her mouth again. The intimate caress of his tongue against hers sent ripples of pleasure down her spine. Jessie locked her arms about his neck; she couldn't let go, afraid the dream might end and she would find herself once more alone. She molded her body to his hard length and felt his arousal pressing through their clothing against her belly. Needing to feel his skin against her own, Jessie slipped one hand down and began to unfasten the buttons on his shirt. When the last had slipped free, she ran her hand up his hard abdomen to the mat of crisp curls spanning his chest. A moan of pure pleasure escaped her. She had thought never to touch him again. Suddenly the aggressor, she pushed Brand back on the blanket and opened his shirt to reveal his naked chest. A tiny, provocative smile curled her lips as she slowly ran her hands over the wide expanse before lowering her head to nibble his neck. She felt him tense as she ran her tongue against his heated flesh, flicking it teasingly until she had made her way through the thick forest to his nipple. She teased him with her mouth and tongue until Brand groaned, unable to endure any more of the heady torture.

In one swift movement he flipped her onto her back and raised himself above her. He gazed down, smiling wickedly. "Ah, love, you'll not have all the pleasure."

Brand lowered his mouth to hers, his tongue thrusting deep within the sweet cavern, moving in and out erotically in the ancient ritual while his hands worked

142

to loosen the multitude of tiny pearl buttons at the front of her gown. Finally becoming impatient, he tore the bodice apart and lowered his head to the bounties that had been hidden beneath.

His mouth closed over one taut nipple as his hands worked the gown down her hips. A few moments later he freed her of her undergarments and tossed them aside before he unbuttoned his jeans and added them to the heap of clothing already on the hay.

Giving Jessie's blood no time to cool, Brand moved over her, spreading her thighs with his knee as he continued to suckle her breast. He tantalized her, pressing his aroused sex against her, moving back and forth slowly, teasing the tiny bud hidden in the moist valley until she writhed beneath him, silently begging him to take her. Still he held himself back as he slowly moved his mouth down her breasts to the tiny concave belly button. He ran his tongue around the small indentation before nibbling his way across her abdomen to the dark glen awaiting him between her thighs. He buried his face against her, drawing in her woman's scent before exploring the depths of the honeyed passage.

Jessie's dark hair fanned out across the golden hay as she tossed her head from side to side and arched her hips against his mouth, moaning in pleasure at this erotic caress. Tiny bursts of lightning exploded through her as Brand worked his magic. The muscles in her thighs and belly quivered, and she cried out his name, begging him to take her. She clutched his bare shoulders, digging her nails into his tanned flesh as she whimpered, "Brand, love me."

Unable to deny himself a moment longer, Brand covered Jessie's soft form with his muscular body and thrust deep within her. He moaned as she closed tightly about him, moist and hot. He moved slowly at first, savoring the silken sheath that caressed his hard length. He watched the expressions play across Jessie's face as his movements carried her toward fulfillment. Her eyes glazed with passion, her mouth soft and parted slightly, her breath panting with the rapid beat of her heart, she arched against him, bringing her legs around his waist, taking him deeper into her velvety warmth. Brand felt himself touch the very core of her femininity and knew he couldn't hold back his own pleasure any longer. Her body caressed him as he moved his hips faster. She stroked his manhood, creating exquisite sensations that sent his senses reeling and pushed him past all coherent thought. Nature held reign. Instinct drove him forward until his cry mingled with Jessie's as their bodies pulsed together with fulfillment.

"I love you," Jessie murmured. She cradled Brand's head against her breasts, tenderly stroking his dark hair as her heartbeat slowed and the last throbbing sensation faded into overwhelming contentment.

"Don't say that," Brand whispered, drawing in a shuddering breath.

"Why shouldn't I tell you how I feel?" Jessie asked quietly, though she didn't really want to hear his answer. Her heart drummed uncomfortably against her ribs as Brand raised himself on his arms above her.

A sliver of pale moonlight filtering through the hayloft door revealed his pained expression. Jessie drew him to her against his will, but he couldn't call what he felt for her love. Intrigue, desire, hunger, or lust could all be used to describe his feelings, but they were not what she wanted to hear. Brand didn't believe he could love any woman; such emotions had been torn from him long ago. Not even Jessie's passionate nature could reclaim a heart that lay in his chest like stone.

Brand released a long breath and moved away from her. He lay back on the hay and covered his eyes with his arm to keep from seeing Jessie's face. "I don't want your love, Jessie. What we've shared has been wonderful, but nothing can come from it. As I've told you before, I don't like to be tied down and I don't want any hard feelings when I decide to move on."

Jessie felt her world rock from the impact of his words. Suddenly ashamed of her nakedness, she struggled to regain her dignity by sitting up and jerking on her clothing. She ran her fingers through her tousled hair before facing Brand bravely. Eyes glittering, she raised her chin in the air. Her voice was icy when she spoke. "I'm sorry I said such a foolish thing. I wasn't thinking. Please don't believe I meant any of it. I've known from the beginning that nothing could come from our relationship except a few hours of pleasure."

Brand peered up at Jessie, wondering why her words brought him no relief. "Then you're not hurt?"

Jessie's false laughter grated in her ears as she shook her head. She had to save her pride; it was all she had left. "I've tried to tell you I'm not some simpleminded miss, Brand. Kate taught me to believe women have the same rights as men, and I firmly adhere to that belief in all things, whether it's owning my own ranch or finding a moment of pleasure with you. Don't be foolish enough to think I would want a commitment from a man who is little more than a saddlebum. I thought you understood my feelings."

Brand's expression hardened. A muscle twitched in

his jaw as he sat up. Jessie had relieved him of any responsibility, but he found himself oddly infuriated by how easily she had accepted his disclaimer. A moment of pleasure be damned! Equal rights be double-damned! What they had shared meant much more than that, and she damn well knew it. Frustrated by his own duplicity, Brand pulled up his britches.

"Damn," he swore aloud, jerking on his boots. He stood and shrugged into his shirt. He frowned at the woman who was driving him berserk with her independence and outrageous ideas. He never knew what to expect from her from one moment to the next. He also wasn't sure what to expect from himself when he was around her. She made him feel as though he were teetering on the brink of some unknown chasm, and once he fell there would be no turning back.

More confused than ever, Brand reached down and pulled Jessie to her feet. He clamped his hand in her hair and drew her roughly against his hard frame. His eyes glittered with silver ice as he looked into her beautiful, moonlit features. He smiled cynically. "I'm glad we have an understanding. It will make it much easier for us, Jessie. We know what we want from each other, so there's no need for any more games between us."

She didn't respond when Brand gave her a harsh kiss before turning and climbing down the ladder. He didn't wait for Jessie but walked out of the barn without a backward glance.

A dry sob escaped Jessie as she collapsed onto the bed Brand had improvised for them. She covered her head with her arms and wept. Although she had managed to keep Brand from knowing how much he had hurt her, she didn't feel any sense of victory. Pain was pain no matter how well you hid it.

When no more tears would come, Jessie lay staring up with red, swollen eyes at the rafters overhead. Like a fool, she had surrendered to Brand even though she knew he didn't care for her. She hadn't helped matters between them by allowing him to believe she wasn't affected by their lovemaking, either. She had managed to protect her tender pride but had also succeeded in making herself look like a bitch in heat. With her own words she had also freed him to walk away. And damn him, he had done so.

Jessie drew in a shuddering breath and pushed herself upright. She had made a complete and utter fool of herself with Brand Stockton tonight. However, Sarah Fleming and Kate Nolan had instilled in her the courage to face bravely what life brought, and she'd not dishonor their memory by being a coward. Tomorrow, when the sun rose over Eden, she would turn her back on her feelings for Brand Stockton. She would make Eden prosper, find her brother, and someday see the man who had killed her parents pay for his crime. Those things would fill the aching void left in her life and heart by Brand Stockton.

Resolutely Jessie combed the straw from her hair and climbed down the ladder. She wouldn't think of what might have been had Brand loved her in return. She'd make herself so busy that she wouldn't have a spare moment to remember the sweetness of his kisses. She would work hard enough to fall into bed at night, too tired to realize how lonely she was without him next to her.

Brushing a wayward curl off her brow, Jessie wandered back to the house. She knew the path she'd chosen might be very rocky in places. In fact, it could be downright dangerous, if she didn't keep her distance from Brand Stockton.

Chapter 9

Slim wiped the sweat from his face with the hem of his apron and squinted toward the couple riding away. Then he glanced at the man sitting at the checkered-clothed table, staring at the cup of coffee in his hand. "I don't rightly understand what she sees in that man."

Brand looked at Slim and frowned. "Did you say something?"

"Hell, I might as well keep my mouth shut around here for all the good it does me. You don't ever seem to listen to anythin' I got to say anymore."

Brand set his cup down and pushed back his chair. He picked up his hat and settled it on his head. "I might listen more to what you had to say if you didn't talk in riddles half the time. You're getting worse than an old woman. I'm going to have to get this job finished so I can get away from here before you go completely senile."

"Damn it, Brand. It wouldn't be hard to understand me if you didn't have your mind on other things. You can't keep your thoughts or your eyes off our tight-britched boss lady."

"I don't know what you're talking about, and I don't

have the time to stand around and figure it out," Brand said, turning toward the door.

"You know damn well what I'm talkin' about. You haven't been yourself since you brought that girl back from Indian territory. I'd like to know just what exactly happened up there for you to act so strange. It ain't like you, Brand. You were always able to handle any job the cap'n gave us until now."

Thick lashes shielding his inscrutable silver eyes, Brand regarded Slim for a long moment before he asked, "Do you think I'm not doing my job?"

"Naw, I ain't sayin' that. I just mean you're not actin' yourself. How long has it been since you've been into town and had a woman, or even a few drinks? You say you're keepin' your eye out for Fleming, but to me it looks like you're keepin' your eye on Miss Nolan and Ramsey. I've seen the way you look when they ride out of here together, and let me tell you, it ain't a pretty sight. Your face is like a thundercloud and your mood ain't much better."

"The way I look and feel is none of your concern. I'm doing my job." Brand's expression darkened even further as he spied the two riders in the distance.

"Damn it, Brand. Look at you now. You need to take a few days off and get this out of your system. You ain't doin' yourself any good moonin' over that woman. She's set her sights on Ramsey, and you're goin' to have to accept it. From what Winnie says they're gettin' closer'n two bugs in a rug. Any day now the old man'll ask her to marry him, and if my guess is right, she'll accept."

Brand flashed Slim a withering look. "I didn't know you and Edwina Roilings were close enough for her to confide in you. And you seem to forget that our Miss Nolan is involved with Fleming.''

''Winnie's loosened up a bit where I'm concerned. We have a jaw from time to time, but that doesn't have anythin' to do with what I was talkin' about, and you damn well know it. As for Jessica Nolan, I haven't forgotten anythin' about the woman. She's trouble if I ever laid eyes on it. I've known that from the first day we come here. She's up to somethin' with all her smiles and sweetness for that old man. He's nearly twenty years older'n her if he's a day, but that don't seem to bother her none. She's prob'ly using her wiles on him to get information for Fleming about the ranches in this area. What better way to avoid bein' caught than to have someone on the inside to let you know where the traps are set?''

Thoughtfully, Brand turned to look in the direction Jessie and Ramsey had traveled. Slim had made a good point. Jessie could very well be leading Ramsey on to help Fleming.

Brand's eyes glittered with disgust. He wouldn't put anything past Miss Jessica Nolan after their last encounter. She'd used him as if he were a whore from Miss Molly's and then had laughed in his face. He clenched his teeth. The memory of that night still rankled. It made him feel degraded. His encounter with Jessie had completely changed his view of whores forever. For the first time he understood what the Indians meant when they said not to judge a man until you had walked a mile in his moccasins. He could nearly envision himself in a whore's red, feather-trimmed wrapper, waiting for Jessie to toss him a few coins for the pleasure he'd given her.

Brand's skin flushed and his hand clenched into a fist at his side. Pride-soothing anger pushed the humiliating thoughts to the back of his mind. His eyes glittered as he remembered his concern for Jessie. He'd been a fool for trying not to hurt that woman. She didn't have any feelings to hurt. Where a human heart should have beat, she possessed a lump of ice. Fortunately he had learned his lesson before he'd let the thing go too far. Unlike Clint Ramsey, who seemed blinded by her beauty, he saw through her charade of being a lady. Jessica Nolan was nothing more than a breed's calculating floozy, who decked herself out in her eastern finery to dupe poor fools like himself.

"Damn her to hell," Brand swore beneath his breath, and stalked from the bunkhouse, his expression grim. Jessie was tearing him apart, inch by inch, digging bewildering emotions out of the recesses of his soul. And, should Slim's suspicions about her be true, he would have even more problems. He'd have no alternative left but to arrest her when he caught Fleming.

Brand's frown deepened. No matter how he felt about her, putting Jessie behind bars didn't appeal to him. After seeing her ride out with Ramsey, he'd like nothing better than personally to ring Miss Jessica Nolan's perfidious little neck, but the thought of someone else putting a rope around her ivory throat sickened him.

Brand released a low growl and ground his teeth together in frustration. He took off his hat and ran a hand through his sweat-dampened hair before swiping beads of moisture from his brow with his shirtsleeve. He squinted in the direction Ramsey and Jessie had traveled earlier. He was a Texas Ranger, and he wasn't supposed to get personally involved in his work. But damn it, in this case he had. He'd let one small woman who didn't give a tinker's damn about him insinuate herself into his life. He couldn't trust Jessie, but he couldn't deny she'd somehow managed to worm her way past the barriers he'd erected around himself through the years.

"What in the hell has gotten into me?" he muttered, setting his hat back on his head and walking briskly toward the barn. He'd never felt so confused in his life. His emotions veered wildly, changing like the breeze, and for the life of him he didn't know why. One moment he wanted to hang Jessie up by the heels from the nearest tree, and the next he felt like stripping her naked and making love to her until she moaned with pleasure.

After leading his horse from the shade, Brand mounted and kicked him in the side, urging him into a trot. The only thing he could be certain about, he reflected darkly, was that he had to catch Fleming and then get as far away from Eden before he went stark, raving mad.

Jessie slipped from the saddle and looked up at her companion, who stood silently watching the longhorns grazing in the distance. She couldn't stop herself from admiring Clint Ramsey. He was the type of man any sane woman would be pleased to have share her company. He was handsome, rich, and powerful. Yes, she mused, tying the reins of her mount to the limb of a cottonwood, most women would be proud to have the attention he'd showered upon her during the past weeks. But I'm not most women, she admitted to herself. I've been branded by a silver-eyed devil, and my heart won't let me forget it.

Clint glanced at Jessie and gave her a slow smile as he raised a hand to encompass the surrounding area with a wave. "What do you think of my spread?"

"The Lazy L is even grander than I expected. I'm very impressed," Jessie said, pulling off her gloves. By habit she tucked them into the rear pocket of her denims. Her gaze swept over the grassy plain where the large herd grazed contentedly. "Someday Eden will be as prosperous as your Lazy L."

Clint's pale blue gaze took in the sweet line of Jessie's profile, the soft curve of her lips, the slender column of her throat down the the V opening of the plaid shirt she wore. His mouth went dry as he envisioned the coral-tipped breasts that would be hidden beneath the soft cotton. He cleared his throat and forced his gaze once more toward the cattle. "Jessica, I know how to make Eden even larger and more prosperous than the Lazy L."

Jessie cocked her head to one side and smiled curiously. "I would be interested to hear your ideas."

Clint looked down at Jessie and took her hand in his. He raised it to his lips and tenderly placed a kiss on each finger. His voice was husky as he said, "My idea concerns a certain merger."

Jessie's brows knit in puzzlement. "I don't understand."

"Jessica, I want to marry you. Together we can join Eden and the Lazy L to build the largest spread in Texas."

Jessie's eyes widened in shock. "Clint— I don't know what to say."

"Just say yes. That's all I want to hear," Clint said, bringing her hand back to his lips.

Jessie pulled herself free and turned away. Edwina had warned her that Clint Ramsey had more on his mind than friendship, but she had not listened. She had enjoyed his light flirtation and his companionship. She had eagerly accepted his invitation to ride and to picnic near Little Creek and had found it soothing to have him sit on the porch with her in the late evening to discuss their ranches. Clint's charming presence had kept her from thinking of Brand, and she had been too grateful for the diversion to note his deepening interest.

Jessie released a long breath and glanced back at Clint. "I'm afraid you've taken me by surprise. I wasn't expecting a proposal, since we've only known each other a short while."

"It's not been a short time to me, Jessica. I've known you existed all of my life, and I've waited patiently until I found you." Closing the space between them, Clint turned her to face him. "I want you to share my life. I want our children to inherit this land."

Jessica swallowed uncertainly. He was offering her so much, but she couldn't accept because another man already possessed her love. Until she could put Brand completely out of her heart and mind, she couldn't marry Clint or anyone. It wouldn't be fair.

"Clint, I'm honored by your proposal but . . ." Clint's finger against her lips silenced her words.

"Jessica, I know I've shocked you by speaking of marriage so soon, and I understand your reluctance. But don't turn me down now. Wait until my shindig to give me your answer. It will give you a little more time to get to know me better. And it'll also give me time to prove that I can make you happy."

Jessica looked into his serious blue eyes and felt herself reconsider. She did need time to know Clint better. She'd already admitted she found his company appealing and, given the opportunity, he might be able to erase Brand from her life. She nodded. "All right. I'll consider your offer, but please understand, I make no promises. I don't want either of us to be hurt."

"I can ask for nothing more. I just want you to see that together we can have everything we've ever wanted. And maybe," Clint said, giving her one of his most charming grins, "we'll have an announcement to make to all our neighbors at my shindig in a couple of weeks." Without waiting for Jessie's response, he hugged her close and smiled triumphantly against her dark head. He had won the first skirmish; now came the true battle.

Clint released Jessie and took a step back. He tipped up her chin and brushed his lips against hers. He felt her withdraw and smiled confidently to himself at the game she was playing. Like most young women, she didn't want to overreact to a man's attention and give the wrong impression. However, he knew she wasn't as unaffected by his touch as she would have him to believe. Soon, my dear Jessica, he mused, you will be in my bed and my problems will be solved. I will bury myself in your silken warmth until I have made up for all the years I've lost. Confident his body would respond once they were married, Clint was determined that nothing in the world would stop him from having Jessica Nolan as his wife.

The sound of horses startled Jessie from sleep. Instantly alert and sensing trouble, she clambered from the bed and jerked her wrapper from the back of the chair as she passed. Slipping on the thin satin robe as she went, Jessie ran through the house and out into the night. She didn't stop until she'd reached the paddock, where Brand was giving orders to the men.

"What's going on?" she shouted over the rush of men saddling horses.

Brand turned to find her at his elbow, hair flowing to her waist, breasts peeking between the satin opening of her robe. He forced his gaze away from the alluring sight, and back to the mount he'd been saddling. Jerking the cinch tight, he answered in a hard voice, "Rustlers hit us tonight, Miss Nolan. One of the nightwatch just rode in to tell us that they got away with nearly half the herd."

"What are you going to do?" Jessie asked.

"My job," Brand said, swinging into the saddle. "This time they've made a mistake by taking so many cattle. They won't be able to just up and blend into the countryside. The trail will be fresh enough to follow." Brand didn't doubt for a minute that Fleming's gang was responsible for tonight's raid, but he kept his opinion to himself because he didn't have proof. If the rustlers headed into Indian territory, that would be all the evidence he needed to lay the blame at Fleming's door.

"I'm going with you," Jessie said, already turning toward the house.

Brand maneuvered his horse in front of her, stopping her in her tracks. "No, Miss Nolan. You are not going with me. It's too dangerous." He couldn't trust Jessie because of her involvement with Fleming, nor could he trust himself to be near her after so many nights of lying alone in the bunkhouse, dreaming of her.

"Mr. Stockton, I am going with you. You will remember that you still work for me," Jessie said, determined not to let anything deter her. She suspected the thieves who had struck Eden worked with her brother, and she couldn't lose this chance to find Wade.

"That can easily be remedied, Miss Nolan," Brand ground out.

"The decision is up to you. Whether I go with you or without you, I intend to find the rustlers' trail and retrieve my cattle. Eden can't afford to lose so many head," Jessie said, tightening the belt to her wrapper. She'd use any excuse to search for Wade.

"Damn it, Jessie. I don't want to see you get hurt," Brand said, exasperated. If he let her ride out alone to find Wade Fleming, all his chances to catch the rustler would be ruined.

"I'm going, Brand," was Jessie's firm answer, though Brand's concern for her sent warm little tingles along every nerve in her body. Her heart fluttered briefly with hope before she staunchly pushed the thought aside. Brand just didn't want a woman in on his chase.

"Oh, hell. All right. Get your clothes on while I saddle your mount," Brand said, swinging down from the saddle.

Jessie hurried toward the house and within minutes was back at Brand's side, dressed in her usual denim britches and shirt. She carried a rifle at her side.

Brand glanced at the weapon and shook his head. "That's not going to do you any good."

Jessie raised her nose in the air and peered haughtily at him. "For your information, Clint has been good enough to teach me how to use this. It's far more than

I can say other people offered to do when they learned I couldn't shoot.''

''We don't have time to discuss any of the lessons Clint Ramsey may have taught you these last weeks. If we want to get your cattle back, we'd better get on the move.'' Brand swung into the saddle and without a backward glance at Jessie urged his horse north toward the open range.

Jessie smiled smugly as she slid the rifle into the sheath of her saddle. If she had any say in the matter, Brand would never learn Ramsey had given her only one lesson with the rifle. Clint had objected at first, but he'd finally relented after a long picnic in the shade of the cottonwoods near Little Creek. That afternoon she had learned to load and shoot the rifle. She had practiced alone since then, but she still had trouble hitting the bull's-eye of the target. Perhaps she wasn't an expert with the weapon, but she felt better knowing she could at least protect herself to some degree, especially if her target was the size of a barn door.

Jessie mounted and followed Brand at a gallop. She caught up with him near the thicket where her parents' cabin lay hidden by the overgrowth. He cast her an annoyed look before pointing toward the north. ''Just as I suspected. It's Fleming who took the herd, and they're headed into Indian territory. If we don't catch them before they reach it, I'm afraid it will be too late. Fleming's friends will scatter the cattle all across the territory until it's safe to take them north to the rail lines for sale.''

''Your optimism is overwhelming. Why did you even set out on this chase if that's the way you think?''

Brand's icy gaze flicked over Jessie. "Unlike some people, I use my head."

"Are you saying *I* don't use my head?" Jessie asked, bristling.

"Take it any way you want. Any fool knows chasing rustlers is no business for a woman."

"Then I am certainly not a fool, Mr. Stockton. So what does that say about you?" Jessie said smugly. Giving Brand a syrupy-sweet smile, she kicked her mount in the side and urged him forward, putting enough distance between herself and Brand to resist the desire to slap his handsome face.

Brand felt the blood rush to his head with such force, he thought it would blow off the top of his skull. Grinding his teeth together, he suppressed the urge to jerk Jessie from her horse and swat her behind until her clever little mouth howled for mercy. Instead he focused his ire on the trail and Wade Fleming, vowing that when he caught up with the half-breed, he'd hang the man to the nearest tree for getting him involved with Jessica Nolan.

At dawn Brand called a halt to the search. Fleming had made it to the Red River and crossed over into Indian territory before they could catch up with him. As a Texas Ranger Brand couldn't legally go into Indian territory to search for Fleming without permission from the federal judge in Fort Smith. Dismounting, Brand hunkered down to sift a handful of finely powdered dust through his fingers. His eyes traveled from the cloud of dirt to the muddy bank on the opposite side of the river. The tracks clearly indicated Fleming had driven the cattle across at this point.

Brand stood, disgust mirrored on his face as his gaze

skimmed the ground at his feet. Fleming's luck never seemed to run out. The man must have a guardian angel watching over him or—Brand glanced toward Jessie—perhaps she was.

"Why are we stopping? Surely we can go on for a few more miles before we rest the horses," Jessie said, rolling her shoulders absently to ease her aching muscles. It had been a long night in the saddle, but she didn't want to take even a small amount of time to rest and risk losing Wade's trail.

"I'm calling off the search. We've lost them."

"That's impossible. Even I can see where the cattle came out of the river on the other side."

"Yes, but in what direction did they go? From the looks of it, they turned directly around and headed back into Texas."

Jessie frowned, noting for the first time that the tracks beneath her feet led in several directions. Brand was right; it did look as if the rustlers had turned around. But that made no sense. She would have passed them.

"I don't understand," she said, puzzled.

Brand cocked a dark brow at Jessie. "You mean only a fool could understand what the rustlers had in mind?"

"If the shoe fits," Jessie snapped, fire flickering in the depths of her sapphire eyes. She was in no mood to put up with Brand's sarcasm. Her brother was only a few miles away, and she didn't have time to waste verbally sparring with Brand.

"Then I must still be the fool because I understand exactly what the cunning bastard did. It's the same reason he always takes only a small number of cattle at a time. Once he crosses the river he divides them up, knowing full well we can't track all of them." Brand smiled grimly. "Like a coyote, he knows how to throw us off his trail."

"Then we'll follow only one trail. Surely it will lead us to them sooner or later."

"We'd be lucky to find even a few head. Fleming's friends were probably waiting here for him. And before the day's over the herd will be spread so thin no one could ever locate them. When it's safe they'll drive them north to sell at the railroad in Sedalia."

"But we can't give up. We have to follow them before they can divide the cattle up."

"It's already been done," Brand said.

Frustration burned Jessie's eyes, and she had to blink several times to clear her vision before she looked at Brand. "Does this mean we won't find Fleming's trail?"

Brand nodded. "We don't know which one is Fleming's. And even if we followed them, they'd all lead to a dead end. Fleming is not fool enough to leave a path to his hideout. That's why he's been so hard for the law to capture. He uses his savage blood well to throw the law off the scent."

Jessie sank onto a nearby rock. Hands limp between her thighs, she hung her head. Her hat shadowed her features, hiding her expression of defeat from Brand. She had once more come close to her brother but had failed to find him.

"It's time we started back to the ranch. The men need a few hours' rest before they bring the rest of the cattle back to Little Creek," Brand said, watching Jessie carefully. He didn't understand why she was acting so strangely. She seemed depressed because he wouldn't continue the search. He frowned. Once again Jessica Nolan wasn't fitting into the mold. A devil's handmaiden would be only too happy to have the search called off.

A cynical little smile curled Brand's lips. Perhaps Jessica didn't approve of the rustler taking what was hers. As long as he took from others, she'd didn't give a damn what he did, but her property was an entirely different matter. Brand's smile deepened. Perhaps Miss Nolan now knew how it felt to walk in someone else's moccasins. He chuckled to himself. It would serve her right to have the renegade turn on her.

Brand's smile faded as reason began to assert itself. Although he'd heard the tenderness in her voice when she spoke of Fleming to Edwina Roilings, and he knew she had gotten herself lost in Indian territory because of the rustler, Jessie's interest just didn't seem to fit with the man's actions. Everything looked as if Fleming didn't even know of her existence.

Brand's encounter with Jessie had proved she wasn't the half-breed's lover. She'd been a virgin. Now the rustler had muddied the waters even more by stealing Eden's stock.

Brand shook his head and swung himself into the saddle. Nothing made sense. He couldn't lay to rest his suspicions about Jessie, but he no longer firmly believed she and Fleming were in cahoots together. Things just didn't add up. Brand tipped his hat to the back of his head and crossed his arms over the pommel as his silver gaze swept the riverbank. Wade Fleming was in Indian territory, and it was time to find a way to smoke him out of his hole. Instinct told him Jessie was still the key he needed to bring Fleming to justice, but exactly how she fit into the scheme of things, he had no idea.

Brand frowned as he pulled his hat lower on his head and stole a look at Jessie from the shadows. Again he felt a strange stirring within his chest at the sight of the weary droop of her shoulders. He ached to reach out and give her the comfort of his arms, to take her against his body and protect her from harm.

Confusion welled in an ever-widening pool. Jessie looked so young, so delicate on the surface, but he knew she was strong and independent beneath that lovely facade. With the look of an angel she was a woman of the earth, intelligent and passionate. In that moment of acceptance, the gray clouds of confusion drifted away to allow him to see his own feelings clearly for the first time. His insides twisted as he realized he wanted Miss Jessica Nolan more than any other woman on earth.

Brand's revelation startled him so much, he abruptly jerked back on the reins. His mount shied and stepped sideways nervously. Surprise and bemusement mingled on his face as he ignored the curious looks Jessie and the men cast in his direction. Calmly he patted the Morgan's sleek neck and then urged the animal forward. At the moment he wanted to be alone with his thoughts.

Chapter 10

From the Red River the rustlers crossed a hundred and fifty miles, moving northeast across Choctaw territory toward their hideout in the San Bois Mountains. Herding the cattle along the river bottom, their progress often slowed by streams and forested hills, they had carefully spread out the cattle a few head at a time among their Choctaw friends for safekeeping before heading toward the mountains. The welcoming sandstone peaks, capped and studded by tall pines, overlooked the old Butterfield stage route and could be seen from the lookout's point above the hideout's stone corral. The corral, a natural formation cut into the sheer face of the sandstone cliffs, kept the rustlers' mounts well hidden.

Tired, hot, and sweaty, Wade and Renegade maneuvered their horses up the trail along the ridge toward a cave that had a history of sheltering stage robbers, rustlers, and other bandits within its rocky walls. It was the perfect place for outlaws. A natural fortress, the lookout gave a clear view of the surrounding area. Few lawmen knew of its existence, and those who had had not lived to tell about it.

Wade reined his mount to a halt at the opening to the cave that they'd used for their hideout for over three years. It had been well over a week since he'd left Texas, and he was eager to see the girl again after the successful raid on the upstart's ranch. Satisfied with his first taste of revenge against those who owned the Fleming ranch, he cupped his hand over the round bulge beneath his shirt and swung a leather-clad leg over the saddle, dismounting agilely. He looked up at his scar-faced friend. "I wonder how the girl has faired while we've been away."

Renegade shrugged. "I'm sure she's managed without us. From the way she acts, she'd just as soon not have us come back at all."

Wade smiled and nodded. "I have to agree she's not too anxious to have us around. I would have thought she'd loosen up by now. She should know we mean her no harm."

A tiny meow came from the squirming bulge in Wade's shirt. Unfastening several buttons, he reached inside and retrieved a small bundle of fur. A tiny head, a tiny nose, tiny ears, and two large green eyes attached to a fluffy, gray ball of a body wormed through his fingers.

Gently Wade rubbed the kitten between the ears. A smile softened his rugged features when the animal began to purr loudly with contentment. He hoped the girl would respond in a similar manner when he gave her this newest addition to their band of misfits. The moment he had seen the litter of kittens in the barn at the last farm where they'd left several head of cattle, he'd wanted the girl to have one. He needed something to help break the ice. He also knew she needed something to care about in her life. He understood as Man with No People what it was like to be forever alone. It wasn't a good feeling.

"The girl," Wade muttered to himself, stroking the kitten. They'd been together now for weeks, yet he hadn't found out her name. She seldom spoke and kept to herself, sleeping and eating in the little space he'd curtained off for her near the back of the sandy-floored cave.

Renegade bent and retrieved the reins to Wade's mount. "I'll see to the horses. You go on and see if the girl is still here. We've been gone for over a week now. She could have decided to hightail it out of here."

Disturbed by the thought, Wade frowned. "I doubt she's tried to escape. There's nowhere for her to go for forty miles. McAlester is the closest settlement around these parts."

"I hope you're right, Wade. When the men arrive I'd hate to be the one to have to tell them she's escaped. Her knowing where the cave is located don't set well with them. Makes 'em uneasy. Should that information reach the wrong hands, we'd be facing Judge Parker at Ft. Smith before we knew what day it was. Our heels would be swinging in the air and our eyes bulging from their sockets."

Wade's frown deepened. "The girl can't harm us, and I'm damned tired of the men's bitching."

"They have every reason to be concerned and you know it. You're going to have to make a decision about her sooner or later. I just hope you don't wait until it's too late."

"Damn it, Renegade, I've already made my decision.

Tell the men I'm keeping the girl because she knows too much and it'd be too dangerous to let her go.''

"Do you honestly expect the men to believe that's your motive when all of us know you can't keep your eyes off her? And what do you think they'll believe when they see you're bringing her gifts?'' Renegade looked pointedly at the kitten curled in Wade's hand.

"I don't give a damn what they believe. Any time they get tired of the way I do things, I'll pay 'em off and they can get the hell out of here. I won't have my every move questioned by you or anyone else. It's my damned business what I do or don't do with the girl.''

Renegade shook his head. "Wade, you've let yourself get too tangled up with her. You haven't been yourself since you brought the girl here. In the past you didn't give a spit for all the white captives put together.''

"This girl is different,'' Wade said, giving Renegade a blank look.

"You're damn right she's different. She's got you wound around her little finger, and that's what makes all the men uneasy. They're afraid you're losing your edge. Getting too deeply involved with any woman is dangerous when you're in our kind of business. Women want stability—a vine-covered cottage and babies. That's something we can't offer.''

"If that's the way they feel, then they know exactly what they can do about it,'' Wade growled, and spun on his heels. The shale underfoot tumbled downhill as he stomped off, his temper high. He had no intention of letting his men make him send the girl away. No more than he had any intention of allowing her to leave him and jeopardize their safety. He was the one who ran things around here, and they'd all just have to live with it.

The cave was still. Finding no sign of the girl, Wade turned and walked back out into the sunlight. Squinting against the bright glare, he searched the surrounding area and breathed a sigh of relief when he spied a flicker of movement near the spring. A smile curling his shapely lips, he wandered down the rocky path to a clump of willows that edged the pool of water. Although his moccasined feet made little sound, the girl heard his approach. Unnerved by his sudden appearance, she stood watching him, eyes wary, her legs poised for flight.

Wade noted her stance with annoyance. He'd rescued her from the Comancheros, he'd gone up against his own men to keep her safe at his side, yet she still acted as if he might devour her at any moment. His patience wearing dangerously thin, he said, "I'm damned tired of being treated like I was the devil in buckskin."

The girl lowered her eyes and hung her head. Her throat worked as she swallowed nervously and moistened her lips.

"Damn it, look at me!" Wade snapped. The girl jerked her head up, regarding him through eyes wide with fright. Wade swore beneath his breath, disgusted with himself. She'd already lived through hell, and he'd vowed not to continue her torment. Abruptly he handed her the kitten. "I'm sorry. I didn't mean to be so sharp with you. I had thought by now you would understand that I won't harm you. But I guess after all you've lived through, it'll take a lot longer than I imagined for you to trust me enough to even tell me your name."

Wade looked at the kitten curling itself into a comfortable ball in the girl's hands and gave her a wry grin. "I thought he might be company to you." He turned away.

"My name is Mercy," the girl whispered.

Wade stopped in his tracks. He turned around to face her, his features awestruck by the sultry voice.

"I'm pleased to make your acquaintance, Mercy," he uttered softly.

Mercy lowered her eyes to the ball of fur in her hands. A timid little smile touched her lips as she stroked the kitten under the neck, rousing his loud purr. "He's beautiful."

Wade smiled back. "I'm glad you like him. I know being here with us has been very lonely for you."

"Does he have a name?" Mercy asked, looking once more at Wade.

Wade shrugged and shook his head. "Not to my knowledge. He belongs to you now, so why don't you name him."

Mercy frowned thoughtfully for a long moment. "I believe I'll call him Smoke because of the color of his fur. He's so gray, he looks as if he's been rolled in ashes."

Wade chuckled appreciatively. His laughter was not prompted by the kitten's name, but came from the knowledge that Mercy could still see humor in her life. In only a few words he saw the strength she possessed, a strength the Indians and the Comancheros had not been able to destroy with their brutality.

Without thinking, he reached out to stroke the kitten. His sudden movement startled Mercy, and she jumped back. Again there was fear in her eyes when she looked at him.

"Damn my stupidity," Wade muttered. He knew Mercy was like a wild animal who had been trapped. It would take time and patience to tame her. A moment ago he'd gained a few inches; now, looking into Mercy's wide blue eyes, he realized his rash movement might have set him back a mile.

"I'm going to the cave. Renegade should be back from the corral by now with the supplies," Wade said, and turned away. He'd not rush things again. The girl needed time, and he'd give it to her no matter how much he yearned to take her into his arms and hold her against his heart.

Her expression pensive, Mercy stroked her new pet as she watched Wade wind his way back up the path to the cave. She didn't know what to think of the rustler. Wade Fleming differed from any man she'd ever known. He had strength, yet he didn't use it to force her to his will. He could be violent when antagonized—his retaliation against Estaban had revealed that side of his nature—but he had only shown her tenderness. He possessed Indian blood, proudly proclaiming himself a savage, though he was far more civilized than the white men who rode with him. Wade Fleming was a man of contradictions.

Mercy glanced at the kitten in her hand and felt her eyes mist over. The tiny creature was the first unselfish act of kindness she had received in nearly twelve years.

Quietly she settled herself on a large round slab of stone jutting out of the earth. The sun caught in her tawny hair, making it shine like spun gold when she bent her head to watch her gift playfully flip onto its back and swat at the long strand of silk falling over her shoulder. Mercy smiled with pleasure and realized how long it had been since she'd felt such a simple emotion. She hadn't truly laughed in many years.

She glanced through the golden veil of hair toward the direction Wade had traveled earlier. He had given her back something she'd thought long dead. Hope now rose from the black depths where despair had thrust it years before. Like the healing balm of herbs the medicine man used on Comanche braves injured in battle, Wade had unwittingly begun to purge the festering wounds in her soul. His kindness soothed the deep hurt that had cankered within her since she'd been torn from her family. However, self-preservation demanded she be wary.

The smell of the campfire and hot coffee flowed on the breeze to Mercy. Gently she cradled Smoke in her arms and rose to her feet. It was time to go back to the cave where she could quietly watch Wade without his knowledge. She had missed looking at him while he was away.

The sound of voices raised in anger stopped her. Quietly she eased toward the mouth of the cave, where she could hear what was being said yet go unobserved. Panic flickered across her beautiful face as she listened. The man called Link wanted her dead!

Swallowing with difficulty, she crept away from the cave and made her way toward the trees. She had to escape—it was her only hope of survival. Mercy glanced back toward the camp only once and felt an unexpected sting of tears. A heavy weight seemed to settle in her chest. She had begun to trust Wade Fleming, but like all the other men she'd known, he'd not go against his own kind for her. Mercy clutched the kitten to her breast

and bolted into the trees, her heart pounding with fear
. . . as well as something else she could not name.

"Damn it, Wade, the girl has to go one way or the
other. It's up to you," Link Parry growled, his face set,
his eyes glittering from the whiskey he'd purchased at
Belle Starr's place on the Canadian. "I ain't risking my
neck so you can have a piece of a white squaw's ass."

His swarthy features flushed a dull red, indigo eyes
flashing with blue fire, dark hair falling long and straight
about his shoulders, Wade resembled an avenging warrior as he glowered at Link Parry. "Like I told Renegade when we arrived, if you don't like my decision
about the girl, then you can pull out."

"Listen, Wade," Joe Sutton said, casting Parry a si-
lencing look, "we don't want to pull out. We've made
a good living with you, but you've got to understand
our position. Belle and Sam have asked us to join up
with them, and it's hard to turn down their offer when
you want us to risk our necks because of a girl."

"I've already told you, you're not in jeopardy. I won't
let her escape."

"If she tries to leave the next time we ride out, I'd
like to know how you plan on stopping her. Or do you
want to slow us down by taking her with us every time
we make a raid?" Parry asked, his long, narrow face
sullen with anger.

"She was here when we returned this time," Wade
said, his own temper near the boiling point.

"But that don't mean she'll be here the next time.
What if she gets a hankering for her white folks? What
then? Are you going to let her go off just as pretty as

you please, or are you going to get rid of her like you should have done weeks ago?"

"I've already told you once today that what I do is my business," Wade growled, a feral light entering his eyes.

"Then I don't guess you leave us any choice in the matter. Link and me ain't about to ride with a man who risks his neck on the slender hope that a woman won't do him wrong. They ain't a one been made that could be trusted. Bed 'em and leave 'em and you'll be safe," Joe Sutton said, coming to his feet. He hoisted his saddle bags over his shoulder.

Wade looked toward Renegade. He raised one dark brow at his friend. "Are you going to stay, or do you ride, too?"

Renegade ran a hand down his scarred cheek. "Looks like I'm here to stay."

"Then you're as much a fool as Fleming," Link Parry said.

"That may be, but I don't rightly cotton to a man like you calling me a fool, Parry. So I suggest you get on that nag of yours and hightail it outta here before I decide to get downright mean about it," Renegade said, eyeing the other rustler coldly.

"Hell, Renegade. I ain't got no fight with you." Link glanced from the scar-faced man to Fleming. "And I wouldn't have any argument with Wade if he got rid of his white squaw."

"You already know my decision, so take your money and go," Wade said, his eyes raking contemptuously over Parry, challenging him to say more. He tossed the man a bag of coins.

"You'll be sorry you've gone against us, Wade. Mark

my words. The girl will be the end of you." Link Parry stuffed the pouch in his shirt and grabbed his saddle bags. He tossed them over his shoulder, and without a backward glance in their direction he made his way toward the secret passage that led to the stone corral. He'd be back at Belle and Sam's place on the Canadian before sundown the next day. He had to admit Belle Starr wasn't much to look at, and compared with Wade's girl she was downright ugly, but at least she didn't let her feelings for Sam get in the way of business.

Renegade watched his young friend. Wade stood with hands folded over his chest, head bowed in contemplation, his features shielded by his dark hair. Renegade shook his head as he reached into his pocket to retrieve a pouch of tobacco to roll himself a smoke. He didn't know why he hadn't hightailed it out of here with Link and Joe. He feared they were right about the girl being the end of Wade Fleming. The man himself might not die, but the outlaw in him certainly would. Like he'd told Wade earlier, women wanted things an outlaw couldn't give unless he gave up his lawless ways.

Renegade licked the thin paper roll closed and placed it between his lips. Lifting a burning stick from the fire, he raised it to the cigarillo and puffed. The strong smoke filled his lungs as he squinted up at Wade once more. "Well, amigo, it seems you waited until it was too late."

Wade didn't look at Renegade but kept staring into the fire. "It's still not too late for you to change your mind."

"Hell, Wade. I made my decision just like you did."

Wade looked sideways at his friend. Renegade lounged against the cave wall, the hand holding the cigarillo relaxed across his bent knee. "Why did you stay?"

Again Renegade shook his head. "Damn if I really know. Maybe my curiosity's got the better of my good sense."

Wade frowned. "What have you got to be curious about?"

"Well, for one thing, I just want to see how long it takes the girl to get you to a preacher. Right now my guess is you're a prime candidate for the bonds of holy matrimony. You've got too much pride to just take what you want from her, and you're too damned horny to turn your back and walk away. It only means one thing in my book." Renegade started humming the "Wedding March."

Wade's frown deepened as he acknowledged Renegade's words. He'd like nothing better than to tell Mercy he loved her, but it wouldn't be fair. As Renegade seemed so fond of reminding him, he could never offer her the security she deserved. Even if she returned his affection, they could never settle down and raise a family without looking constantly over their shoulders. Neither the law nor bounty hunters would leave them to live in peace.

Damn it to hell, Wade swore silently. He could offer Mercy nothing, yet he couldn't just set her free. She meant too much to him. During the past weeks he'd allowed himself to look beyond the lawless life he led to a future filled with Mercy.

He drew in a long breath. Even her name meant a relief to suffering. He closed his eyes, savoring the flavor of the word and the images it aroused in his mind. Ten long years of hard living had wearied his soul; lately he'd begun to crave the love and peace he'd known as a child. He had taken to a life of crime to avenge his parents' death, yet now, after finding Mercy, his need to make his parents' murderers pay had lost some of its intensity. His thoughts had turned toward the future for the first time since the fatal night his parents had been killed.

Wade looked back at Renegade and smiled sheepishly. "It might be the way I feel, but there's little I can do about it. You've pointed that out often enough."

Renegade shrugged. "I could be wrong about something sometime."

"Not in this. I've allowed myself to fall in love with Mercy, but there's no future for us. I can't ask her to live like we do, Renegade. She's survived hell already, and I won't put her through more."

"Perhaps you should let her make her own decision. Give her the freedom to decide her future for once in her life. Give her something no one else has ever given her. It'll be a much better gift than a cat, Wade."

"How did an ugly old rustler get so damned smart about women?" Wade asked, smiling down at his friend.

Renegade thoughtfully rubbed his scarred cheek as he looked sideways at his companion. "Even an old rustler like me has had a woman or two in his lifetime."

He didn't add that the scar along his cheek had been made by a Yankee's bayonet—a wound inflicted when Renegade had learned his wife and child were dead. He'd attacked the guard on duty in that hellhole of a prison, wanting nothing more than to die himself. The scar was a daily reminder of what he had lost.

Yes, he knew something about women. His beautiful

Abigail had taught him much about the fairer sex during their short marriage. Through her he had learned how to live. Then he had lost her to the inhumanity of war. She and their daughter had died during Sherman's campaign across Georgia. Feeling like a walking dead man himself, Renegade hadn't returned to the South after the war ended. He'd headed west, determined to end his misery one way or the other. A bullet or a hangman's noose would someday put his body to rest. Then it could join his heart and soul in death.

"I think I'll take you up on your advice," Wade said. He didn't wait for Renegade's answer but turned and walked from the cave. He wanted to find Mercy, to give her her freedom.

His steps light with hope and eagerness, his moccasined feet making no sound, Wade strode toward the spring where he'd last seen Mercy. Finding no sign of the girl, he called out her name and scanned the deepening shadows enfolding the forest. The sun had already crept behind the mountains, leaving twilight to blanket the landscape in muted tones.

Wade's call went unanswered. A furrow marked his brow as he again searched the shadows. Struggling to remain calm, he followed Mercy's tracks back to the edge of the cave. Wade's heart pumped furiously against his ribs as he realized what she must have overheard. Nearly strangling with emotion, he turned and followed Mercy's trail into the forest.

His keen gaze taking note of a broken twig, an overturned stone, a blanket of pine needles disturbed by her passage, Wade closed the distance between them. The moon rose high in the sky before he found Mercy crouched behind a large rock in a stand of pines. Shadows webbed her hiding place, but her tawny hair was like a beacon in the moonlight.

Wade went limp with relief as he quietly moved across the layers of thick pine needles to where she huddled, kitten to her breast, her pale eyes wide with fear and her face ashen.

"Mercy, I mean you no harm," Wade said, not touching her. His heart twisted at the look on her face.

Mercy's answer was seen in her movements. She crouched farther back against the rocks.

Wade drew in a steadying breath, again forcing away the urge to take her into his arms. He had to handle the situation with care, or he would destroy any chance he had with her.

"Mercy, I know what you overheard at the cave, but I promise you no one wants to harm you." Wade hunkered down on his heels, putting himself at eye level with Mercy. "I admit Link and Joe were nervous about you telling the law about the hideout, but you don't have to worry about them anymore."

Mercy looked at Wade, her eyes shining with the light of the moon as well as the questions he'd left unanswered. Wade nodded. "Link and Joe pulled out a little over an hour ago because I wouldn't agree to get rid of you."

The tension seemed to flow out of Mercy. Her lips remained silent, yet the pale blue depths of her eyes spoke volumes. Mesmerized by her beauty, Wade unconsciously released a sigh of longing. At the present moment he wanted nothing more than to reach out and caress the smooth line of her cheek. The words came before he realized he'd spoken them aloud. "Do you know you are beautiful?"

Mercy's inquiring look faded, and she eased backward. Wade suddenly realized that the Comanchero Estaban had probably told her she was beautiful, too.

"Mercy, forgive me. I don't mean to frighten you, but every time I open my mouth, I say the wrong thing." Wade got to his feet. He looked at the girl who had stolen his heart and wondered if he'd ever win her trust. At the moment it seemed an impossible dream.

He turned away and glanced through the tall pines at the round globe lighting the night. He didn't look at Mercy as the hard, thick words poured from him. "Mercy I've decided to set you free." He crammed his hands into his pockets to keep them from balling into fists against the pain welling within his heart.

"You don't want me anymore?" Mercy asked quietly.

Wade drew in a deep breath, but he didn't turn around. He answered honestly. "I want you more now than I've ever wanted anything on earth, yet I can't keep you here any longer."

Silence closed in around them while moonbeams dappled the thick pine needle carpet beneath their feet. An owl hooted in the distance as a gentle current of air stirred the long green needles overhead. At last one simple word challenged every emotion within Wade.

"Why?"

Unable to stand the agony any longer, Wade spun about, his action startling Mercy back against the rocks. "I can't keep you against your will. It's not right. Your life is your own, and you should choose where you want to be and who you want to be with."

"I don't understand," Mercy whispered.

"I know you don't. And that's my point. You've never

known how to make choices. You've had to live so long as a slave, you don't understand what freedom is.''

''Must freedom mean that I leave you?'' Mercy asked, her heart welling with joy.

Wade wet his lips and released a long, agonized breath. ''Yes, Mercy, it does. No matter how much I love you, I can't ask you to live like I do. Nor can I ever give you the security you need. I'm an outlaw: that's the way I make my living. And I'll never be free of those who want to see me hanged.''

''But what if I don't want to go?' Mercy asked, her lips curving into a tender smile.

''It doesn't matter. You need to be with your own people and not some half-breed rustler who can offer you nothing more than a cave and a worn blanket to call home.''

''Do you think I care that you are only half Indian or half white, Wade?''

Wade turned away, knowing he didn't have the strength to keep his distance. ''Damn it, Mercy. You should hate me because of my blood. Half of it is Indian. They are the people who made your life a living hell.''

''Yet I lived with them longer than I did with my white family. I was only a child of eight when the Comanches murdered my family and took me captive. I still feel pain when I remember my parents and brothers, but for twelve years I have lived as a Comanche, and had I been given to White Wing, as his wife, I would have been content. I know it's hard to understand, but I now feel more Indian than white. I know nothing of the white world from which I came, and I have no desire to go back to it.''

"But you must go. I'm giving you your freedom. It's your only chance to live the life you deserve."

Timidly Mercy reached out and placed her hand on Wade's arm, drawing him around to look at her. "You have given me my freedom, Wade Fleming, and I accept the gift with much gratitude. And I will use it as it was given, to make my own decisions."

Unable to stop himself, Wade reached up and cradled Mercy's cheek in the palm of his hand. He swallowed the emotion clogging his throat.

"I'm glad. Someday you will be grateful you didn't remain with me."

"Someday will never come, Wade, because I choose to stay with you," Mercy whispered, looking up into Wade's shadowed face.

Battle weary, he could no longer fight himself or Mercy any longer. His battered heart could sustain no more torment. His arms came up about her, drawing her into his embrace as he had dreamed of doing for so long. He felt her stiffen and he eased away, not wanting to frighten her ever again.

Mercy slowly moistened her dry lips and took a tentative step closer. Trust was reflected in her eyes as she looked shyly at Wade. Again a timid smile touched her lips as she raised her arms and curled them about his neck. "You have given me my freedom, Wade Fleming, and in return I give you my heart."

Wade felt the thrill begin at his temples and work its way over the entire length of his body. He threw back his head and laughed aloud for the joy of being alive and in love. He thanked the gods for their blessings and vowed silently he'd never again do anything that might jeopardize the beautiful woman in his arms.

"I gave you your freedom, Mercy, but I can't give something that is already yours. You have possessed my heart since the first moment I saw you across the campfire."

A pained expression touched Mercy's beautiful features as she caressed Wade's cheek. "I bring shame to you, Wade. I want to be your woman, but I cannot erase what has happened in the past."

Wade's hand covered hers, and he drew her closer against his lean body. He wanted to shield her from the memories of the past. "You bring no shame with you. You are as innocent to me as a newborn babe. You have nothing to regret because you were not responsible for what happened. And I'm honored you see fit to give me your love."

"But I wish I could come to you untouched," Mercy said, her throat choked with tears.

"In my eyes you *are* untouched. I am the only man you've given your heart, and I will be the first to love you. Let our love vanquish the memories of the past, because it no longer exists. All that matters now is the future." Gently Wade lowered his head and brushed his lips across hers. Though his body cried out to know her, he would not rush her. He had not lied when he'd told her she was innocent. She was no longer a virgin; her violation had taught her about the sex act. Yet she knew nothing of the beauty of love between a man and woman. In time he would show her, but for now he was satisfied to hold her close and knew he was the luckiest man alive because he also held her heart.

Chapter 11

The afternoon sun rode low in the sky as Jessie led her horse down the hillside toward the pool she'd discovered the previous afternoon. After tying her mount to one of the tall sandbar willows along the creekbank, Jessie delved into her saddle bags and took out the towel and bar of soap she'd secretly brought from the ranch house. She smiled, picturing Edwina's expression if she ever learned that Jessie had bathed in the creek.

Jessie pushed her way through the thick shield of yellow-green foliage and stepped onto the sandbar that jutted into the still water where driftwood and brush had made a haphazard dam, slowing the creek enough to form a pond. Narrow-leaved cattails, their fuzzy cob-like blooms raised to the sun, grew in fanned clumps along the water's edge to further isolate the pool.

The sand under Jessie's boots crunched as she crossed the narrow strip of land to where a tree, its limbs gnarled and white from being exposed to the elements, had fallen. Using a broken limb as a towel rack and soap dish, Jessie sat down on the slick tree trunk and pulled off her boots. A sigh of relief escaped her as she dug her hot toes into the cool, moist sand and slowly unbuttoned her shirt. She relaxed and raised her face to the slight breeze that stirred the cattail fronds, closing her eyes to savor the tranquillity.

The recent weeks had been so unbearably hot that the heat rose in waves above the land, distorting the horizon. Everything suffered from the severe temperatures. Men and cattle alike tried to find relief from the sun, which drained energy and moisture from their bodies.

Jessie glanced up at the cloudless azure sky. The last time it had rained she and Brand had been together in the line shack. Jessie frowned. She didn't want to remember how it felt to be held in Brand's arms and the sweet pleasure his body gave to hers. In the past weeks she'd been unable to stop the memories from coming back at all times of the day and night. Nor had she been able to stop the pain that came with them.

Jessie swallowed hard and squared her shoulders. Fortunately she'd managed to avoid being alone with Brand since the night he'd told her he didn't want her love. She realized the distance she'd kept between them was the only thing that had saved her from once again making a fool out of herself where Brand Stockton was concerned. She'd lain awake too many nights, trying to dredge up the courage to leave her lonely bed and go to the bunkhouse. The bravado to offer herself brazenly to Brand had never come, and she was grateful for being a coward. She wanted to keep at least a smattering of pride. It was all she had left since Brand tossed her love back in her face.

Jessie's gaze skimmed over the quiet glade. The gurgle of flowing water barely disturbed the stillness. How she wished she could find such peace within herself.

She wanted to put Brand from her heart and look toward the future with a husband who wanted to share her dream of building Eden into one of the most prosperous ranches in Texas. Yet she could have neither wish without pain.

Jessie slowly shook her head and looked once more at the glassy pool of water. Much like the pond, which appeared tranquil on the surface, she harbored disturbing currents beneath her calm exterior, tearing at her resolutions just as surely as the water ate away the sand and stone of the creekbed. Jessie knew she was going to have to come to terms with the turmoil. She could allow herself to take whatever Brand offered, or she could stand firm and suffer the pain of losing him. Neither choice pleased her.

"I'm going to have to make a decision before tomorrow night," she murmured. The minutes were ticking by, and in less than a day Clint would expect an answer to his proposal.

"But I still don't know what to tell him," Jessie muttered, coming to her feet. Disgruntled with herself, she shucked off her britches and shirt. She knew a marriage to Clint would be the logical answer to all her problems. But as she'd feared, her heart didn't heed her mind's logic.

Perhaps a bath in the cool creek would help clear the heat from her befuddled brain. After hanging up her clothes to wave in the breeze, Jessie recovered the bar of soap and crossed to the water's edge. She tested the temperature with her toes, and with a smile of pleasure curling her lips, she waded in. The water felt wonderful against her skin.

Jessie lathered herself from head to toe, stretching

her lithe body toward the heavens as she savored her bath. Her thoughts occupied, she was completely unaware of the silver eyes watching her from the willows.

Brand felt his blood run hot and his mouth go dry at the sight of Jessie. His eyes swept over the nymph rising from the water, his gaze devouring the naked white skin glistening with beads of moisture, the arms raised to wash the long dark hair, firm breasts thrust forward proudly, their nipples hard from the cool touch of the water. He allowed his gaze to linger on the enticing sight for a long, ravenous moment before his eyes slid down to her flat belly and on to the softly rounded hips that disappeared into the water swirling gently about her naked glory.

Brand's body pulsed and throbbed, and his breath came hard. His heart pounded against his rib cage like an Indian drum. He'd followed Jessie when she rode out, using Wade Fleming or any other excuse he could invent to be near her. He'd done his best to keep his distance, but after admitting he wanted Jessie more than any other woman on earth, it had been a continuous battle with himself to stay away. He still didn't call what he felt love, but he believed it was as close as he'd ever come to experiencing such an emotion. To have Jessie, he was willing to forget her involvement with Wade Fleming and everything else in her past. Satisfied with his decision, he gave himself a mental pat on the back. Few men would have the strength of character to overlook a white woman's association with a half-breed.

Brand eased through the willows and quietly crossed to the water's edge. He'd fought the battle to stay away from Jessie as long as he could. She belonged to him, and he was determined to help her realize it. He looked at the beautiful woman, whose white-frothed body made him ache. A wicked grin curled his lips. "May I join you?"

A cry of surprise escaping her lips, Jessie spun around and sank into the water in the same instant. Hands crossed protectively over her breasts, dark hair floating about her, she looked up at Brand, who stood with hands braced casually against his lean hips, hat tipped to the back of his head, feet spread.

"How dare you sneak up on me? Get out of here this minute!" Jessie screamed, fury and embarrassment flushing her skin a delicate rose. She sank farther into the water at the appreciative look Brand flicked over her. After one wishful glance at her clothes, she glared at him once more. "Are you deaf? I told you to leave."

Brand's grin deepened and his eyes sparkled with a devilish light. "Surely it would be much nicer to have someone scrub your back?"

Eyes widening, Jessie sputtered, "I don't need anyone to wash my back!"

Brand tossed his hat onto the limb of a fallen tree. "Then you can scrub mine."

"I most certainly won't scrub your back!"

Brand frowned. "That's not nice, Miss Jessie. I'm certainly willing to return the favor."

"Brand Stockton, this is ridiculous. Now if you're through playing your little game, I'd certainly appreciate being left alone to finish my bath. Then if you still want to have one, you can use my soap." Jessie eyed Brand from head to toe, inspecting him slowly. She made a moue of disgust, wrinkling her small nose primly. "And you certainly look like you could use a good scrubbing. Do you realize I've never seen you clean-shaven?''

Brand ran a hand over his beard-stubbled cheek. "I might manage to shave if you'd agree to hold the mirror so I won't cut myself."

Jessie regarded him through narrowed lids, drops of moisture glistening from the tips of her thick lashes. "Let me get my hands on your razor and I'll guarantee you won't have to worry about shaving yourself ever again. You'll have a permanent smile just below your chin."

Brand grinned and slowly began to unbutton his shirt. "My, you certainly are bloodthirsty today. But I'm glad you warned me. Now I know to keep all sharp objects away from you."

Eyes widening in alarm, Jessie watched Brand's fingers swiftly unfasten his shirt and then begin to work on the buttons of his Levi's. "What . . . do . . . you think . . . you're doing?"

Brand shrugged out of his shirt and pulled off his boots before answering. "I'm going for a swim."

Jessie couldn't take her eyes off the wide expanse of his chest. The crisp mat of hair narrowed into a dark trail that disappeared down his hard, lean belly into the open fly of his britches. She shook her head. "No! You'll not swim while I'm here."

Brand cocked one dark brow at Jessie. "The only way you can avoid sharing the water with me is to come out."

Indignant, Jessie countered, "I most certainly will not come out while you're here."

"It seems, Miss Nolan, you have a predicament on your hands. You can't stay and you can't go."

"But you can go, Mr. Stockton, and if you want to remain in my employ, you will do as I ask and leave here this minute," Jessie snapped, finding nothing humorous in the situation.

Brand jerked off his britches and waded into the water toward Jessie. She saw his intent and made a futile effort to escape him, but the water held her back. Brand easily captured her in his arms and pressed her flesh against his body. "I've been meaning to talk to you about my job at Eden, but I think it can wait for a little while longer."

Stunned by the electricity that shot through her at the mere touch of his hands, Jessie stared up at Brand and watched, mesmerized, as he slowly lowered his head toward her. Her mind ordered her to resist the lips and tongue sending sweet torment through every inch of her being, but her heart and body again resisted logic. Once more she was in the arms of the man she loved. Surrendering to need, Jessie slowly wound her arms around Brand's neck and molded her slick body against his. She felt his arousal pressing against her belly. No matter how he had acted during the past weeks, Brand still desired her.

All resistance gone, Jessie entwined her fingers in the dark hair at the nape of his neck as his silken stubble grazed against her tender flesh. She regretted chiding him about not shaving. It didn't matter to her whether he ever shaved again or not. She'd love him any way he came.

Needing no foreplay to arouse them further, they deepened their kiss as they strained together. The current of the water swirled about their hot bodies, moistening the tender places already damp with need. Jessie felt Brand press his sex against hers, and she opened to him, slipping her legs about his waist as he lifted her to sheathe his hard shaft. She clung to his shoulders, her expression rapt at the intense sensations coursing through her as he plunged into her depths. Head back and face raised to the sky, she rode the stallion, the muscles inside her belly quivering as they caressed his satiny length, holding him tight as he stroked her.

Brand groaned his pleasure. Cupping her buttocks in the palms of his hands, he held her small body, driving himself within her warmth, glutting himself as he'd dreamed of doing so often in the past weeks.

Together they soared toward the fiery orange ball in the western sky. They crossed man's universe and reached for the heavens of the gods. They captured the sun, the moon, and the stars in one quivering explosion of ecstasy. Cool water flowing around them, they stood joined, hearts beating furiously against their ribs, bodies pulsing and eyes closed against returning to the world of mortal man.

"Jessie," Brand murmured, lifting a hand to brush a wet strand of raven hair from her cheek. "God, how I've wanted you. All these weeks I've lain awake at night, dreaming of burying myself deep within your sweetness."

"Why didn't you let me know?" Jessie asked quietly, her eyes holding Brand's captive.

"I wanted to, but I thought you didn't want me. You've avoided me since the night in the barn."

Jessie raised a hand to caress his cheek. "I'll always want you, Brand."

Brand's lips curled at the corners. "It seems we've been at cross purposes, Miss Nolan."

Jessie raised herself on tiptoes and brushed her lips tenderly against Brand's. "No, we've not been at cross purposes. Until now we've used our heads. You and I both know nothing can come from our relationship."

Brand's smile faded and his arms fell away from Jessie. His suspicions flaring back to life, he looked down at her. "What makes you say that?"

"You do. You said you didn't want my love, and I won't be just your plaything. I will have all of you or nothing at all," Jessie said suddenly voicing the decision she'd been dreading all along.

"Jessie, isn't it enough to know I want you more than any other woman on earth?" Brand asked.

Jessie looked up into Brand's astonished face and realized he had given her all she would ever have of him. Sadly, she also realized she wanted much more. She needed security. She needed a life not filled with confusion. She wanted the stability of a man who would always be there for her. And she would follow her head and not her heart, no matter how much it hurt.

"No, Brand. Your desire is not enough. Since the last time we were together I've had time to think about what's important to me. I've decided life is too short to waste on games that mean nothing more than a few minutes of pleasure. I won't share my life with a man who may be gone when I awake every morning. You made me a woman, Brand, and as such I won't settle for less than your full commitment to our relationship."

"Damn it, Jessie. I am committing myself to you as much as I can," Brand said, his expression darkening. Didn't she realize how much he had already given her? Why couldn't she be satisfied?

Jessie reached out and tenderly caressed his beard-stubbled jaw. "I know you are, Brand. And that is the sad part."

"Don't patronize me," Brand said, jerking away from her hand. "I've offered you more than I've ever offered any other woman, and if you can't accept it, then perhaps you're right about us not having a future."

Jessie released a long, slow breath. Her eyes reflected the pain welling in her heart as she looked up at Brand. "At least you've helped me make up my mind about one thing."

Brand arched one dark brow in question.

Jessie shrugged and stepped closer. "I'll tell you about it later."

She looped her arms about Brand's neck and drew his head down to hers. She knew she shouldn't give in to her emotions again, but she couldn't leave Brand before he made love to her one last time. It would be all she'd have to carry her through the years as Mrs. Clint Ramsey. She would make Clint a dutiful wife and partner, never giving him any reason to doubt her devotion to their marriage. Yet at this moment in time she could think only of herself and her own needs.

Unable to resist the temptation of her sweet lips, Brand swept his arms about Jessie, instinctively crushing her against his hard body as his mouth claimed hers. He lifted her into his arms and walked to the shallows. There he laid her down and covered her silken flesh with his own. Again and again he claimed her until the moon rose high in the sky and they lay exhausted and sated in each other's arms upon a bed of moss.

"Jessie," Brand said, staring up at the stars overhead. "You said you had come to a decision earlier and would tell me about it." He felt Jessie's body tense.

"It's nothing now," she whispered. How could she tell him she intended to marry another man after what they had just shared? Their hours of lovemaking had not changed Brand, nor had it altered her decision to marry Clint. She just didn't want to spoil her memories by watching the tender look on Brand's face turn to hatred. For he would hate her after tomorrow night, when Clint announced their wedding at the party. He would believe the worst of her, and it would be best for all concerned. He would have an excuse to leave Eden before she had to tell him to go. Because after today she knew that as long as Brand remained at the ranch, she'd never be able to totally commit herself to marriage with another man.

Brand stretched his long legs over the rim of the tub and laid his head back. The blue smoke from the cigar he held between his teeth rose lazily toward the bunkhouse roof as he hummed a bawdy little ditty beneath his breath. A rakish grin curled his lips as he thought about his plans for the evening. After leaving Jessie the previous night, he'd lain awake, trying to sort out his feelings about his boss lady. Near dawn he had finally realized there was only one decision he could make about their relationship, and tonight he was going to enjoy himself to the hilt.

Brand chuckled at his invitation to Ramsey's yearly get-together. It hadn't been given with the rancher's usual finesse. Obviously, like any animal marking his territory, the older man sensed he had a rival for Jessie's affections and wanted to keep Brand as far away from her as possible, especially in a social situation. However, it would have been bad manners not to invite him at all.

Squinting against the smoke, Brand snuffed out the cigar and laid it on the table beside the tub. Taking the cloth and soap, he began to scrub himself from head to toe. Tonight Jessie would have no reason to complain about his appearance. He had laid out a brand-new pair of Levi's and shirt.

Brand glanced from the clothes on his bunk to his aproned friend near the stove. "I'm ready for more water, Slim."

Slim picked up the kettle and crossed to where Brand sat lathering his head. A smug grin touched his lips as he poured the steaming water into the tub.

Brand's eyes widened and he let out a loud yell. "What in the hell are you trying to do? Make stew out of me?"

Slim chuckled and cocked one eye at Brand. "Naw. You're too rangy and too damned tough to eat."

"Then why are you trying to scald me to death?" Brand asked, stirring the water to cool it.

"I just thought I'd put you out of your misery," Slim said as he refilled the kettle and set it back on the stove to heat.

Brand frowned at his friend. "Slim, what kind of burr has gotten under your saddle now?"

"I'm not the one with the burr under my saddle. You're the one whose jumpin' around here like a stallion smellin' a mare."

"All right. Damn it. No more riddles. What's on your mind?"

Slim untied the stained apron and hung it on a peg

beside the dry sink. He drew a chair away from the table and straddled it. Propping a hairy arm over the back, he appraised Brand for a long moment before he nodded his understanding. "You've gone and let yourself fall in love with that girl, haven't you?"

Brand rinsed himself free of soap, rolled the washcloth into a ball, and tossed it into the tub as he stood. Bath water splashed over the sides of the tub as he reached for a towel and draped it about his hips. "You might call it love, but I'm not exactly sure what to call it."

"Brand, the cap'n ain't goin' to approve of what you've done if Jessie is involved with Fleming."

Brand shrugged. "I don't really give a damn anymore what people think, Slim. All I know is I can't just walk away from her."

Brand crossed to the washstand and peered into the cracked mirror hanging on the wall. He frowned and ran a hand over the dark stubble on his chin before he glanced over his shoulder at Slim. "Tonight I'm going to ask Jessie to marry me."

Slim blinked at his friend and shook his head as if to clear it. He couldn't have heard Brand right. The Brand Stockton he knew was pure Texas Ranger. He didn't give a damn about settling down and raising a passel of brats. He loved the adventure of the chase too much to abandon his job for a woman. And there was one more thing that kept him from settling down: the search for his sister.

Again Slim shook his head and tapped his ear with the palm of his hand. "I don't believe I heard you right. Did you say you were goin' to ask Jessie to marry you?"

Brand grinned and nodded before he peered at his

reflection once more. "You heard right. I'm going to ask Jessie to marry me before it's too late and Ramsey horns in on my territory."

Brand reached for the straight razor lying on the shelf beside the soap cup. He stropped it, bringing a fine edge to the blade before he poured water into the tin pan. He moistened the shaving brush and then swirled it into the soap cup until it foamed with lather. He spread a generous amount over the lower half of his face. Tonight he would go to Jessie clean-shaven and wearing his heart on the sleeve of his new shirt.

"What about Mercy?" Slim asked softly.

The hand that held the razor stilled. "I haven't forgotten Mercy. I'll keep searching for her until I know there's no hope left. But I'm tired of the life I've lived for the past twelve years. Jessie has made me feel things that I haven't felt since I was sixteen years old. She's brought a part of me back to life."

Slim nodded sadly. "I thought as much. I've seen it comin', but until now I didn't realize how much you cared for the girl." He got to his feet and swung the chair back into place beneath the table. "I just hope you know what you're doin'. We still don't know how Jessie is connected with Fleming. You've let yourself get involved in a situation that could tear you apart by the time it's all over."

"I know, but it still doesn't change my mind."

"I didn't figure it would," Slim muttered. He would have liked to be happy for his friend, yet until they finished the job they'd come here to do, he couldn't. He feared Brand would end up brokenhearted before everything was said and done. The beautiful Jessica Nolan could end up destroying what the Comanche and the war had left of Brand's soul. And should that happen, Slim knew his friend would never recover. He'd be left an empty shell of a man, driven by hate.

Slim bent and tested the cooling bath water before he began to unbutton his shirt. He didn't want to go to Ramsey's shindig, but Brand's announcement had changed his mind. He'd spruce himself up, dance a few jigs with that straitlaced old woman, Winnie, and pretend to enjoy himself while keeping a close eye on Brand. Should his friend need him, he'd be there to give support.

Brand glanced at Slim in the mirror. "I thought you didn't want to go to Ramsey's."

"I changed my mind," Slim said, tossing his denims and long underwear in a pile on the floor. He gingerly stepped into the tub. A look of something akin to disgust flickered across his face as he began to scrub himself. He'd had a bath in the creek only last week, and he didn't want to weaken his muscles with too much washing.

"Afraid another man is going to steal Edwina away from you?" Brand teased as he bent to splash his face with water.

"Any man who can handle that ill-natured creature is more'n welcome to her," Slim said, lathering his thin hair.

"I thought you and Edwina were becoming friends," Brand said as he swiped the last of the water from his face.

"Friends, humph! No man can be friends with a woman as contrary as Miss Edwina Roilings. Just when I think I'm breakin' through all that cold and stiffness to find a warm woman, she freezes up on me again."

"Perhaps a few dances and some nice words at the right moment tonight will change your luck."

"I ain't got much hope of that happenin'," Slim said, vigorously scrubbing a hairy leg. He paused and looked up at Brand, a wry grin curling his lips. "But I'd kinda like it if it did. If she'd let herself go, Winnie could make a man happy 'cause there's plenty of woman there to love."

Brand's laughter spilled into the afternoon air like a refreshing breeze. "It would seem I'm not the only cowpoke around here who has his eye on one of Eden's women."

"Humph!" Slim said, his face flushing a beet red. "I suggest you attend to your own affairs and let me see to mine."

"I intend to follow your advice to the letter," Brand replied, pulling on his new indigo denims. "Jessie will get all of my attention tonight, so you'll have to worry about Winnie all by yourself."

Chapter 12

"Everyone is already here and eager to meet you," Clint said as he swung Jessie down from the buckboard and set her on her feet upon the flagged walk that led up to the white, two-storied framed house. He turned to assist Edwina. "They also want to meet you, Miss Roilings."

Edwina adjusted her gloves, dusted the draped fabric of her skirt, and secured a wayward strand of graying hair that the breeze had pulled from the tight chignon coiled just above the stiff lace collar of her high-necked gown. Now prepared to face anything, she looked to Clint to proffer his arm but found his attention centered on Jessie.

"Humph!" she muttered. Clint Ramsey looked at Jessie like a man starved. But she'd made a promise to herself to mind her own business and stay out of Jessie's love life. Jess was a grown woman and could make up her own mind about the men in her life. Lifting her skirt, Edwina strode off in the direction of the music and laughter. She paused at the corner of the house and glanced back to where Jessie and Clint still stood. Tonight, she suspected, he would propose.

A sick feeling settled in the pit of Edwina's belly. She didn't know what it was about the man, but he gave her the willies. He was just too damned good to be true, and as Edwina had learned thirty years ago, good-looking rich men could be so deceptive you couldn't see their flaws until it was too late.

She glanced up at the velvet sky. Yes, she'd learned that lesson the hard way, having years before foolishly given her heart to one of Boston's wealthy men—only to find out he already had a wife.

Edwina jerked her thoughts from the past and raised her head proudly in the air. She'd made one mistake, but she hadn't been that foolish again. She knew men and their wants, and she had no use for the male of the human species. She had as yet to find one you could trust. They were all intent on having their own way without a thought to the women they used. Giving a sniff of disdain, Edwina wandered toward the music and laughter drifting upon the evening breeze.

Unaware of Edwina's departure, Clint cupped Jessie's cheek in the palm of his hand. His voice was little more than a hoarse whisper as he said, "You are more beautiful each time I see you, and I'm already begrudging my guests the time they will spend with you tonight. I want you all to myself.'

His warm gaze swept over Jessie appreciatively, taking in the soft swell of the firm breasts peeking above the modest, heart-shaped neckline of her gown. Silver lace edged the small puffed sleeves, bodice, and draped skirt, which was swept up in back to fall in layers of sapphire-and-silver ruffles. The sleek cut of her gown accentuated her slender body to perfection, the rich sapphire fabric deepening the color of her eyes until they were fathomless indigo pools in which a man could lose his soul.

Jessie blushed under Clint's direct appraisal and suppressed the shiver of apprehension that tingled its way up her spine. Tonight she intended to tell this man she would accept his proposal of marriage, yet the warm look he gave her made her want to get as far away from him as possible. It reminded her of the hunger in Brand's eyes before he made love to her, though she felt no thrilling response. Jessie forced a smile to her lips. She had to put Brand from her mind. She'd made her decision, and she wouldn't allow herself to succumb to the memories.

"Excuse me," Brand drawled, reining the Morgan to a halt. "I don't mean to interrupt, but I thought you might want someone to remind you there's a party going on."

Jessie jumped guiltily and stepped away from Clint. A blush tinged her cheeks as she looked up at Brand to find him grinning down at her. Her mouth went dry as the glow from the lanterns revealed the clean-shaven planes of his face. The effect was devastating. Beard-stubbled, he had been ruggedly handsome in a roguish kind of way, but now he took her breath away. She'd never seen a man with such beauty. The years seemed to have vanished with the dark shadow of beard. He looked young and carefree and utterly charming as he flashed her a devilish smile. Jessie again felt her cheeks heat when she realized Brand knew exactly what effect he had on her. Glancing away, she centered her attention on the man at her side, and as her gaze came to rest on Clint's handsome features, she couldn't stop herself from comparing the two men. Clint was attractive, but now she realized he looked old and worn compared with the man mounted on the ebony Morgan.

Jessie glanced down at her tightly clasped hands and silently scolded herself for her wayward thoughts. She couldn't continue such comparisons between the two men, or she'd never be able to go through with marrying Clint.

Noting the brief look that passed between Brand and Jessie, Clint took Jessie by the arm and drew her against his side possessively. His eyes sparkled with challenge as he looked up at Brand. "Thank you for reminding us, Stockton. Now, if you will excuse us, I'll show Miss Nolan her way." He flashed Brand a contemptuous look. "I'm sure you can find your own way."

Brand tipped his hat and gave Jessie a wicked smile. "I wouldn't get lost tonight for the world." As Clint led Jessie away, Brand's silver gaze turned to ice and the smile slowly faded into a scowl. He slid from the saddle and tied his mount to the hitching post, all the while cursing Clint Ramsey under his breath.

The sound of music and laughter filled the night as Clint introduced Jessie to the men and women who had gathered at the Lazy L, eager to meet their newest neighbor. After the introductions were made, Clint led Jessie onto the bricked patio to dance. Oil lanterns showered them in golden light as they swirled to the music.

The intoxicating fragrance of yellow jasmine filled the air as the rest of the Lazy L's guests joined them to dance. So seldom did their lives give them a chance to enjoy themselves, they didn't waste a moment when they all came together. The ladies dressed in the finest gowns, and the men with their hair slicked back, string ties knotted neatly about the collars of their ironed shirts, and boots polished to a high sheen, danced together until thirst drove them from the dance floor for refreshments.

The unmarried men, waiting their turn to dance with the few ladies present, lined up at the long table that had been placed discreetly beyond the hedge of roses that edged the patio. Out of sight, it gave no offense to the sensibilities of the Lazy L's female guests, while it offered beer, home brew, and whiskey to quench the male thirst and fortify the spirit for more dancing. Near the porch, which wrapped around the entire first floor of Clint's home, another table had been filled to the brim with ice and fruit punch. For the few ladies who preferred something slightly stronger, a silver wine bucket held a bottle of Madeira that Clint had had shipped in from Spain.

Beyond the lace-covered tables set with china and silver for the guests, several men worked to baste a large haunch of beef spitted above a pit of glowing mesquite and hickory coals. The tantalizing smell mingled with the sweet scent of roses and jasmine, making the guests hungry for the feast to come.

When the dance ended, Clint led Jessie to the refreshment table, where a dark-skinned Mexican girl served them punch. Sipping the cool, sweet drink, he surveyed his accomplishment with pride. "What do you think, Jessie?"

"Everything looks wonderful, and everyone seems to be having a good time," Jessie said, smiling her pleasure. Until that moment she hadn't realized how much she'd missed the social events she'd attended in Boston.

Parties had been nearly a nightly occurrence, and when she had left the city she'd been so bored with them, she'd believed she'd never miss such frivolity. Now it seemed an eternity since she'd heard music or laughter.

Clint's smile deepened at her answer. He wanted Jessie to see she could be happy as his wife. He'd spared no expense to make everything just right this year for his shindig. The musicians had come all the way from San Antonio, and he'd had ice brought down from the Rockies and fresh fruit shipped in from Galveston just to impress her.

"Then, Miss Nolan, will you honor me with another dance?"

"I'm afraid you're going to have to share," Brand said, coming up from behind and taking Jessie's hand. Before Clint could protest, he swept her out onto the dance floor.

Jessie's eyes snapped fire as she looked up at Brand. "Of all the gall! Exactly what do you think you are doing?"

"Claiming what's mine before that horny old bastard steals it," Brand said, gracefully waltzing Jessie around the dance floor.

"For your information, I don't belong to you. And you just can't come in here and take over as if I do," Jessie said, doing her best to ignore the thrill Brand's words created.

"You and I both know exactly where you belong, but I'll wait until later to make you change your mind," Brand said. "It would be bad manners for me to sweep you away from here before you've finished your second dance." A slow, provocative grin curled Brand's lips as he looked down at her.

"Bad manners! What on earth do you know about manners or anything else that deals with polite society?"

Brand's grin deepened and he spread his hand at the small of Jessie's back, possessively drawing her near. "Not much, to be truthful. But I do know what I want."

Against her will Jessie felt another thrill of excitement ripple along her nerves as Brand's warm gaze dipped into the V of her gown. She gave herself a sharp mental shake. She had to get control or she'd make a complete fool of herself in front of every rancher for a hundred miles. "Stop it, damn you. Don't look at me like that."

"Tsk, tsk. Such language from a lady. What would Clint think if he heard you?" Brand drew her closer. His words were spoken softly and meant for her ears alone. "But what does it matter what he thinks; you belong to me, Jessie."

Jessie's steps faltered and she stumbled against Brand's body. She knew he could feel her heart pounding as she pushed herself away from him. "I don't want to dance anymore."

Brand wouldn't release her. His fingers a vise on her hand and waist, he said, "Ah Jessie. No matter what you say about the future, you and I both know there's something between us which can't be denied. Call it love or lust, it's there, and you're going to have to accept it."

"I don't have to accept anything of the kind, Brand Stockton," Jessie said as the music came to an end. Shaken to her core, she jerked her hand free and nearly ran from the dance floor before the music could trap her again in Brand's arms. Heart pounding furiously, she crossed to the refreshment table and gladly took the proffered cup of punch. She managed only a few sips before the musicians began another tune and she found herself surrounded by men of every age, shape, and size, all wanting a dance.

Brand watched from the sidelines as Jessie was swept onto the dance floor time and time again. The night wore on, the whiskey making the party and the dances more lively. He winced on several occasions when he saw Jessie's face screw up in a pained frown after a heavy foot trod upon her toes. But he didn't go to her rescue. He'd give her a while longer to ignore him before he stepped in and showed her as well as everyone else at the Lazy L exactly who she belonged to.

Brand smiled to himself as his gaze drifted to Clint Ramsey. At least he wasn't the only man Jessie had ignored tonight. She'd had the first dance with Ramsey, but since then he'd been unable to steal her away from his other guests. The man was doing his damndest to hide his frustration, but Brand could read the tension in the lines about his mouth. Brand could also see the mounting anger in the other man's eyes. He chuckled. Clint would have a seizure when he learned of Brand's plans for Jessie tonight.

Jessie knew her feet would fall off. She'd never danced so much in her life, nor had she ever run into so many men who thought they could dance. Her toes ached from being trod upon by heavy boots, and the muscles in her legs felt like rubber. Exhausted and in need of a quiet place to recuperate from the abuse of the last few hours, Jessie managed to slip away while Clint was overseeing the final preparations for dinner.

Moving stealthily through the concealing shadows, she made her way along the planked porch until she found an empty room in which to rest her aching feet. She eased opened the French doors that led into the large room and paused upon the threshold to take her bearings. She immediately realized that she'd entered Clint's private study. The masculine smell of leather and tobacco permeated the air. Deer antler trophies from Clint's hunts graced the chimney above the stone fireplace, and a large steer-hide rug was spread across the floor in front of it. There was a huge mahogany desk across the room, a leather-and-horn chair behind it. A settee covered in burgundy leather and several heavily padded leather chairs made up the rest of the room's furnishings.

Quietly closing the door behind her, Jessie crossed to a chair and gratefully sank onto it. She breathed a sigh of relief as she slipped off her shoes and wiggled her toes to make sure none were broken before massaging her battered appendages. Relaxing back into the chair, she worked to ease the discomfort. Her gaze moved over the room once more, coming to rest on the wall behind Clint's desk. Rifles, pistols, sabers, and revolvers of every description, as well as Indian spears and hatchets decorated with feathers and beads, lined the pine paneling from floor to ceiling.

Jessie took in the arsenal, her interest only mildly piqued until her gaze came to rest on the rifle hanging directly behind Clint's desk. Something about the weapon drew her from the chair and across the room. Tentatively she reached up and ran her fingers over the intricately carved stock. Her heart went cold and she jerked her hand away as if the dark wood had suddenly turned venomous. She swallowed hard and drew in an unsteady breath. The rifle was the same as the one she'd seen ten years ago. Jessie backed away slowly. She could never forget the rifle. It had haunted her dreams since the night of her parents' murders.

Jessie felt the blood slowly drain from her face. Her skin grew cold and tingled as dark shadows swirled before her eyes. She gripped the desk behind her for support, unable to take her eyes from the weapon of her nightmares. The man she'd been searching for could be none other than the one she'd decided to marry, Clint Ramsey.

Jessie shook her head. It was impossible. The man she knew couldn't be the same vicious animal who had slain her parents. There must be dozens of carved stocks like the one she'd just found. It was the only reasonable explanation.

"Jessie, is something wrong?" Clint asked as he entered through the French doors. "You look faint."

Jessie swallowed her suspicions and turned to look at Clint. What reason could this man have for killing her parents? He had power and wealth. He didn't need to murder for a few head of cattle. Jessie forced a smile to her stiff lips. "No, there's nothing wrong. I just slipped away for a few minutes to rest my aching toes. I hope you don't mind."

Clint chuckled. "Of course I don't. I should have come to your rescue hours ago. Every man here wants to go home tonight and be able to say he's danced with the most beautiful woman in Texas. However, it does seem to have created a problem for you, especially when they've had a few drinks to make them believe they're light on their feet."

Jessie turned once more toward the rifle of her nightmares. "I was just noticing your collection."

Clint crossed to where Jessie stood. His face glowed with pride. Each weapon held a special place in his heart. Noting Jessie's interest in the rifle, he took it down and proudly showed it to her. A wide smile spread his lips as he caressed the oiled wood. "My father made this gun for me. It's the only one like it." He lifted the rifle to give her a better view of the intricate carving. "It took months for him to carve the stock. If you look close enough, you can see his initials just inside the bear's mouth. He gave it to me on my fifteenth birthday, and from that day I've never allowed anyone else to use it." Again Clint ran his hand lovingly down the rifle before he returned it to its place on the wall. "Someday I will give it to my son."

Jessie felt the world shake beneath her feet and grabbed for the desk. Alarmed, Clint swept her into his arms and carried her to the settee beneath the wide double windows. Gently he set her down before throwing open the sash. Anxiously he bent over her prone figure, his face grave with concern. "Are you all right, Jessie?"

Jessie swallowed the bile in her throat and laid her head against the soft leather. She closed her eyes, shutting out the sight of the man whose masked image had haunted her dreams for ten long years. "I'll be fine in a few moments. Would you please get me a cool glass of punch?"

"Of course," Clint said, and hurried from the room.

The music drifted through the open window as Jessie relived the horror of her parents' murders. She had finally found the man who had killed them, but how could she prove it after so many years? The law would never believe Clint Ramsey was a cold-blooded murderer. The man had been masked, and she had been only a child of ten on that fateful night. It would be his word against hers, and she was a newcomer who hadn't revealed her true identity, while Clint was one of Paradise's most upstanding citizens.

Jessie pressed her lips into a hard, thin line. She was determined to see Clint Ramsey pay for his crimes one way or the other. But how?

She had not managed to find the answer to her dilemma when Clint returned with the punch. She took the cool drink, drained the contents of the cup, and started to rise. "I feel much better now. I think the heat and the dancing were just a little too much for me."

Clint placed a hand on her shoulder. He sat down beside her and draped an arm around her, drawing her against him. "Perhaps you should rest awhile longer before you rejoin the party."

At his touch, Jessie had to fight the urge to cross the room and take down the rifle Clint had used to kill her parents. She knew she'd feel no remorse if she turned it upon him and pulled the trigger. She pushed the thought aside and drew in a deep, steadying breath. She wanted revenge, but she had to use her head. She couldn't allow her emotions to have the upper hand. Until she could find a way to make Clint pay for his crimes, she had to keep him from guessing her true feelings.

Jessie clenched her teeth, and her nails bit into the palms of her hands as she balled them into fists of silent rage. It wouldn't be easy to keep from putting a bullet in Clint. She hated him to the core of her being. However, death would be too easy for the man responsible for destroying her family. He needed to suffer. He needed to know what it was like to lose everything he loved.

An idea exploded in Jessie's mind, making her feel slightly giddy. She knew how to destroy Clint Ramsey.

She forced a smile to her lips. "Clint, I appreciate your concern, but you shouldn't worry about me."

Clint turned to face Jessie, one broad hand resting on the soft skin of her shoulder. "Jessie, I want to worry about you. I want to take care of you forever."

Jessie lowered her lashes, afraid he would see the hatred in the depths of her eyes. "Clint you've been so wonderful to me since I've come to Paradise."

Clint's face lit with excitement. "Does that mean you'll accept my proposal, Jessie?"

"I don't know." Jessie kept her gaze upon her tightly clasped hands. "There are many things that we don't know about each other."

Clint laughed and opened his arms. "What you see is what you get, Jessie. I know I'm quite a bit older than you, but I can still make you happy."

"It's not your age or your looks that I'm uncertain about," Jessie said, and watched Clint visibly relax. "I'm worried I might not please you."

Clint threw back his dark head and laughed aloud. "My God, Jessie. There isn't a thing about you that doesn't please me. You are the most beautiful woman I've ever met."

"But you know nothing of my background or past."

"I know enough by looking at you. Your blue eyes tell me you come from good stock, not from some wigwam. And anyone can tell you're a lady. Just like my Thoroughbreds, you've got breeding, Jessie.''

Jessie smiled sweetly at Clint and thought, You're right. I do come from good Indian stock, as you'll soon learn. Raising her chin proudly in the air, she said aloud, "My family was among the first settlers in America.''

Again Clint chuckled. "I could tell. Like I said, breeding shows.'' He brushed his knuckles against the smooth line of her cheek, and his face became serious. "So say you'll marry me, Jessie. I promise, I'll do everything in my power to make you happy.''

Jessie lowered her eyes demurely. "I'll marry you, Clint.''

Clint let out a loud whoop and captured her in his thick arms. Before she could stop him, he swooped down and covered her mouth in a smothering, wet kiss. Jessie forced down the gag in her throat. She had to control her revulsion until she had Clint so firmly trapped in her web that he'd never escape. Using every ounce of willpower she possessed, she endured the kiss, though she couldn't pretend to respond.

Thrilled by Jessie's acceptance, Clint didn't note her lack of enthusiasm. He was too busy mentally making plans for the finest wedding Texas had ever seen. Afterward there'd be no more jokes going around at Miss Molly's that the name of his ranch wasn't the only thing Clint Ramsey owned that could be called Lazy. His marriage to Jessie would show all the damned gossips in Paradise that he was a man in every way.

Releasing Jessie's lips, he smiled triumphantly. "Let's get married next week.''

Jessie forced a smile. "Clint, a wedding can't be

planned in a week. There are too many things to do. I have to send to Boston for my wedding gown and trousseau.''

''Then when would you like to set the date?'' Clint said, the first glow of excitement fading.

''I should think by the end of next month, I can have everything ready.''

Clint nodded and grinned. ''I don't guess it's too long to ask a man to wait.''

Jessie raised her hand and caressed his craggy cheek. ''I hope not. I wouldn't want anything to hinder our plans.''

Clint captured her hand and brought it to his lips. ''I promise you nothing will.'' He smiled at her. ''Shall we tell our guests the good news?''

Jessie drew in a deep breath and braced herself to face the one guest who had already laid claim to her heart. She nodded. ''I don't see why not.''

''Where's your little lady?'' Slim asked, lounging back against the table at Brand's side.

Brand tossed the shot of whiskey down his throat and turned his cool silver gaze upon his friend. ''I could ask the same of you.''

Slim shrugged and raised a mug to his lips. He took a long sip of beer and then wiped his lips free of foam. ''Winnie's somewhere around here. I've managed to get her onto the dance floor twice tonight, but I don't know if I'm man enough to do it again. It's like draggin' a heifer to a brandin'. She don't want to go.''

''It seems my luck hasn't been much better. I managed one dance with Jessie before every man in the county decided it was his time to dance with her. Now she's up and disappeared.''

Slim's gaze swept over the gathering as he raised the mug to his lips once more and downed the last of its contents. "I don't see Ramsey anywhere, either."

Brand flashed Slim a look that boded ill. "I ought to go and find our Miss Nolan."

Slim tapped Brand on the arm and nodded toward the porch. Jessie stood next to Ramsey, her hand on his arm, her eyes sweeping the crowd until they found Brand. He couldn't read the look she gave him, but something in her face made his breath freeze in his throat. Tension coiling his insides into knots, he watched Ramsey raise a hand to silence the musicians. The word *No* rose to his lips even as Ramsey cleared his throat and opened his mouth to speak.

"Friends, I have an announcement to make. . . ."

All heads turned in Ramsey's direction. "Tonight Miss Nolan has honored me by accepting my proposal of marriage. And you're all invited to the wedding next month."

Brand felt the blood rush to his brain and a shield of red cover his eyes. He made to step forward to tell Ramsey to stop making an old fool of himself. Jessie wasn't going to marry him because she was going to become Mrs. Brand Stockton just as soon as he could get her away from this farce.

Slim's hand on Brand's arm stopped him. "Leave it be, Brand. She's made her decision. You can't do any-thin' now but make a fool of yourself."

Ramsey's announcement was like the keen blade of a knife twisting in his gut. Brand nodded, his nostrils flaring as he drew in an unsteady breath of air. Lips compressed and eyes the color of a stormy sky, he flashed Jessie a look of loathing before he turned and strode off into the night.

Jessie absently accepted everyone's congratulations, but all she could think about was Brand. She'd seen hurt, anger, and confusion mingle briefly in his eyes before he had cast her a venomous look and stalked off. Her heart cried out to go after him and tell him she didn't love Clint Ramsey. Yet reason held her, and she smiled warmly at each person who hugged her or shook her hand. She owed it to her parents and to her brothers to follow through with her plans. Once she had succeeded, she would have time to make Brand understand.

Edwina stood to one side as Clint's guests clustered around Jessie and her fiancé. Tears burned the backs of her lids while she watched Jessie accept their congratulations. She wished she could go to her young friend and tell her she was happy about the engagement, but she couldn't in all honesty say the words courtesy demanded. She just didn't like Clint Ramsey. In truth, he'd always been a gentleman in her presence, but every instinct she possessed warned her against the man. Now Edwina realized she should have told Jessie about her feelings. Had she done so, perhaps Jessie wouldn't have accepted his proposal without giving herself time to know the man better.

"It seems to me that we're the only ones here who ain't so happy about the comin' nuptials," Slim said softly at Edwina's side.

Edwina drew in a shuddering breath, and her features crumpled under the strain of trying to remain composed. Slim's compassion undermined her hauteur. Her lower lip quivered and she dabbed at her eyes with a lace-edged lawn handkerchief.

"I know I should be happy for Jessica, but . . ." Her words ebbed away, and she shook her head sadly before turning away. She strode into the shadows, silently giving way to her tears.

A callused hand came to rest on her shoulder. "But you love the girl like your own and don't want to see her make a mistake. Is that it?"

Edwina nodded and sniffed into her handkerchief. "I wish to God we had never come to this place. Jessica could have had any man she wanted in Boston, but no, she had to come back to Texas. Now she's going to marry a man who's twice her age and only the Lord knows what else. God, Kate would turn over in her grave if she knew Jessica had lost her mind."

"Winnie, we may not approve of her choice, but that doesn't mean she's lost her mind. Miss Jessie could love Ramsey," Slim said.

"My name is Edwina, as you well know. And I would thank you to remember it," Edwina said, drawing herself up. The nickname brought her to her senses. Disquieted by her lack of control, she raised her chin in the air and sniffed. "I'm sorry I have detained you, Mr. Johnson. I'm sure you would like to return to the men's refreshment table now. You seemed to have imbibed quite freely tonight. If you will excuse me."

Having regained a modicum of composure, Edwina stepped past Slim and made her way toward the crowd still surrounding Jessie and Clint. She couldn't believe Jessie loved Clint Ramsey. The girl had shown no signs of being in love with anyone except Brand Stockton. Only Stockton made Jessie's eyes light up when he came near. Edwina shook her head and looked closely at her young friend. No, Jessica Nolan didn't act or look like a woman in love. She couldn't hide her feelings from the woman who had watched her grow from a gangly-limbed girl into a beautiful woman. Edwina saw the tiny lines of tension fanning Jessie's eyes and the taut line of the girl's mouth. Yet it was the haunted, pained expression in her eyes that told Edwina there was far more to Jessie's acceptance of Clint's proposal than anyone knew. Relief and concern mingled as one, confusing Edwina even further as she made her way to Jessie's side.

Slim scratched his head as he watched Edwina walk away like a ship under full sail. He didn't know what he'd said or done to bring down that icy facade, but Winnie wore it like a badge of honor. For a few moments in time he'd managed to touch the woman beneath the barrier. He'd seen her pain and worry, until she realized she'd let him get too close. Slim shook his head. Miss Edwina Roilings could be a bitch, but the Winnie he'd glimpsed tonight was a woman who loved and hurt like everyone else. She needed someone to lean upon, someone to share the burdens of her life.

"Ah, Winnie. I would be that man if you'd just give me a chance." Sighing, Slim turned toward the refreshment table. A wry grin curled his lips as he refilled his mug with beer. He and Brand were a pair. Both had come here to do a job, and both had let themselves get hooked up with women who didn't give a fiddler's damn about them.

Slim gulped down the dark golden brew and wiped his mouth on his sleeve. After this job was finished, he was going to have to rethink things. He'd thought at one time his life was set. Now he wasn't at all sure if he wanted to continue roaming the countryside hunting bandits and savages. He wasn't getting any younger. Next year he'd be fifty-five. And oddly enough, he liked being settled down at Eden.

Chapter 13

Quietly Jessie pulled off her nightgown and tossed it to the foot of the bed. The coverlet was uncreased and drawn to its full length, the pillows undented, exactly as Edwina had plumped them the night before. Jessie glanced toward the chair where she'd spent most of the night. After pacing the room to outdistance her thoughts, she had curled up on the chair to await the dawn.

Fortunately last night Edwina had believed her excuse of a headache and had refrained from asking questions about her sudden betrothal to Clint. However, Jessie knew her reprieve would last only until Edwina awoke that morning. Winnie would not be satisfied until she knew why Jessie had decided to marry a man she didn't love.

Jessie pulled on her denims and shirt. Absently she braided her long hair and tied it with a ribbon before jerking on her boots. She had to escape before she was forced to face Edwina's badgering.

Jessie raised her chin defensively and narrowed her thick-lashed eyes. Blue fire glowed in their sapphire depths as she looked at her own reflection in the dressing table mirror. Last night she'd learned who had destroyed her family, and now no one was going to stop her plans for revenge.

During the long dark hours she had been assaulted by memories of that horror-filled night ten years ago until she was drained. By early morning she had begun to formulate her revenge upon Clint, and now, as dawn lightened the eastern sky, she knew exactly how she would bring him to his knees.

However, Jessie's emotions were too battered and raw to keep up the pretense for much longer. She needed time to strengthen her resolve and bolster her aching heart. The next few weeks would test her willpower to the limit.

Jessie picked up her gloves and slipped out of the house. She made her way to the barn and saddled her mount. She swung herself into the saddle, cast a brief glance at the bunkhouse where Brand slept, and then urged her mount in the direction of her family's cabin.

A pair of glittering, bloodshot silver eyes watched Jessie ride out. Lips tight, his face granite planes, Brand stepped out of the shadows. He hadn't been able to sleep a wink since he'd come back from the Lazy L. All through the long hours of the night he'd prowled about Eden, watching the light in Jessie's window, pondering the easiest way to throttle her. Yet even as he considered each option, he knew he could never hurt her, no matter how much he longed to put his hands about her slender neck and shake some sense into her brainless head. By the time he saw her ride out, he knew his only option was to ride away from Eden and never look back.

Brand strode into the barn and saddled his mount.

He would leave Eden, but not before he told Miss Jessica Nolan exactly what he thought of her and her plans to marry Clint Ramsey. Swinging himself into the saddle, he urged the Morgan in the direction Jessie had taken only moments before.

The sound of snapping twigs disturbed the morning stillness as Jessie maneuvered her horse through the underbrush toward the crumbling walls of the cabin. The gray sky was lightening to blue and the first rays of the sun streaked over the horizon, splashing her in golden light, as she slipped to the ground and tied her mount to the limb of a small tree. She tucked her gloves into her rear pocket and drew in a deep, bracing breath as she turned toward the decaying timbers and sagging roof.

Again the pain rose unbidden, tearing through her heart. Tears brimmed in her eyes as she made her way toward the door and stepped inside the shadowed interior. Her gaze moved over the cobwebbed corners, the leaf-strewn floor, the glassless windows, and up through the hole in the roof to the blue gray of the morning sky. Here the memories of what had once been a home filled with laughter and love, were far more poignant to recall.

She hadn't wanted to come back, but she knew this place would give her the strength required to set aside her love for Brand and to follow through with her plans to ruin Clint Ramsey. The sight of the rotting remains of her father's dreams rekindled her need to avenge her family. Clint Ramsey had cut her parents down in the prime of their lives, leaving her and her brothers to fend for themselves in a world prejudiced against those with the taint of Indian blood in their veins. She would not, could not, allow him to escape unscathed. He would keep his life, but she would make him suffer. Jessie stiffened her spine and her expression hardened. She would do what she had to do to keep the promise she and her brothers had made at their parents' graves.

Her thoughts upon Clint Ramsey's destruction, Jessie didn't hear the soft tread of footsteps approach the cabin.

"Damn you to hell, Jessica Nolan," Brand said.

At the low growl of Brand's voice, Jessie spun about, her hand going automatically to her pounding heart. As she looked into the silver ice of his eyes, the blood drained slowly from her face, leaving her ashen. There was no warmth within their glittering depths for her— only cold hostility. Jessie lowered her gaze and turned away. She didn't have to question his reason for damning her to hell. She already knew the answer.

"It seems you make a habit of sneaking up on me," Jessie said, her voice even, though her insides trembled with the need to throw herself at his feet and beg him to understand her actions. She squared her shoulders against his rage and waited for it to erupt.

"It seems we both have a way of sneaking things up on each other."

Jessie didn't answer but raised her chin and stared out into the golden morning. The muscles between her shoulder blades burned from the glare directed at her back. Her nerves screamed with tension at the sound of Brand's boots on the leaf-strewn floor. She felt him pause behind her and braced herself for the touch of his hands. Her mind demanded she be strong and not give way to the heart whimpering within her breast for his touch.

Brand stood looking down at the dark head tilted proudly in front of him. Again he was reminded of the first time he'd seen her in Paradise: so haughty, so determined, so independent.

God! How he wanted this woman. No matter how angry she made him, he craved her like an opiate. He ached with his need of her. He wanted to place his lips against the silken flesh of her throat and taste her skin as he wrapped his arms around her, covering her breasts with his hands, cupping them in his palms to feel their coral crests harden in response. Yet he kept his hands at his side, afraid to touch her. In his present state of mind he didn't trust himself to know exactly what would happen should he give way to his desire. His voice was gruff as he asked, "Can't answer me, can you?"

"I don't have to answer to you about my actions," Jessie said, ignoring the urge to turn and throw herself into his arms.

"Didn't it ever occur to you to have the decency to tell me you and Ramsey were getting married?"

Keeping her back to him, Jessie stepped away. "What did it matter whether you knew or not? Nothing would have changed between us."

Before Brand could stop himself, he reached out and captured Jessie's long braid. He drew her slowly back against him. His breath was hot against her throat as he said, "It would seem your love for me didn't last long up against Ramsey's wealth. But I have something he can't give you, Jessie, and you know it." He rubbed against her, his actions insulting. His words were low and laced with contempt as he continued. "Do you think you can find the same kind of pleasure in that old man's arms as you did in mine?''

"Let me go, Brand. I've made my decision and nothing you can say or do will change it.'' Jessie held her voice steady, her tone aloof, even as the pain of Brand's words ripped through her heart.

Brand's hands fell away. "God, you're a cold bitch.''

Jessie spun around to face him. "How dare you say such a thing to me!''

"I dare, Miss Nolan, because it's damned well true! A woman with a heart not made of stone wouldn't marry a man she didn't love. You're not much better than the women at Miss Molly's. But with them a man knows where he stands. They're honest about what they want. That's more than I can say about you.''

Jessie blinked to stay the tears that burned the backs of her lids, but she couldn't stay the pain his words created. She swallowed hard and moistened her lips as she asked, "How do you know I don't love Clint?''

"Because, damn you, you love me,'' Brand ground out between clenched teeth. Before Jessie could stop him, his hands clamped down on her shoulders and he drew her roughly against him. His mouth descended in a devastating, punishing kiss.

Jessie's heart soared at the touch of his lips against hers. A whimper of defeat escaped as a streak of passion seared through her, singeing every nerve in her body. She trembled from the force of it as her arms crept up around Brand's neck and she molded herself against his hard, sinewy length. Her mind fought a brave battle, but her heart rose in victory over the bloodied bodies of logic and intent. All thoughts of revenge fled before love's triumphant flag. It rippled and fluttered wildly in the winds of desire surging between herself and Brand.

As swiftly as he had taken her into his arms, Brand set her away from him. "Remember that when you're in Ramsey's bed," he growled before he turned and walked purposefully toward the lopsided door.

"Brand," Jessie said, his name the only word to pass the tightness in her throat.

Brand paused at the anguished whisper and looked back over his shoulder at the woman he loved. A muscle twitched in his jaw, and he felt the need to go back and beg Jessie to tell him she wouldn't marry Clint Ramsey. But even as his gaze rested on her beautiful face, he knew he couldn't obey the urgings of his heart. He'd not open himself up for more rejection, more hurt by this fickle-hearted woman.

"I'm leaving Eden, Jessie. I just came to tell you good-bye." The sardonic grin that tugged the corner of his mouth did not reach his silver eyes. "May you and Ramsey be happy. You deserve each other."

"Brand, you can't leave Eden," Jessie said, running after him as he strode into the sun-splashed morning.

Brand didn't slow his pace until he'd reached his mount. He swung up into the saddle and looked down at the woman staring at him with jeweled sapphire eyes. "It's time I moved on, Jessie. And we both know it. You don't need me anymore. You have Ramsey to fill your bed and take care of your ranch."

"Brand, you don't understand," Jessie said, clinging to his saddle. She couldn't let him ride out of her life, especially now that she knew Clint was responsible for destroying her family. She needed him.

Brand dislodged Jessie's fingers. "I understand enough."

"No. You don't," Jessie said.

Brand released a long breath and bent forward to look her in the eyes. "Then tell me what I don't understand, Jessie. Tell me you're not going to marry Clint Ramsey."

Jessie gulped back her tears and drew in a shuddering breath as she stepped away from Brand's mount. Her hands fell to her sides and she shook her head. "I can't tell you that. But you have to understand this is something I have to do. It has nothing to do with how I feel about you. Please don't leave Eden, I need you."

"You don't need me. You don't need anything except Ramsey's money." Brand jerked his horse about and kicked him in the sides. His battered heart couldn't take much more punishment. He had regained his emotions only to find how much it hurt to love. It would have been better had his heart remained untouched within him. It would have been far less painful to keep it frozen in the icy scars created by the war and the loss of his family.

"It's a debt I owe to my family," Jessie whispered helplessly to herself as she watched Brand ride out of her life. Slowly she turned and walked back into the cabin. Her legs refused to hold her upright any longer and she sank down amid the dry leaves. She drew her knees up to her chest and wrapped her arms about them. Her eyes burned, but no tears would come. It was to late for tears. Brand was gone. She drew in a deep breath and her expression hardened as she gave herself a sharp mental kick. She could stay here all day feeling sorry for herself, but it would gain her nothing. It would not bring Brand back, nor would it finish what she had set out to do. She had come here to reaffirm her hatred for Clint Ramsey and had found another heartbreak to lay at his door.

Jessie pushed herself to her feet and squared her shoulders. When her debt was settled with Ramsey, she could turn her attention to Brand. She would follow him to the ends of the earth if necessary to make him understand he alone possessed her heart and soul.

Jessie cast one last glance over the dilapidated cabin before turning to the door. The next time she came here, the debt she owed would be paid in full and she would be able to look toward the future.

Her attention centered on pulling on her gloves, Jessie stepped through the doorway. She didn't see the figure poised beside the door with arm upraised. Nor did she see the butt of the pistol descending toward her. It clipped her on the back of her head, sending her spiraling into the dark void of unconsciousness.

Brand strode into the bunkhouse and began stuffing his belongings into saddle bags. Slim, a bemused frown screwing up his lined face, watched his friend until Brand tied the leather thongs and swung the bags over his shoulder. "Looks like you intend on stayin' gone a spell."

"I'm pulling out," Brand said, heading toward the door.

Slim's eyes widened in surprise. "Just like that?"

Brand nodded. "I'm heading to Fort Smith to get federal permission to go into Indian territory after Fleming. I've wasted too much time here as it is."

"Don't you think you could have at least told me of our plans?"

"You're not coming with me this time. I need you to stay here," Brand said, staring out the door. He didn't add that he needed to be alone to come to terms with his emotions. Perhaps by the time he reached Fort Smith he'd know how to deal with his feelings for Jessie.

Slim's frown deepened. "We've been ridin' together for nearly fifteen years, Brand. It's my job as well as yours to go after Fleming."

"The captain put me in charge of this mission, Slim. And you'll be more valuable to me here at Eden."

"So you still think the girl is involved with Fleming?" Slim asked, wiping his hands on the front of his grease-stained apron.

"I don't know what to think of her anymore. I just know I have to get away from here before I do something I'll regret."

Slim took a red bandanna out of his back pocket and wiped the sweat from the back of his neck. He'd just finished feeding the crew a huge breakfast of steak, eggs, fried potatoes, and flapjacks with molasses, and the heat from the iron stove made the bunkhouse as hot as Hades. "So you're gonna ride off into Injun territory without me to back you up if you run into trouble up there? Damn it, Brand, you're gonna git yourself killed because of Jessica Nolan."

A muscle twitched in Brand's cheek as he turned his silver gaze upon his friend. "I can take care of myself without you, old man."

"Damn right you can when you got your mind on business. But I'm afraid you're thinkin' with a far lower part of your anatomy now and not your brain."

"I've never let a woman interfere with my duties before and I'm not now." Brand turned toward the door. "Keep your eyes open for anything unusual. I'll be back before the nuptials take place." He walked from the bunkhouse without looking back.

"Damn," Slim muttered in disgust as he watched Brand ride away.

Renegade caught Jessie before she sank to the dust at his feet. He lifted her limp body easily into his arms and carried her to her horse. Tying her across the saddle like a bag of flour, he retrieved his horse from the thick clump of underbrush that had hidden them while the girl and her lover argued.

Renegade swung into the saddle and glanced at his unconscious hostage. A thoughtful frown creased his brow and he shook his head. He couldn't figure it all out. From what he'd overheard, the girl intended to marry Clint Ramsey. But the rest of what he'd heard didn't make a whole hell of a lot of sense to him. Renegade shrugged. He'd let Wade figure it out when they got back to camp.

Renegade maneuvered the horses through the thicket of loblolly pine and north toward the camp Wade had set up near the Red River. His sun-darkened skin creased with tiny lines about his eyes as he squinted toward the horizon. Wade would be wondering what had happened to him. He should have returned to camp a couple of hours ago. He had sent Renegade to watch the ranch so they would know when it would be best to make a raid. He'd been on his way back to camp when he'd seen the girl ride out. His curiosity had gotten the better of him, and he'd followed her to the cabin. He'd just managed to hide his mount in the thicket when the man had ridden up. Curiosity gnawing great chunks out of him, he'd eased his way through the underbrush until he'd maneuvered himself beneath one of the broken windows, where he could overhear their conversation.

Renegade glanced once more toward the girl stretched across her horse. He didn't know how Wade would feel when he brought her back to camp, but from what he'd overheard, she was connected with Clint Ramsey. And that meant she was valuable. If they used their heads, they might not have to make a raid on the girl's ranch tonight. They could ransom her to Ramsey for enough money to build each of them a ranch in New Mexico or the Arizona Territory.

Renegade ran a callused hand down his scarred cheek and frowned. The only problem he saw was Wade's need for revenge. This was to be their last raid because Wade wouldn't leave the territory until the people who had bought his family's land had paid a high price. Tonight he planned to burn the barn and house, and then, while everyone was fighting the fire, they would round up the livestock and head north. When that was done they would sell the cattle and horses and head west to make a new life for themselves.

"Well, that was our plan until I kidnapped the girl," Renegade mused aloud to his horse. Again he rubbed his cheek. With luck Wade would see reason and they could be on their way west without burning the ranch the girl called Eden.

The willows along the Red obscured the camp from view. The moist earth silenced the sound of the horses' hooves as Renegade maneuvered them through the yellowish green jungle toward the outcropping of rock and earth that jutted out over the water. A narrow trail led down along the steep bank to the water's edge, where erosion had eaten away the earth, leaving a sandy-bottomed cave large enough for several men and horses beneath the outcropping. In rainy weather, when the river rose, the water filled the cave and gouged it out deeper. However, it had been weeks since the last rain-fall, and the sandy cave made a perfect camp for the rustlers.

Renegade's horse waded the last few feet to the sandy shore, where Wade stood watching him, rifle in hand.

"I expected you back near dawn. What took you so long?" Wade asked, setting aside the Winchester.

"I got a little sidetracked," Renegade said as he swung down from the saddle. He cocked his head toward the burden draped across the horse.

Wade frowned as he stepped around Renegade. "What in the hell. . . ?" he swore when he saw Jessie.

"It's a girl," Renegade answered as he led his horse into the cave and secured him alongside of Wade's mount.

"I can damn well see that," Wade said. "Is she dead?"

"Naw. I just tapped her a little too hard on the head, that's all."

"Damn, Renegade," Wade said, already busily un-tying the ropes, "why in the hell did you hit her? And why in the hell did you bring her here?"

"One question at a time," Renegade said, turning his attention to the pot of coffee brewing on the fire. He bent and poured himself a cup of the steaming liquid and then took a long sip before he looked once more at Wade. "To answer your first question, I hit her to keep her quiet. For the second, she's the girl who owns your pa's land. I saw her ride out at dawn and decided to follow her. And when I heard her and her man arguing over Clint Ramsey, I decided it might be profitable to us to bring her here.''

Wade lifted Jessie down and carried her to the bedroll he'd left lying near the entrance to the cave. He laid her down and gently felt through her hair for the lump left by Renegade's blow. He found it on the right side of her head: a swelling the size of a hen's egg. ''Damn, Renegade, it's a wonder she's still alive.''

''She's supposed to marry Ramsey,'' Renegade said, ignoring the censure in Wade's voice.

Wade's head snapped up. ''You said she was arguing with her man about Ramsey. You mean she's not married to the man we saw her with?''

Renegade nodded. ''As far as I can tell, she's supposed to marry Clint Ramsey. The man didn't like the idea too much and left her.''

Wade sat back on his heels and looked down at the dark-haired woman. She had bought his family's property, and Clint Ramsey thought he'd get it by marrying her. Old demons rising from his past, Wade's expression hardened. He smiled coldly. ''Perhaps you were right to bring her here. I might be able to kill two birds with one stone.''

A chill rippled up Renegade's spine. ''I didn't bring her here for you to kill, Wade.''

The gaze Wade turned on his friend looked like black glass. ''I don't intend to kill her. But Ramsey might not want her when I'm through.''

''Let it be, Wade. You now have Mercy to think about. You don't want to leave here with the girl on your conscience. So far we've never actually harmed any innocent people. And I don't want us to begin now, when we've got a chance to start over.''

Wade released a long breath as he looked back down at the unconscious girl. The hatred that had been ingrained through the years had nearly made him forget his promise to himself and Mercy. He nodded. ''You're right. I can't let the past ruin the future. I've been given a second chance at life with Mercy.''

Renegade smiled. ''That's what I thought. And I thought since Ramsey intends to marry this girl, he might be willing to pay to get her back.''

Jessie's moan halted further conversation between the two men. Her lashes slowly flickered open, and she blinked several times to clear her vision before she realized the darkness before her eyes were the muted gray tones of earth and stone. She moistened her dry lips and sought to orient herself. She turned her head to the side to stare up into the face she hadn't seen in nearly ten years, but the sharp pain that careened through her skull made her gasp back her brother's name.

Wade smiled down at her. ''You don't have to be afraid. We won't hurt you.''

''Wade?'' Jessie finally managed as the pain in her head eased.

Wade frowned and glanced uneasily at Renegade before he said, ''I don't know any Wade.''

Jessie squeezed her eyes closed and raised a hand to her injured head. Confusion swept over her. The man was the image of her brother, or was he? Was she seeing things that didn't exist? Had the blow to her head addled her senses? Drawing in a deep breath, she looked once more at Wade. Her eyes hadn't been playing tricks on her a moment earlier. The man had to be her brother and none other. "Wade, don't you know me?"

Wade's frown deepened as he peered down into the puzzled dark sapphire eyes. A long-lost memory resurfaced, and the years seemed to drop away as he looked at the girl before him. The image of his mother's face rose up in his mind, and his breath left him in a *whoosh* as he realized the identity of the beautiful woman.

"Jessie?" he breathed, unable to believe what his eyes told him.

A tremulous smile tugged the corners of Jessie's lips as a surge of relief swept over her. She had finally found her brother.

"Wade? I can't believe it's really you!" Jessie said, and watched his lips curl into a grin. "Oh, Wade!" Ignoring the searing agony that banded her skull, Jessie threw herself into her brother's arms. They sat on the sandy floor of the river cave, laughing, hugging, their faces glistening with tears of joy, until Renegade interrupted their reunion.

"It would seem you two know each other," Renegade said.

Jessie and Wade looked at the scar-faced man hunkered down by the fire and laughed. "Jessie is my sister," Wade replied, draping a loving arm about the woman at his side. "She's grown quite a bit since the last time I saw her, but she has Mother's eyes. And I'd know them anywhere."

Renegade stood and dusted off his britches. "Then I guess you two can stand some time alone to get reacquainted. I'll just mosey on down the river a ways and see if I can catch a fish or two for our supper."

Wade stuck out his hand and grabbed Renegade's. He

shook it vigorously. "You don't realize what you've done for me. I never dreamed I'd ever see Jessie again."

"I'm glad it worked out this way, but it wasn't my intention to reunite brother and sister, as you'll recall. I was thinking of the money from Ramsey."

The smile faded from Wade's face. He nodded but didn't look at Jessie again until Renegade had left them. His smile was reserved as he settled himself once more at her side. "Jessie, it's been so long and so much has happened since I left Boston that I don't know where to begin."

"You could tell me why you never wrote to me, Wade. Until I came back to Texas and saw a Wanted poster at the jail, I thought you were dead."

Wade looked up at the ceiling and then down at the sandy floor before his eyes once more came to rest upon Jessie's pale features. His face was grim as he released a long breath. "I wanted to write, but I thought it best for you to believe me dead."

"But why? You're my brother and I missed you."

"Jessie, believe me when I say what I did was best for all concerned. The life I've led since running away from Kate's isn't something to be proud of. I've done everything necessary to survive, and now I'm wanted by the law for rustling."

"But you could have come back to Kate's. You wouldn't have had to steal to make a living. And you would have been a rich man when she died," Jessie said, trying desperately to understand Wade's reasoning for abandoning her all those years.

Wade looked toward the river, his chiseled profile like an ancient god's molded from granite. "Jessie, I didn't fit in. The people in Boston don't like little half-breed boys around their kids any more than Texans do. We may look as white as the rest of them, but it's our blood they hate. It's easy to blame us for all the wrongs both sides have committed against each other.''

''But people in Boston always treated me fairly,'' Jessie said. Until that moment she'd never realized Wade had suffered in Boston because of their Cherokee heritage. ''I always had friends. Kate saw to that.''

Wade nodded grimly. ''Kate would have seen that I had friends as well, if she'd known how people treated me. But I was older and I didn't tell her how her so-called friends reacted when they had daughters of a similar age who I might taint with my attentions. I was quickly put in my place. I could come to their houses with Kate, eat at their tables with Kate, but without Kate I wasn't welcome.''

Jessie stared at her brother. She knew of the prejudice against her Indian blood in Texas, but she'd never known it existed back east. She'd naively accepted so much, though now, as she thought back, she realized the prejudice had been there all along. After Kate's death, the invitations to the parties and dances had dwindled. Only a few of her overly ambitious suitors had come to call at all. She'd been so busy making her plans for Texas that she'd believed her friends were giving her time to mourn. Now she realized even the boys who had escorted her to all the season's social events had been hand-picked by Kate. At the time she hadn't cared enough about the opposite sex to wonder why Kate had to choose her dates. Now she understood. The half-breed girl just wasn't quite proper enough to fit into society, yet her adopted mother possessed so much wealth, she couldn't be snubbed completely.

"I didn't realize," Jessie whispered.

Wade placed a comforting hand on Jessie's shoulder and gave it a reassuring squeeze. "You were only a child. And I didn't want you to know. Kate was rearing you to be a lady, and I thought things would go differently for you. Since the day you were born, you were always beautiful, and I hoped your looks would make people forget about our Indian heritage."

Jessie raised her chin in the air. "I'm proud of our heritage. And we owe it to Mother's memory to hold our heads up and make people accept us for who we are."

"You're right, but that's not the way life is out here or anywhere else."

Jessie looked away from Wade. She knew he spoke the truth. Attitudes were slowly changing, but there were far too many people who were still hostile toward anyone possessing Indian blood. To ensure Eden's success for the time being as well as her quest for her parents' murderer, she'd kept her real identity a secret. She nodded. "I know you're right, and I've gone under Kate's name since my return. But the time is nearing when everyone will know I am Sarah and Earnest Fleming's daughter."

Wade's frown deepened as he recalled what Renegade had said about Clint Ramsey. "Jessie, Renegade said you were going to marry Clint Ramsey."

Jessie looked her brother directly in the eyes, blue sapphire clashing with shining indigo. She didn't want to tell him the truth about Clint. He was already wanted by the law, and she couldn't risk losing him again. No matter how much she would like to see Clint Ramsey dead, she couldn't allow Wade to end his miserable life.

Wade would then be wanted for murder and he'd be hunted down like an animal and hanged. No, Jessie realized. Revenge for her parents still lay upon her shoulders. She wouldn't lose all her family to Clint Ramsey. At last, she answered, "That is my intention."

"Damn it, Jessie. You can't do it," Wade said, coming to his feet. "You don't know the man. The way he treated Pa and Ma, he could be one of the men responsible for their death."

Jessie couldn't meet Wade's eyes. "Do you have proof of his guilt?"

Wade ran a hand through his dark, shoulder-length hair. "No. I know he hated Pa for marrying an Indian, but that's all. Had I proof, he would have been dead long ago."

"Then I intend to follow through with my plans," Jessie said, releasing a breath of relief.

"Jessie, the man is no good. He'll never marry you when he learns who you really are."

"That may be so, but before the wedding takes place he will know my real name. I won't go into any marriage with a husband who can't accept my family." Jessie's thoughts were no longer on Clint Ramsey, but on the man who had left her that morning: Brand Stockton.

"Damn it, Jessie. I'm your brother and I forbid you to marry Ramsey."

Jessie came to her feet and glared at Wade. "You are certainly taking a lot upon yourself for someone who didn't let me know he was alive for nearly ten years. You should realize I don't need your permission. I can marry anyone I please."

Wade ran a hand over his face and shook his head.

"Jessie, for God's sake and our own—let's not argue about this. Just say you'll not marry Ramsey."

"I will not tell you that, Wade. I love you, but you are going to have to believe I can lead my own life. I know what I'm doing." Jessie's voice cracked as Brand's image rose in her mind. "I've already given up too much to turn back now. At the end of next month I will walk down the aisle of Paradise's church to meet Clint Ramsey."

"Jessie, I promise you, if you marry Ramsey, he won't live to come to your bed on your wedding night," Wade said, his face set with resolve.

"You won't have to kill him, Wade," Jessie said.

Taking her answer to mean she agreed to cancel her wedding plans with Ramsey, Wade crossed to his sister's side and swung her into his arms. "God, it's good to be with you again! I can't wait until you meet Mercy. Jessie, she's wonderful."

Hands on Wade's wide shoulders, her feet dangling in the air, Jessie looked down at her brother. "You're married?"

"Not yet, but I soon will be. Just as soon as we get out west I'm going to make Mercy Mrs. Wade Fleming, or whatever name I choose." Wade lowered Jessie to her feet.

"What do you mean?" Jessie asked anxiously.

Tenderly Wade cupped Jessie's cheek in the palm of his hand. "Sis, you know I'm wanted by the law here. My only hope to have a chance at a normal life is to move farther west, where no one will know us. And just as soon as I can get enough money, we're heading out. I love Mercy, and I won't ask her to live an outlaw's life with me. She deserves better."

"But can't you just change your name and stay here? I don't want to lose you now that I've finally found you."

Wade shook his head sadly. "My face is plastered on posters all over north Texas. We must go. We have no other choice."

Jessie nodded. "I understand, but you will keep in touch."

"Of course. Since I've found you again, I don't want to lose you, either. Someday my children will need their aunt Jessie to spoil and love them."

"Then you'll let me help you. Kate left me all of her wealth, and I have far more than I can ever spend. You are her son as much as I'm her daughter, and it's only right I share my inheritance with you. She would want it that way."

"God, Jessie. You're a blessing in more ways than one. I'll gladly accept your offer. It'll mean Mercy and I can get started on our future much sooner than we thought."

"Thank you," Jessie whispered, and hugged him close.

"I'm the one who should be thanking you. You've reclaimed our heritage and are giving me a chance to live a normal life again."

Jessie cocked her head and looked at her brother. An impish smile touched her lips. "You mean the life of an outlaw isn't filled with adventure and gold, like it says in the penny novels we read back east?"

Wade gave a snort of disgust. "If you mean living like an animal in a hole in the side of a mountain with men who'd just as soon cut your throat as to look at you, then it might be. As for all the adventure and gold

. . . adventure is sleeping out in the cold under a thin blanket or always sitting with your back to the wall to keep someone from shooting you for the reward on your head. And there's usually only enough gold to buy a bottle of whiskey and some supplies to keep you from starving to death. No, Jessie. My life isn't like one of the penny dreadfuls the well-fed easterners read in their comfortable houses.''

Jessie hugged Wade tighter about the waist and buried her face against his chest. ''I didn't realize.''

He patted her comfortingly on the back. ''It's not your fault. I chose the life I've led, but now I'm ready for a change. I'm wanting to settle down and raise another batch of Flemings.''

''Will you be safe until I can get the lawyers in Boston to transfer all my holdings to the bank in Paradise?''

''How long will it take?''

''I should have everything completed by the end of next month.''

''We hadn't figured on pulling out before then,'' Wade said.

''Will I find you here?'' Jessie asked, glancing about the cave.

''No. Send word to me at Sam Starr's place on the Canadian River. Our hideout is not too far from there in the San Bois Mountains. That's where Mercy is waiting for me now.''

''Is she safe there?'' Jessie asked, wondering at her brother leaving the woman he loved alone in the mountains.

''Mercy is safe. I've taught her how to use a rifle, and I assure you she'll take care of herself.'' Wade chuckled. During the past weeks Mercy had come out of her protective shell. She was no longer the meek, frightened rabbit. She was a woman in full bloom, a woman sure of herself. There were times when he glimpsed the Mercy he'd found in the Comanchero camp, but those times were becoming fewer and farther between. Wade smiled to himself. Soon he would also know her in all the ways a man could know the woman he loved. . . .

At the look on her brother's face, Jessie smiled sadly. How she wished Brand's face had held such a look for her. But she didn't mention the man she loved to her brother. There would be time for that later. "I'm looking forward to meeting this woman who has tamed the savage outlaw."

The smile faded from Wade's face. "Never call me savage, Jessie."

"I'm sorry. I didn't mean anything by it. I understand your feelings, but you have to try to put your hatred aside. Don't let the past taint your future with Mercy, or you'll regret it someday."

Wade caressed Jessie's cheek. "It isn't going to be easy, but I'll try."

"It's for more than just us, Wade. It's for our children."

"So wise and so beautiful," Wade said, and nodded in agreement.

Jessie hugged him close. If all went as she planned, by the end of the next month she too would be able to put the past behind her.

Her mind on Wade, Jessie didn't see Clint's horse tied to the hitching post in front of the house until it was nearly too late to avoid meeting him. Her head throbbing from her earlier encounter with the man called Renegade, she was in no mood to pretend any great affection for her enemy. Casting a quick glance in all directions, she quickly urged her horse toward the barn. Perhaps she could hide there until Clint decided to leave.

The shadowy interior of the barn was a welcome relief after the long hours she'd spent in the saddle. The afternoon sun had pounded down upon her unmercifully, giving no quarter for her aching head. Dismounting, Jessie led her horse into a stall and loosed the cinch. She dragged the saddle from the animal's back and lugged it into the tack room. While she was hiding from Clint, she would use the time to rub down her mount. There was no reason both of them should suffer because she didn't want to face Clint Ramsey.

"I thought I saw you ride in here," Clint said, coming up behind Jessie.

She stiffened at the sound of his voice and shut her eyes as she drew in a slow, resigned breath. Forcing a pleasant smile to her lips, she readied herself to face her enemy.

Before she could move, however, Clint slipped his arms about her waist and drew her back against him. His warm breath stirred the silken strands of dark hair that had slipped free of her braid and clung enticingly against the slender column of her throat. He brushed his lips against her soft skin as he murmured huskily, "God, Jessie. You feel so good." He spread his hands across her flat belly, aligning her even closer to his body, and drew in a ragged breath. "You don't know how long I've waited for you to come into my life. It's been years since I've felt so alive, and it's all because of you.

And I promise, you'll never regret marrying me. Once the vows are spoken, I'll show you what it's like to be loved by a man.''

Jessie couldn't hide her grimace of disgust. She squeezed her eyes closed and swallowed the bile of revulsion that rose in her throat at the images Clint's words roused in her mind. The very thought of bedding the man who had brutally killed her parents made her stomach churn, and she fought to restrain the urge to vomit. Her nostrils flared as she drew in several deep breaths. For now, she knew, she had to hide her feelings. Clint must never suspect that they were anything but what he believed, until it was too late.

Seeking to regain control of her composure, yet needing to get as far away from the monster as possible, Jessie moistened her lips and eased out of Clint's embrace. She plastered a smile on her face as she turned to look up at him and said honestly, ''Clint, I know I'll never regret marrying you. I've known that since the moment I accepted your proposal. And you don't know how many years I've waited for you to come into my life.''

''Ah, my beautiful Jessie,'' Clint said. Taking a step closer, he raised a hand and brushed his knuckles down the line of her cheek. ''I know it's proper for us to wait until our wedding night, but it's damned hard to when you're so sweet.''

Jessie cast a nervous glance at the tack room door, judging the distance for flight if it became necessary to escape Clint's ardor.

Seeing the uncertainty on her face and the direction of her gaze, Clint chuckled and shook his head. ''There's nothing for you to fear, sweetness. I know you're a decent young woman who wouldn't allow a man who wasn't your husband to take liberties. And I respect your maidenly feelings; I'll not press my suit. We will be together soon enough.''

Jessie felt her cheeks heat, and she lowered her lashes to hide a look of guilt. Fortunately she was the only one to know exactly how much she lacked maidenly sensibilities when it came to the man who set her blood on fire and made her heart ache with love. But that man was now gone, and she was left with making Clint Ramsey pay for destroying her family.

Mistaking her blush for modesty, Clint chuckled again and draped an arm comfortingly about Jessie's shoulders. ''Enough of this talk. We'll have all the time in the world to discuss our feelings when we're married. Now give me a kiss and I'll be on my way.''

The muscles in Jessie's throat worked as she swallowed once more against her rising revulsion. Yet she obediently draped her arms about Clint's neck and kissed him. His arms went about her possessively, pressing her once more against his muscular body. Unable to control the shiver of disgust that raced over her, Jessie pushed herself out of Clint's arms.

Again arrogantly misconstruing her reaction to his touch, Clint smiled. ''Sweetness, our time will come. Just be patient.'' He brushed his lips against her brow and walked from the barn, leaving Jessie sick to her stomach.

Edwina met her at the door, looked her up and down, and firmed her lips into a narrow line as she braced her hands on her hips. ''Jessica, I've tried to mind my own business about your relationship with Mr. Ramsey, but from the way you look, it's time I spoke my mind. I know you don't love that man, so why on earth are you so determined to marry him?''

The dull ache now a pounding pain in her temples, Jessie's composure—already strained by the past few minutes and the events earlier in the day—snapped. She turned on Edwina, her blue eyes sparking fire. ''If I want your opinion, I will ask for it. I've already told you I intend to marry Clint Ramsey, and I wish to God you'd accept it!''

''Jessica, what's wrong?'' Edwina said, noting the look of pain that flickered over Jessie's face as she absently rubbed at her temples. ''Are you ill?''

Jessie released a long breath and shook her head. A rueful grin curled up one corner of her mouth. ''If being ill means I have one hell of a headache from being bashed over the head and knocked unconscious, yes, I'm ill, Edwina.''

''What? But how? Who?'' Edwina sputtered as Jessie slumped on a chair and covered her face with her hands.

''It's a long story,'' Jessie said. She leaned back and looked up at her friend. Again she shook her head. ''But I can see I won't get any rest until I tell you.''

Edwina, her eyes wide with worry, nodded.

''I found Wade today,'' Jessie began, and watched Edwina's eyes widen even farther as her friend sank onto a chair.

Jessie smiled. She could now reveal to Edwina a small part of her plans for the future.

Chapter 14

Jessie neatly rearranged the plaid skirt of her gown and folded her hands primly in her lap while she awaited the bank president, Mr. Langtree. A smile touched her lips as she peered at the leather satchel on the floor beside her chair. Within it lay most of her wealth. As directed, her lawyer, Abrams Smith, had transferred all her capital to Paradise.

Jessie's smile deepened as she imagined the look on Mr. Langtree's face when he opened the bag. He'd be as shocked as Edwina had been when she'd learned of Jessie's orders to her lawyer in Boston. She'd demanded to know why Jessie was taking all her money out of the bank Kate's family had trusted to handle their affairs for so many years. Jessie had reluctantly explained her sudden need for the large sum, using her intentions to help Wade as an excuse. Fortunately Edwina had understood and had asked no further questions. She would have been appalled had she learned of the staggering amount Jessie had requested the lawyer to send to her.

Jessie released a long breath, and her expression hardened. Her gloved hands balled into fists and her lips thinned into a narrow, ungiving line. Everything was nearly in place for the final act of the game she'd been playing. It hadn't been an easy ruse to perpetrate, yet it had worked to keep her mind on business and away from thoughts of Brand. Oddly, Clint had also helped in his own way. He had turned into an ardent suitor who showered her with his attention every day. Only during the long, lonely hours of the night did she have time to think of the man she loved.

During the past weeks it had taken every ounce of willpower she could muster not to reveal her hatred of Clint Ramsey. Her feelings, so explosively near the surface, were like a bin of wet corn in hot weather. They fermented, growing stronger and more virulent with each passing day. And the only thing that had sustained her was the knowledge that she didn't have much longer to wait until Clint was at her mercy.

"Miss Nolan," Mr. Langtree said, closing the frosted-glass door behind him and drawing Jessie away from her reverie. "It's good to see you. How may I be of service today?"

Jessie smiled sweetly at the roly-poly man. "Mr. Langtree, I have some property I wish you to purchase for me."

Langtree leaned back against his desk, his grin deepening. "More property? Miss Nolan, when you and Clint marry, you'll own nearly all of north Texas."

Jessie nodded innocently. "I know we will have extensive holdings, but I would like to purchase a few more tracts as a surprise for my husband on our wedding day."

Langtree gave an envious shake of his head and moved around his desk to the heavily padded chair. Settling his bulk on it, he bent forward, clasping his pudgy hands in front of him on the desk. "What property do you have in mind?"

Jessie opened the satchel and took out the map of the land in the area. She unfolded it carefully in front of Langtree and pointed to the acreage surrounding the Lazy L. Langtree's eyes widened.

"Miss Nolan, you want to buy all of that property?"

Jessie nodded. "Can you arrange it?"

Langtree's breath whistled through his teeth as he leaned back on his chair and looked at her. He ran a hand thoughtfully over one smooth cheek. "It won't be easy, nor will it be cheap. You're wanting some of the best grazing land around the Lazy L and Eden as well as all the rights to the water."

"Please say you'll help me, Mr. Langtree." Jessie lifted the satchel onto the desk in front of him and spilled out its contents.

Langtree gaped at the huge pile of bills. He'd be damned! Clint Ramsey's luck never seemed to run out. Any man would feel proud to marry a beautiful woman like Jessica Nolan without her having a cent to her name. But that bastard, who already owned the largest spread west of Fort Worth, had found a woman who wanted to make him richer than he already was. It wasn't fair, Langtree thought, but he didn't voice his feeling to Jessie. He plastered another grin on his pudgy face. "It would seem you've come prepared for bear, Miss Nolan. Clint's a lucky man."

"Then you will help me purchase the land?"

Langtree nodded. "Of course. How could I come to your wedding knowing I was responsible for spoiling Clint's wedding gift from you?"

"I would like the land deeds made out to the Redman's Cattle Company for the moment. I don't want Clint to know who has been buying up the land until I show him the deeds on our wedding day.''

''It shouldn't be any problem to put it under the name. Quite a few large breeding companies use other names when they buy land. It helps keep the price down.''

Jessie again gave Langtree one of her most charming smiles. ''Then you will keep my secret as well?''

Langtree raised a hand and laid it over his heart. ''You have my word upon it. Clint would have to skin me alive to get the information out of me.'' He chuckled and realized the man would do exactly that should he suspect who was behind the purchases. ''I can't wait to see his face. He's going to be dumbfounded when you present him with the deeds.''

''I can't wait to see his face either,'' Jessie said, her smile deepening with satisfaction. She visualized the noose slowly tightening about Clint's neck. She came to her feet and took several large-numbered bills from the pile on the desk. She extended the bills to Mr. Langtree. ''I hope this will show a measure of my gratitude for all your help.''

''You've always been more than generous, Miss Nolan.'' Langtree said, smiling his pleasure at the hefty commission she'd just placed in his hand. ''Should there be anything else you require, please feel free to see me any time.''

''I will keep it in mind. Now if you will excuse me, I need to stop by the post office to see if my wedding gown has arrived.''

''Of course. I know how busy you must be. Maybelle and I are looking forward to attending. And we wish you and Clint every happiness.''

"Thank you, Mr. Langtree," Jessie said, and left him staring at the pile of money on his desk. She stepped onto the planked sidewalk and turned toward the general store. The post office was located in one small caged corner of the building.

"Jessica," Clint said, taking her arm. "I was just coming to look for you. I stopped by Eden to see if you wanted to drive into town with me. Miss Roilings said you had several errands in Paradise, so I thought I'd join you and we could ride back to Eden together."

Jessie forced a smile to her lips. "I would love to have you join me, but I'm afraid you can't accompany me on my errands. They concern our wedding and I want everything to be a surprise for you."

Clint shrugged and smiled like a small boy awaiting a treat. "All right. You go about your business. I won't tag along and chance ruining your surprise. Anyway, I need to see if Langtree has had any word from Austin about those damned Rangers. They were supposed to have been up here a couple of months ago to get rid of Fleming and his gang. But we haven't seen hide nor hair of them."

"You mean you've called in the Texas Rangers?" Jessie asked, her heart thumping uncomfortably against her ribs. It was one thing to have the local sheriff and the ranchers after you, but another entirely when the Texas Rangers were involved. Even in Boston she had heard wild tales about their exploits. They didn't give up until they got their man, alive or dead. A chill of trepidation raced up her spine.

"We asked the governor several months ago to send in the Rangers to take care of the rustlers. But as far as we know they've never shown up in Paradise."

"You will let me know what you learn, won't you?" Jessie asked.

"Of course. You forget that we will soon be partners in more ways than one. And what you lose, so do I," Clint said, and cast a surreptitious glance about. Seeing no one watching, he quickly brushed his lips against Jessie's brow. "I will see you this evening, Miss Nolan."

Jessie's stomach churned at his touch as she forced another smile to her lips. "I will be looking forward to it, Mr. Ramsey." Before he could say more, she turned and made her way toward the general store. Edwina had given her a list of supplies to purchase, but there was one other item she intended to order today that no one would know about until it arrived from back east.

Another notch slipped on the rope about Clint's neck as Jessie opened the door and stepped inside the store. The bell tinkled overhead as she turned toward the post office, where the store clerk was sorting letters behind the iron-barred window.

"Did I have any packages arrive today, Mr. Miller?"

"Yes, ma'am. It's come all the way from Boston," the clerk said, lifting the brown paper package.

Jessie smiled. "It's my wedding dress."

"I suspected as much from the fancy name on the return address," the clerk said, and grinned. "Will there by anything else, Miss Nolan?"

"Yes, I need the things on this list, and I want to mail this." Jessie placed the letter on the counter and held her breath. Should he read the address, she knew that before the day was done the entire town would know what she intended.

The store clerk nodded and postmarked the envelope

without a glance at the address. Jessie breathed a sigh of relief. She'd dreaded the prospect of trying to find a reasonable explanation for her writing to a company that sold barbed wire. Nor did she like the thought of the reactions she'd receive once it was learned. In the past four years fencing grazing lands had turned neighbor against neighbor and had caused range wars that had magnified the hatred for barbed wire.

"I'll see to that list now," the clerk said, more intent upon making a profit than serving the U.S. government as mail clerk.

"Thank you, Mr. Miller," Jessie said, and handed him Edwina's list. She glanced back at the postal cubicle, where her letter had been put in a bag with others headed out on the next stage east. Everything was now in motion. When Langtree purchased the land and when the barbed wire arrived, she would have her revenge upon Clint Ramsey.

Lifting the package that contained her wedding gown, Jessie smiled. She had sent detailed instructions as well as drawings to her dressmaker in Boston for her gown. It would ensure that no one in Paradise would ever forget the day Clint Ramsey stood at the altar in the small church at the end of town.

Jessie's lips twitched, and she had to suppress the urge to laugh aloud and startle poor Mr. Miller. Her gown would be far different from anything the good citizens of Paradise had ever seen.

Sitting on one of the high-backed rockers, Jessie heard the approach of Clint's mount and braced herself for her next encounter with the enemy. Her fingers curled about the wooden chair arms as she watched him dismount and tie the reins to the hitching post. Every evening for the past month he had been at her side, making plans for their future. She had listened politely, and he'd believed she was as interested in seeing Eden and the Lazy L merged into one large spread as he was. However, all the time he talked, she consoled herself with her own plans.

Jessie watched Clint stride up the walk and readied herself to plaster another welcoming smile upon her lips. However, the expression on Clint's face forestalled the gesture. His pale eyes glowed, and his skin was flushed a dull, angry red. He carried a piece of paper clutched in one gloved hand.

"Where's Stockton?" he asked without preamble.

"You mean Brand?" Jessie asked, surprised by the question yet slightly apprehensive. The thought flitted through her mind that somehow Clint had found out about her relationship with her foreman.

"Damn right. I've a bone to pick with him." Clint's tone didn't soften.

"What's the matter?" Jessie asked, her voice shaky.

"This is what's the matter," Clint growled, and thrust the piece of paper at her.

Jessie forced her hand to remain steady as she unfolded the telegram and read. Her eyes widened in shock and she looked back to Clint. "Brand's a Texas Ranger? That can't be. He worked for me."

"Damned right. He snuck in here just as pretty as you please without letting anyone know who he was or what he was up to. I had to get the truth from the governor himself."

Jessie looked once more at the paper in her hand and shook her head, still unable to believe what she had read. "Surely there's some mistake. Brand Stockton couldn't be a Texas Ranger. What reason would he have for working here?"

"I suspect he thought one of the ranchers in the area was in cahoots with Fleming and his gang."

Jessie's head snapped up. "What do you mean?"

"Hell, Jessica. The way Fleming has managed to escape into Indian territory without being caught makes anyone wonder if he hasn't had help. He's been far too lucky."

Jessie paled, drawing a steadying breath and feigning bewilderment. "Then why would Brand come to work for me? I know nothing about the Fleming gang. Surely he doesn't suspect me of helping them?"

The anger seemed to drain from Clint. He shook his head, and a grin curled his lips. "Of course not. You're a lady. We all know you wouldn't have anything to do with a half-breed rustler. He took the job you offered because it was the only way he could stay around these parts without drawing too much attention to himself."

Anger began to prickle a hot path along Jessie's nerves as memories of her conversations with Brand resurfaced. His concern about the rustlers, the offhand remarks, all the times he'd appeared when she didn't know he was anywhere around, the time she'd lost her way to Indian territory—the time he'd made love to her—he hadn't been following just to give her protection. He had hoped she'd lead him to Wade.

Everything began to fall into place, and she realized he had used her from the beginning. No matter what Clint said, Brand had suspected her of being in league with Wade from the first day he'd arrived at Eden.

"Brand Stockton doesn't work here anymore. He left several weeks ago," Jessie said, striving to sound calm.

"Jessica, I hope this hasn't upset you," Clint said, noting her pallor.

Jessie shook her head. "No, I'm not upset. I should feel grateful I had a Texas Ranger guarding Eden. However, his presence didn't stop the rustlers from stealing my stock, did it?"

"It would seem Stockton didn't accomplish anything while he was here. And I intend to speak with the governor about his methods. The ranchers in the area deserve to know what's going on under their noses. Working together, we might have been able to catch Fleming."

Jessie looked away from Clint. She couldn't tell him that Brand had accomplished far more at Eden than he knew. He had made her into a woman. He also had succeeded in making her love him, no matter how hard she tried to wipe him out of her heart and mind. Jessie's anger faded. She couldn't condemn Brand for keeping his identity from her. She had done the same with him. She had allowed herself to fall in love with the mysterious stranger who had ridden into her life on an ebony Morgan. And even now, knowing the truth about him and the danger he represented to her brother, she couldn't stop the way she felt.

Her emotions in turmoil, Jessie looked at Clint and wondered if she would ever find a man she could completely trust. The two men in her life had both turned out to be something other than she'd first thought. Yet again, she herself wasn't guilt free. Soon everyone in Paradise would learn she wasn't what they believed her to be. Unable to bear Clint's company a moment longer, she came to her feet and raised a hand to her temple. "I hope you will forgive me, Clint. I'm afraid I've suddenly developed a headache."

"I understand," Clint said solicitously. "This has all been too much of a surprise for you. It's hard to learn the man you've trusted has lied to you."

Jessie nodded, for the first time in full agreement with Clint Ramsey.

"Then I'll bid you good night. I will stop by tomorrow to see how you are feeling. We can't let you get sick this close to the wedding." Clint brushed his lips against her brow and left her standing on the porch.

Jessie remained where he'd left her until he rode out of sight, then she lifted her skirt and stalked down the steps. She was determined to get some answers, and Slim Johnson would be the the man to give them to her. She was also so hungry for news of Brand, she'd use any excuse to find out about him.

The heavy scent of fried steak and potatoes hovered in the bunkhouse air as she stepped through the door to find Slim up to his elbows in flour, mixing a batch of sourdough biscuits for the men's breakfast the next morning.

A look of surprise flickered over his face, but he quickly hid his feelings by turning his attention back to the work at hand. "What can I do for you, Miss Nolan?"

Jessie glanced at the table, where several of the men sat playing poker. "Would you mind if I spoke with Mr. Johnson in private?"

The men cast a curious look at Slim, tossed their cards on the table, and then shoved back their chairs. Within moments the bunkhouse was empty.

"What's so important that we have to discuss it in private?" Slim asked, scraping the gluelike dough from his hands.

"We need to talk about Brand," Jessie said, her tone brooking no argument.

"What's to talk about? He's gone," Slim answered with a shrug as he crossed to the dry sink to wash his hands.

Jessie's eyes sparkled with ire. "I think you know there is far more to discuss than that, Mr. Johnson. I've just been informed that he is a Texas Ranger working undercover to capture the Fleming gang."

Slim stiffened visibly and slowly turned his head to look at Jessie fully for the first time. "Who told you such nonsense?"

"There is no longer a reason to lie, Mr. Johnson. I know it's the truth. It's been confirmed by the governor of Texas himself."

Slim released a long breath and untied the apron about his waist. He tossed it over the back of a chair and shook his head. "I guess that means you want me to pull out as well?"

"I've said nothing about your leaving. I just want to know where Brand is now."

"Can't rightly say," Slim said, looking away from Jessie.

Jessie sank onto one of the straight-backed chairs. "Then he's out searching for the Fleming gang?"

"I can't rightly say that, either," Slim said, tension crinkling the skin at the corners of his eyes.

"Damn it!" Jessie slammed her fist on the checkered-clothed table. "Can you tell me anything?"

"I'm afraid not," was Slim's dry answer.

Tears burned the backs of Jessie's lids. She swallowed hard and drew in a shaky breath. "Is he coming back?"

Slim frowned at the expression on Jessie's face and the tone of her voice. She had agreed to marry Clint Ramsey, but from the way she was acting, she had more feelings for Brand Stockton than she wanted to admit. Slim's frown deepened. "As long as he gets the job done, what does it matter to you if he comes back here?"

A great tear rolled over the tips of Jessie's dark lashes and down her cheek as she answered, "Because I love him."

Deep lines gouged a path across Slim's forehead, and his brows lowered to shadow his eyes as he frowned at Jessie. "I don't believe I heard you right, Miss Nolan. You're engaged to marry Clint Ramsey, if you'll recall."

"I know," Jessie said, her words a mere whisper.

Slim pulled out a chair and sank onto it. He shook his head. "Do you know what you're sayin' ?"

Jessie nodded.

"Then, damn it, woman, why in hell did you accept Ramsey?"

Jessie drew in a shuddery breath. "I can't answer your question."

Anger flickered across Slim's face. "You can't answer my question? That's just like a damned fickle female. Do you realize what you've done to Brand? The man has had enough pain in his life without you addin' to it with your willy-nilly, so-called affections. Just leave him alone, Miss Nolan. The boy has been through hell since the war. What with havin' his family massacred by the Comanche and then lookin' for Mercy all these years, he's suffered enough already.''

''Mercy?'' Jessie said, feeling the hair at the nape of her neck prickle. The girl Wade planned to marry possessed the same name. She pushed the thought aside. It couldn't be the same girl; there were other women named Mercy.

Slim nodded. ''She's his baby sister. The Comanche captured her when they killed the rest of his family, and he's been lookin' for her ever since.''

''How long has Mercy been missing?'' Jessie asked.

''Since before Brand came back from the war.''

Jessie breathed a little easier. Mercy couldn't be Brand's sister. Too much time had passed. It was sad, but she doubted Brand would ever find his Mercy. Unlike their civilized brothers, the Comanche hated the white man and wanted to annihilate them. It would be a miracle for a small child to have survived this long in captivity with them.

''I don't want to hurt Brand,'' Jessie said, pushing herself to her feet.

''No? You could fool me. You say you love him, but you're goin' to marry Ramsey. Woman, that's not what I call love.''

''I know it's not easy to comprehend my actions, but believe me, I never meant to hurt Brand or anyone else. And I only want the chance to try to make him understand.''

''I'll tell him that when I see him, but I can't guarantee he'll want to hear it from you, Miss Nolan. There's not a hell of a lot a man wants to hear from a woman set on marryin' another.''

A spark of Jessie's spirit returned at the censure in

Slim's voice. She paused at the door and looked back at the him. "Slim, I love Brand, but I'm not the only one at fault in this situation. Brand told me he didn't want my love long before I accepted Clint's proposal."

Relenting at the look of pain that flickered in Jessie's eyes, Slim said, "Then he's also a fool."

Jessie left Slim wondering exactly what was going on. Brand was turned wrong side out over Jessica Nolan, and now Slim had found she felt the same way. The entire situation left him in a quandary. He didn't know which side to support. Both seemed evenly matched in stupidity.

"Damn," he muttered, and turned back to his sourdough biscuits.

By the time Jessie reached the house her mind was made up. Slim had not told her Brand's whereabouts, but her every instinct told her he'd gone into Indian territory to find Wade. She had to warn her brother before it was too late.

"Edwina," she called as she entered the house and headed toward her bedroom to change into her denims. "I want you to pack my saddle bags."

Edwina, her face flushed, came hurrying out of the kitchen. She rolled her eyes toward heaven and shook her head as she followed Jessie to her bedroom. She paused upon the threshold. "I'm not even going to ask what you intend to do this time."

"Good," Jessie said, slipping out of her gown and tossing it onto the chair. "I don't have time for explanations."

"Jessica, will you at least tell me in which direction

you're going so I can send out a search party when you don't come back?''

"I'm going to warn Wade that Brand is a Texas Ranger.''

Edwina's features screwed up into a puzzled frown. "Brand Stockton is a Texas Ranger?''

Jessie nodded as she pulled on her Levi's. "Clint told me tonight. Brand was sent here to catch Wade.'' She shrugged into her shirt. "I don't have time to waste. If Brand finds Wade before I can warn him to leave the territory, it will be too late. Wade will hang and that will be the end of everything.'' She didn't add that it would be an end to Wade's chance at life and happiness as well as her own. She would never forgive Brand if he caused her brother's death.

Jessie watched the man in the sombrero as he rode along the trail ahead of her. His head lowered against the bright afternoon sunlight, he let his body sway gently with the movements of his mount. Oddly enough, Quillon Diaz was the only concession she'd had to make to Edwina before she left Eden. She had been prepared for the woman's objections, but none had been forthcoming, and within the hour, after making sure Quillon knew the way to the Canadian River in Choctaw territory, they had set out toward the north.

Now four days into the journey, Jessie was bone weary. Every muscle in her body ached, and her eyes burned from trail dust as well as lack of sleep. When they made camp at night, she found little rest with the hard ground as her bed. She glanced once more at the silent man ahead of her. She might be one big ache from head to toe, but she couldn't complain about her traveling companion. Quillon had made an excellent, though reticent, guide. He spoke in his halting English only when she spoke to him. He never ventured any conversation of his own and stayed to himself even as they sat within feet of each other around the same campfire.

Jessie urged her mount alongside Quillon's. He cast her a shy glance and then turned his black gaze to the trail ahead.

"How much farther?" Jessie asked for what seemed like the thousandth time since they'd left Eden.

Quillon shrugged. "Less than a half day, maybe."

A half day more to reach the Starr place on the Canadian and then, if things went well, perhaps another day to find Wade. The excuse she'd told Edwina to give—that the boss lady was ill and unable to see anyone—would be wearing thin by the time she returned to Eden.

Jessie allowed her mount to fall in behind Quillon's once more. She had known when she'd decided to warn Wade of Brand's intentions that she was risking everything she'd set into motion for Clint Ramsey. She also knew she really didn't have any other choice to make. She wanted to see Ramsey pay for killing her parents, but she couldn't sacrifice Wade's life to satisfy her need for revenge.

Several hours later Quillon drew his horse to a halt on a small rise overlooking the river. "Señorita Nolan, we have reached the Canadian River." He raised a hand and pointed toward a dilapidated looking cabin alongside the road that followed the winding watercourse. "I think this is the place you want to go. See, there are many horses in the corrals." He flashed Jessie a worried look. "It is said Sam Starr is in cahoots with horse thieves."

"Will it be safe for us there?"

Quillon frowned as he turned his dark gaze in the direction of the hostelry Sam Starr had made of his cabin. His voice reflected his concern for Jessie. "That I do not know."

Undaunted by the prospect of meeting horse thieves, Jessie checked the rifle in its scabbard before stuffing her braid beneath her hat. She knew her efforts did little to disguise her true gender, but perhaps she wouldn't draw too much attention to herself if at first sight people thought her a young man. She glanced at Quillon. "Let me borrow your poncho."

The young Mexican frowned as he handed Jessie the woven, multicolored cape, yet a moment later, when she slipped it on, he smiled broadly. A look of relief crossed his swarthy features. "*Sí*. It is much better."

"Then, amigo, we go," Jessie said, giving Quillon a mischievous grin at her play of words and earning a tiny smile in return.

A few minutes later Jessie and Quillon reined their mounts to a halt in front of the Starrs' hostelry. Assuming the role of Quillon's male companion, Jessie swaggered inside. The light from the doorway and the oil lanterns hanging from the rafters overhead revealed several rough-hewn tables and an improvised bar made of overturned barrels and boards laid lengthwise. The wall behind the bar was lined with whiskey bottles, while several kegs of beer sat on the floor. The acrid smells of smoke, cured animal skins, and unwashed bodies filled the air.

Jessie suppressed the urge to hold her nose against

the offensive smells. She swallowed hard and propped one elbow on the bar as she took in the hostelry's customers at a glance. Several unsavory-looking characters lounged at the bar, drinking the rotgut Sam Starr sold his nefarious customers at an exorbitant price. At one table four men played cards, their weatherbeaten faces screwed up in concentration over the hands they had been dealt.

A woman, her dark, oily hair pulled away from her harsh-featured face, stirred a pot hanging over the fire. Dressed in a worn velvet coat, a stained white blouse, and split skirt, she resembled the waterfront doxies Jessie had seen when she and Kate had visited the Nolan shipping offices. However, the Boston doxies didn't carry a revolver strapped about their waists like the woman who covered the Dutch oven and then spat a squirt of tobacco against the back of the firepit.

Amazed, Jessie watched the woman wipe the corners of her mouth with the back of her hand before she hung the spoon on a nail and turned toward the bar. The wrinkles in her leathery face deepened as she looked Jessie over and smiled knowingly. "What can I get you, fine sir?"

Jessie glanced at Quillon and lowered her voice. "Two whiskeys."

The woman poured two shots of rotgut into grease-filmed glasses. "That'll be four bits."

Jessie slapped the money on the bar and lifted the glass. She looked from it to Quillon and then back. She set the glass down. No matter how hard she tried, she couldn't drink from the dirty glass.

A smile stretched the woman's wide mouth, and she lowered her voice so her words were audible only to

Jessie. "You can't fool Belle Starr, little lady. One look at your fussless face tells me you didn't come here to drink our fine whiskey. So do you want to tell me why you're here, or should I inform the boys of what they might find beneath that poncho? They'd enjoy a little sport since we don't get many females in these parts."

Jessie moistened her suddenly dry lips. "I—I—came here looking for my brother."

The dark eyes narrowed upon Jessie's face. "And who might he be?"

"Wade Fleming," Jessie said evenly, though a shiver raced up her spine.

"You don't say," Belle said, her lips spreading to reveal large yellowed teeth. "Well, I'll be damned. Didn't know Wade had any kin since the Indians call him Man with No People."

Jessie ignored Belle's attempt to draw her into conversation. "Do you know where I can find him? He told me to send a message here and he'd get it."

"Wade comes by for a few drinks every now and again, but I ain't seen him in several months now."

"Can you tell me how I might reach him?"

Belle eyed Jessie for a long, thoughtful moment. "I don't reckon it would hurt, but I won't guarantee you'll find him still there."

"I'll take the risk. I have to warn him that he's in danger."

Belle chuckled and shook her head. "Where you been living, girl? An outlaw is always in danger. That's nothing new."

"I know," Jessie said, feeling foolish.

"For a price, Sam can show you the way to Wade's hideout."

"I'll gladly pay whatever he asks," Jessie said.

"Sam," Belle hollowed over her shoulder. "Get out here. I've got a job for you."

Sam Starr, his bony features harsh planes and ridges, his red clay skin flushed deeper from the whiskey he'd consumed, poked his head around the curtain separating the living quarters from the hostelry. "What in the hell do you want now, Belle?" he snarled.

"I've got a job for you. This, uh"—Belle's tongue stumbled over the word *lady*—"this fellow needs you to show him up to the cave. He's Wade's brother."

"Ain't never heard Fleming had any kin. Thought he was a loner."

"Now you know different. And he's willing to pay," Belle said as Sam ran a hand through his shaggy hair and hiked up his britches.

"Well, that's a different matter," Sam said, eyeing Jessie speculatively through narrowed, lashless lids.

A prickle of suspicion tingled along the base of Jessie's spine. Something in Sam's demeanor made her suspect he wouldn't think twice about taking her money and leaving her before she ever reached Wade. "I'll pay you when we reach Wade's hideout and not before."

Belle chuckled. "He ain't the greenhorn he looks, is he, Sam?" She glanced once more at Jessie. "Ain't no reason to worry yourself none. He'll take you up to the cave."

Belle was correct: Sam led them to Wade's hideout without any problem. Wade saw them coming from the lookout's point, and by the time they made their way down the trail to the cave, he and Renegade were awaiting them. Wade's eyes widened when he recognized Sam Starr's companion.

"What in the hell are you doing here, Jessie?" he asked as he swung her down from her horse. "I told you to send word to me at Belle's place, not to come yourself."

"I had to. I couldn't risk anyone learning of your whereabouts."

"Sis, you don't realize the danger you've put yourself in," Wade scolded. "The kind of people I deal with wouldn't think twice about shooting a woman."

Jessie glanced to where Sam Starr and Renegade stood talking a short distance away. "I understand your concern, but I couldn't send a message and chance it not reaching you. It was too important for you to know that a Texas Ranger by the name of Brand Stockton is looking for you."

A gasp drew Wade's and Jessie's attention to the woman standing white-faced behind them. Wade's face softened as he looked at Mercy and held out his hand. "Mercy, come and meet my sister, Jessie."

Mercy came forward and clutched Wade's hand. He felt her tremble as he drew her against his side. Protectively he slipped an arm about her shoulders. "Mercy, what's wrong? Jessie won't harm you."

Mercy drew in a shuddering breath and clutched Wade's hand. Her soft blue eyes were bright with unshed tears as she shook her head and said, her voice little more than a whisper upon the wind, "It can't be. . . ."

Jessie released a long breath. When she'd learned of Brand's sister, she had hoped for Wade's sake that this girl was not the one Brand had sought for so many years. Now she knew her hopes had been in vain. She also knew Wade's heart would be broken should Mercy return to the world where he would be an outcast. At last Jessie said, "It is true."

"No. I can't believe Brand's alive. He would have come for me. He wouldn't have left me with the Comanches for all these years," Mercy said in desperation.

Jessie watched Wade's face pale, and her heart went out to him. She wanted to protect him from hurt, but there was nothing she could do to save him from it. "Brand is alive, Mercy, and he's been looking for you for twelve years."

Mercy's eyes misted with relief, and a tremulous smile touched her lips. "Then he didn't forget about me?"

Jessie shook her head. "No, Brand never forgot about you."

"For the love of God, would you tell me what's going on here?" Wade asked, feeling suddenly uneasy.

"Should I tell him, or would you like to be the one?" Jessie asked.

Mercy swallowed and looked up at Wade. Her voice reflected her joy as she said, "Brand Stockton is my brother."

Wade stared down at Mercy and felt dread settle in a cold, hard lump in the pit of his belly. "I thought all of your family was dead."

Mercy glanced uncertainly at Jessie before once more looking at Wade with tear-bright eyes. "Until now I thought the same thing."

Wade's shoulders sagged visibly, and he drew in a long breath. He should have known things had been going too smoothly. Now his luck had finally run out. Mercy would leave him. Resigning himself to the fact, he smiled at her tenderly. "I'm happy for you, Mercy. I know what it's like to think you'll never see any of your family and then to find them again."

Mercy threw her arms about Wade's neck. "Oh, Wade. My dreams have come true."

Wade wrapped his arms about her tightly as he met Jessie's gaze over Mercy's shoulder. The indigo depths of his eyes showed the misery in his soul.

Jessie's eyes burned with tears of sympathy. She understood all too well what he was feeling at that moment. She'd felt the same excruciating agony when she'd watched Brand ride out of her life. She looked away. She was responsible for bringing this misery upon Wade. Had she used her head, she wouldn't have blurted out Brand's name in front of Mercy, and then no one would have been the wiser. She turned away.

"Jessie," Wade called. "Can Mercy ride back to Eden with you?"

Jessie slowly turned to look back at her brother and the woman who stood looking at him as if he'd suddenly started to foam at the mouth. She opened her mouth to tell Wade that she'd see Mercy reunited with her brother, yet before any words could pass her lips, Mercy let out a screech of rage.

Hands on her hips, Mercy turned on Wade. She stamped her foot. "I won't let you send me away, Wade Fleming!"

Surprised by Mercy's fury, Wade stared at her, bewildered. "You know your brother is alive now, Mercy. There's no reason for you to stay here with me."

Mercy drew back her hand and thumped Wade in the chest with her balled fist. "I have the same reason as I had before I learned Brand was still alive."

Wade blinked at her for a long moment before a slow smile curled the corners of his lips. "You mean you don't want to leave me? That nothing has changed?"

Mercy glanced at Jessie before she looked once more at Wade in exasperation. "The only thing that has changed between us is that we now have a sister and a brother."

"But your brother is a Texas Ranger. When he learns you're alive, he'll come after you. He'll never allow you to stay with me."

"Then he will never know I'm alive. My place is by your side, Wade. I am your woman, and nothing can change that." Mercy looked once more to where Jessie stood, smiling her relief. "When you return to your land, I beg you not to tell anyone I am here. My brother can make a life of his own, but my place is here with the man I love."

Jessie nodded. She would keep Mercy's secret. She would not be the one responsible for tearing the lovers apart. Though she could not be with the man she loved, she would not deny Wade and Mercy their chance to be together. In some small way she would find solace in knowing they were happy.

"God, Mercy," Wade said, swinging her off her feet and spinning around. "How I love you!"

Their laughter filled the afternoon air.

Chapter 15

Clint slammed his fist on Langtree's desk. His pale eyes shot pure venom at the banker. "All right, Langtree. I want to know who in hell is behind this so-called Redman Cattle Company."

Langtree swallowed uneasily as he looked at the furious rancher. He could feel beads of sweat popping out beneath the stiff collar of his shirt but suppressed the urge to run his finger beneath it to relieve the tightness. Clint looked ready to explode. At last Langtree shrugged and lied, "All I know is what I've been told. The Redman Cattle Company is a group of buyers from back east."

Clint's features deepened in hue as a new rush of fury suffused his face. "If they think they can choke me out, then they're mistaken. I've lived here far too long to allow a group of strangers to come in and take over without a fight. They may have bought up the water rights, but they'd better not even attempt to stop the supply to my stock or they'll be sorry they ever came to Texas."

"Clint, maybe everything isn't as bleak as you've painted it. You don't know who is behind the land grab. Perhaps they mean no harm."

Clint looked at the banker as if he'd suddenly gone mad. "No harm? What in hell do you call fencing in the grazing land? Barbed wire isn't a friendly gesture, Langtree, no matter how you look at it. And neither is the way they sneaked in and strung it up on the south range without a soul knowing. Until yesterday when my men were driving the herd down for new grass, I wasn't even aware of what they had done. But now I am, and I know what they've got planned. Whoever is behind the land grab also intends to strangle the life from the Lazy L until I'll be forced to sell. But they're in for a damned big surprise. I ain't a man who can easily be run off land he's fought Indians, drought, and the elements to keep."

Langtree's eyes widened and he gave a mental shake of his head, unable to believe Miss Nolan would intentionally put up barbed wire fences around the grazing land. Yet even if she had, he still couldn't tell Clint who owned the Redman Cattle Company without revealing he'd played a major role in buying up the land for her. In Clint's present state of mind, he'd shoot first and ask questions later.

Again Langtree mentally shook his head. All of this had to be some kind of mistake. Miss Nolan probably thought she was doing Clint a service to have their land fenced. That had to be it, he reflected. There was no other explanation for the woman's actions.

Langtree cleared his throat and braced himself for Clint's next explosion. "Speaking of dollars, Clint. Your loan is due this month and I'll need your payment in full by the thirty-first. The stockholders are raising a fuss because I've let you be delinquent on your payments."

"You'll get your money as usual," Clint said, his stony gaze raking over the banker. When he married Jessica he'd have the money he needed to pay off his debts and to do the improvements he'd planned for the Lazy L. "And you can tell your stockholders to go to hell!"

"Clint, you know all of them are your friends, but we can carry your credit for only so long. I'm sure everything will be fine after the next roundup. We all know you wouldn't be behind now were it not for Fleming stealing so many of your herd."

Clint's glacial expression chilled Langtree to the bone. He shifted uneasily on his chair and smiled at the menacing rancher. "Well, now that we've got our business out of the way, let's turn to something far more interesting. Maybelle and I are looking forward to your wedding this afternoon. It's the talk of the town, and it seems as if everyone for a hundred miles around has come to Paradise for the event. The hotel is filled to the rafters."

Clint's expression didn't soften. He'd be damned if he'd let Langtree off the hook so easily. The man said he didn't know anything about the Redman Cattle Company, yet from the rumors flying around, he was the one buying up the land. "Damn it to hell, Langtree! I intend to find out one way or the other who's behind the Redman Cattle Company—and who here in Paradise has been helping them. And when I do, they'll both be sorry they ever crossed my path."

Langtree came to his feet and absently tugged his waistcoat over his large belly. He took out his pocket-watch and flipped it open. It was ten o'clock, and the wedding was set for twelve. Only two more hours to keep Clint in the dark. Langtree cleared his throat and looked once more at the rancher. "I understand your concern, but I'd not fret too much about it until after your wedding. And if nothing changes within the next few days, I'll be more than glad to help you learn who owns the Redman Cattle Company."

Clint clapped his Stetson on his head. "I'll give you until tomorrow, and that's all the time you have before I bring in my own man."

"But surely you don't want me coming out to the Lazy L to disturb you and your new bride so soon after the wedding?"

"If you know anything sooner, you'd better tell me, Langtree. Business is business, and Jessica will just have to understand I can't let things come apart at the seams because we are married."

Langtree nodded grimly. He'd thought Jessica Nolan would change Clint Ramsey, but nothing could alter the coldhearted bastard. The man thought more of the Lazy L than he did of the woman he planned to make his wife. And he wouldn't allow anything as simple as his own wedding to interfere with business. The Lazy L possessed Clint Ramsey more than any woman ever could.

Until he'd announced his plans to marry Miss Nolan, Langtree had thought he understood the reason behind Clint's obsession. Several years ago, on one of his infrequent sneak visits to Miss Molly's, he'd heard the rumors circulating about Clint's lack of virility. The rancher had become something of a joke around the whorehouse because he reacted like a jealous lover when it came to the Lazy L. Langtree had assumed Ramsey had directed his energies toward his ranch because of his lack of manhood, but now he realized the man's actions stemmed from nothing more than his greed for power. He wanted to control everyone and everything the way he did the Lazy L and most of the people in Paradise.

The banker felt an unfamiliar pang of sympathy for the young woman who would soon be Mrs. Clint Ramsey. "Clint, I'm sure I'll have the information you need by tomorrow. Let's forget about it for now. It's nearly time for you to get married. Let me buy your last drink as a single man," Langtree said as he lumbered around the desk and clapped Clint on the back.

Clint relented slightly. "I guess business can wait just a few hours." The two men walked out of the bank and down the planked sidewalk toward the saloon.

The morning sun streamed through the window, gilding the room as Jessie fanned the deeds on the bed beside her wedding gown. Only a few hours more and her revenge would be complete. Smiling, she unfastened her robe and tossed it aside. She lifted the gown she'd kept so well hidden from Edwina and slipped it on. Fastening the small opening at the nape of her neck, she crossed to the full-length cheval mirror and looked at her reflection. A tiny satisfied smile curled her lips at the image that stared back at her.

Her seamstress in Boston had followed her orders to the letter. There were few places in the city to buy white doeskin, so she had used white satin as a substitute to create the design specified. However, instead of taking away from the beauty of the garment, the gleaming material had only enhanced it. The expensive fabric contrasted vividly with the multicolored beadwork that edged the neck, the V-shaped design across her breasts, the fringed elbow-length sleeves, and the pattern on the fringed skirt. Strips of white rabbit fur attached by beaded leather thongs hung from the beaded front of the gown, which had been cut straight from neck to hemline in Indian fashion.

Relishing the feel of the loose garment against her skin, Jessie bent and pulled on the white suede, knee-high moccasins she'd directed her shoemaker to send with the gown. Fringed at the top, their beaded leather laces crisscrossed in front, they hugged her leg to just below the knee.

Jessie's smile deepened as she carefully braided her hair and placed a beaded band around her forehead. She doubted her wedding ensemble held any resemblance to the actual attire worn by an Indian maid, yet it would be authentic enough for Clint Ramsey and the people of Paradise to recognize her heritage.

"Jessica Nolan!" Edwina said from the doorway, where she stood dumbfounded upon the threshold. "What on earth are you doing?"

Jessie turned slowly to look at her friend. "I am preparing for my wedding."

Shocked, Edwina accused, "You've planned this all along, haven't you?"

Jessie nodded.

Edwina released a long, slow breath as she came into the room and sank onto the chair. "I should have known you had some wild scheme brewing in that head of yours. I knew you didn't love Clint Ramsey, but like a fool I took you at your word."

"Forgive me for not telling you of my plans, Winnie, but I was afraid to tell anyone."

"Does Wade know you're doing this?"

Jessie shook her head. "I couldn't even tell him. I was afraid when he learned Clint murdered our parents, he'd kill him. He's already in enough trouble with the law without adding murder to his crimes. I hope he and Mercy have used the money I left with them and are too far away by now to hear of what will take place today."

"How do you know Clint Ramsey killed your parents?" Edwina asked, her eyes widening with surprise.

Jessie crossed to the bed and picked up the deeds. "I found the gun, Edwina. The gun specially made for Clint, which no one else has ever used. It's all the proof I need." She looked back to her friend. "I think it's time for us to go to the church."

Edina blinked up at Jessie, visibly shaken by her explanation. It took her a moment to recollect her wits and come to her feet. Worry lines etching her mouth and eyes, her skin ashen, she drew in a deep, steadying breath. "Jessie, you can't mean to go through with this. Let the sheriff handle Ramsey."

"It's too late for the law. And I owe this to my parents. I can't see Clint hanged for his crimes, but I can make him suffer. He's already begun to pay, though he's not aware of it yet."

"Jessica, I don't like this. You've pitted yourself against a powerful man. Clint Ramsey won't just lie down and take what you dish out to him. He'll fight back. And he'll not rest until you've paid for humiliating him today in front of the entire town."

Jessie smiled sweetly, though her eyes held a hard,

ungiving light in their sapphire depths. "Nor will I rest until I see him ruined. And after today, Edwina, Clint won't be the man with all the power in Paradise. With these"—Jessie raised the deeds and waved them in the air—"I have the power to destroy him and everything he holds dear."

"Jessica, please. I fear you're asking for more trouble this time than you can handle," Edwina said, desparate to make her young friend see reason. Clint Ramsey had murdered in the past, and she didn't doubt he'd do so again.

"It's far too late to change things now even if I wanted to. Today Clint Ramsey will meet Jessica Fleming for the first time, and he will also get the first taste of my revenge." Jessie took down a dark cloak and slipped it over her shimmering wedding gown. Until she walked down the aisle of the church, she wanted no one to see her gown.

Edwina felt a chill race down her spine. Kate had made Jessie strong and independent, but her inner strength would do her little good against a bullet. "Jessie, please reconsider. There should be some other way. You're going to get yourself killed."

Jessie paused at the door and looked back at her friend. "I'm not afraid of Clint Ramsey, Edwina. You can't get a snakebite if you keep your eyes open and see the snake before he sees you."

Edwina shook her head. "You fail to realize he may strike when you're not looking. That's the problem."

"I am grateful for your concern, but there's nothing you can say or do to stop me from meeting Clint Ramsey at the church today." With that Jessie turned and walked out of the house to the buckboard. She climbed up and took the reins. In less than an hour she was due at the church.

Edwina seated herself beside Jessie and glanced at her young friend as she raised a parasol over her head. "Fool that I've always been where you and Kate are concerned, I'll be at your side when the trouble comes."

Jessie hugged her. "I'm grateful for your friendship, Edwina Roilings, even through all of your grumbling."

Brand downed the whiskey and held his glass out to the bartender for a refill. He'd been in Paradise less than an hour, but already six gossips had informed him that the big event was scheduled to take place that afternoon. Today Miss Jessica Nolan would marry Clint Ramsey. The clink of the bottle neck against the rim of the shot glass shattered the stillness hovering over the saloon. Everyone in town was either inside the church or waiting outside to get a glimpse of Clint and his new bride as they rode back to the Lazy L, where Ramsey had ordered a huge celebration banquet prepared for his wedding guests.

Brand lifted the glass to his lips and tossed the whiskey down his throat. It burned all the way to his stomach, yet it didn't relieve the hard knot created in the pit of his belly by the thought of Jessie marrying anyone other than himself. He'd tried in the past weeks to put her from his mind and heart, but he hadn't succeeded. He still loved the woman no matter how hard he tried to deny it.

He'd gone to Fort Smith to see Judge Parker and had received the permission he needed to enter Indian territory. He should have been there now, looking for Wade

Fleming. A man named Link Parry, recently arrested near Fort Smith, had told him that Fleming had his hideout in a cave in the San Bois Mountains. He didn't know how much faith to put in the thief's words, but they were the first real clues he'd had about the rustler's whereabouts. But instead of being where he was supposed to be, he was back in Paradise to see Jessie. Now it was time for him to finally face the fact that he would soon lose her forever to Clint Ramsey.

"Leave the bottle," he growled at the bartender.

The bartender readily complied and moved to the far end of the bar, where he busily began polishing glasses. He wanted no trouble from the steely-eyed stranger. He'd bet his last dollar that before the day was out, some unfortunate fellow would end up on the stranger's bad side. The man reminded him of a coiled rattler just waiting to strike.

Brand poured himself another drink and leaned against the bar. He cupped the glass in his hands as he rested his elbows on the wooden surface and stared up at the painting on the wall over the rows of whiskey bottles. The scantily clad beauty, her bosomy, robust figure revealed to perfection by the artist, served only to remind him of another beautiful woman and the small breasts that fit perfectly in his hands. He'd suckled them greedily, unable to get enough, wanting to consume her like the tempting morsel she was.

Jessie, his mind cried. Jessie belonged to him. He had been her first lover, and the very thought of Clint Ramsey burying himself deep within her sweetness was sacrilege. He was the only man who should taste her nectar and feel her surround his hard length with her satiny flesh. Brand nearly groaned aloud at the thought.

He shifted to ease the sudden discomfort in the crotch of his Levi's, swallowed hard, and drew in a shuddering breath. His knuckles whitened as he gripped the glass.

Brand again downed the fiery whiskey before refilling the glass with the amber liquid. He knew he had to stop thinking about Jessie, but for the life of him, everywhere he looked he saw things to remind him of her. The twilight sky . . . her eyes; the morning dew upon a pink rose . . . her passion-swollen lips; a bubbling brook . . . her laughter; the scent of wild jasmine . . . her heady smell. Jessie surrounded him day and night.

Brand took a drink and felt a slight buzz in his temples as he lifted the bottle to refill his glass. His expression hardened as he watched the last amber drops fall. He flashed the bartender an annoyed look. ''Bring me another bottle and make it full this time.''

The bartender set a bottle on the bar and shoved it down the slick wooden surface to Brand. He had no intention of getting any closer to the menacing-looking stranger than necessary.

Brand uncorked the bottle with his teeth and spat the cork into the brass spittoon on the floor as he poured himself another drink. He tossed it down his throat and then staggered over to one of the deserted tables. Were it not for Ramsey's wedding, every table in the place would be full of cowhands hoping to get rich on the lucky draw of a card. Brand kicked out a chair and sank onto it. He leaned back and propped his booted feet on the table as he poured himself another drink. It too burned down his throat and made his blood careen wildly through his head.

He narrowed his silver eyes as he raised the bottle of whiskey and studied the liquid inside. A few drinks had made him feel slightly giddy, but they couldn't make him forget the ceremony that would soon be taking place. A muscle twitched in his jaw. He should be the one marrying Jessie.

Ignoring the glass, Brand raised the bottle to his lips and guzzled the burning liquid. If he drank enough, maybe he could forget—forget Jessie, forget the ache in his heart, just forget. That's all he wanted.

The peal of the church bell drew his attention. Bleary-eyed, he stared at the bat-wing doors. Only a few hundred feet separated him from the woman he loved, and he'd be damned if he'd let Clint Ramsey have her without a fight. When the preacher asked if there was anyone who had anything against the marriage, he damned well planned to speak his mind.

His decision made, he lifted the bottle to his lips once more and drew in a long drink before he set it on the table and rose to his feet. Surprisingly, he showed no sign of the effects of the whiskey he'd consumed as he walked out of the saloon and turned toward the church.

Brand glanced at the crowd milling about outside the church. Some stood in small groups, talking quietly, while others laughed and joked together as if it were a holiday. Cowhands from Eden and the Lazy L sat were mounted on their horses near the windows, hoping to get a glimpse of the ceremony that would unite their ranches. Ignoring them, Brand strode up the steps and into the church. He closed the door behind him and slipped onto the last seat on the rear pew. The church was filled to capacity. Businessmen and ranchers, along with their wives decked out in all their Sunday go-to-meeting finery, packed the hard wooden benches. In front of the altar stood Clint Ramsey, talking with Reverend McBeard, while Mrs. McBeard played the organ.

A steely light entered Brand's eyes as his gaze rested once more on Clint Ramsey. If he had his way, the day would not turn out the way Ramsey thought. Smiling, he folded his arms over his chest and settled back to await the arrival of the bride.

Chapter 16

The crowd outside the church quieted as the buckboard rolled to a stop. Several of the cowhands who worked for Jessie stepped forward to assist her down. With the regal dignity of a queen, Jessie raised her head in the air and slowly loosed the the ties of her cape. As the garment slipped from her shoulders, an audible gasp passed among the onlookers before a curious silence settled over them like a thick, hot blanket.

Ignoring the stares she could feel boring into her back, Jessie kept her gaze centered on the white doors as she ascended the steps. The sweet organ music filtered out into the afternoon air as she quietly opened the church door and stepped inside.

All eyes turned in her direction. An eerie stillness rippled from pew to pew toward the front of the church as the wedding guests took in her attire. Along the aisle the guests' faces mirrored shock, horror, and bewilderment as they stared at Jessie. Yet she had eyes only for the man before the altar. Upon first seeing her, Clint's face had split into a wide grin, but as his gaze moved over her, his face darkened. By the time she reached his side, he stood pale and taut, his chiseled features granite hard, his icy blue gaze the only color in his rigid face.

Jessie smiled sweetly at Clint and then gave Reverend McBeard a nod to proceed with the ceremony. McBeard, his eyes wide with shock, glanced uncertainly at Clint and nervously moistened his lips.

"Ah . . . ah," the preacher began, clearing his throat, "we are gathered here . . ." He stuttered to a halt, his eyes beseeching Clint for some sign to continue. He went unnoticed by the man glaring at Jessie.

"What is the meaning of this, Jessica?" Clint hissed, his voice low with suppressed fury.

"Meaning, Clint?" Jessica asked innocently. "I don't understand."

With a sweep of his hand, Clint encompassed her from head to toe. "You know exactly what I'm talking about. I want to know the meaning of that Indian getup you've got on."

Feigning innocence, Jessie glanced at her shimmering gown before she looked once more at Clint. "I thought you would approve of my choice of gown."

"Approve!" Clint exploded, forgetting in his rage that he was the center of attention of nearly the entire population of Paradise. "How can you think I would approve of you coming in here dressed like a squaw? I demand an explanation."

"Then you will have one," Jessie said. Shedding the act she'd perfected over the past few weeks, she allowed her true feelings to show for the first time. Eyes flashing her rancor, she smiled coldly at Clint. "I have come to my wedding as what I am."

Clint's frown deepened. "This is no time for jokes.

287

You're making a scene in front of the entire town. We all know you're a lady, not a savage.''

"I am a lady, Clint, but I am also half Cherokee."

The only sound in the church was a sharp indrawn breath from the back pew. Clint shook his head. "What kind of game are you playing? You're no more a half-breed than I am."

Jessie raised her chin proudly and glanced back at the congregation. Everyone stood frozen in place, listening intently to their exchange. "I was born Jessica Fleming."

Langtree gave an audible groan and slowly sank onto the pew. He covered his face with his hands and shook his head in disbelief. Jessica Nolan—Fleming—or whatever her name was had just destroyed his future in Paradise.

Jessie looked back to the man at her side. "You recall Sarah and Earnest Fleming, don't you, Clint?''

Clint's face suffused with color, but he made no comment.

"I'm sure you remember them," Jessie continued softly, her words audible to his ears alone. "I remember them well, and I also remember the man who killed them. He shot them with the gun his father made for him on his fifteenth birthday."

Clint jerked as if he'd been stuck by a pin but made no other visible sign that he knew what she was talking about. He glanced toward the crowd that had come to witness his marriage and swallowed the uncomfortable lump of embarrassment in his throat. "There will be no wedding. I won't marry a woman who has lied to me."

Jessie smiled and raised the hand that clutched the

deeds. "Before you go, there is something else I would like you to know."

"There is nothing more to be said between us, Miss Fleming," Clint growled, and started to turn away.

"I think there is," Jessie said, catching him by the sleeve.

Clint looked at the hand on his arm in disgust. He shook it off. "Then spit it out. I've far more important things to do than stand around and talk to some half-breed squaw."

Jessie's expression hardened, as did her smile. She waved the deeds beneath Clint's nose. "You may be interested to know that I'm the Redman Cattle Company."

"Bitch," was Clint's low growl before he turned his ire upon the cowering bank president. "You and Langtree will pay dearly for crossing me."

"I paid dearly ten years ago. Now it's your time to suffer," Jessie said between clenched teeth. "It's too late to turn you over to the law for what you did to my parents, but I will see that you know how it feels to lose something you love."

"You are going to be sorry you ever came back to Texas, Miss Fleming."

"Are you threatening me, Mr. Ramsey?" Jessie said loudly enough for everyone to hear.

"I don't threaten, Miss Fleming. I make promises and I keep them." Clint turned and stalked down the aisle and out of the church.

Jessie felt a chill of apprehension ripple down her spine. Edwina had been right: Clint Ramsey would not lie down and let her walk over him. But she'd expected nothing less from the man. She had known from the beginning that he was ruthless, but she would not let him defeat her. She would see him pay for his crimes if it was the last thing she ever did.

An uneasy silence hung over the congregation as they slowly filed out of the church. Jessie received several curious glances, but no one made an attempt to offer her their friendship or support. The inhabitants of Paradise were wary of the woman who had humiliated Clint Ramsey. They didn't want his wrath to fall upon them by association. They were all too aware of what happened to those who went against the man.

Jessica remained at the altar as the door closed. Only one man had not moved from his place on the last pew. He stared at Jessie, his silver eyes shining with an unreadable light, his face chalky from shock.

Jessie felt her heart leap into her throat at the sight of Brand, yet the look he gave her kept her standing there. She moistened her lips and smiled timidly. "I tried to tell you that I wouldn't marry Clint before you left."

Brand's nostrils flared as he drew in another sharp breath. He swallowed the disgust that rose in his throat as he looked at Jessie. Dressed like an Indian princess, she represented everything he despised. The blood in her veins was tainted by the savages who had massacred his family.

Brand's lips turned down at the corners as he fought the urge to strangle her. All his instincts had warned him against her from the beginning, and now he knew why. She wasn't Fleming's lover, as he'd first suspected, but his sister.

Brand felt his insides lurch sickeningly. He had given his heart to this woman. He had loved her as he'd loved no other, and she had betrayed him by the very blood in her veins. Brand squeezed his eyes closed to shut out the sight of Jessie in her Indian attire. He felt he'd suddenly fallen into a pit of rattlesnakes. The venom shooting through him burned to his very soul, annihilating every emotion in its path but hate.

Brand clenched his teeth and pressed his lips together to keep from spewing out his bitterness. He couldn't allow himself to feel anything beyond his hatred for her Indian blood, or he knew he'd never survive. It had been agony believing she would marry Clint Ramsey, but now he realized he'd known nothing about true pain until this moment. Deserts of despair opened before him as he realized Jessie was now lost to him forever just as surely as if she had died. He had loved an image, something she had pretended to be.

"Brand," Jessie said, frightened at the look on his face, "can you forgive me for not telling you?"

Brand didn't answer, couldn't answer. He stood stiff and straight, even though he was dying inside. The liquor he'd consumed less than an hour ago had abruptly left him cold sober at the shock of seeing Jessie walk down the aisle, looking more beautiful than he'd ever seen her, yet more despicable to him than a rotting carcass in the noonday sun. Unable to say or do more, he turned and left the church.

"Brand," she cried, running after him. She caught him at the foot of the church steps. "What's wrong?"

Brand's lips curled back in disgust and he shook her hand from his arm much the way Clint had a short time before. "Stay away from me, Jessie. I won't be responsible for what I do if you don't."

Jessie let her hand fall to her side. "Brand, you have

to understand. This was something I had to do. Clint is the man responsible for my parents' death and for having my brothers and me sent to the orphanage in Indian territory. Don't you see, I couldn't tell you or anyone of my plans. Can't you understand and forgive me for keeping the truth from you?''

''I could forgive you for not telling the truth about your marriage to Ramsey. What I can't forgive is the very blood in your veins.'' Brand turned and stalked away.

Numb, Jessie watched Brand mount and ride out of town. She now understood what drove Brand Stockton: hatred. She'd seen it in his eyes as he looked at her. Jessie shivered and wrapped her arms about herself. She had been foolish to believe her love would be enough for Brand and that together they could overcome anything in their pasts. Now she knew too many years of hatred had been ingrained within Brand's soul. His prejudice against an entire race of people would not allow him to love her in return.

Jessie released a long, resigned breath and turned back to the buckboard, where Edwina waited. It was over. She had begun to tighten the noose about Clint Ramsey's neck and had lost Brand forever because of her heritage. Jessie looked at her friend with a sad little smile. ''I guess we've done everything here that we came to do.''

Edwina nodded, her own heart aching for her young friend. She had suspected Jessie's feelings for Brand Stockton were more than the girl wanted to admit, and now she knew the truth. Jessie's eyes reflected the pain in her heart, though she tried desperately to keep up a brave front.

Edwina placed a comforting hand on Jessie and squeezed, silently conveying her sympathy. She knew all too well how it felt to have a broken heart. She also knew there was nothing she could say to give her young friend comfort. Only time would heal what Jessie now thought shattered. Yet even time wouldn't erase the scars left by Brand today. They would stay forever etched across her heart to remind her of the silver-eyed man who had just ridden out of her life.

Jessie swallowed against the tears clogging her throat, picked up the reins, and clicked them sharply across the horse's back. She couldn't allow herself to give way to her emotions. There was still too much left for her to do. She had to concentrate all her energy on her plans for Clint Ramsey. Soon the barbed wire would be strung, and then she would have the course of Little Creek changed. It would take only a few days' labor to dig a trench at the fork where their properties joined. That small ditch would end the water supply to the Lazy L.

A frown creased Jessie's brow at the sight of several of her men awaiting her arrival at the gates of Eden. She drew the buckboard to a halt and looked at the mounted men curiously.

"Has something happened while I was in town?" she asked.

"Naw, Miss Fleming. We just come up to ask for our wages."

Jessie's frown deepened as she glanced at Edwina. She knew the woman's worried expression mirrored her own. "Your wages? It's not the first of the month."

"Yes, ma'am. We know it ain't the first of the month,

but we're pulling out," answered the spokesman for the group.

Jessie released a long breath and nodded. "All right, I'll give you your wages, but before I do I want to know exactly why you're leaving. Is it something I've done? Or is it who I am?"

The spokesman glanced at his silent companions and shook his head. "Not exactly, ma'am. We ain't got nothing against you personally, but we just don't want to be in on no range war. We hired on here as cowhands, not gunfighters."

"There's not going to be a range war," Jessie said, surprised and relieved at the man's answer. She'd feared their decision had stemmed from the fact that she was half Cherokee Indian.

"That's not the way it looks to us. Ramsey is a mean son of a bitch, ah—excuse me, ma'am. I mean, he's a mean bastard, ah—darn it to hell. You know what I mean. He ain't going to let it rest about what you done to him. He'll hire every gunslinger west of the Mississippi to keep you from choking out the Lazy L. And we just don't plan to be their targets."

"Isn't there anything I can say to change your mind? I need you here at Eden."

"Naw. We've made up our minds, and we want to be out of here before dark."

"Come by the house in an hour and I'll have your money," Jessie said, and clicked the reins, setting the horse to trot down the dusty road. She'd not beg the men to stay at Eden. She was in no mood to plead, not to a cowhand or to the man she loved. Kate had taught her to be independent, and she'd be damned before she'd grovel at any man's feet. Stiffening her spine, she glanced at her silent companion. "So it's already started?"

Edwina nodded grimly. "It would seem so. I told you Clint Ramsey wouldn't just lie down and let you walk all over him. What do you plan to do now?"

"Exactly what I set out to do in the beginning," Jessie answered, her eyes never leaving the sandy roadway. She'd be damned if she'd cower at the first sign of trouble. Every last man could leave Eden and she'd not stop her plans for Clint Ramsey. She'd gone too far, and if it took a range war to bring Ramsey down, then he'd get one.

From the bunkhouse Brand watched Jessie rein the buckboard to a halt and climb down. Feeling his insides twist painfully, he turned his back on the sight and looked back to the man who sat sipping a cup of coffee at the table. "If we leave tonight, we can be in the San Bois Mountains in three days' time."

Slim shrugged and took another long sip of the steaming brew in his cup. "I've chased my last outlaw, Brand."

"What do you mean?" Brand's brow furrowed in bewilderment. Slim had been his partner for nearly fifteen years.

"Just what I said." Slim tugged a piece of paper from his shirt pocket and tossed it onto the table. "There's my resignation. As of this moment, I ain't a Texas Ranger."

Brand picked up the piece of paper and unfolded it. He scanned the words Slim had scrawled and shook his head. "You're making a mistake, Slim. Rangering is in your blood as much as it's in mine. We're too much alike. You won't like settling in one place any more than I would.''

''Don't be so cocksure,'' Slim said, setting aside his cup and looking at his young friend. ''I ain't had your incentives, Brand. I ain't lookin' for nobody. And you'd feel different about settlin' down if it weren't for your search for your sister. I'm tired, Brand. My old bones hurt from havin' slept far too long out under the stars. It's time for me to find a home. And I believe Eden is it.'' Slim looked Brand up and down. ''And you can't deny that the thought of settlin' down ain't crossed your mind in the last months. If you'll recall, you were goin' to ask Jessie to marry you before Clint beat you to it.''

Brand's face hardened. What a fool he'd been—a stupid, gullible fool who had fallen in love with a halfbreed. Dark lashes narrowed against the sudden pain that ripped through him. Brand shook his head. ''It was fortunate that Ramsey beat me to it. It probably saved me from hanging for murder.''

Slim gave a sad shake of his head. He'd heard about what had happened at the church. Cowhands gossiped worse than a bunch of old women. The news had reached Eden within the hour of Jessie telling the world she was half Cherokee. ''I thought you loved that girl.''

Brand turned his back on Slim, afraid his friend would catch a glimpse of his pain. ''I did until today.''

''Can you tell me just exactly how she's changed now that you've learned Indian blood flows through her veins? As far as I can see she's no different except maybe she's got more sense than I gave her credit for.'' Slim knew he was treading upon dangerous ground and expected Brand's temper to detonate at any second. But no matter; he couldn't leave things as they were. He braced himself, preparing for the storm ahead as he continued, "She loves you, Brand."

The explosion came. Brand swung around, his face flushed with fury, his eyes glistening silver orbs, his hands balled at his side. "I don't give a damn *what* she feels! And I didn't come here to discuss Jessie. I came to tell you I'm going after Fleming, and if you're determined to stay here and be an old woman, then you have my blessing. If you change your mind, I'll be in Indian territory."

Slim came to his feet, his own temper beginning to simmer. "Then, damn it, get the hell out, but don't say I didn't try to make you see reason. Jessie is a fine woman. It's taken me awhile to realize it, but it's true. She's done nothin' more than you would have done if you'd been in her place. And be damned to the blood in her veins. It's not what counts." Slim thumped himself on the chest. "It's what's in here that matters, but you're too blinded by hate to see it."

"Thank you for your sage advice. I put great store in it since you've learned so much about love from your visits to the likes of Miss Molly's. I'm sure whores know what really counts in life." Brand stalked from the bunkhouse and swung himself onto the saddle. He looked back to his traitorous companion and tipped his hat. "It's been nice working with you." Without a backward glance he kicked the Morgan in the side and headed north.

Slim pressed his lips into a thin line as he watched Brand ride away. He hadn't wanted things to end like this, but he couldn't leave Eden, not with all the other cowhands cutting out on Jessie. Brand was too hurt and angry now to realize what the girl had done by pitting herself against Clint Ramsey. Since coming to Eden he'd heard enough about the man to know she was putting her life in jeopardy.

Slim shook his head and turned back into the quiet bunkhouse. Maybe the few cowhands who were riding nightwatch over the herd wouldn't desert Eden when they learned that their friends had quit. If they did, though, he and Quillon would be of little protection against Ramsey's men.

Slim crossed to his bunk and took down his Winchester. He loaded it and then hung it back on the wall. He knew he would need the rifle before all was said and done between Ramsey and his fiery boss lady.

"Jessie! Wake up!" Edwina screamed, pounding on the bedroom door. "The barn is on fire!"

Jessie jerked upright and was already scrambling from the bed before she came fully awake. She grabbed her wrapper and hurried to the door to find Edwina ashen-faced, her nightcap askew, her bare feet peeking from beneath the hem of her nightgown.

"Wake the men," Jessie ordered, hurrying past her housekeeper and out the door. Barefoot, she ran toward the blazing structure. Her heart skipped a beat at the whinnies of terror coming from the frightened animals inside. Thinking only of saving them, Jessie ran into the barn.

Flames licked upward along the walls and the wooden pillars supporting the hayloft, greedily devouring everything in their path. The fresh hay overhead exploded into an inferno, raining smoke and glowing ash down upon her as she raised her arms to shield her face against the heat singeing her skin. The agonizing screams pierced the night air, rending Jessie's heart as she tried to reach the horses trapped in their stalls. The flames drove her backward toward the door as Slim ran forward and covered her in the heavy woolen blanket he'd doused in the watering trough. He lifted her into his arms and staggered into the cool night air. Breathing heavily, he set her down at Edwina's side.

Face smudged with soot, his expression furious, he glared at the young woman who stood staring helplessly at the barn. The wrapper she wore was burned and full of holes. "If that ain't the damn foolishest thing I've ever seen anyone do in my entire life! Ain't you got one bit of sense in that pretty head of yours, woman? You could've been killed."

Jessie coughed and wiped her burning eyes. "I couldn't just let them die without trying to save them. But it was already too late."

Slim nodded and cast a grave look at what had been the barn less than an hour ago. He didn't doubt it had been set by one of Clint Ramsey's hirelings. It was Ramsey's way of making Jessie understand how easily he could destroy her. Next time, it could be her life instead of her horses'.

The fiery glow lit the early morning sky as the flames consumed the barn and all within. The putrid scent of burned horseflesh rose sickeningly in the air, yet neither Edwina nor Slim could convince Jessie to go back to the house. She watched as the roof collapsed and then the walls tumbled inward, crumbling into blackened ash. Wisps of smoke still rose from the mess when the first rays of the sun crept over the eastern horizon to drench Jessie, Edwina, and Slim in the sparkling light of a new day.

Edwina glanced worriedly at Slim and then placed her arms about Jessie's shoulders. "Come away now, Jessica. There is nothing more for you to do here. It's all over."

Red-eyed from smoke and lack of sleep, Jessie looked at her friend and shook her head. "Damn him, he's not going to get away with this. If he believes one fire will stop me from ruining him, then he's sadly mistaken."

Jessie pulled away from Edwina. She smiled coldly. "I can't have the law arrest him for killing my parents, but I can have him arrested for burning my barn."

"Miss Jessie, the sheriff won't arrest Ramsey for barn burning."

Jessie frowned at Slim. "But he's guilty of it."

Slim nodded. "I don't doubt it one bit, but you don't have any proof. You didn't see or hear him here last night. For all the sheriff knows, it could have been burned by rustlers."

"Then do you think I should just forget about this?" Jessie said with a wave of a hand toward the heap of charred timbers.

"I ain't sayin' that. I'm just sayin' the sheriff won't do you any good. The man ain't goin' up against Ramsey. He's just like most of the folks in Paradise. He knows who helped him get elected and he wants to keep his job."

"Then who should I go to if I can't go to the sheriff?" Jessie asked, suddenly feeling like a warrior deserted upon the battlefield to face an entire army. Ramsey's control over the people of Paradise was far more extensive than she'd imagined. It wouldn't be quite as easy to bring him down without the support of the sheriff to back up her claims.

"You'd have to call in the Texas Rangers."

Jessie cast Slim a sharp look and saw his lips curl into a curious little smile. He too was thinking of the only Texas Ranger whose help she wanted. But she knew it was futile even to hope that Brand would come to her aid against Clint Ramsey. He was so consumed with bitterness, he'd ridden away the previous day without even a thought of her or Eden. "I don't believe even they would help me in this situation."

"It's their job, Miss Jessie. They can't let their personal feelings get involved."

"Can you get in touch with him?" Jessie asked, and held her breath until she saw him nod.

"It'll take a few days. He's gone after the rustlers in Indian territory."

"Tell him it's no use looking for Wade. He's gone."

Slim scratched his beard-stubbled chin. "So you did know where Fleming was all along? You were warnin' him just like Brand suspected?"

"No. I only learned where my brother was a few weeks ago, Slim. Until I came back to Texas I thought Wade was dead. And now that I know Wade is out of Brand's reach, I don't have to keep our relationship a secret any longer," Jessie answered honestly. The time for lies and deceit had ended the previous day. She would now tell the truth, and be damned to what anyone thought.

Slim frowned. Oddly enough, he believed the girl. But he seriously doubted Brand would feel the same way. Her past and his feeling for her wouldn't allow him to give her the benefit of the doubt. He would immediately believe the worst and arrest her for conspiring with a criminal. Slim gave a mental shrug. He didn't want to see Jessie arrested, but he didn't want to see her dead, either. Without Brand's help, he was afraid that would be how she'd end up.

"I'll ride out within the hour," Slim said. "Brand only has a a day's lead. Maybe I can catch him before he reaches Indian territory."

"I'll pack some food," Edwina said, giving Slim a tiny smile.

Slim looked at the robust older woman in her prim, soot-stained nightgown. Several wispy hairs curled about the gathered edge of her nightcap, making her face look much younger than her fifty years. He nodded and returned the gesture with a lopsided grin of his own. Somehow during the long night's vigil with Jessie, they had come to understand each other. Perhaps it stemmed only from their mutual feelings toward the young woman, yet it was there, budding into a friendship that time could only deepen.

Chapter 17

The sound of a snore drew Jessie's attention to the woman dozing on the chair beside the fireplace. Edwina, her head down, her chin resting on her chest, had finally succumbed to sleep. A tender, understanding smile touched Jessie's lips as she set aside the rifle and stood. She stretched her own aching muscles before crossing to Edwina's side. She shook her lightly on the shoulder.

"Edwina, go to bed. I can keep watch for the rest of the night."

"Huh, ah," Edwina muttered groggily, rousing from her slumber. She blinked at Jessie through reddened eyes and then came alert. "What's wrong?"

"Nothing. But it's time for you to go to bed. One of us has to get some rest. We can't keep up a twenty-four-hour vigil until Slim returns with help." Jessie didn't mention Brand's name. She wasn't as certain as Slim had been that he would come to her aid against Clint Ramsey. She couldn't allow herself to hope that he would. She might then begin to believe there was a chance to work things out between them. And she couldn't let that happen. It would only bring more pain to a heart already battered and bruised. Brand had made his feelings very clear at the church, and she had to accept them no matter what her heart said. She had to keep reminding herself that whatever happened in the future, Brand's feelings would not change because of her heritage.

"Jessie, you go and rest. I'll be fine," Edwina said, and attempted to hide a yawn.

"Edwina, you're exhausted. You didn't sleep last night and you can't keep up this pace," Jessie said, seating herself once more on the chair she'd occupied since early in the evening. She glanced at the small porcelain clock over the mantel. It was two in the morning. "Now go to bed."

Jessie lifted the rifle and laid it across her lap. She felt more secure with the weapon close at hand. Pulling back the lace curtain, she peered out the window. Her gaze swept over the moon-drenched landscape, seeking out any sign of Clint Ramsey or his hirelings. It had been two days since Slim had left Eden. And in that time Clint Ramsey had managed to frighten or buy away the last of her men. Quillon was of no help whatsoever. He and his family stayed barricaded in their little house. It was left to her and Edwina to protect Eden until Slim returned.

Jessie's expression hardened at the thought of Clint Ramsey. The man had burned her barn, driven away her help, and last night had come again in the cover of darkness to steal her horses. Had she not known better, she would have thought from the signs she'd found this morning that Indians were making the raids on Eden. However, she wasn't a simpleton. She knew that Ramsey was carrying out the promise he'd made to her at the church. He wanted to frighten her into believing she didn't have the power to go against him.

"But you won't succeed," Jessie murmured softly.

"What did you say?" Edwina asked, shoving herself to her feet. She rubbed absently at the dull ache in her back.

"I said sleep well. I'll wake you when it's daylight."

Edwina yawned. "Jessica, are you sure you don't want me to stay?"

Jessie smiled at her friend. "Yes. After you've rested, then I will sleep."

"Call me if you see or hear anything," Edwina said, suppressing another yawn.

"Good night," Jessie said, her attention returning to the moon-silvered landscape. When she heard Edwina's door close, she rose from the chair and with rifle tucked under her arm opened the door and stepped onto the porch. She lifted her face to the ebony sky and drew in a long breath. The quiet stillness reminded her of that fateful night ten years earlier. On that night, too, the world had seemed at peace. Like tonight, not even the sound of nocturnal animals disturbed the illusion. Yet Jessie knew the peace to be as fleeting as the wispy clouds blowing across the moon. For the devil lurked in the shadows, just waiting his chance to destroy her as he had done her parents.

Jessie jerked herself from her reverie and tightened her grip on the rifle. She'd be waiting to give the devil his due when he came again to Eden.

She tensed at the sound of horses galloping down the road toward Eden. A foreboding chill raced up her spine when the phantom riders came into view. Without seeing his face, she recognized Clint Ramsey in the lead.

Mounted upon his white stallion, he appeared out of the night like an apparition from hell.

Undaunted by her thoughts, Jessie stepped into the shadows and raised the cocked rifle to her shoulder. She waited patiently for the dark images to come into range. The loud report of her rifle echoed through the still night as dust sprayed at the hooves of Clint's mount. The riders jerked their horses to a skittering halt and looked frantically for the gunman.

"Get off my property, Clint Ramsey," Jessie ordered from her shadowy haven. "Or the next bullet will blow your head off." Her attention centered upon her enemy, Jessie didn't note the rider who eased from the saddle and quickly blended into the night.

"You're a bloodthirsty little bitch, aren't you, Jessie?" Clint said, and laughed, the sound raising goose-flesh on Jessie's arms.

"I wouldn't think twice about putting a bullet in you, you murdering bastard. You certainly didn't have a second thought when you killed my parents," Jessie said with all the bravado she could muster.

The moonlight glinted off the polished barrel of the rifle in Clint's hands. "That's right, Jessie. I killed that Indian-loving bastard and his squaw. Had I been smart, I would have exterminated you and your brothers that night as well. It would have saved me a whole hell of a lot of trouble. But I intend to take care of that mistake right away."

"Is that one of your promises, Clint?" Jessie asked, her fury renewed by his brazen admission of guilt. She aimed the rifle at his chest. "If it is, I'm afraid it's not going to be one you can keep. You're not going to live long enough." She began to squeeze down on the trigger when a sound behind her drew her attention. Her rifle still leveled on Clint, she glanced over her shoulder to see Edwina, her face bleached white, her eyes bulging from their sockets, a gun barrel at her temple. A grinning man held her trapped against his body, his arm choking off her breath and voice.

Jessie felt a sinking in the pit of her belly as she glanced once more toward Clint and lowered the rifle. She heard Clint's triumphant chuckle as he urged his horse forward. The animal trampled the bright blooms in Edwina's flower beds as he came alongside the porch. Jessie fought the urge to go for the man's throat as he casually folded his arms over the saddle pommel and smiled at her. Jessie shuddered in disgust at the assessing look he gave her. She wanted nothing more than to spew out all the bitter hatred boiling within her, but she knew she had to control herself. She had more to consider now than her need for revenge. Edwina's life was at stake. She had let Ramsey outsmart her, and now she would pay the price. All that was left was to try to save Edwina. She knew she had forfeited her own life the day she had humiliated Clint at the church. "Let her go, Clint. This is between you and me. Edwina has nothing to do with it."

Clint's lips curled back against his teeth and his gloved hand lashed out too quickly for Jessie to avoid the impact. The crack against her cheek echoed through the night as she staggered backward and tumbled onto one of the high-backed rockers. The rifle fell from her hands and slid off the porch to land in the dust at the bottom of the steps.

"You red bitch. You really thought you could get away with it, didn't you? You thought I'd let you take everything I've worked to build and not do anything to stop you?'' With the fluid grace of a man used to long days in the saddle, Clint dismounted. He strode up the steps to where Jessie sat glaring up at him. He towered over her, his shadowy features livid with rage. His gaze flickered briefly to the woman and man in the doorway before it settled once more upon Jessie. ''How much is her life worth to you?''

Breathing heavily, her heart pounding against her ribs, Jessie asked, ''What is it you want?''

''You know damn well what I want and intend to have before this night is over,'' Clint said, his voice a low growl.

''You want the deeds to the land I bought.''

Clint nodded. ''And I want the deed to Eden. I've waited long enough to get my hands on this land. It should have been mine after I got rid of your parents, but the state took it over, so I had to be satisfied to use it as grazing land. Then when you managed to wheedle it away from the state, I decided it would be to my advantage to marry you.''

''But that didn't work out, did it, Clint?'' Jessie said, a faint smile curling the corners of her provocative lips.

The contempt in her tone and gesture was obvious. Clint ground his teeth together and clenched his fists at his side to keep from smashing her face. He didn't want to mar her beauty until he had finished with her. Her beauty had made him believe he could be a complete man, whole and healthy, and he'd not risk ruining her looks until he'd reaffirmed his virility by sinking himself into her soft, warm flesh.

Clint clamped his hand on Jessie's arm. His fingers bit into her flesh as he jerked her from the chair. He glared at her. "Our marriage didn't work out, but I will have a taste of the wedding night before I'm through with you, Jessica Fleming. Be assured you won't cheat me out of it, any more than you cheated me out of the Lazy L. The past few nights were only a sample of what's in store for you, my dear little squaw."

For the first time Jessie felt her courage falter, but she raised her chin in the air with false bravado. "You can threaten me all you like, but I won't sign over the deeds unless you release Edwina."

"You have no choice," Clint said, tightening his hold on her.

"I do have a choice. I don't have to sign the deeds over to you." Jessie fought against the biting pain in her arm.

"Then you will die an ugly death."

Jessie drew in a deep breath. "And you'll never get your hands on the land you want unless my signature is on the deeds. I've given instructions to my lawyers to see you never get my land should anything untold happen to me, such as an unusual accident."

"Perhaps I'll just forget about the land and kill you for the sport of watching you die. It's been a few years since we went hunting red vermin, and I miss seeing them crawl in the dust before I blow their heads off," Clint growled, a muscle twitching in his cheek. He lowered his head and looked Jessie directly in the eye. "You know, I was only fourteen when I killed my first Indian, but I ain't never had a piece of squaw before. You're going to help me find out if red meat is any different from white, Jessica."

Jessie tried to jerk away from his hurtful grasp but found herself imprisoned against his body. "Do what you will, but release Edwina. She has no quarrel with you.''

"Take the old bat inside," Clint said, and jerked his head in the direction of the house. "Tie and gag her so she won't give us any trouble." He looked down at Jessie once more. "I want the deeds, Jessica."

Jessie shook her head. "You'll not have them."

"Payton," Clint called to the man inside the house. "Tear this place down if you have to, but I want those deeds found." He turned to the men still mounted. "I want you to burn the bunkhouse and then round up the cattle and head them north. The trail should lead into Indian territory because we want everyone to believe our dead little squaw was murdered by renegade Indians. Payton and I will join you in a few days."

"You forget, Clint, I'm half-Indian. No one will ever believe I was attacked by my own people," Jessie said.

Clint shook his head. "You are naive, Jessie. Having Indian blood in your veins doesn't stop the Comanches. They hold nothing but contempt for you tame Indians."

Jessie swallowed uneasily. It was true. She was naive in many respects about her heritage. Unlike Wade, she'd never felt the need to concern herself with the history of her mother's people.

Clint felt Jessie cringe and chuckled. "And don't think your white neighbors will ask too many questions about your demise. They won't. You humiliated me the other day at the church, but you also made the people who befriended you in Paradise look like fools. They'll be more than glad to see you gone. They don't want any half-breed squaws living next to them any more than I do. Texans have long memories. They all have lost relatives and friends in Indian raids. It's not easy for them to forget the horrors they've witnessed while trying to conquer this land.''

"If they hate me so much why are you trying to make everyone believe it was Indians who raided Eden? You should be a hero to the people of Paradise for killing me.''

The muscle twitched in Clint's cheek again. "It's none of your damned business what I do. Now tell me where the deeds are.''

Jessie shook her head and glared at him. "Release Edwina first.''

Jessie felt the blow explode in her brain. She reeled from the impact of Clint's gloved hand against her cheek. Her head snapped back and she blinked to clear her vision of the wildly gyrating shadows. She swallowed as the taste of her own blood filled her mouth. Unable to stand erect, she sagged against Clint, her knees threatening to give way beneath her.

"I've had enough of this, bitch. Either you tell me where the deeds are hidden or I'll beat you until you beg me to kill you,'' Clint said. Capturing a handful of Jessie's hair, he jerked her head back and stared into her dazed eyes. "But before I do, I'll let you watch my men enjoy themselves with that old bat you seem to care so much about. How would you like to see her staked out, spread-eagle and naked as the day she was born? She ain't much to look at, but my men have had worse at Miss Molly's. We can show you what the Comanches do to their enemies.''

"The deeds are in the bottom drawer of the desk in my bedroom,'' Jessie whispered through swelling lips.

"Get them,'' he ordered, and shoved her ahead of him into the house.

Jessie cast about frantically for Edwina but didn't see her. The door to her bedroom opened as she passed. Clint paused to speak with the man he'd called Payton and then roughly pushed Jessie forward, giving her no time to see how Edwina fared.

Jessie opened the desk drawer and took out the small metal box where she kept the deeds as well as other valuable papers. She drew in a deep, steadying breath and opened the lid. She flashed Clint a look of hate before she reached inside and retrieved the packet of papers. She tossed the deeds on the desk in front of him. "There they are, but I won't sign them until I'm sure Edwina will not be harmed."

Clint smiled coldly as he picked up the deeds and tucked them carefully into his coat pocket. "I've already left instructions that the old bat is to remain here when we ride out. But you're coming with us."

Jessie nodded. She had expected no less. She knew Clint wouldn't allow her to live. But she was relieved that he had agreed not to harm Edwina. "May I say good-bye to her?"

Clint shook his head. "I don't have time for your sentimental gestures."

"I want to see Edwina," Jessie said firmly. "I want to make sure she hasn't been harmed."

Clint grabbed Jessie by the arm and propelled her roughly toward Edwina's room. He opened the door enough for her to see her friend sitting, tied and gagged, on a straight-backed chair. Jessie breathed a momentary sigh of relief before Clint jerked the door closed and ushered her outside. He took her up in front of him on his white stallion and wrapped an arm about her chest, covering one breast with his hand. He chuckled under his breath when he felt her cringe from his touch. "Bitch," he whispered in her ear, "I'm going to enjoy taming you."

Clint urged his mount into a gallop. He had planned Jessica Fleming's demise so precisely, no one would ever know he was responsible for her death. Should her body ever be found, it would look like the renegades had killed her after raiding Eden.

Clint smiled his satisfaction. He'd have his revenge upon Jessica as well as the damned redskins who had raided the Lazy L. His smile deepened at the thought of the papers in his pocket. Jessica Fleming would never know how much she had given him. He'd wanted to buy up the land surrounding the Lazy L for many years, but he hadn't been able to afford it.

Clint's smile faded. He was the only man who deserved the land, because he'd been the only man in Paradise with enough balls to get rid of Fleming and his squaw. In his opinion, exterminating vermin wasn't murder—even if the vermin walked on two legs and looked like a man.

Jessie cast one last look toward Eden, knowing it would be the last time she saw it. This land of her birth had brought her great joy as well as great sorrow. She had few regrets. Wade and Mercy were now headed west, where they would be safe. And Brand . . . Jessie closed her eyes at the thought of the man who still held her heart. Brand would go on searching for his sister and hating anyone with Indian blood. Jessie released a long breath. Had she one thing to regret, it would be the chance she'd never had to make Brand realize that their love, had it been given an opportunity to grow, could have overcome all else, even the blood in her veins. And once he'd accepted the truth of what she'd said, she would have told him of Mercy and Wade and the great love they shared.

But Clint Ramsey had destroyed everything. When Brand came back to Eden, she would already be dead.

The shaley rock slivered beneath Brand's boots as he crept along the crest of the ridge overlooking the hideout. Parry's directions to the cave had been perfect. Now, as he looked down into the valley below, he could understand how the rustlers had managed to keep their hideout so well hidden. It would be nearly impossible for anyone to happen upon the cave. In the twelve years he'd worked as a Texas Ranger, Fleming's hideout had been the hardest to find.

Brand crouched behind a large tree and checked his revolvers and rifle. They were all loaded and ready. He glanced at the sky and then settled down to wait out the afternoon. He couldn't risk going in until dark. From what Parry had said, all that was left of Fleming's gang was him and another fellow called Renegade. Two men would be easy enough to take by surprise; however, Brand didn't necessarily trust Link Parry's word, even if he had told him where Fleming's hideout was located. The thief could now be sitting in his jail cell at Fort Smith laughing his head off at the stupid Texas Ranger he'd sent here to get himself killed. No, it was best to wait until he could be certain how many men Fleming had.

A blazing red-gold ball, the sun sank slowly below the mountains, leaving the landscape in the deepening shadows of night. The eastern star, more brilliant than all the rest, rose and challenged the full moon that crept over the tops of the tall pines to shed its silver light across the valley floor. The time had come. Brand slowly uncoiled his sinewy body to relieve his cramped muscles and then quietly made his way down the hillside toward the light coming in from the bowels of the cave.

Using stealth garnered from years of experience, he crawled forward, his steps as weightless as a stalking panther's, his senses attuned to every sound and movement. As he neared the cave he heard a soft feminine voice as well as two distinctly male ones. Brand frowned. Perry hadn't mentioned a woman. That could make things more difficult. He crouched near the cave entrance and listened until he ascertained that Parry had not misled him. Quietly he eased forward. Alone, his only chance to capture Fleming and his friends would be to take them by surprise. If what he'd overheard was true, tonight would be his only opportunity. Fleming and the others planned to leave the cave and head west by dawn.

His decision made, Brand moved along the rocky wall until he reached the cave entrance. He leveled his rifle at the tall man with shoulder-length hair before the three were aware of his presence. "Don't make a move, Fleming. You're under arrest."

All three froze. Heeding the warning, Wade slowly raised his head to look at the man framed by the night and knew instinctively he was facing Brand Stockton: Mercy's brother. He glanced at the woman at his side and knew by the way her body tensed that she too had recognized him. Wade drew in a long breath as his gaze flickered to where Renegade sat, unperturbed by the sudden appearance of the Texas Ranger. They had foolishly allowed their dreams of the future to make them careless. They had been so caught up in their plans for tomorrow that they had let down their guard.

"Get your hands over your head," Brand ordered, his gun still trained on Wade. He glanced at the scar-faced man and motioned toward Wade. "Get over there with him and don't make any sudden moves."

Renegade shrugged and pushed himself to his feet. "You ain't got anything to worry about, lawman. We're unarmed."

"I've heard that before, and the reason I'm still alive is that I didn't believe it then, any more then than I do now," Brand said, his gaze flickering over the golden-haired woman. She looked harmless enough, but a man in his profession couldn't go on looks. He'd seen too many men die from the mistake of trusting women, especially women who hooked up with outlaws. Most were as mean and tough as their men, and some were even more vicious when cornered. "Girl, get your hands in the air."

When Wade, Renegade, and Mercy stood with hands over their heads, Brand circled around behind them. He set aside the rifle and withdrew his revolver. With it cocked and ready to fire in one hand, he searched his prisoners for hidden weapons. Finding none, he allowed them to lower their hands. He reached into the pocket of his coat and withdrew two sets of wrist irons. "Girl, lock these about their wrists."

Keeping guard on the two men, Brand paid little heed to the young woman who moved quickly to obey him. She took the wrist irons and clamped them about Wade's and Renegade's arms. When she'd finished she took her place once more by Wade's side.

"What do you plan to do with us?" Wade asked, eyeing Brand through narrowed lids.

"Take you back to Texas," Brand said, hunkering down by the fire. He poured himself a cup of the coffee. He hadn't eaten since early that morning, and his stomach was rumbling in protest.

"There are beans and fatback in the pot," Mercy offered.

Brand looked at her fully for the first time, puzzled by her friendly offer. A frown etched a path across his brow as he stared into her pale eyes. A memory niggled at the back of his mind, and he wondered where he'd seen the girl before. He shook the thought away. He didn't have time to sort out the memories of every woman he'd met in saloons and whorehouses over the years. He had to keep alert. Fleming and his friend were acting far too calm to suit him.

Ever wary, Brand picked up one of the tin plates sitting nearby and lifted the lid of the pot. The heavenly scent of beans and meat met his nostrils and made his mouth water. Wasting no more time, he holstered his revolver and filled his plate. He devoured the beans and fatback, but his attention never wavered from his prisoners.

Wade shifted, earning Brand's direct regard. "You don't have any authority in Indian territory, lawman."

"Judge Parker at Fort Smith says I do," Brand said. Finishing the last few bites of his supper, he set aside the plate.

Mercy moved to pick up the plate to clean it, but Brand's revolver appeared in his hand as if by magic. He aimed it at her. "Just leave things as they are and get back over there with your man. I'd hate to have to shoot a woman.''

''Damn you, Stockton. She isn't going to hurt you,'' Wade growled, and strained at the manacles binding his hands. The thought of anyone, even her brother, threatening Mercy infuriated him nearly beyond reason.

Brand cocked a brow at Wade, and a cold smile curled his lips at the corners. ''So your sweet little sister has told you of me?'' His expression darkened at the thought of Jessie. ''Did you think I wouldn't know about Jessie and you, Fleming? I suspected from the first day I saw her in Paradise that she was in cahoots with you, but until last week when she arrived at her wedding decked out in her Indian finery, I didn't know she was also a half-breed.''

Brand's revelation made Wade feel suddenly old. He shook his head sadly and his shoulders sagged in defeat. ''I thought I'd convinced her not to marry Ramsey.''

''She didn't,'' Brand said, his voice toneless as the memory of Jessie walking down the aisle to meet Clint Ramsey returned to haunt him. He'd relived that moment over and over during the past days, and no matter how hard or how fast he rode, he couldn't outdistance it. He was always left sick to his stomach and with a dull pain where his heart had once been.

''She didn't marry Ramsey?'' Wade asked, his concern for his sister making him forget his precarious position as Brand's prisoner.

''No,'' Brand said, his features stormy granite. ''She told me she never intended to marry Ramsey because he was the man responsible for killing your parents. But it was Ramsey who called off the wedding when he learned the truth about her.''

Wade's swarthy features paled. "My God! If what you say is true, Jessie's life is in danger. Ramsey can't let her live. She knows too much."

Nostrils flaring, Brand felt a sudden wave of fear pass down his spine. The thought of Jessie's life being in jeopardy made his blood run cold. He couldn't love her because of the blood in her veins, but he didn't want to see her harmed.

"Listen, Stockton, you have to do something. You can't just let Ramsey kill her," Wade said, working his wrists furiously in a futile attempt to free his hands. "And if you won't do something, then I beg of you, let me go and I'll help her."

Brand's look told Wade what he thought of his idea. "Just like that"—he snapped his fingers—"I'm to let you go to rescue your sister?"

"Damn it, Stockton. I give you my word that I'll turn myself in once Jessie is safe. Don't you understand, Jessie is going to die for what she knows!"

"Brand, please listen to him. If you won't help Jessie, then let Wade go," Mercy said. "He's given you his word he won't escape, and I promise you, he'll keep it."

"Damned if I've ever encountered an odder lot than the three of you. You expect me to take a thief's word and then his doxy's promises that he'll keep them." Brand shook his head. He couldn't allow Fleming to play upon his feelings for Jessie. It would jeopardize the job he'd come to do. He'd already made one mistake with Jessie, and he wouldn't do so again, no matter what Fleming and his woman said.

"She's not a doxy, you fool. She's your sister," Renegade snapped, unable to keep silent a moment longer. He watched Brand through narrowed, unforgiving eyes.

Brand jerked as if he'd been slapped. His gaze came to rest on the scar-faced man. "Keep my sister out of this, scum. I won't have her mentioned by the likes of you."

"Brand, I am Mercy," the girl said quietly.

Brand's face darkened with rage as he turned his heated gaze upon the woman standing beside the half-breed. "If you think you can get me to let you go by pretending to be my sister, then you're mistaken."

"I'm not asking you to let me go. All I've asked is for you to allow Wade to go to his sister's aid, as you've tried to come to mine all these years," Mercy said. Though his gaze scorched her, she held her ground. This was her brother, and she didn't fear him. No matter how be acted now, he was still the same gentle-hearted person he'd been the day he'd left for the war.

Brand balled his fists at his side to keep from throttling the half-breed's whore. How dare she try to use his search for his sister to her own advantage! "I'm no fool, woman. And you're not Mercy."

Mercy looked at her brother and felt her heart go out to the tormented man he had become. The protective barrier of his hatred prevented him from seeing the truth. He couldn't accept her as his sister, or he'd also have to accept the fact that she loved a man with Indian blood. She smiled sadly at the handsome man with the haunted eyes. "I have no proof of my identity, Brand. I can only tell you that on the day you left home to fight in the war, I cried my heart out. You were my favorite brother and I didn't want you to leave me. I loved Russ and Charles, but you were always special, even when you teased me about my eyes.''

''Eyes like a clear Texas sky,'' Brand breathed, still unable to believe he had come to the end of his quest and his sister now stood before him.

Mercy nodded and smiled at him tenderly.

Forgetting about his prisoners, Brand stared at Mercy as he finally accepted the truth. He raised his arms to her and struggled to keep his tears at bay. It was a futile effort. They spilled down his cheeks as Mercy slowly came to him. He hugged her close and squeezed his eyes closed as he silently sent his thanks to God for giving him back his sister.

''Brand, will you help Wade?'' Mercy asked, looking up into his tear-bright eyes.

''Mercy, I am a Texas Ranger. I can't release a prisoner to go roaming the countryside out of some misbegotten belief that his sister might be in danger.''

''I'm not asking you to release us, but to help Jessie,'' Mercy said.

Brand frowned at her. ''Release you? You've done nothing wrong. You're not under arrest.''

''Brand, I go where Wade goes. He is my husband.''

Brand's expression darkened once more. ''You can't be married to that half-breed?''

''No preacher has spoken words over us, but we are man and wife in all other ways. And nothing anyone can say or do can change how we feel about one another.''

Brand shook his head. ''You can't mean you love him, Mercy? Do you know what you're saying? He's a savage just like the murdering lot who captured you and killed Ma and Pa.''

The strength that had seen her through the years of deprivation and abuse with the Comanche seemed to glow like a golden aura as Mercy looked at her brother. "I love Wade more than anything else on this earth, Brand. And you must realize I lived with the Comanches for nearly twelve years. I am more Indian now than I am white."

Brand shook his head. "You don't know what you're saying. You've just been away from civilization too long. Once you're back with your own kind, you'll see that you don't really love Fleming. And I won't hear any more of this."

"You must listen to me, Brand. Wade is my life. I will die when he dies."

"Then prepare to die, Mercy," Brand said, unable to accept her vows of undying love for the half-breed. "Because Fleming and his friend here will swing after they're tried in Paradise for rustling."

Brand glanced toward his prisoners. "Get a few hours' sleep if you can. We leave for Texas at dawn." He placed an arm about Mercy's shoulders to lead her away from his prisoners, but she shook it off.

"My place is beside my man, brother," she said. She turned and walked back to where Wade had slumped down on the sandy cave floor. She sank beside him and rested her head against his shoulder.

Brand's fingers itched to kill Wade Fleming, yet he suppressed the urge. For now he would allow his sister to stay with Fleming, but once they returned to civilization he'd hear no more of her love for the half-breed. And no matter what she said, she was a white woman, not an Indian squaw.

Brand settled himself across the cave from his prisoners and allowed his gaze to rest once more upon Wade and his sister. He could sympathize with Mercy's feelings, but like him, she would have to put them aside.

Brand leaned his head back and stared at the cold, brownish gray stone overhead. He couldn't stop himself from wondering what Jessie was doing at that moment. Was she in danger, as Fleming believed? The hair at the nape of his neck prickled with apprehension, and he glanced toward the mouth of the cave. Dawn could not come soon enough for him. He wanted to be on his way back to Texas at the earliest possible moment. Should he learn Ramsey had harmed Jessie, he'd kill the man with his bare hands.

The second night on the trail south, Slim Johnson rode into camp. He cast only a curious glance at the prisoners, raised an eyebrow at the sight of the beautiful blond woman next to the dark-skinned man, and then launched into his story about Jessie. When he finished, Brand's face reflected the turmoil tearing his insides apart. He glanced at Wade, who had listened to Slim's story without comment. "You were right. Jessie is in danger."

Wade lifted his iron-bound wrists. "Let me go, Stockton. I give you my word, I'll not escape."

Brand glanced toward Slim and pressed his lips into a thin, tight line. He didn't know what to do. He was torn between his duty and his heart. Releasing a long breath of disgust, he looked at Slim, his expression daring his friend to stop him. "All right, Fleming. I'll release you, but on one condition. We ride together, and once we make sure Jessie is safe, you'll turn yourself over to me again. Is that agreed?"

Wade nodded. "You have my word."

"I'll shoot you on the spot should you decide not to keep your word," Brand said.

"Oh, Brand. I knew you'd help us," Mercy said, throwing herself into her brother's arms and startling Slim Johnson. Wide-eyed he gaped at his friend and saw Brand grin.

"This is my sister, Mercy, Slim."

Slim blinked at the golden-haired girl and then back to Brand. "How in hell did all this come about in just a few days?"

"Have a cup of coffee and I'll tell you all about it," Brand said as he fished the keys to the wrist irons out of his pocket. He tossed them to Mercy, and she quickly released Wade.

"What about me?" Renegade asked. "I have a stake in all this, too."

"Do I have your word you'll surrender once we've made certain Jessie is safe?" Brand asked, and watched Renegade nod his agreement. Brand shrugged. "Just remember, I won't hesitate to shoot either one of you if you try anything suspicious."

Mercy gave her brother another approving smile before she released Renegade's wrist irons.

Slim cast a wary glance at his friend, wondering what had come over him. He certainly wasn't acting like the hard-bitten lawman he'd become over the past twelve years. Slim glanced toward Mercy. She was the only answer he could find to his friend's odd behavior.

The bunkhouse was still smoldering when Brand, Slim, and their prisoners rode into Eden. They had made better time than expected. On their trek south they had stopped only long enough to give their horses time to rest and feed. Mercy, used to long, hard days of travel, had endured the miles without complaint. Yet all four were exhausted by the time they reined their horses to a halt in front of the ranch house.

Edwina, disheveled and bruised, burst into tears as she ran down the steps to meet them. "Thank God you've come! I've been out of my mind."

"Where's Jessie?" Brand asked, ignoring the housekeeper's obvious distress. He couldn't think of anyone else until he saw that Jessie was safe and sound.

"Ramsey has her. He—he—had me tied up and gagged so I couldn't help her. But he didn't count on the sewing scissors I keep on my dressing table. I finally managed to move my chair close enough to reach them. But it took me nearly all day to cut through the rope and get free," Edwina said, sniffling back another sob.

"Here now," Slim said, distressed to see her tears. Dismounting, he crossed to the housekeeper and draped a comforting arm about her robust shoulders. "That's enough of that. Tears ain't goin' to do Jessie no good."

"But he means to kill her. I heard him say it," Edwina said, on the edge of hysteria. "He's going to make it look like Indians raided Eden and captured Jessie. I know he'll come back here and kill me after he's murdered Jessie. That's why he left me tied up. He didn't want me to go for help or tell anyone what he's planned." Another shaky sob escaped her, and she dabbed at her reddened nose.

Brand glanced toward the barn and then to the empty paddocks before he looked at the silent man mounted at his side. "We need fresh horses."

Wade nodded and flashed Brand a roguish grin before

he motioned for Renegade to follow. They knew the best stock on every ranch in the vicinity. And they would bring back the best horses the Lazy L possessed. Wade laughed at the irony of using Ramsey's horses to help catch him. Wade's eyes reflected only the intensity of his hatred for the man who had killed his parents and now threatened his sister's life.

Brand dismounted and helped Mercy down. "Slim, when Wade and Renegade return, I want you and Mercy to stay here with Edwina. She shouldn't be left alone, especially if Ramsey's men do take it into their heads to come back. And I don't know how long we'll be gone. I don't intend to come back without Jessie."

"I go with Wade, Brand," Mercy said.

"I can't allow it. It's far too dangerous. You could be hurt," Brand said, realizing this was his chance to get Mercy away from Fleming without making it look like he'd intentionally come between them. It would be much simpler to separate them now than wait until he could take Wade back into custody.

Mercy gave her brother a tender, understanding smile. "I know all about danger, brother. And I assure you I can take care of myself. I go with Wade."

Brand took off his hat and ran his fingers through his tousled hair. "Mercy, can't you understand I'm only thinking of your welfare?"

"I know how you feel, but my place is with Wade."

Brand released a long, exasperated breath. "What am I going to do with you? You've grown up to be as stubborn as a mule."

Mercy's smile deepened. "I fear it's a trait that runs in the family, brother."

Brand threw up his hands. He'd just have to find another way to get Wade Fleming out of Mercy's life. "All right," he said in disgust. "You can go with us. But I'm warning you, I'll tan your backside until you can't sit down if I catch you putting yourself in danger. I've found you now and I don't intend to lose you again."

Chapter 18

The trail ended abruptly, and Brand reined in the Morgan. He scanned the earth for any sign that might indicate the direction Ramsey had taken, but it appeared as if the man had vanished into thin air.

His face dark with worry, he glanced back at Wade. "Their trail ends here."

Wade urged his horse alongside Brand's, looked down at the set of tracks, and smiled. "Ramsey's trying to make us believe he's Indian, Stockton."

Brand flashed Wade a disgusted look. "I already know his intentions, Fleming. It still doesn't change the fact that we've lost his tracks."

Wade's white teeth gleamed as he gave Brand a taunting grin. "You may have lost his tracks, white man, but I haven't." He pointed in the direction Ramsey and his hostage had traveled only a few hours earlier. "He's separated from his man to throw us off the scent." Wade indicated the faint markings where Ramsey had used brush to wipe away his tracks. "He may want us to believe he's an Indian, but he doesn't realize only a white man would use such a stupid trick. An Indian wouldn't have left a trail from the beginning."

Silver gaze clashed with indigo. Both men knew what Wade had left unsaid. Neither Texas Rangers nor anyone else had been able to follow his trail.

Urging his mount in the direction Wade indicated, Brand found the faint tracks of Ramsey's passing within minutes. The iron-shod horse left distinctive markings in the sandy soil.

Brand rode ahead, leaving Wade, Mercy, and Renegade to follow. He was in no mood for Fleming's taunts. The references to his heritage had already added to the burden of prejudice now strapped to his back like a bundle of thorns. He had sought to ignore his own emotions by focusing his attention on the dilemma of Mercy's love for Wade. However, he'd not succeeded. They fermented and boiled to the surface against his will. His insides felt like raw meat from the turmoil ripping through him.

A muscle worked in his jaw as he clenched his teeth. He couldn't keep his mind off of Jessie. The very thought of her in danger sickened him. He didn't know what he would do should Ramsey harm her. His heart told him he couldn't live without her, but his head told him he couldn't live with her. He was torn by his conflicting feelings.

At trail's end, Brand drew his mount to a halt. Feeling like a volcano about to explode, his face the mask of the angel of death come for retribution, he dismounted and took his rifle from its scabbard. With a flick of his wrist he worked the lever, setting a round into the chamber. Intent upon killing Ramsey, he turned toward the path that would take him down to the line shack.

"Where in hell do you think you're going, Stockton?'' Wade asked, his voice low, his hand restraining Brand.

Brand flashed him an angry look and shook off his hand. "To do my job."

"Damn it! I thought you Texas Rangers had more sense. You may not give a damn about my sister, but I do. If you go in there, Ramsey will kill her."

Brand gave himself a sharp mental shake. He'd allowed his emotions to overshadow all common sense. If Wade had not stopped him, he would have been the cause of Jessie's death. Brand swallowed and looked at Wade, unable to apologize for his actions without revealing far more than he wanted to admit even to himself. He nodded, turning his attention to the small shack sitting in the valley below. "It won't be long before dark. We'll wait until then to go in." He flashed Wade a taunting smile to equal the one he'd received earlier in the day. "Unless you Indians are afraid your spirit won't make it to the happy hunting ground if you die fighting at night."

Wade took the barb and grinned. "Remember, Stockton. I'm just half-Indian, so part of me will make it no matter when I fight."

The moment of crisis over, Wade relaxed. Fortunately Stockton had seen reason. Had he not, Wade feared he would have had to resort to methods of which Mercy would not have approved. But no matter how she felt, he couldn't have allowed Stockton to go in after Ramsey without first being sure Jessie would be safe.

Brand glanced up at the waning light and set aside his rifle. Hidden by an outcropping of rock, he turned his attention back to the shack below. If all went well, he'd soon have Jessie with him again. Brand did not delve deeply into the thought. He had done enough soul-searching for one day. It was time now to focus all his energy on making sure Jessie was safe.

Jessie moistened her dry lips and turned from the dusty window. Her gaze swept over the line shack, looking for anything she could use as a weapon against Clint Ramsey. But, like the line shack she and Brand had shared, this place was furnished with only a minimum of furniture: one pot-bellied stove, one broken chair, one wobbly three-legged table propped against the wall, and a narrow, rat-eaten bunk.

Jessie snorted in disgust. She had nothing with which to defend herself against the man who now stood talking with his hireling, Payton, who had arrived a few minutes earlier. She couldn't stop Clint from carrying out all the threats he'd made on the long ride from Eden. During those hours he had entertained himself by tormenting her with his descriptions of every perverted sexual act he could conjure up.

Jessie squeezed her eyes closed and massaged her throbbing temples. A bruise purpled the side of her face from the corner of her swollen mouth to her ear. The blow Clint had given her the previous night was clearly marked by the imprint of his fingers upon her skin.

"Damn him to hell," she muttered, wincing when she accidentally touched her face.

"Did you say something, squaw?" Clint asked as he entered the cabin and closed the door securely behind him.

"Nothing you would want to hear," Jessie snapped, glaring at him. She'd be damned if she'd give him the satisfaction of knowing she was in pain.

Ignoring her retort, Clint crossed to the bunk and jerked off the rat-chewed blanket. He looked back to Jessie. "Take off your clothes and lie down, squaw."

Jessie glanced at the lumpy mattress and then back to Clint. She shook her head. She'd die before she'd willingly submit to Clint Ramsey.

"Bitch, I'm tired of waiting," Clint growled, and reached out for her.

Jessie avoided his rough hand. Her eyes shot blue fire as she moved out of his reach and spat, "You can wait until hell freezes over, for all I care. Kill me and get it over with, because I'm not going to degrade myself with you."

Clint's face mottled with fury. "I've waited long enough to have you, Jessie. And I'm not going to wait any longer. You can do as I say, or I can have Payton help me hold you down. It's your decision."

"If either of you comes near me, I'll scratch out your eyes," Jessie threatened. For the thousandth time since she'd arrived at the line shack, she searched frantically for a way to escape. And like the other times, there was none.

Clint moved toward her. His face set with determination, he withdrew his revolver and aimed it at Jessie. "I said get on the bed, squaw."

Jessie looked down the barrel of the gun and swallowed with difficulty. She cast one last, fleeting glance toward the door but knew she would die before she reached it. Drawing in a steadying breath, she walked slowly toward the narrow bunk.

"Take off your clothes," Clint ordered, motioning with his revolver.

Jessie closed her eyes. The time had come to make a

choice between life and death. She could refuse to obey Clint and die. Or she could do as he bade and live a few hours longer, until he decided it was time to kill her. She moistened her dry lips. The decision between life and death was not easy. The spirit that craved life willed her to live as long as possible, yet her heart rebelled at allowing Clint to totally destroy her before he put an end to her life.

She looked at the man leering at her. The thought of him touching her as Brand had done sickened her. She looked at the revolver he had trained on her and raised her chin in the air. Her decision made, she bolted toward the door. She would not die meekly.

Engrossed with his plans for Jessie, Clint was taken by surprise at her sudden flight. A low growl of outrage emerged from his throat as he pulled the trigger.

The bullet that had been meant for Jessie's heart missed its mark by several inches, entering her back between her shoulders and tearing a jagged hole through her as it exited just beneath her collarbone above her right breast. The impact slammed her into the rough timbers of the door. Eyes wide with pain and shock, her fingers instinctively clutching the wood for support, she slowly sank to the floor.

"Bitch, I warned you." Calmly Clint holstered his revolver and crossed to Jessie's limp body. Contempt reflected in every line of his face, he rolled her over with the toe of his boot. He sneered at the red stain spreading across the front of her chest but made no attempt to aid her.

"Only good Indian is a dead Indian," he muttered in disgust, and opened the door to come face to face with Brand and Wade. Renegade stood over Payton's lifeless body. Ramsey's hireling had made the mistake of believing he could take Renegade with a knife.

Without considering his options, Clint instinctively reached for his revolver. It was a mistake he didn't live to regret. Brand's bullet hit him in the heart. A look of surprise flickered briefly over his paling features before he crumpled into the dust, his lifeless eyes staring toward the darkening sky.

At the same instant, Brand saw Jessie lying in a pool of her own blood. His heart lodged in his throat, he rushed forward. Shoving Wade out of his path, he knelt and lifted her into his arms.

"My God, Jessie," he whispered, his voice filled with fear. He carried her to the bunk and laid her down gently. One glance toward Wade made his heart freeze. The look on the outlaw's face held no promise of hope. Brand shook his head and said, "She's going to live. So get that damned forlorn look off your face and get Mercy. Jessie needs attention."

Wade nodded and rushed out the door. He called out frantically to Mercy as he reached the edge of the clearing. He feared Jessie was near death, no matter what Brand said.

Brand slumped on the doorstep and hung his head. Red-eyed from lack of sleep, his face shadowed by several days' growth of beard, he buried his face in his hands, pressing his fingers against his eyes to stem the tears that burned the backs of his lids. He drew in a haggard breath and once more sent a silent prayer toward heaven for Jessie's life. Praying, it seemed, was all he had done since finding her wounded. Mercy had seen to her care, leaving him to pace, worry, and pray.

A sound at his side drew Brand's attention, and he took in a steadying breath before he looked up to find Mercy sitting there. She reached out and took his hand, giving it a gentle, reassuring squeeze. Her smile was tender with understanding.

"Jessie's fever has gone down," she stated simply.

Brand let out a long breath. "Is she going to live?"

Mercy glanced up at the star-studded sky and shrugged. "It's now up to God and Jessie. I've done all I can do."

Brand's fingers tightened upon Mercy's. "You know how I feel about her?"

Mercy nodded. "The same way I feel about Wade."

Still unable to reconcile his feelings about Wade, Brand glanced away. "Mercy, Fleming is an outlaw who will probably hang when I take him back to stand trial."

"Brand, I'll go back with you if you'll let Wade go free."

Brand's head snapped around and he stared down into his sister's lovely face. Illuminated by the lantern light filtering through the doorway, she looked like a golden angel. He hated to deny her anything, but he had no choice. "I can't do that."

Mercy nodded sadly. "You know I had to try. I love Wade."

Brand draped a comforting arm about his sister's shoulders. "In time you'll be able to forget about all this and make a new life for yourself."

Mercy jerked away. Her voice shook with suppressed emotion. "I don't want to forget. Should Wade die, then I shall die as well."

A shiver raced up Brand's spine. He had heard of the grief rituals of the Comanche women. He remembered well the story of Cynthia Ann Parker. With her small child, she had been brought back to her white family after twenty-five years with the Comanche. When the child died she had mutilated herself by cutting off her breasts, prayed to the Indian spirits, and then starved herself to death.

He could not let that happen to his sister, but he didn't know how to stop it. She had been with the Comanche twelve years, and no matter how hard he tried to deny it, the years had bred many of their ways into her.

Brand jerked around at the sound of his name. It was little more than a whisper upon the breeze, yet it was far more than he had ever expected to hear again from Jessie. His joy making him forget about Mercy and Wade, he hurried into the cabin. He knelt at the side of the bunk and gently brushed a dark strand of hair from Jessie's bruised face. "Do you want something, Jessie?"

Jessie gave a nearly imperceptible nod and motioned with one finger for him to come closer. The bullet had missed all her vital organs, but she had lost a great deal of blood and it took all her strength to speak. "Let Wade and Mercy go, Brand."

Brand jerked back and frowned at her. Even in her weakened condition all she could think about was her brother. She had no words for him. Annoyed, he shook his head. "You know I can't do it."

Jessie closed her eyes, and for a long moment Brand thought she had slipped into unconsciousness once more. He started to rise, but Jessie's words stopped him.

"Brand, don't let your hatred ruin their lives. Give

336

them the chance to find the happiness that we've been denied. They love each other. Let them go west, where it's safe for them.'' Jessie's thick lashes fluttered open and she looked up at Brand. Her eyes dark sapphires, her bruises the only color to her ashen skin, she silently begged him to understand.

''Jessie, you don't realize what you're asking of me. You want me to turn my back on everything I've believed for the past twelve years. It's my job to bring Wade to justice. He is a criminal.''

Jessie gathered the last of her reserves. She had to make Brand realize that what he was doing wasn't because of his job as a Texas Ranger. His prejudice was driving him to destroy her brother and Mercy. ''Let them go, Brand, and let go of your hatred. Mercy doesn't hate and she has far more right to do so than you. She loves my brother and wants only to make a new life with him.''

Brand ran a hand through his hair in exasperation. ''This isn't the time to discuss this. You need to rest and recover. We nearly lost you.''

Jessie drew in a shaky breath. ''I can't rest knowing that the man I have given my heart and soul to is also the man who will see my brother hanged.''

Brand stilled. After a long moment he asked, ''You can still love me after all I've done to you? After all I've said?''

Garnering her strength, Jessie reached out a trembling hand and took Brand's. ''I have never stopped loving you, even when you told me you didn't want my love.''

''God, Jessie,'' Brand said, torn between old hatreds

and new loves. "I've been such an ass. I don't see how you could still care for me."

A tender smile touched Jessie's lips. "Sometimes I've wondered the same thing, but I only have to look into your eyes to know why. I see within them a man who has suffered, a man haunted by the past, a man who yearns for love yet who believes he has no heart."

Brand lifted Jessie's hand to his lips and kissed it tenderly. "Jessie, I'm afraid. I don't know if I can put the past behind me. It's driven me for so long, I don't know how to cleanse myself of all the years of hatred."

"It's simple. All you have to do is to love."

"I do. I love you with all my heart and soul. I've done my damnedest to deny my feelings, but during the past days of not knowing whether you were going to live or die, I've had to face the truth. And I'm not proud of what I've seen about myself. But if you will give me a chance, I'll do my best to put the past behind me and look toward the future."

Tears brimmed in Jessie's eyes. She had waited so long to hear those words. She moistened her dry lips. "There is only one shadow left between us now, Brand. And I fear it will darken our future forever."

Brand understood. "Wade Fleming has to die."

Jessie drew in a sharp breath and then cringed from the searing pain that shot through her chest. She closed her eyes, unable to look at Brand any longer. He was determined to take Wade back to stand trial, and nothing she could say or do would stop him.

"And so does Mercy," Brand said quietly.

Jessie's eyes flew open and she stared at Brand, wondering about his sanity. He'd just spoken of his love for her, then a moment later he was talking about killing his sister and her brother. "Brand, you can't mean what you say. Take Wade back to stand trial, but don't execute him yourself."

"But it has to be done, Jessie, or we'll never be happy," Brand said, his eyes sparkling with devilment.

"No, Brand, please," Jessie said, her breath coming in small, shallow pants.

Realizing his jest was upsetting her far more than he'd intended, Brand relented. "Don't you see? Wade Fleming and Mercy both have to die before they can be reborn with new names and new lives."

Jessie gaped up at Brand and tried to sort out everything he'd just said. A tiny smile touched her lips. "You mean you are going to let them go?"

Brand shook his head. "No. Wade Fleming and Mercy, as well as the one called Renegade, were killed in a gunfight while trying to save you. The three people who will ride away from here have nothing to do with the outlaws. They are newlyweds."

"I love you, Brand," Jessie whispered, and reached up to caress his beard-stubbled jaw. She released a long breath and then curled her hand against his chest. Her eyes closed slowly and her breathing became even. She slept, soundly and peacefully. All was well within her world at last. Brand loved her, and Wade and Mercy would have their new life together.

Several days later Jessie stood in the doorway of the line shack and watched her brother and his wife ride out of sight. She waved one last time and then looked up at the man supporting her with his strength and love. She smiled. Soon she and Brand would begin their life together. She knew it would not be perfect. She and

Brand were both too strong-minded. They would al--ways have differences, but they had one thing that would sustain them when their tempers got out of control: their love.

Brand brushed his lips against Jessie's brow as he bent and lifted her in his arms. He carried her back to the bunk and tucked her snugly beneath the rat-chewed blanket. He smiled tenderly. ''Rest, love. In a day or two we'll be on our way back to Eden.''

''Eden'' Jessie murmured softly, and closed her eyes. Like the first, their Eden would be the place where new lives would begin.

ABOUT THE AUTHOR

Cordia Byers was born in the small north Georgia community of Jasper and lives there still, with her husband, James. Cordia likes to think of her husband as being like one of the heroes in her novels. James swept her off her feet after their first meeting, and they were married three weeks later.

From the age of six, Cordia's creative talents had been directed toward painting. It was not until late 1975, when the ending of a book displeased her, that she considered writing. That led to her first novel, *Heather*, which was followed by *Callista*, *Nicole La Belle*, *Silk and Steel*, *Love Storm*, *Pirate Royale* (winner of a *Romantic Times* Reviewer's Choice Award), *Star of the West*, *Ryan's Gold*, *Lady Fortune*, and *Desire and Deceive*. Finding more satisfaction in the world of her romantic novels, Cordia has given up painting and now devotes herself to writing, researching her material at the local library and then doing the major part of her work from 11:30 P.M. to 3:00 A.M.

Regency...

HISTORICAL ROMANCE *AT ITS FINEST*